ALEXANDER'S
SONG

ALEXANDER'S SONG

BY
PAUL F. OLSON

CEMETERY DANCE PUBLICATIONS

Baltimore

❖ 2022 ❖

Alexander's Song
Copyright © 2022 by Paul F. Olson

Cover Artwork © 2022 by Jill Bauman
Cover Design © 2022 by Desert Isle Design, LLC
Interior Design © 2022 by Desert Isle Design, LLC

All rights reserved. No part of this book may be reproduced in any form or by any electronic or mechanical means, including information storage and retrieval systems, without permission in writing from the publisher, except by a reviewer who may quote brief passages in a review.

Trade Paperback Edition

ISBN:
978-1-58767-847-9

This book is a work of fiction. Names, characters, places and incidents either are products of the author's imagination or are used fictitiously. Any resemblance to actual events or locales or persons, living or dead, is entirely coincidental.

Cemetery Dance Publications
132B Industry Lane, Unit #7
Forest Hill, MD 21050
www.cemeterydance.com

For writers Peter Straub, Charles Palliser, Jonathan Carroll,
Thomas Tryon, and Wallace Stegner.
Without whom, indeed.

AUTHOR'S NOTE

This book is a sort of time machine. The first drafts were written more than thirty years ago, in the basement of a house in Wheaton, Illinois. Much has changed since then, but the novel remains very much a creature of its time, those last golden years before the internet, smart phones, and other so-called advances irrevocably altered the world. It may be disorienting at first to journey back across the decades, but I hope you'll enjoy the trip.

In other matters:

Rock Creek, Michigan, and the Quad Lakes will not be found on any map.

The books of the writer featured in these pages will not be found in any library, nor will the writer himself ever appear in any encyclopedia.

This is a work of fiction. Any real people or places are therefore used fictionally and are mentioned for the purposes of entertainment only.

The concept of the Doppler Effect of history, brought up briefly in the final section of the novel, is not mine. I originally came across it in Wallace Stegner's marvelous book *Angle of Repose* – surely a candidate for Great American Novel if there ever was one. I took Mr. Stegner's idea and twisted it, manipulating it for my own purposes. But that twist in no way diminishes the admiration with which I blatantly stole the concept in the first place.

PFO

THE PAST...

THE DEATH OF A FAMOUS WRITER

"Endings are all the same," he said to her, raising his glass as though making a solemn toast.

She blinked, hoping against futile hope that the tears in her eyes were caused only by the thick smoke from his pipe.

"I disagree," she said, although she wasn't sure if she did or not. "Life is always full of surprises. Didn't we hear that just a day or two ago? Isn't it true that the only thing you can expect is the unexpected?"

"Romantic rubbish, my dear." His voice was firm but not completely without kindness. "No matter how we try, no matter what, there's only one choice, one way. In the final counting, the only shades are shades of black."

Alexander Bassett
from *Doctor Howell* (Novel, 1943)

THE DEATH OF A FAMOUS WRITER

1

He put down the phone and turned on the light over his desk, startled and more than a little dismayed that he'd been talking long enough for it to grow dark outside. It wasn't so much that a great deal remained to be done before the start of his journey, but rather that he felt the need to sit and rest awhile, dwell on what he was about to do, and perhaps even give himself a chance to change his mind.

With a trembling hand, he pulled back the drapes and gazed at the street below, unsettled by its strangeness; it looked like an avenue in a foreign town. He had only been back in Manhattan for a few days, and it had been so many years since he had lived here that everything he saw both inside and out of the virtually empty apartment gave him a feeling of trespassing, a sensation of being somewhere he wasn't wanted or needed, where no one even knew he was alive.

At least that's going to change, he thought, and was aware of his lips pulling into a wry smile, despite the fact that there was really nothing funny about it at all.

With a sigh, he turned from the window and limped into the bedroom. His heart fluttered a little, but that was nothing he wasn't used to. He waited for it to die down, then flexed his stiff fingers, like a man mimicking the preparations of a concert pianist, and popped the latches on his suitcase.

Inside, hidden beneath a stained white towel, were the things he hadn't already shipped ahead, the pitifully few items that would be going on the road with him. There was a single change of clothes and a sliver of Ivory soap. There was his razor, unused for weeks, rust coating the old blade, flecks of whisker clinging to the rust. There was a 1969 desktop calendar. There were pages and pages of typewritten manuscript, the fruits of nearly ten years work, all of it unfinished, unpublished, maybe even unpublishable. There were three unopened packs of Pall Mall cigarettes and two bottles of cheap bourbon tucked beneath a jumbled sheaf of essays on the politics of John Steinbeck.

It was the bourbon he was after.

He carried one of the bottles to the chair across the room, sat down, broke the seal, twisted the cap, lifted the bottle to his lips, and drank deeply. The pain in his belly flared like fire.

"Ahhhh...shit."

He was an old man and he was dying. He knew it even if that long-haired, hip-talking doctor (if he really *was* a doctor; he wore bell-bottomed jeans and a tee-shirt advertising something called The Purple Monkey Coffee House) had not.

He had gone to the clinic, after years of avoiding the medical profession as much as possible, with the simple intent of confirming his own diagnosis—and maybe seeing if something could be done about it. The waiting room had been painted a hideous shade of yellow. The walls were covered with VD posters and warnings about the dangers of bad acid. There were two doctors on duty and more than two dozen people waiting to see them: boys with fantastically long hair, young girls glassy-eyed from drugs or pregnant or both, a few young couples. One young man with a shaved head sat all alone in a corner, gently stroking the leaves of a dusty plastic philodendron and murmuring to it in a slow, crooning voice.

He had been both amused and saddened to note that he was forty years older than anyone else in the place, and he had thought (not for the first time) how odd it was that the eternal wheel had turned again. The

ALEXANDER'S SONG

time for so many of his ideas was back, and yet he found it increasingly difficult to express them. His politics were in vogue, but the spoiled children who espoused them seemed alien to him, a generation of ciphers. His beliefs were in fashion, while he himself was dying. He had become, in effect, a dated relic. And he had long since run out of words.

"Dying?" the long-haired doctor had said after a cursory exam. "No way, no how, man."

"But—"

"You might be a lot of things, but dying you're not."

"But my heart—"

"Horse-doody. You listen to me, gramps. Eighty-six the smokes and lay off all the firewater. You do that and you're going to live to see a hundred… well, maybe ninety-nine. But you keep on going the way you are, then you're right, it's time to pick the lilies. You dig what I'm saying? It's a lifestyle thing. You've got to take care of yourself a little, that's all."

On his way out of the clinic, something had caught his eye, a pamphlet blown by the wind and trapped, fluttering, in the gutter. Gritting his teeth against the pain, he bent to retrieve it—white paper, a clenched black fist, a glaring blood-red title: THE MARXIST CURE FOR A SICK NATION. For just a moment, the black fist appeared to him to be a mighty tree, and the word MARXIST seemed to be something else entirely. But either way it was just as bad, and he dropped the pamphlet, which seesawed lazily back into the gutter like a wind-tossed seed.

He hurried away, fleeing as quickly as he could on legs that had long since lost the strength to run.

Now, working diligently on the bottle and listening to the sounds of traffic outside, he thought about the clinic and about the rude doctor and about dying (he had wanted to for so long, and now that he was, did not) and about going back to Michigan. Going back, going home. Returning to a place he hadn't been in thirty years, to a place where he had no family or friends, a town whose streets would seem new to him, whose customs and schedules would be as strange as Manhattan felt now.

Home.

He lit a cigarette and watched the smoke crawl toward the ceiling.

I'm coming.

His body shuddered, and he raised a clawlike hand to wipe away a single, saltless old man's tear.

2

HE AWOKE AT three A.M. to the sound of someone chopping wood nearby. He was still in the chair. The bottle had slipped from his hand some time before and lay amid a drying bourbon stain on the carpet. The room reeked of alcohol, tobacco, and sweat.

He realized immediately that there was no wood chopping going on—that had been part of a dream, nothing more—but the knowledge did nothing to slow the quick bursts of his breath or calm the stampede of his racing heart.

A dream, the same dream he'd been having for weeks now, ever since his decision had been made. A dark nightmare full of shadowy visions of his hometown, a town substantially the same as the one he had left so many years ago. There were none of the changes that he was sure must have occurred there. There had been no progress, no development, no modernization. It was frozen in time, this hometown of his dreams, and down its streets someone moved, coming silently, creeping stealthily. It was calling to him without words, summoning him, drawing him back.

A ghost of terror entered his body, midnight cold.

He wouldn't go, he decided. It was simple, really, as simple as the word *no*. He had avoided it this long; he could avoid it a little longer. He didn't want to die. He wanted to work. Keep hiding. That wouldn't be so bad. He was an expert, after all; it's what he was best at. It was an attractive idea, but he knew that it was just talk, empty thoughts. The time for hiding was over, and he had made that choice himself. There was no avoiding it now.

ALEXANDER'S SONG

He tried to get back to sleep, but was still sitting there, wide-eyed and trembling, when morning came.

3

HE LEFT MANHATTAN in his shiny new car at eight o' clock, under a cloudless sky, in bitter January cold. It had been many years since he had done any substantial amount of driving, but he found himself enjoying the trip nevertheless. He settled into the rhythm of it (or it settled into him) and the miles rolled by smoothly, easily, the road stretching ahead, a perfect thing to hold him in empty concentration, free for the most part from doubt and worry.

The snow began that afternoon, about the time he reached the Ohio line. Dialing around on the radio, he found a powerful Cleveland station where an announcer was saying, in breathless tones of excitement, that it was shaping up to be the worst blizzard the lower Great Lakes had seen in many years. He dialed again, found soothing music instead, and hunched over the wheel, wishing his vision would sharpen to compensate for the rapidly thickening curtains of white.

Not long after dark he came to a roadblock, flares and barricades and bundled, shivering troopers telling him to get off the turnpike, follow the old state route two miles east, and stop at the motor lodge there, where the owners would be serving complimentary coffee and food, bedding travelers down in the lobby for the night.

It was just as well. He had planned on exiting the turnpike anyway, not here but a few miles farther along. He had no intention of stopping, however. Michigan was still a long way off. There were many miles yet to go, and someone would be waiting for him when he got there.

The state highway was badly drifted, the shoulders and centerline lost, whatever scenery might have dressed up the view hidden in an endless blowing cloud. The lights of the motor lodge appeared briefly on his left, like a beacon along a storm-swept shore, and vanished again immediately.

He rubbed his eyes, which felt grainy and dry. The car bumped and slithered, shook and slid, grinding on.

He ground on, too.

When the car went off the road at twenty minutes of ten that night, it made very little noise as it tumbled end over end down into a snow-choked gully. Even the explosion that followed seemed muffled, there for a moment, swallowed up and gone the next.

It was a long time before the rescue vehicles arrived, and by then the flames had begun to die, licking slowly, feebly around the charred hulk of the car, already finished with the body inside.

"Look at that, willya," the first policeman on the scene said to his partner.

The partner, a rookie, nodded wordlessly. His stomach lurched as he stared at the diminishing flames, and he was struck by an image that came out of nowhere, without explanation, without sense.

It seemed to him that the flames were suddenly moving across the snow, actually coming toward him, approaching in a way that was not menacing but not entirely benign. He couldn't explain it then and never talked about it later. But for that one brief moment it seemed as if those fading, flickering tongues of fire were trying to tell him something, trying to communicate, speaking to him with a message he could not quite hear and could not hope to comprehend.

THE PRESENT...

PART ONE

CHASING A MYSTERY

Searching was the axis of her life. It was just as her father had always told her. The quest was everything, the quest for truth, for happiness, for meaning. She wondered why he hadn't warned her, then, that at the end of the road you never found what it was you had been looking for when you started out.

Alexander Bassett
from *Helen: A Tale* (Novel, 1947)

ONE

HISTORY, PEACE, AND A BETTER WORLD

1

On a warm, windy Friday in late April, a thirty-year-old schoolteacher named Andy Gillespie looked down on Rock Creek, Michigan. He had been in the town for more than a week, and so far his overriding impression of the place was that it was hopelessly out of touch with the rest of the world.

Get with it, people, he wanted to shout to every last one of Rock Creek's twenty-two-hundred residents. *Don't you read the papers? Don't you watch the news? The Berlin Wall is down. Germany is one. Poland's free—they've had real elections. The Soviet republics are in revolt. Castro's a dinosaur. The cold war is over.*

To which he was fatalistically sure the reply would be: *Not around here, buddy boy. Not around here it ain't.*

Those thoughts, which had been drifting through his mind for several days, solidified as he maneuvered his pickup truck around the rising twists and turns of a dirt trail the locals called Silver Mountain Road. The road began innocently enough on a flat stretch behind the parking lot of Waterland Realty, but soon enough became a steep and difficult climb.

The switchbacks were frequent and tight enough to make even the ascent seem a little like a carnival ride. Andy couldn't imagine what the trip back *down* was going to be like.

At the summit, he breathed a sigh of relief and allowed the truck to coast across the crushed gravel of the scenic overlook. A hundred yards away, set atop another little rise (in other words, on the highest spot of ground for perhaps fifty miles in any direction), were the dry bones of an old gift shop, the one Maxine Turner had told him closed a dozen years ago due to lack of business. Pale letters above the door read THE VANTAGE POINT GIFTS SOUVENIRS ANTIQUES, and in slightly smaller strokes, *Snacks Film Cold Pop*.

He stared at the building for a moment or two, gripped by the romantic notion that ancient ghosts would appear through the open doorway to bid him welcome. When nothing of the sort happened, he shut off the engine, climbed out, and walked to the edge of the cliff, where his heart actually skipped a beat and his breathing quickened.

To call the view spectacular was to be a libelous piker. Andy tried to come up with some word, *any* word, to describe what he saw and failed miserably.

Directly below was the town with its homes and stores and streets laid out on a not-quite-perfect grid, as though by several generations of mathematicians. The hawk's eye view was enlightening, but not exactly inspiring. The inspiration lay beyond the gradually diminishing sprawl of houses, cabins, and trailers, where the wilderness of the western Upper Peninsula unrolled dramatically.

From the edge of town, rounded hills far smaller than Silver Mountain went on forever, dappled with valleys and meadows and the occasional craggy gorge still filled with pure white snow. The lakes that gave the area its marginal fame sparkled among the hardwoods like jewels— Preston Lake and Green Lake, Carver Lake and Lake Manabozho. To the north was a thin, gray, hazy line that he knew was the biggest lake of all—Superior.

ALEXANDER'S SONG

He lit a cigarette and walked along the cliff edge, following a footpath that was really just a narrow trail of matted, spring-dead grass. It meandered in a lazy circle around the entire hilltop, and by the time Andy had made it back to where he'd started, he felt a nervous little flutter in his chest. The sense of isolation was overpowering. It was like the giddiness of being drunk with none of the exhilaration or joy.

He had never expected it to be like this. Driving up to the U.P. from Illinois, traveling the state of Wisconsin from south to north, you saw a lot of trackless woodland. Once you were north of Green Bay, there were few towns or villages. But confined to the highway, Andy had thought that surely, somewhere back behind all those trees, civilization had been lurking. It might be a mile away, or ten, or thirty, but it was there. Now, however, seeing the view from Silver Mountain, he understood for the first time that he was in the middle of…nothing…miles and miles of nothing. Looking to the northeast, toward the town of L'Anse twenty-five miles away, he saw only what looked like a large patch of darker forest. Due north, up the Keweenaw Peninsula, the larger cities of Houghton and Hancock were an invisible dream.

He crushed out his cigarette and immediately lit another, unsure what surprised him more: that one of the greatest writers of the twentieth century had come from this area, or that *he* had left Chicago and come all the way up here to research that great writer. Or was it some combination of the two? All he knew for sure was that he, a private man, essentially friendless and comfortable with that, felt suddenly lost and unsteady and almost fatally lonely.

He stayed there a few minutes more, held and frightened by the view, wanting to return to town but not quite able to accomplish the seemingly simple acts of going back to the truck, getting in, turning the key, heading down the mountain. The scent of distant wood smoke seemed to permeate the air, making it heavier than normal, and after a time he began to think that he could reach out and physically grasp a chunk of it. The sound of birds—what kind, whether large or small, native or transient, he didn't know—was simultaneously nearby and endlessly far away.

The sudden sound of crunching gravel made him spin around in time to see someone approaching him at great speed. The shift from staring dreamily out over miles of wilderness to looking at something so close turned whoever was there into a blur of color—red and gray and blue, all washed together. For a panicky split second he imagined someone charging into him, his feet slipping, his body stumbling awkwardly backward, toppling over the knee-high fence that ran around the overlook, dropping downward into an oblivion of oak branches and pine needles. Then he heard rasping breath and a rusty squeal of brakes.

"It's you," a voice said.

2

SHE WAS RIDING a bicycle, an old blue Schwinn haphazardly touched-up with rust-colored blots of primer. After one final second of startled disorientation he recognized her.

"It's Virginia, isn't it?"

"Ginnie, yeah."

Red-faced and puffing, she planted her feet on the ground and sagged over the handlebars. A full minute went by while she gathered the strength to continue.

"Shit, I haven't been up here in two or three years. I forgot what a climb it is."

"It's quite a mountain, all right."

That made her laugh. "This is no mountain. Where my dad lives, in Utah, *those* are mountains. There's nothing in Michigan but big hills."

"*Really* big hills," Andy said with a smile.

He had met her last night, over dinner at Turner's Bed and Breakfast—another one of Maxine's stupefyingly large spreads of roast and potatoes and salad and corn and several dishes he couldn't even remember. Her name was Virginia Turner. She was Max's seventeen-year-old daughter, a high school junior who spent winters in Provo with her father, Max's

ALEXANDER'S SONG

ex-husband, and summers in Rock Creek with her mom. She had just returned to Michigan yesterday, a full six weeks early, because her father had been suddenly called to a temporary four-month stint on an offshore oil rig in Louisiana.

"You're probably wondering why I'm not in school," she said. Andy hadn't been wondering anything of the kind, but he nodded encouragingly for her to go on. "I'm starting on Monday. Hard enough to switch schools when it's practically the end of the year. I didn't want to start at the end of the week, too."

He flashed a vague smile and checked his watch. It was a rude thing to do, but it was hard to muster any shame. One of the benefits of being on a leave-of-absence from teaching was that he didn't have to talk to seventeen-year-olds for a few months, and when he did, didn't necessarily have to pretend to be interested in everything they said and did.

"You're pretty brave," he told her, "bringing an old bike like that, with no gears, all the way up here."

She nodded, absently straightening the hem of her Utah Jazz sweatshirt. "Mom said you came up here. I wanted to talk to you."

She might as well have said she wanted to buy a forty-foot yacht and sail to the moon. He gave her a blank, uncomprehending stare.

"I was helping her with the breakfast dishes when she let it slip. She said you were interested in Alexander Bassett."

He frowned.

"Are you?"

"Am I?"

"Are you interested in Bassett?"

"Yeessss," he said cautiously. "But what do you—"

"I'm a fan of his. I thought maybe we could talk."

"A fan? You mean you've actually read his stuff?"

"Oh, yeah, all of it. I even did a paper on *To Raise Brave Men* for American Lit last semester."

"But your mother calls him—"

"Bassett-the-commie, I know. Hey, what can I say? Appreciation of fine art isn't genetic. My mom wouldn't know a great book if it bit her on the ass, and my dad's favorite reading is a back issue of *Popular Mechanics*, when he can swipe one from the dentist's office."

Andy felt his initial wariness crumble a little, but it was replaced by an even more discomforting sense of confusion. For seven days he had been trudging around Rock Creek, banging his head against walls, trying fruitlessly to find anyone with information about the town's most famous son. Information, hell. In all honesty he had been trying to find anyone who would even mention the man's name without attaching a pejorative. And now here she was, surprising him on what was supposed to be a morning off, a seventeen-year-old, a student, a kid. She was a Bassett fan, and she had written about him, and she considered his work fine art.

It would doubtless come to nothing, but he couldn't help feeling a little like a prospector who packs up after months of useless searching only to find nuggets of gold lying in the road on the way back to civilization.

"Are you a critic?" she asked.

He shook his head. "I'm a writer. Well...actually, that's not exactly true. I *want* to be a writer. What I am is a high school teacher. I've been reading Bassett for years. I've collected him, studied him, even taught most of his work in class at one time or another. I decided to give myself a birthday present this year, so I took some time off to write about him."

"A book?"

"Not at first." He hesitated, not fond of the direction the conversation was taking as it veered away from Bassett and headed straight for him. "I don't...I mean, I'm not sure I can find enough material for a full book, and frankly, I don't know if I have the ability to write one. I thought I'd see what information I can gather, put it all together, and try a series of articles." He stopped again, and shrugged. "If someone came along and wanted to collect them in book form, I certainly wouldn't say no."

"That's great," she said, and he realized by the tone of her voice that she meant it.

ALEXANDER'S SONG

Andy looked at her closely, interested in her eyes. They were dancing with scholar's fire. It was a look he had always wished more of his students would display, but now it made him uneasy. His feet itched. He wished that he could back away from her without falling over the cliff. He could feel intensity radiating from her like waves of heat.

"I'll bet you're not having an easy time of it around here," she said.

He laughed in spite of himself. "Whatever gave you that idea?"

"Why do you think Bassett moved away? My mom's not the only narrow-minded person in this town. Let's face it, I don't think there's been much enlightened thought in Rock Creek since Hell Time."

Andy blinked. "*What* time?"

"Hell Time, you know, the lumbering days back in the 1800s."

"I never heard—"

"In those days, if you wanted to catch a train to Rock Creek, you asked the station master for a ticket to Hell."

He smiled thinly.

"No, it's true. There were a lot of towns like that. You ever hear of Seney? It's east of here, near Newberry. Seney was the *real* Hell Town, but Rock Creek was a strong runner-up. In the 1890s, the population here was triple what it is now. There were bunches of logging camps and lumber mills, maybe a dozen hotels, more than twenty saloons, God only knows how many tattoo parlors and whorehouses, and I'll bet a lot of undertakers, too. It was crazy back then, but once those days were gone, they were really gone. The closest thing we get now is a couple of winos punching each other out in Allie's Bar on payday."

Andy didn't know whether to be amused or impressed by the span of her knowledge, and finally decided he was both. "Did you really write a paper on *Brave Men?*"

Ginnie nodded, which caused a thick shock of red hair to fall across her eyes. She brushed it back, and said, "Thirty-five pages. It was great. I'll show it to you sometime, if you want. It contrasted the play to the novel it was based on, and to all his other works too. I also tried to answer a question that always bugged me: Why did he write only that one play? Why not a stage version of one of his other books—*Seascape*, maybe, or *Doctor Howell*? Unfortunately, my teacher's idea of activist literature began and ended with Upton Sinclair. She gave me a C+"

"Forever misunderstood," Andy said softly, and with just a trace of humor. A thought occurred to him, and he brightened. "Since you're a fan, maybe you'd know of anyone else around here who shares your enthusiasm. A teacher, maybe? Someone like that?"

Ginnie gave a harsh, snorting laugh. "Not many, but your best bet would be Liz Rappala over at the library. She always—"

"Forget it. I stopped at the library my first day here. They have the books, all tucked away on a little shelf in the back, but it seems Mrs. Rappala retired just after Christmas and moved to Florida to live with her son. Her replacement's a college dropout by the name of Connie Something."

"Connie LeMay? I know her. She was a couple of years ahead of me in school. Don't tell me she hates Bassett, too?"

"She doesn't hate him. She didn't even know his books were in the building. She's never even heard of him."

"Well, I guess that about sums up Rock Creek." She sighed. "This might sound lame, but what kind of information are you after? I've been into Bassett since I was ten, ever since I found out a real writer once lived here. Maybe I can help."

Andy shook his head. "What I really need is to talk to someone who knew Bassett when he was in Rock Creek, someone who maybe went to school with him, who remembers what he was like, what kind of grades he got, what he talked about, what he liked to read." He paused, lighting a cigarette. "So far, I've found four...four people who were around here way back then."

"And?"

"Let's see. There was Albert Anson."

"From Allie's Bar?"

"Right. He's ninety-two, but surprisingly he was the most lucid one in the bunch. He claims to remember everything about our man, even what his parents were like, what clothes he used to wear, things like that."

"That's good."

"It would be, I guess, but he refused to talk. Oh, he'd ramble on endlessly about anything else under the sun. I'll bet he spent twenty minutes complaining about the potholes on Carver Lake Road. But when it came to Bassett, he said he wouldn't spare two words on any treasonous, fairyboy scum—or words to that effect. The names he called Bassett make your mother sound like a speaker at a testimonial dinner."

"Who else?"

"Evelyn Van Wyck. Do you know her? She's eighty or eighty-one, just about the age Bassett would be if he was alive. She lives all by herself in a trailer out on some back road."

"King Oak Road. Yeah, I know her. What'd she have to say?"

"She remembers going to school with Alex and his older sister, Ruth. She remembers him as a bright boy, inquisitive, eager to learn, not like the others in her class."

"That's all?"

"That's it. She wanted to know why I was interested. I told her there were always people interested in the pasts of great writers, and she said, 'Writer? Is *that* what became of him?'"

Ginnie smiled faintly. "You must be awfully frustrated."

"That's one word for it, yes."

"Well, don't worry. I'm sure we'll be able to nail something down, if we try hard enough. It's just a matter of looking in the right places."

Andy swallowed a mouthful of smoke and coughed. It seemed that he must have heard her wrong. *We'll* nail something down, if *we* try hard enough? The thought of it didn't so much make him wary again; it ignited a spark of anger. He had already been at this for three months. He had spent countless hours in libraries back in Chicago, countless long nights pouring over Bassett's works for the thousandth time, countless phone calls to university collections and the New York Public Library and various publishers. The notebooks back in his room at the bed and breakfast (seven of them so far, each filled with history and biographical tidbits and trivia) were his. He didn't like what he was feeling now, the utterly irrational selfishness of a little boy trying his best to keep a trunk full of toys from his playmates, but he couldn't help himself.

"I don't know," he said slowly. The selfishness was all mixed up in his mind, tumbled and jumbled together with the incredibly lonely sense of isolation he'd been dealing with just a short time before. He felt trapped. "To be honest with you, I've been thinking of—"

"I'll make a list," she said, as though he hadn't spoken at all. He wondered if he had, or if the words had only been in his mind. "Things to check, people to talk to. We'll find something you can use. I guarantee it."

The weight of her smile pressed down on him. He spread his hands and shrugged and grinned. Helpless, he thought. Trapped and helpless.

3

EIGHT DAYS AGO, on his way down Rock Creek Road from Highway 41, Andy had passed a billboard for a hotel with the ridiculous name of the Sleep-Tite. The sign advertised king-sized beds (waterbeds available), cable TV, free HBO, movies, continental breakfasts, and a lounge. What would you call the lounge in a place like the Sleep-Tite? he had wondered. The Drink-A-Lot? And then, because it seemed as good as any of the many advertised alternatives (Jefferson's Motor Court, Camp Sleepaway Cabins, Kim Washburn's Wilderness Hideaway, Lake Manabozho Resort and Boat Rental, Chief Stop-In-Here Motel), he had decided to give it a try.

The hotel was a not-very-impressive three-story building at the far end of Michigan Street, Rock Creek's main thoroughfare. The only place to stay in what passed for a downtown business district, it anchored a block between Baraga and Iron Streets that contained a hardware store,

ALEXANDER'S SONG

Watterson's Appliances, the Commercial National Bank of L'Anse - Rock Creek Branch, and Shelby's Quad Lakes Outfitters.

The lobby was a long, dark, high-ceilinged room where all the furnishings looked dusty whether they were or not. It smelled faintly of oil-based paint and stale fried food. There were two shelves of souvenirs for sale and a spinning rack of free brochures advertising area attractions on the wall opposite the registration desk. A dirty brass chandelier high overhead had seven of eight sixty-watt bulbs burning, just enough to highlight the frayed edges of the large floral-pattern rug laid in the center of the room.

Andy tapped the service bell, waited a minute, rang it twice more, and had turned away to study the brochures when a voice from behind made him jump.

"The sign says 'Please Ring Bell For Service.' It doesn't say play a goddamned symphony."

He found himself looking at a little old woman who had materialized from some back room behind the desk. Except for her jeans and a sweatshirt that said I CAUGHT A LUNKER ON THE QUAD LAKES! his immediate impression was that she was a troll—not an actual fairy tale troll, but one of those silly rubber dolls he remembered from his childhood. She might have been five feet tall, though that seemed overly generous. Her hair was long, thick, straight, snow white. It zoomed down to her shoulders and then took off at right angles, bristling outward. Her face was tanned and lined, her eyes tiny dark beads almost lost within creased pouches of flesh.

"Name's Marilyn," she said. "Don't wear it out." Before Andy could respond to this, she went on: "I suppose you want a room."

"If you have one, yes."

"Hon, I got rooms dripping out of my asshole." She cast out a withered hand and reeled in a dusty leather register. "How long?"

"I beg your pardon?"

"How *long*? How many nights?"

"I...I'm not sure. At least a week, maybe longer. If that's a problem, I—"

"You want a week, you got a week. You want the effing summer, you can have that, too. Sign here."

"What about rates?" he said, taking the pen she offered but not quite touching it to the book.

"What about them?"

"What are they?"

She sighed, as though displeased with the effort such an answer would require. "Off-season like this, it's fifty a night. You go by the week, I can let you have a single for three-hundred."

"That's a lot."

"Fifty?" She laughed, and it was indeed a troll's laugh, a sharp, humorless sound that suited her perfectly. "What decade you from, darlin'?"

"It's not that," he said, stung, wanting to defend himself without quite knowing why. "It's only that...well, I'm going to be here quite a while. I've got to save every dime I can."

Marilyn was unimpressed. Her eyes seemed to sink deeper into her head. He imagined he could see her impatient displeasure pulsing away beneath the flesh of her forehead like an artery. "Not going to do much better anywhere else," she said. "There's only two or three other places open. The rest don't start up till next month. Not much competition, if you know what I'm saying."

Andy nodded; he knew. "Maybe I better look around."

"Suit yourself."

"I might be back."

"I'll be here."

"Thanks for your help."

"Hon, Help is my goddamned middle name."

He was almost out the door when something occurred to him. He spun back and caught her just before she vanished into whatever office there was behind the desk.

"Excuse me? Marilyn? I know this is a long shot, but did you ever know a man by the name of Alexander Bassett? He was—"

"I know what he was. He was a commie."

"A *what?*"

This time her laugh seemed to have more genuine humor in it, although Andy still thought that if he could somehow touch it, the sound would cut him like a razor blade.

"You heard me," she said. "He was a commie—a red."

"But he wasn't! Or at least that's not exactly what he was. He was really more of a socialist, or—"

"Hon, I don't give a flying you-know-what if he was a communist, a socialist, or a what-all. Isn't any of my business."

"You knew him?"

Her troll head bobbed once. "A little."

"Did he—"

"Knew his father, too. Rich man, more money than God."

Andy felt lightheaded. He seemed to be floating several inches off the ground. He imagined the lobby of the Sleep-Tite revolving slowly around him. He felt the urge to grab onto something for support and was disappointed that the nearest object was the main door, still eight or ten feet away. "You knew...what was his name? William Bassett?"

"That was him, all right."

"And you knew him?"

"Knew *of* him."

"Could you ...." He hesitated, trying to rein himself in before he got swept giddily away. He felt woefully unprepared. His notebooks were still in his suitcase, tucked behind the bench seat of the truck. His tape recorder was there, too, and he didn't trust himself to remember whatever she might tell him; his mind and body were too road-weary for that.

"I guess the time's not right," he said, "but if you wouldn't mind, I'd like to talk more about all of this. Maybe tomorrow? Or the next day? Whenever it's convenient, I could—"

"Save your strength, hon. I don't know what you want and I don't care why." She shook her head firmly. "Isn't anything to talk about. The man had more money than God. I mean the old man, not the commie. He could do whatever he wanted. He could get away with anything. That's all I know."

"But—"

"Good luck finding a cheap room. You're going to need it."

She refused to say another word, and that was how Andy not only received a foretaste of the trouble he would have in Rock Creek, but also how he ended up spending forty-four dollars a night for a place at Turner's Bed and Breakfast on Victory Street.

4

OVER DINNER THAT Friday night, Maxine entertained them with stories of Rock Creek's early days, both the Hell Time Ginnie had told him about and the years prior to that, which could best be described as a rugged period of settlement. Besides Andy and Ginnie and Max herself, there were five other people at dinner, two young couples on early-season vacations and a salesman named Sheridan traveling through on his way from Sault Ste. Marie to Duluth, Minnesota. ("I always stay at B&Bs when I'm on the road," Sheridan had said. "It's cheaper, and you usually get dinner thrown in, too, at least in the off-season. Best food going is at these places. You can shove your Ramadas and Red Roofs in a nice dark place, lemme tell you.")

Andy listened to Max's stories with morbid interest. The history of Rock Creek and the Upper Peninsula, from the earliest fur trading days up through the eras of logging, iron and copper mining, seemed to be composed entirely of bloodshed and unhappiness, of poverty and hardship, struggle and death. Listening to Max's stories was like reading a historical record carved in cold and unforgiving granite. The others didn't seem to mind. They joked and laughed a lot. One of the young men, a Detroit insurance adjuster by the name of Tony Chizmar, said "Yeah!" and pumped his fist in the air every time Max told of a logger felled by his own axe or

ALEXANDER'S SONG

a miner lost forever in a dark, uncharted ore drift. When she came to the story of two saloon keepers gunning each other down in the mud of the main street, apparently over a dispute involving a shipment of whiskey and a pretty woman, the salesman Sheridan said, "Ah, those bastards really lived on the edge back then," in an awestruck, admiring tone.

For his part, Andy lost much of his appetite and held his gestures to an occasional nod or faint smile. He found himself able to appreciate the horrendous difficulty of life back then without taking pleasure in that understanding, and he saw images of Rock Creek in its infancy superimposed on the landscape he had studied that morning from the top of Silver Mountain. He knew the resulting pictures were accurate. The land hadn't changed much in the last hundred years. It probably wouldn't change much in the *next* hundred. There would be the town, a spot of dim light in the middle of darkness, a quiet island in the center of an even quieter wilderness that just went on and on. The town and the trees—no more.

Afterward, while Ginnie helped her mother with the dishes, Andy went out on the porch. The warm day had been swept aside by a bitter evening, with temperatures hovering somewhere just below forty and a shrill northwest wind delivering snow flurries all the way from Lake Superior. He pulled the collar of his jacket up, found that it did no good, shoved his hands in his pockets, and sat on the steps, where he could watch rowdy teenagers coming and going from a party across the street, carrying bottles in plain brown bags and twelve-packs of beer like suitcases. He felt depressed, the frustration and the time-is-running-out anxiety of this trip north pressing between his eyes like a throbbing headache. His leave of absence had begun after Christmas. In August he would have to return to work. His freedom was half gone, and yet he had so little information and next to nothing down on paper. Worse, he wasn't sure he cared anymore.

And yet he knew that wasn't true. As he gazed across the street at the tall white house, it was frighteningly easy to allow the partygoers and cars and stereo music to dissolve, to let everything swirl together into a silent, monochrome background, like a movie screen on which he saw projected another trip to Rock Creek. He arrived, he asked questions, the locals were knowledgeable and friendly, interested in helping him with his project. In this trip-that-never-was he accumulated pages of notes like snowdrifts, each page filled with his small, cramped handwriting covering details of Alexander Bassett's childhood and adolescence. His articles formed themselves in a kind of weird, spontaneous way, an evolution over which he needed no control. They grew from locals' mouths to printed, published page with eerie, easy speed.

"There you are. You're going to freeze your ass off out here, don't you know that?"

The movie vanished abruptly, but he was still reluctant to turn away. When he did, he saw Ginnie poking her head out the door, her red hair pink and punklike in the glow of the porch light. "I've been looking all over for you. Phone call."

"For me?"

"Yeah, of course. Long distance. You better hurry; she's already been holding for four or five minutes."

She, he thought. His mind felt gummed and sticky; he didn't seem capable of making the necessary connection to understand what all this was about.

"Do you want me to have her call back?" Ginnie asked in an exasperated tone.

"What's that? Oh. No...no, of course not. I'll take it."

The phone was on a small wooden table in the corner of the living room, across from the couch where Sheridan was entertaining one of the young couples with tales of his life on the road. When Andy lifted the receiver to his ear, he heard a hiss of static.

"Hello?"

The static grew louder for a moment. He thought he heard a voice say a few words, but he only caught the last two: "...that you?"

"This is Andy Gillespie. Who is this, please?"

"Me...damn fool...you think...is?"

The line was so clogged now with bursts of electrical interference that the person on the other end sounded young, old, male, female. He was reminded of trying to listen to an AM radio during a bad thunderstorm and being unsure if the broken voice came from a live announcer, a taped commercial, or maybe even a song.

"Could you speak up, please? We've got a really bad connection here."

There were no words at all this time, just a hoarse explosion of white noise followed by an empty metallic rattle.

"Hello?"

"...me, Andy, who...oh, goddammit...on...back!"

The line suddenly went dead, and the rapid transition from sound to silence was like sailing off the edge of the world.

"Everything okay there, pal?" the salesman called from across the room. Andy nodded slowly, staring at the receiver and finally putting it back in its cradle.

Without having anything solid to base it on, he had the impression that he'd been talking to the old troll woman from the hotel; Marilyn, she'd said her name was—don't wear it out. The faint possibility that she'd decided to talk to him about Bassett after all was immediately overcome by the knowledge that she didn't know where he was staying, or even that he was still in town. Even more obviously, he'd never had a chance to tell her his name.

The phone rang again before he stepped away from it, but this time when he picked it up, the connection was as sharp and clear as winter sunlight.

"Well, thank god, this is better."

He came back onto solid ground with a jarring thud. The muscles of his jaw felt like worn-out rubber bands, slack and powerless.

"You are there, aren't you?"

"Jo? Is that you?"

"Not tonight," said his ex-wife. "Tonight, I'm your fairy godmother."

"Jesus Christ," he thought and said at the same time.

"Yeah, I figured you'd be overjoyed." Her laughter sounded a little like the static that had jammed the line before. "I tried reaching you in Chicago—spent two days trying. What the hell are you still doing up there in Podunk Creek?"

"Rock Creek," he said automatically.

"Yes, Andy, I know the name of the town. My question was, what in God's name are you doing there?"

"The same thing I came to do. What did you think? I'm doing research."

"Of course you are."

"Jo...where are you? How did you find me?"

"I'm in New York. And finding you wasn't hard. I don't know about there in Stone River, but here in the real world we have something called 'information.' Sometimes we call it 'directory assistance,' but it's the same thing when you come right—"

"Jo, c'mon. How'd you know where I was staying?"

"I didn't." She laughed again. "Pebble Stream only has fourteen places listed under hotels-slash-motels. I got the numbers one at a time and dialed alphabetically. Most never even answered the phone."

"Closed for the season," Andy said softly, and felt a weight beginning to press on his chest. Whatever had made Joanne spend—what? Half an hour? An hour? Whatever had made her spend that amount of time dialing numbers, trying to reach him, it couldn't be good. At the same time, he was aware of being watched closely, scrutinized. The combined gazes of the threesome on the couch and Ginnie in the doorway made his palms sweat and the back of his neck itch.

"What's wrong, Jo?"

"Nothing's wrong, Mister Suspicious. I called to help you out. I know you probably find that next to impossible to believe, but it's true. I thought I'd give you a hand."

"A hand," he heard himself say. His mind started bumping down illogical tracks. "Why are you in New York? Why aren't you in Orlando?"

"Bob had to come up here on business, so I tagged along."

ALEXANDER'S SONG

"Bob."

"Yes, Andy, you remember. Bob. The man who replaced you. The man you could never be." She paused, then added in a here's-the-proof tone: "We're spending two weeks at the Plaza."

His lips felt thick and dry. "What a lovely, perfectly Bob-like place to stay. Did you mention something about giving me a hand?"

"As a matter of fact, yes." She paused again, and in that moment, Andy had a snapshot-clear picture of her in her hotel room, sitting on the edge of a huge bed, her bare feet cushioned by thick, rich carpeting. He saw her playing with her hair, twirling the ends of several long, dark strands around her index finger. She was smiling, he realized. It was the same thin smile she'd always had when she knew she was making a fool of him. He wondered quickly if Bob Jackowicz was in the room too, watching her from an easy chair across the way, drink in hand. Just wondering chased the entire image away.

"I suppose you haven't found many of your pet writer's diaries up there in Gravel Pond," she said mildly.

Andy's heart sped up, but slowed again a second later. "No, but I know all about the collection of Bassett's journals at Columbia. That's one of the reasons I'm heading to New York when I'm finished here."

"Well, bully for you. I'm not talking about something in a stuffy old library. I'm talking about the diary I found for sale, in a decidedly *un*-stuffy used bookstore."

He saw the words she had just uttered printed on some mental screen in black block type, but the letters were all jumbled and he couldn't grasp their sense. "What did you say?"

"Please, Andy, don't waste my time. You heard me. Do you want me to get it for you or not? I've been having the proprietor hold it two days already, and he's none too happy about it."

"Uh," was all he managed to say for several seconds. Then the mental log jam broke and the words tumbled out. "Yes, yes, of course. Get it. If you're sure you've got the name right, I mean if you're sure it's Alexander

Bassett and not someone else, and if the bookstore's willing to stand behind its authenticity, get it right away. How much?"

"Thirty-five dollars. I suppose that's not a lot, is it? Not for something from a writer so many people are nuts about."

He heard something in her voice and recognized it as a combination of disdain and grudging respect; in all the years he had known her, he'd never been able to get her to share his enthusiasm for Bassett's work, or even to finish one of his books.

"Are you kidding?" he said. "It's probably worth four times that. Can you...do you remember how many years it covered? What time period?"

She sighed, sending the message that she was unable to care less. "I think it was 1926 or '27."

"Oh my god." He felt dizzy, as though he were standing high above the sitting room, looking down. The journals in the Columbia University collection were all from the forties, when Bassett was a very famous man. 1927, on the other hand....

"Are you there, Andy?"

"I'm here. I just realized—that's from when he was a kid, before he went to the University of Wisconsin, even. It's from when he lived—" He paused, briefly forgetting the name of the town. "—when he lived here in Rock Creek. Did you have a chance to read it? What did it say?"

"Oh, really now. When did you develop such a sterling sense of humor?"

He nodded, as though she were there with him. "I guess you'd rather read the Tokyo phone book, wouldn't you? It doesn't matter. Jesus, it's enough that you even found it."

"So you *do* want it?"

"Of course! Buy it! I'll send you the money when you get back to Florida. Mail it off to me here. I can give you the address and—no, wait. Don't mail it. Express it."

"You mean they actually have express service to Granite Swamp?"

"Yes, Jo, yes, they do."

ALEXANDER'S SONG

The dizzy feeling refused to leave. He thought he might float through the roof any minute, out into the windy night.

He told her to wait while he asked Ginnie for the full address and Zip code. She disappeared from the doorway and came back a minute later with a glossy postcard that showed the big three-story house surrounded by a blaze of autumn color. On the back it said, *Turner's Bed and Breakfast, a great place to stay in the heart of the Quad Lakes Country!* along with the address, phone number, and information on rates.

"You there, Jo?"

"Hanging on."

"Even if you can ship the book tomorrow, I guess I won't get it till Monday, but that's still faster than mailing it. I'll reimburse the express charges too."

"You're damn right you will."

He gave her the address, and before she could go, said, "Why are you doing this?"

Her voice turned soft, distant, dreamily innocent. "Doing what, Andy?"

"You know what I mean." He cleared his throat, trying to rid himself of that dizzy floating sensation, ordering his mind, wanting to get the words absolutely right. "Why did you have the bookstore hold the journal? Why did you try so hard to get hold of me? When I told you about my articles, you called me a kid who wouldn't grow up. You said the whole thing was a crazy, irresponsible goose chase. Why go through so much trouble to help me now?"

There was a long moment of nothingness on the line. The receiver was like a rock against his ear.

"I guess six years of marriage has to mean something," she said at last.

He had a bit of difficulty breathing as he murmured, "But what about two years of divorce?"

He was still waiting for an answer when he understood that the line was dead and that this time she was gone for real.

5

"I WANT YOU to know something," Ginnie said on their way up to the third floor. "I don't make a habit of visiting strange guy's rooms the very first day I meet them."

"I'm sure you don't," Andy said, recognizing the joke for what it was but still flying in the fog of Joanne's call. He was glad the upstairs hallway was dark; it made avoiding further conversation easy as they fumbled along to his room.

"You're not still thinking of leaving, are you?"

He ushered her into the room and snapped on the overhead light. "How did you know I ever was?"

"Oh, hey, was it supposed to be a secret? I could see it all over your face this morning, up on the mountain. You had the towel in your hands, just waiting to throw it in."

He nodded. She was right. "It's not that I wanted to, but I was dead-ended. I didn't know what else to do. I thought the whole trip was a waste. I was beginning to think I could've learned more about Bassett by staying home, and I *knew* I could learn more by going on to New York."

"Until your wife called."

"Ex-wife."

"Sorry."

He waved the apology away. "My guess is that journal's going to be full of things I can use. In 1927 he was…eighteen, I guess. There should be names, places, all sorts of leads to follow. It'll tell me a lot about what kind of person he was back then."

"And point the way to people who can tell you more."

"Well, yes." He nodded. "With any luck, yes."

"And in the meantime—" She dug in the back pocket of her jeans and produced a folded sheet torn from a yellow legal pad. "—we can talk to these guys."

ALEXANDER'S SONG

Andy took the page, glanced at it quickly, but didn't recognize any of the four names Ginnie had scrawled there. He had a feeling about the first one, though. "This Marilyn Borg...she doesn't, by any chance—"

"She owns the Sleep-Tite. That's a hotel down on Michigan Street. Not the friendliest person in the world. When we were kids, we used to go in there on summer afternoons—the lobby was so dark and cool, it was great—but she always chased us out with a golf club she kept under the counter. She was about eighty back then, I think; she's got to be a hundred and fifty now."

"I was afraid of that," Andy said. In his mind he heard the troll woman saying, *Hon, I got rooms dripping out of my asshole* and *I don't know what you want and I don't care why ….Isn't anything to talk about.* He quickly told Ginnie about his first day in town. "I had it in the back of my mind to go there one more time before I left, but I doubt it would do any good." He checked the list again. "Who's 'J.L. and husband'?"

"That's Jeanette Lammi. I think her husband's name is Toivo, something weird like that, something Finnish. They live on Keller Road, and they might not be as old as Marilyn Borg, but I know damn well they're old enough to have been here in Bassett's time. Toivo's grandfather was one of the men my mom was talking about tonight, one of the town founders."

Andy lowered himself into the straight-back chair by the desk. He fumbled a cigarette out of his pack, lit it, and said, "Ed Hoffer?"

For the first time since she'd come puffing up Silver Mountain Road that morning, a look of uncertainty crossed Ginnie's face. "He's a long shot. I don't know anything about him except that he's old. He lives in a cabin on Wolf Island."

Andy heard this as *golf highland*. "Where?"

"Wolf Island. It's out in the middle of Green Lake. I've never been out there or anything. It's all private; I guess he owns it all. But it looks real pretty from shore, real rugged and woodsy, you know what I mean? Kind of desolate."

"You think he knew Bassett?"

Her red hair swung rhythmically back and forth as she shook her head. "All I know is what I told you. He's old. I'll tell you this, though—going out there will be a real adventure."

Andy glanced down at the growing column of ash on his cigarette. He felt the tug of gravity and knew that he was starting to come back to earth after the excitement of the phone call.

Planning new interviews, especially with so little to go on, made the memories of his failures clearer. He wasn't sure he was up for another round of frustration, hearing Rock Creek's assessment of Alexander Bassett—*The man was a bum, he was a no-damn-good commie creep, don't you know that, fella?*—repeated over and over.

The fact that Ginnie's enthusiasm was like a hammer, chipping steadily away at his reserve, didn't necessarily help. She saw this search for information as a game, or as she had just said, an adventure. That wasn't a bad thing in itself, but what was going to happen when the weekend was over and she had to return to school?

He sighed. "Islands now. I suppose that means renting a boat or something? And all to find out what color shirts Bassett wore in elementary school."

"Or maybe hear how he used to preach Marxist philosophy on the playground after class," Ginnie said.

That prospect, as dim as it was, brought back a little of his cheer. "Maybe so," he said. "That would be something, all right."

He looked at the last name on her list: Martin Visnaw.

"I should have thought of him earlier," Ginnie said. "He owns a store in town—The Trading Post. Sells rubber tomahawks and plastic ashtrays, mostly, sweatshirts and moccasins and postcards, all the usual stuff."

Andy nodded. He had seen the place a few days earlier—a small store, outwardly indistinguishable from the three or four other gift shops in the same block. "He's old?"

"You'd never know it, but yeah. He runs every day, or at least he did, and I used to see him hiking a lot out near the lakes. He's in great shape."

ALEXANDER'S SONG

She quickly told him the rest. She had met Martin Visnaw four years earlier, before her parents' divorce, when she was still a full-time resident of the Creek. She had known who he was, of course—everyone in town knew everyone else, at least by face and name, often by reputation—but had never spoken to him until one afternoon when she'd run into him at the library, reading a piece called "The Nature and Meaning of Sorrow" in *The Collected Essays of Alexander Bassett*.

"He didn't know Bassett, but he'd been a hardcore fan for years. We talked for a couple hours that first day, and when I ran into him a month or two later, taking a walk out near Carver Lake, we talked again. He invited me over to his house." She closed her eyes, remembering. "It just blew me away. The guy has the most incredible collection—all the books in first editions, poems and stories in the original magazines, book reviews, newspaper articles, an interview that ran in *Publishers Weekly* back in the forties. He even had an opening night *Playbill* from the Broadway version of *Brave Men*. "I'm not saying he can help you. I don't know, he might not have anything you haven't already seen. But he's been collecting longer than you've been alive, and even better, he's been *here*. Ten bucks says he's worth our time."

Andy nodded, although he wasn't really thinking about Martin Visnaw's collection. Absurdly, he was feeling pushed, manipulated, and he couldn't help thinking about another essay in Bassett's only non-fiction book, one entitled "Service and Selfishness." Its thesis (roughly stated: that man has a duty to work for humanity, but that to do so he must ignore the wants and desires of those around him, acting only on the true guiding messages spoken by his own heart) seemed all tied up with what they were talking about, with his search, with Ginnie's eager ambition, with Joanne's call, with the six-year-old's single-minded greed he had been feeling earlier in the day.

Ginnie wanted to help, but she wanted something from him in return. She needed him to give her the key, the tools to unlock the secrets of her literary hero. He wondered why that should matter, and he wished that it did not.

"It's not the world's greatest list, I know," she said, obviously seeing the uncertainty written all over his face. "Give me another day or two and I can come up with more names. Jesus, this town's full of old people. But it's a start, right? If nothing else, it ought to fill the time till that journal gets here."

He heard the eagerness to please in her voice, and when he looked into her eyes he felt both a thud of recognition and the powerful snap of something cold in his heart loosening its hold. For the first time he understood that she wanted much more than just the key to Bassett's hidden past. He saw her as a whole person, alive, complex, full of pushing and striving contradictions, bristling with desires. Her face held an expression he had seen only half a dozen times before in all his years teaching. It was the look of the uncommonly bright high schooler, the silent plea beneath whatever mundane topic was being discussed: *Tell me there's room in the world for someone who likes to think. Tell me there's a place for someone whose concerns run beyond classes and parties. Tell me. Prove it to me.*

This realization made him feel ugly, stony, uncharitable, sad...and a little nervous.

"Ginnie," he said after a moment, "have a seat." He pointed to the unmade bed behind her. "I've got something special I want to show you."

6

"THIS PROBABLY ISN'T my most treasured possession," he said, reaching into the suitcase that sat in the corner on a stand of aluminum with black nylon webbing. "That would be my first edition *Bleak House*. But this is close." He gingerly produced a small hardcover book and handed it to her.

She took the copy of *A Daughter's Song* with a bland, noncommittal smile. "I've got an old copy of this too. I picked it up at a garage sale in Provo for two dollars."

"I doubt it's quite like this. This is a first edition—but that's not all. Flip to the title page."

ALEXANDER'S SONG

She did, and Andy couldn't help matching her smile, relieved to find pleasure from her pleasure.

He knew the inscription by heart:

To Danny,

Thank you for dinner and the most stimulating conversation. You are a fine young friend, and I suspect our bond will endure—forged in sadness, never to be broken. You have all my best wishes as you sail forth.

Yours for peace and a better world,
Alexander Bassett
12/21/41

"Where in the world did you find this?" Ginnie said after reading the inscription at least three times. Her eyes were glowing and her cheeks were flushed. Her hair was as bright as fire. "Where did you find it and how much did you have to pay?"

"I dug it out of the stacks at a hole-in-the-wall used bookstore in Chicago. Unfortunately, I paid through the nose for it. The Bassett market's really increased in the last ten years. Hell, all American first editions are hot. I tried dickering, but the owner wouldn't hear of it. She charged me eighty dollars."

"Hey, I'd call that a bargain." She studied the title page again. "Any idea who Danny was?"

He shrugged. "It's damn near impossible to trace old inscriptions. It's just another of those books that somehow found its way onto the antiquarian market. My best guess would be that Danny died, his family didn't know or care what they had, and bingo—they sold it off along with his entire library, probably for one lump sum that worked out to pennies per book."

Her right index finger trailed lightly across the lettering and lingered on the signature. "Yours for peace and a better world," she murmured.

"Yes, he was always looking," Andy said. He was going to add that the search for peace (both individual and societal) was a theme that popped up repeatedly in Bassett's work. That sentiment—*Yours for peace and a better world*—actually appeared word for word in *The Biggest Angel*, one of the writer's longest novels. He also used it to sign off most of his correspondence with friends and business associates, most notably the letters that now resided in the library of Princeton University, fifteen years literary chatter with other famous writers of the time. He was going to add all of those things, but then realized that Ginnie surely knew them.

He watched her staring with loving fascination at the title page, and heard her voice in his mind saying, *it will be a real adventure.* Hard on the heels of that he thought, *Tell me there's room in the world for someone who likes to think.*

He restrained his first impulse and allowed her several more minutes with the book before reaching out gently and taking it back.

7

HE AWOKE IN the middle of the night and found himself in another world, or more precisely, he found himself in two worlds simultaneously. He could see the dim shapes of the furniture in his room, outlines of the dresser and nightstand and desk that had become familiar to him. He could see a dark shadow with a brighter center—the mirror on the wall across from the bed.

The other world (though he was still not sure he could accurately call it that) seemed to exist side by side with this first one. No. Not side by side, he thought, but superimposed virtually on top of it. It only showed itself in one or two places where the edges did not quite meet properly—as though the dresser top had five corners instead of four, as though there was a third drape overlapping the two now pulled across the window.

This second world manifested itself more as a feeling than as something he could actually see. As he sat up in bed and rubbed sleep from

ALEXANDER'S SONG

his eyes with one stiff hand, he believed quite strongly that he could hear sounds and smell scents without truly hearing or smelling anything. He was aware of the second world's vibrations as a slight pulsing that reached him in a place below his skin, tingling through his bone marrow.

Instinctively, his hand found the light switch on the wall. He wasn't surprised at all to see his ex-wife standing beside the desk.

"Hello, Joanne."

Her head swiveled lazily in his direction and her gaze flicked across him with the ultimate disinterest.

"I thought you were in—"

She raised a hand to silence him. The gesture was languid, as though she were a corpse floating just below the surface of a cold lake. Her hair seemed to be floating too, the dark strands that normally fell several inches below her shoulders now drifting around the base of her neck.

"Jo—"

She turned slowly away, faced the window, and went to her knees. She pulled the drapes open and peered down into the darkness of Max Turner's back yard. The sensation of being in two different worlds seemed to strengthen, and Andy wondered if it was a coincidence or if her turning away had something to do with it.

He was confused, torn between sitting silently in bed, saying something more to her, or perhaps even getting up and going to her side. He tried to imagine what she was seeing through the window, but with the low cloud cover of the night, he doubted it was much: one or two phantom trees and the barest outline of the back yard storage shed, perhaps.

The door swung open then, and he turned to see Alexander Bassett come striding into the room. Like the sight of Joanne, this appearance caused him no surprise. With a second world laid over the top of the real one, Andy supposed that things like this were common and ordinary. When he glanced quickly back at his ex-wife, he saw that she was gone. The drapes were back in their proper position.

Bassett didn't look like any of his numerous photographs, many of which Andy had photocopied over the years and which were now tucked neatly into his research notebooks. He had the sensation of looking at several Bassetts, a young one and an old one, a happy and sad one, a strong one, a weak one, a light one and a dark, all melded into one human being.

"I came here to thank you," Bassett said. His voice was not soft and cultured, but flat and harsh. Andy had an unkind image of two jagged stones grinding together in the man's throat. "It's a nice thing you're trying to do for me, create an Alexander Bassett history. No one's ever done that. Oh, there have been critical studies galore; I'm sure you've read most of them. But nobody's ever attempted to draw a complete, conclusive picture of me as a man, a real human being."

Andy nodded wordlessly, thinking, where the hell is Ginnie now? She wouldn't want to miss *this* adventure.

"I have to tell you something," Bassett said. "Your objective is noble, but you're going about it all the wrong way. You're looking in the wrong places, at the wrong things."

"Rock Creek—"

"Oh, no. There's nothing wrong with looking here in Rock Creek. It's the things you're looking at. *That's* the problem."

"But I did everything I could think of—the library, the senior citizens. It's a small town. I didn't know where else to turn."

"You should have gone straight to the horse's mouth. Come."

Bassett reached out and took Andy's hand. His touch was cool and dry, and for the first time Andy felt fear. It entered his chest like a small, sharp blade being slipped neatly between his ribs. Something undeniable lay in his throat, not moving, making it hard for him to breath. He shrank away from Bassett but found himself propelled forward nonetheless, out of bed, across the room, out into the third-floor hallway.

"My clothes—" he began, but the words died in his throat when he saw that he was already dressed.

ALEXANDER'S SONG

The bed and breakfast was quiet, dark. They went down stairs that felt soft and unstable underfoot, and passed through the shadowy living room, heading for the front door. They were almost there when the furnace in the basement kicked on with a terrific *whumpf*, and Andy's suddenly glassy nerves almost shattered; he had to bite back a ragged scream that would have awakened the dead.

He stared at Bassett as the author led him outside. Snowflakes and ice pellets whirled in the whitish-yellow halo of light surrounding the coach lamp at the end of the sidewalk.

"This won't take long," Bassett said.

"But you—"

"Hush, Andy."

"But you're dead!"

"Shhhh."

The admonition was useless. The undeniable thing in his throat had bubbled to the surface and escaped. "No! You're dead. You died twenty years ago, in that snowstorm in Ohio."

The author kept walking, footsteps crunching on the icy walk. He didn't say anything, but turned and flashed a quick, meaningless smile.

"That's always been one of the mysteries surrounding you," Andy babbled on. He was aware that he was talking too fast and saying too much, but he couldn't seem to help himself on either count. "Why were you in Ohio? That was the big mystery. Why were you so far from New York? Were you on your way back to Rock Creek? That's what *I* always thought. I figured you knew you were dying, you were sure your heart was about to give out, and you wanted to see your hometown one last time. Am I right? Was that it?"

Bassett made a gurgling sound, like a heavy smoker clearing his throat. The wind whipped around them and carried the sound away into the night. Andy felt frustration and fear and dizzying confusion whirling through his mind, threatening to rip the top of his head off.

They were driving in the pickup now, Bassett behind the wheel while Andy slumped on the passenger's side of the long bench seat. The headlight beams sliced through the darkness. The windshield wipers clacked back and forth. He caught the mingled odors of motor oil, old fast-food burgers, and hot metal, but wasn't able to find the smell of that second world anymore. It seemed that even the steady pulsing of its hidden currents had stopped.

"That's because you're there now," Bassett said, without looking at him.

Andy didn't know Rock Creek well enough to know where they were going, but he was aware that they had left Victory Street, where the bed and breakfast hunkered at the end like a guardian, and had crossed over Michigan Street to the west side of town. Houses flashed by like flickering slides but eventually vanished and were replaced by lumpy shrubs and needle-like trees. The road unwound, changing from asphalt to gravel beneath the tires, then from gravel to dirt, dirt to mud. At one point they passed a huge abandoned building that sprawled along the side of the road, tall windows like black slitted eyes, and he caught a quick glimpse of a sign that read MANITOU PULP MILL in dull, faded letters.

"Please," Andy said, with no real idea what he was asking. He felt another emotion—anger—though he had to admit that it was anger with no real focus or cause, vague and misty, diffused.

At last they stopped, pulling off the muddy road into the overgrown driveway of a big house surrounded by the muscular shadows of large, dark trees. At first Andy thought he saw lights burning in several of the downstairs windows, but realized that what he was seeing were ghostlike reflections of the truck's headlights.

"This is it," the author said. "This is the house where I grew up."

They were inside before he was even aware of leaving the truck, and Andy immediately understood that the place had been empty for a great many years. The stench of rot was heavy, as was the tangy aroma of spreading mold. Off in the corners, the smell of animal urine lingered. There were a few pieces of furniture remaining, namely a couch, two chairs, and a small end table, but they were draped beneath multiple layers of grayish cobwebs that cloaked them like shrouds.

"This way, please."

ALEXANDER'S SONG

Bassett tugged on Andy's hand again and led him through the living room, through what might have been a dining room, and into the kitchen. Sometime, a month or a year or a decade earlier, the ceiling and a portion of the outer wall had collapsed. Rubble was strewn everywhere. Plaster dust puffed up in little clouds as they walked. Snow had drifted in the corners of the room, and much of it still remained, as though summer was years away instead of weeks. They negotiated a jumble of broken beams and studs in front of an old iron cookstove and reached a door on the far side of the room. It swung open on noisy hinges, showing a stairway that led down into absolute blackness.

"Down there?" Andy blurted, hating the sound of horror he was unable to keep from his voice. "But I can't see!"

"I can."

Step followed step followed step, until Andy, with no visual references to contradict him, felt as though they had descended miles into the belly of the earth. The air had grown colder by many degrees, and his lungs felt heavy with moisture, almost waterlogged. After a time he lost all sense of motion or direction and felt alternately as though he were floating or climbing or dropping straight down at great speed. Sometimes it seemed that he was going around and around in wide, lazy circles. Eventually, when he felt as though they would descend forever, or perhaps had *already* descended forever, there were no more stairs and they stepped off onto a hard, smooth floor.

There was a soft hiss and pop from somewhere to his left, and the room was suddenly alight. He felt spears of fire being driven into his eyes. He made a strangled sound and fought to keep his balance. When he could see again, he realized that the light wasn't all that bright; it was just the sudden change from that center-of-the-earth darkness that had gotten him. He rubbed his eyes and saw Bassett standing next to him holding an antique lantern with a large circular lens. Its yellow gas flame swayed and danced.

"W-where are we?"

Bassett smiled another of his unreadable smiles and told him to look around.

They weren't in a cellar, as Andy had first assumed. Or at least it wasn't like any cellar he had seen before. It was a huge room, lushly decorated, richly appointed—a library, he realized. The floor was a highly-polished parquet, the walls lined with fine hardwood bookshelves, each shelf sagging beneath the weight of books. There were no light fixtures on the walls or hanging from the ceiling—the only illumination came from Bassett's old lantern—but other than that he might have been standing in any fine private library in the world.

"Feel free to look around."

There was something odd about Bassett's voice this time. It wasn't flat and harsh anymore. It had grown softer, for one thing. For another, the words were not just tossed off casually but emphasized, each and every one, as though they might contain some key or clue to what was going on, something he wanted Andy to discover for himself.

Andy hardly noticed. He was too busy pacing up and down the length of the room, taking in everything. Amazingly, every book in the place had been written by Bassett himself. There were hundreds of copies of every novel, every volume of poetry, the essay collection, the play. There were hardcovers. There were paperbacks, large and small. There were foreign language editions—French and German, Italian and Spanish, Russian and Chinese and Japanese and Korean. There were copies in Braille and audio copies on records and cassettes. The effect was startling. It made Andy's head feel heavy and his heart feel strangely weightless. He was sure that somewhere in this underground room was a copy of every edition of every Alexander Bassett book ever published.

He reached out and gingerly picked up a slim yellow paperback that was lying face down on the shelf in front of him. He turned it over and felt laughter float into his mouth like a bubble when he realized that he was looking at the Cliff's Notes for the novel *Seascape*.

He turned to make some comment to the author (he wasn't sure what he was going to say, but something would come out, of that he was certain), but Bassett was no longer there. The lantern sat in the middle of the parquet floor, unattended, casting its soft yellow glow.

"You see?" Bassett said softly, invisible, hidden somewhere near. "I told you, didn't I? You're already there."

8

HE CAME TO with his face buried in his pillow and perspiration coating his body like oil. His mind felt brittle, as though it were about to shatter into millions of pieces. He imagined the smell of rich leather embedded in his nostrils. He tasted gritty dust on his tongue.

He remembered a dream, a lost sensation of utter confusion swirling through a mist of irrational fear. But when he tried to pull it together in his mind, he could only remember a few random things: snow, old furniture, darkness, stairs, a soothing yellow light, the word 'hidden.' It was like trying to work a jigsaw puzzle with no picture to guide him.

"Something about a second world," he muttered, the surprise of hearing his own voice making him jump. *A second world...something hidden...not far...something nearby.*

He rolled over and pushed the dream fragments away, irritated to be disturbed in the middle of the night.

Too much work to do tomorrow, he thought. Can't bother with nonsense tonight.

And so thinking, he was back to sleep in just a matter of minutes.

TWO

WOLF ISLAND

1

"**D**idn't you rest well last night?" Maxine Turner asked Andy as she ladled a second, unnecessarily large helping of scrambled eggs onto his plate. "I don't like to say these things, but you look like you went through the ringer."

"I slept fine." He was honestly taken aback by the question. "I was up a little late, though, doing some reading."

"Ah. More research, I suppose."

He glanced across the table at Ginnie, who flashed him a sly wink. "You suppose right."

"For the life of me, I can't see why you're wasting your time." Maxine moved away to serve her other breakfast guests. "Don't you see by now? You're not going to learn anything about Mister Bigshot Radical Writer here in the Creek."

Andy frowned. For no apparent reason, he had an image of windshield wipers clacking back and forth across icy glass. "I'm not so sure about that," he said.

PAUL F. OLSON

"But I am. You should have more sense, like that fellow from downstate who was up here...my goodness, was it really ten years ago? I think it must have been. He came up from Kalamazoo. He was writing a book about famous Michigan murders, and he came here to look into the Haag murder and that other terrible thing, those two boys who were killed back in the twenties. He found what there was to find and left two days later. He didn't spend an entire blessed week tromping around town, bothering good people, looking for things that weren't there."

Andy, who didn't know anything about any murders, and who didn't care, reached for his glass of orange juice. "I guess I'm just hard-headed. I don't like to quit until I'm sure I've exhausted all the possibilities."

"Possibilities?" Maxine laughed once, sharply. "Your writer left here fifty years ago, Mr. Gillespie. Now you tell me: what possibilities could be left after all that time?"

He ignored another secretive wink from Ginnie, wondering why the rhythmic sound of windshield wipers was still with him, now accompanied by the smells of dry dust and sour mold.

"I don't know, Max," he said. "I guess that's what I'm trying to find out."

2

FOUR HOURS LATER, Ginnie turned to him and said, "Now I know firsthand what you've been up against."

Andy's laugh was hollow. "Not pretty, is it?"

The Trading Post, Martin Visnaw's store, had been closed when they got there. A hand-lettered sign in the window said, GONE TO WHOLESALE GIFT SHOW!! BACK ON MONDAY!! SORRY WE MISSED YOU!! The trip to Keller Road had been no more productive. They had spent only twenty minutes with Toivo and Jeanette Lammi. If Andy had been forced to find something good to say about the meeting, it would have been this: at least the old man's variations on the standard theme had been amusing.

"Bassett?" Lammi had said, both his tone and expression clearly indicating that he thought a man would have to be insane to show an interest in such a topic. "What you wanna write 'bout him for? Why doncha do sumpin' 'bout a real writer? Louis L'Amour, mebbe. Now *he* was an American. That sumbitch Bassett—shit, fella, if he'da had his way, we'd all be talkin' Russian right now. We'd all be eatin' rice with them Red Chinee."

"The man was a great writer," Andy had said feebly, feeling the familiar sensation of traveling nowhere fast.

"Great writer? Listen, fella, great writers don't be sellin' their souls to Mister Lenin. Great writers don't be jumpin' into bed with Mister Marx. Don't you be givin' me that great writer horseshit. Comrade Bassett was scum. D'ya get me? S-C-U-M."

"Just another lesson in small town civics," Ginnie said now. "Turn here, then left at the next corner. The outfitter's south of town on Castle Road."

The forest that had already swallowed them once that morning, as they'd gone north on Keller Road, closed in around them again. Andy had an uncomfortable flashback to the view from Silver Mountain, a picture of tiny, orderly Rock Creek as an island in a huge, unfriendly sea. He squeezed the steering wheel a little harder and tried to take comfort from the cabins and mobile homes that sprang out of the trees every thousand yards or so; they weren't much, but any sign of civilization was soothing.

"Uh-oh," Ginnie said. "Hang a quick left." She leaned forward and pointed down a side road marked with two signs. The first was made of yellow-painted metal. It had been riddled with bullet holes over the years. The holes had rusted, spreading like cancer, dripping ribbons of ferrous blood over the letters.

CASTLE ROAD
GREEN LAKE
5 MI

The second sign was much newer, or at least better maintained. It was made of wood cut into the shape of a large canoe, onto which had been painted in cheery red and white lettering:

SEWARD'S OUTDOOR ADVENTURES
SALES AND RENTALS
COMPLETE QUAD LAKES OUTFITTERS
AT THE TIP OF HARKER'S LANDING ON GREEN LAKE

Andy made the turn and felt the pinch of his breath snagging in his throat. Almost immediately the forest had thickened. The trees and dense underbrush formed high, dark walls that pressed menacingly close against both sides of Castle Road. Overhead, naked spring branches stretched outward, grasping for the light, meeting, touching, forming an arch like the entrance to a primeval worshipping ground. He knew the woods were alive, churning with birds and wildlife, but he couldn't shake the feeling that if he were to stop the truck, shut off the engine, and roll down the window, he would hear nothing but a vast, dead, suffocating silence.

The road was narrow, pitted with potholes. He threw all his concentration into keeping them heading straight, wondering what would happen if a car came along in the opposite direction. They might just be able to make it, he supposed. Slow down enough, steer perfectly, and two vehicles could squeeze past each other without sliding off the muddy shoulder—but it would be a close operation indeed.

"—how that is."

He grunted. "What?"

"I said, I'm sorry for the way my mom acted at breakfast."

The road curved sharply. He battled the wheel and shrugged. "I've been getting that from her from day one."

"Well, if you ask me, it's pure ignorance."

"Ginnie—"

"She just doesn't appreciate anything worthwhile, and if you think—"

"Ginnie, for godssakes, I'm kind of busy here. Would you just forget it?"

He didn't dare turn to her, but he felt the heat of her gaze. Her voice was soft, frail, and wounded as she said, "Okay, fine. Whatever you say."

Castle Road swooped to the right and immediately arrowed straight again. He sighed. "Look, I didn't mean...." He wasn't sure what he had meant and what he hadn't. "This is a bad road," he murmured at last. "I wonder how this place ever does any business."

The silence in the truck became the same silence he had imagined for the wilderness outside, heavy and impenetrable. He lit a cigarette but was afraid to take a hand off the wheel long enough to take more than a few quick puffs. The cigarette burned away slowly in the dashboard ashtray, curls of smoke being sucked into the vents.

He wanted to let the silence go, allow it to blow over by itself, but his mind was uncooperative. It didn't want to be left alone. It wanted to continue its unstoppable journey to discover something new for him to worry about—for instance, the fact that never in his life had he stepped foot into a small boat. He needed a quick distraction, a change of subject.

"Do you know anything about that writer your mother was talking about? The one who did the murder book?"

Ginnie gave him a stony stare. He thought she hadn't heard him and was about to repeat the question when she said, "His name was David Kumlien. It wasn't much of a book, just a little self-published thing, that's all it was. *Michigan Mayhem* was the title, I think. I used to have a copy, but I lost it a long time ago."

"There were murders in Rock Creek?"

"Oh, sure, there've been a lot of them. Every few years some husband comes home all liquored up and knocks off his wife. Sometimes a guy and his buddies are deer hunting and something happens and it doesn't look entirely accidental, you know? Small town stuff. But the *big* murder—"

"Something about some boys?"

She shook her head, slowly brightening. He was glad to see it. "I don't know what mom was talking about when she said that. I suppose Kumlien never got it in the book. I certainly never heard about it. The thing I'm talking about is the Royal Haag story."

"Royal Haag...an interesting name."

"He was a millworker, a foreman or something at the Northstar Mill out on Negaunee Road. This was, oh, sometime just after the turn of the century. 1900, maybe 1910. Back in those days there were a whole bunch of sawmills and pulp mills in town. Most of them went bust years ago, but one called the Manitou was actually still in business when I was a little kid. When they finally closed it, the town took over the building and tried to turn it into a youth center, you know, with ping pong and foosball and roller skating on Friday nights. They couldn't get enough adults to volunteer as supervisors and it folded after five or six months. The building's still there, but it's been empty ever since."

Andy nodded. His stomach did a lazy flip-flop, but he didn't know why and chose to ignore it.

"Anyway," Ginnie said, "Royal Haag was Michigan's first union organizer. Well, all right, not the first, but I'll bet he was one of the earliest guys working in this area. He had this idea that all the men at all the area mills ought to get together for negotiating strength. He used to run around holding meetings, agitating for higher wages, stricter safety requirements, a five-day work week, all that kind of stuff."

"What happened?"

"What do you mean, what happened? He got killed, what did you think? They found him out back of his cabin in the woods. He'd been dead a few days, and the wild animals had been having quite a feast, if you know what I mean. Apparently, someone had sliced him open with a knife, pulled his intestines out, and left him to die—which probably didn't take all that long." She paused, and when Andy was able to take his eyes off the road long enough to glance in her direction, he saw a thin, humorless smile stretching across her face. "The murderer also castrated him, by the way. His…well, you know…they'd been stuffed halfway down his throat."

"Jesus," Andy whispered. "They caught the killer?"

"Well, yes and no. No one ever came forward—big surprise, right?—and nobody had any clues. You can imagine what law enforcement was like back then, especially around here, which was really just the wild frontier. It might as well have been the dark side of the moon or something. It looked like the murderer was going to get off free and clear. I'll bet that didn't surprise a lot of people in town. After all, it seemed kind of obvious that one of the mill owners had killed Haag, or hired someone to kill him, same thing. What better way to get rid of the troublemaker, you know? And the mill owners were all powerful back then. They literally owned the town and everything around it. Everyone worked for them. They were like gods. Most people probably figured one of the rich guys had done it and used his influence to hush it up."

"But you said 'yes and no.' I take it they finally caught him?"

"Caught's not the right word. About six or eight months later a local bum put a bullet through his head. He was a real lowlife, a drunk, a brawler, always out of work. He left a note behind explaining how he couldn't live with himself anymore. He said he'd killed Haag over a card game."

"Disembowelment and castration?" Andy said. "Over a card game?"

"Hey, I told you this was Hell Town, didn't I? Strange things happened every day." She chuckled. "I'll bet the local bigwigs were relieved to be out from under suspicion."

"No doubt," Andy said, and thought that if one of the wealthy mill owners *had* been involved, such a confession-by-suicide would have been considered terribly convenient. "Do you remember the killer's name?"

"Uh-uh. You can get all the gory details from the Kumlien book. My mom's probably still got a copy hanging around the house, and I know they have it at the library."

A page of his own scribbled notes floated into his mind. He saw dates and names and places, a handful of numbers. "Did you know Bassett's father owned a mill?" Ginnie sucked in a breath and shook her head. "The man was almost insanely wealthy. He'd started out with small shares in two of the mills—the one you mentioned, the Manitou, and the Johannson Brothers'. Eventually he gained a controlling interest in both. As I understand it, he merged them sometime around 1900 under the Manitou name. You ever hear anything about him?"

"No, but that doesn't mean much. It's really ancient history, isn't it?"

"I suppose it is, yes, but it could be important. One of the theories I was hoping to prove when I got here was my feeling that Bassett's social consciousness arose as a backlash against his father's success."

"You think it did?"

"I don't know. It's just a wild guess right now. I'd need some pretty solid evidence to prove or disprove it, and as you know, hard evidence doesn't exactly grow on trees around here."

She said softly, "Maybe Martin Visnaw could help you with that one. He's certainly been around here a lot longer than I have—about six decades longer." She paused. "If Bassett's dad was that rich, with two mills, or one big one, or whatever…if he was that powerful, don't you think that would've given him a pretty big stake in the outcome of Royal Haag's union campaign?"

A dazzling flash of light that seemed to be suspended in the trees was their first view of Green Lake.

3

THE BOAT RIDE turned out to be a great deal more enjoyable than Andy had expected. After a few awkward minutes on the tiller and throttle, he found handling the purring fifteen-horse Evinrude outboard to be a snap. The lake was almost eerily calm. Along the north shore a solitary angler was trolling the edge of a large weed bed, but otherwise they had the water to themselves. While Ginnie hunkered in the bow, her hair flying in the breeze, Andy steered them southwestward, navigating between the last floating chunks of winter ice, savoring the strangely powerful scents of moss and cedar that reached them from shore.

Wolf Island was now less than half a mile away. Their view of it had been gradually changing from an amorphous patch of black and dark green to something that resembled a craggy hilltop on the horizon. Now, finally, they were beginning to see details.

It was a big place, larger than Andy had expected. He saw a narrow pebbled beach that rose abruptly into a sheer cliff of knobby gray rock. At first he wasn't sure how he was going to bring the boat ashore, or how they would mount the heights once they got there, but he soon made out a long wooden pier jutting into the lake and a set of wooden steps that seemed to hang improbably against the cliff, zigzagging upward. He scanned the heavy growth of conifers atop the island for any sign of a house, but the place looked wild, utterly trackless.

He guided them past a final ice floe fifty feet from shore, throttled back, and coasted toward the dock. When the bow nudged the wooden pilings, he killed the motor and used the tiller to hold their position while Ginnie scrambled out and secured them with a length of frayed nylon rope.

"Are you sure somebody actually lives here?" he said as he stepped out.

"Of course." She laughed and pointed at the two other boats tethered to the dock—a sixteen-foot aluminum with a Mercury outboard and a green Old Town canoe. "Who do you think those belong to? The woodland pixies?"

There were a least a hundred of the steep, narrow steps leading to the top of the cliff, but they had climbed no more than half a dozen of them when a thin voice whipcracked out at them from somewhere high above their heads: "Halt and identify!"

Andy froze, his foot poised above the next riser, his hand tightening around the rough, splintered railing. *Halt and identify, identify and halt*, his mind repeated in a confusing singsong. The surprise of hearing the words and the force with which they had been belted out made it impossible for him to immediately understand them. He glanced quickly at a pale and wide-eyed Ginnie before going up another step.

"Identify! Now!"

This time he got the meaning of the words, but still could see no reason for them to be spoken. It was as though their voyage out into the middle of Green Lake had transported them to a place where the language of choice came from late-show war movies.

He leaned against the railing and tipped his head back, trying to spot movement along the top of the cliff. There was nothing up there but rocks and trees. Whoever had barked at them was very well hidden. He felt a crawling warmth on the back of his neck. Madmen hid, he thought anxiously, lunatics hid. Normal men came out into the open to conduct their conversations.

"Goddammit, *identify!*"

A response bubbled up from the fear churning in his stomach. "My name's Andrew Gillespie," he called.

"Drew Who?"

"Andrew! Andrew Gillespie! I've got Ginnie Turner with me! I...I mean, we...we'd like to...we'd appreciate it if we could come up and talk to you!"

"Why?"

Andy looked at Ginnie again. She rolled her eyes and mouthed the word *Jesus*.

"We'd like to ask you a couple of questions about someone!" Andy shouted skyward.

There was a brief pause. "Don't know why you'd want to do that!" said the voice at last. "I live alone! Don't know anyone!"

"Thanks for nothing," Andy muttered. He assumed the person above could see them, so he gave a dismissive wave and started back down the steps. Ginnie tried to catch his hand but he brushed it away, already adding Ed Hoffer to his list of failures and thinking about the boat ride back to the mainland.

"Did you ever know a man named Alexander Bassett?" Ginnie shouted. Andy whirled back, wondering why she would ask him such a question in such a ridiculously loud voice. As soon as he saw her, he realized that she wasn't talking to him at all. Her question had been directed to the cliff top and the old man hiding in the trees.

There was a long silence. Andy's gaze drifted back and forth from Ginnie to the heights. Hoffer wasn't going to respond. It was possible he hadn't even heard the question. If he had, he was probably leaning against a tree, scratching his head, thinking, *Bassett? Who in God's name is that?* Or even, *Why would they want to know about that lousy commie hack?*

"Who?" the thin voice finally said.

"Alexander Bassett!" they both shouted back.

"Don't think I know him!"

"He was a famous novelist!" Andy yelled. "He lived in Rock Creek a long time ago! He was born here, moved away in the late thirties! We thought you might have known him back then!"

This time the pause was even longer. Andy began to think the old man had given up on them and gone away. The early afternoon sun seemed warmer than it had a moment ago. The island was almost completely silent, the only sound the soft gurgle of water sliding companionably around the wooden dock pilings.

"Looks like a strikeout," Ginnie said at last. "We came all the way out here for nothing. I'll take the blame for—"

"You two watch your step on the way up!" Hoffer called suddenly. "Those stairs are old, rickety as hell! We sure don't need any broken necks out here, almost three miles from shore!"

It was as close as they were going to get to an invitation, and it didn't need to be repeated.

4

THE ASCENT WAS long, difficult, and mentally numbing—provided you didn't look down too often and dwell on a tumbling fall to the rocky beach below. There were ten steps, a change of direction on a narrow landing, and another flight of ten, over and over. As they climbed, Andy developed a rather grudging admiration for Ginnie's inexhaustible supply of oxygen. Not only did she manage to stay five or six steps ahead of him the whole way, she also kept up a running monologue in which she congratulated herself for thinking of Ed Hoffer. It looked as though the man knew something after all, she said repeatedly. Why else would he have told them to come up?

He agreed with her the first time she asked, then dismissed the rest of it as rhetorical. He didn't feel inclined to participate in any unnecessary chatter. Twelve years of smoking was turning the climb into a very interesting physical challenge, and his mind was wandering backwards across the landscape of the last year, to the two weeks when he had been teaching *Helen: A Tale* to the juniors and seniors of his third period Advanced American Lit class.

Bassett's sixth novel, the story of a young farm girl who leaves her Indiana home and travels to New York City to work with the poor, was perhaps the writer's most difficult novel from a teaching perspective. Lean and tight, the story moved from Helen Dortmunder's eighteenth birthday party to her tragic death at the age of twenty-six with uncharacteristic speed. The story and Bassett's usual political points were virtually the only elements; the multitude of interesting characters, the rich symbolism, the sprawling time-frame, the juicy metaphors of the author's other works were all absent. All but one.

Staircases figured prominently in the course of the novel. From the time young Helen grandly descended from her bedroom to the living room in the opening scene, to the moment when she lay at the bottom of a Harlem fire escape, gunned down by a corrupt police lieutenant, the image of steps came up again and again: inside the Statue of Liberty, in an unlighted tenement hallway, leading up to a fountain in Central Park.

When Andy had asked his students just what the image meant, he had gotten the usual variety of answers he had come to expect from teenagers who were bright but unwilling or incapable of putting their brains

ALEXANDER'S SONG

into overdrive. "They symbolize Helen's attempt to reach a higher state, like divinity or something," had been perhaps the most enlightened of the bunch. His favorite, however, had come from a heavy metal fanatic by the name of Kevin Caspian. "Them steps don't mean nothing," Kevin had said with his usual cockeyed grin, an expression that seemed to say *I know ten times more than you'll ever get out of me.* "Then why do they appear every few chapters?" Andy had asked, to which Kevin had responded, "Cause all the buildings in New York are tall, why else?"

When Andy had suggested to the class that Bassett's use of the staircase image might represent the struggle of the underclass to get ahead, their endless efforts to *climb beyond* the state of permanent oppression in which they were imprisoned by the rich and powerful, he had been met with blank stares, an unmistakable signal that it was time to move on to more fruitful territory—namely *The Grapes of Wrath*, one of the more teachable books of the twentieth century.

Andy didn't know why he was thinking about these things now, besides the obvious fact that he was working his way up one of the taller staircases he had ever climbed. Somehow, the steps seemed bound to the mental picture of windshield wipers he had seen earlier, to those smells of dust and rot. All of those things together seemed to form a memory of some sort, a vague, half-real *something* that he could almost but not quite touch, the way he sometimes remembered an incident from his distant childhood in a hazy, jumbled, unconscious way. It was a little bit fascinating and completely frustrating.

He supposed the other reason he was thinking about his lit class was that Kevin Caspian had been the last person from whom he had seen that rare look of burning intelligence—before he had met Ginnie, anyway. Comparing the two was ridiculous. While Ginnie was proud of her knowledge, Kevin dared not show his, except when he could be positively sure that nobody else would see. He would write flawless essays, turn in perfect test scores without effort. In class, however, he said nothing that wouldn't make the smart kids roll their eyes and the other metalheads laugh.

Andy thought the only real similarity between the two was their dogged determination, reason enough to compare them now. Kevin Caspian had always made him uncomfortable. Silly, but true. Andy was steady and competent in the classroom, but he would never make anyone's list of most effective and inspirational teachers. He had difficulty mustering the empathy for the kids that was necessary to be a great leader, finding the enthusiasm to deal with the problem cases. Easier, he sometimes told himself, to push the kid through and hope they could find their inspiration from someone else in another class, another year.

That inability to get truly involved meant that he had never quite been able to reach Kevin. He had been able to draw out the work, but not the future man that hid behind the façade of the uncaring clown, and that made him uneasy. It didn't, however, stop him from having a little fun when the boy was around. Kevin never backed down from his fool's masquerade, and despite the fact that it hid his potential, disrupted the class, and just generally made his job more difficult, Andy had to admire him. It was impossible, after all, not to feel at least a trace of respect for someone so dedicated to playing a role.

If Kevin never wavered in his quest to be the smartass, Ginnie simply never wavered at all. She too made Andy uneasy, but he appreciated the way she had pressed Ed Hoffer after he had already surrendered. The reason they were climbing these steps now, going to meet whatever answer, or *portion* of an answer, waited above, was because she hadn't given up. Would he have done the same thing at seventeen? he wondered. It was an embarrassing thought; he hadn't even done it today.

They were in the last flight now, nearing the top. He could see the straight rock face curving away from them, leveling out, actually sloping downward a little as it met the trees. Just to the right of the staircase there was a simple bench made of flat pine boards nailed to four logs, and sitting on the bench was something so out of its element that Andy would have given a startled laugh had he had any wind left to do so.

It was a tall, loose-jointed scarecrow that someone had dressed in a blue flannel shirt and overalls. Its face had been made to look old and creased, with heavy, sagging pouches of flesh below black-bead eyes. Its mouth was a crude red slash, and some kind of white strawlike material bristled like hair from beneath the sides of a red baseball cap. Its sculpted, gnarled hands were closed tightly over the head of a crooked walking stick.

Andy was briefly reminded of the apple dolls you saw for sale at craft fairs and church bazaars—increased to full life-size, yes, and a little more realistic, but the same basic design and craftsmanship. Yet as they reached the top of the stairs and stepped out onto the hard packed dirt of the cliff top, the scarecrow's hands moved, tightening around its walking stick. Its arms flexed, its legs shifted, and it began to stand. Andy groped behind him for the railing, but missed. He felt lightheaded, unsteady, in danger of tumbling over the edge and dropping to the lake below.

"Helluva climb, isn't it?" Ed Hoffer said.

5

THE APPROACH TO the cabin was down a winding footpath through the woods. The cabin itself was fairly typical, a stone foundation with log walls and a roof shingled with cedar, set in the middle of a wide clearing. But once they had gone past the outhouse-like storage shed and the chopping block and the towering woodpile, once they had passed a simple bench like the one that overlooked the lake, once they had mounted the rickety steps and crossed the sagging front porch, once they had actually gone inside, Andy was stunned.

Clinically speaking, the place was a hybrid, a combination home-warehouse-attic-museum. More romantically, it was an assault to Andy's senses, an explosion of color, a speedy and disorienting journey through time, an absolute marvel.

The main room housed mountains of junk that wasn't really junk at all. There was a huge collection of rocks and minerals, some glued to descriptive cards, others scattered loosely in open boxes sitting on shelves. There was an equally large collection of driftwood. There were stacks of old magazines and newspapers. There was an impressive display of faded campaign buttons from the turn of the century. There were old postcards in shoeboxes and old stamps glued to sheets of cardboard. There was a wall of antique tools. There was a window ledge lined with glass inkwells of various colors and another ledge with early medicine and elixir bottles. There were old 78s and a large Victrola. There was a nineteenth century penny-farthing bicycle hanging from the ceiling.

And there were the books. Two walls were devoted to them. They filled shelves that went from pine floor to beamed ceiling. They spilled off the edges of the shelves and lay piled beneath. Andy took a cursory glance and saw Shakespeare and Byron side by side with Raymond Carver and Bobbie Ann Mason, Homer next to John D. MacDonald, E.L. Doctorow nestled between a Janet Dailey romance and the plays of J.M. Synge.

Looking at the shelves gave Andy a strange, uncomfortable feeling of floating without a rudder. In a way that shouldn't have been familiar at all but was, familiar like an old movie he may or may not have actually seen, he felt the sensation of being *somewhere else*. He knew he was in a cabin on an island in the middle of a northern Michigan lake, but he felt as though he were somewhere else on earth, or on another planet, or in a different universe. He felt like a visitor, awkward and unsure of himself, completely out of place.

Second world, he thought distantly, but was unable to attach any meaning to the phrase.

There wasn't much to see in the rest of the cabin. There were four or five other rooms, but they were all closed. The kitchen that opened off the main room was unremarkable—cupboards, a butcher block, a stove, a refrigerator, a sink. That sensation of being in another reality or actually *beyond* reality came exclusively from the main room and its incredible clutter of contents.

After brief formal introductions, Ed Hoffer went into the kitchen to get them something to drink. When he came back, Andy took a good long look at him for the first time. Ginnie was undoubtedly right. Hoffer was

ALEXANDER'S SONG

certainly old enough to have known Bassett during his childhood. His back was severely bowed, cutting his considerable height by almost a quarter. The hands which had been hooked over his walking stick and now carried an old silver tray holding two bottles of Pabst and a can of Diet Coke never seemed to open completely; they were, in a way, like claws. He walked with the shuffling limp so common to the aged, a limp that came not from a pain or injury in either leg but from an overall, run-down, worn-out infirmity. His eyes were rheumy and dim, like pale marbles floating in milky fluid.

"I'm going to get this out right up front," he said. His voice had the same thin quality they had heard from the top of the cliff, but it was softer now and sounded more strained, as though it were an effort for him to merely force it up from his throat. "I allowed you up here out of pure selfishness. I don't know why you're asking about that old author, and even more than that, I can't imagine why you're asking *me*. I don't have much of anything to say about the man, but I'm curious as hell why you asked."

Andy took a larger swallow of beer than he'd intended, and to his dismay felt it shoot directly to his brain. He shifted his position on the couch, put the bottle down next to a pile of 1950s *Life* magazines on the coffee table, and nodded slowly. "I understand," he said. "Frankly, just the fact that you knew Bassett's name and are willing to talk about him, for whatever reason...well, that's a step in the right direction for us."

Ginnie agreed. "Not many people in Rock Creek even want to *think* about him."

"That so? You mean they're not proud of their native son?"

"Some are, not many," Andy said, and as neatly as he could outlined for the old man both the reasons for his research and the results so far.

Hoffer gave a gentle half-nod and poked one of his stiff hands into the front pocket of his overalls. He groped for something, a faint frown crossing his face. Andy sensed that the man was moving instinctively, reaching for cigarettes that he had given up long ago.

"It sounds like an interesting project, all right," Hoffer said, finally lacing his fingers together and resting his hands in his lap. "I once thought I'd like to do a literary biography. My heroes changed quite a bit. One day it was Ezra Pound, another Robert Frost. I admired Sinclair Lewis, too, and even Hemingway—talk about strange bedfellows, all of them. I'm sorry to say, my project never got beyond the dreaming stage. I didn't have the brains or balls to tackle something like that. You could say I was never attuned enough to literature."

"Oh, I doubt..." Andy started, and finished by casting a questioning glance at the bookshelves on the opposite wall.

"Ah, don't be fooled by those, young man. There's a difference between a dilettante and a disciple. Don't you know that? I've always loved being surrounded by books—I love the look of them, their touch, even their smell—but I'm a lazy reader and an even lazier thinker. I do a fair bit of reading, but more browsing than anything. A paragraph here, a chapter there, now and then a few poems. I'm no scholar. I'm just an insurance man turned bucolic homesteader."

"Insurance?" Ginnie said.

"Yes'm. Had my own agency in Detroit. Made a nice living. That's what enabled me to indulge my various collecting passions—rocks, stamps, even books—adding to what I'd already inherited from my folks. When I sold the agency back in '68, I came away with enough money to buy this place free and clear, and to spend the rest of my days just like this, doing a lot of everything and not much of anything, alone, unbothered. It's perfect."

"You lived in Detroit until 1968?" Andy said. "I suppose that puts the kibosh on any chance that you actually knew Alexander Bassett."

"Now you know why I felt guilty having you climb all those steps. I'm afraid I was thirty or forty years too late to actually know the man. I won't say I'm not interested in him, though. I've read some of his books. I even have a few of them up there." He pointed to the section of shelving nearest the kitchen. "But not only didn't I ever meet him, it was an accident I even discovered him."

"How do you mean?"

ALEXANDER'S SONG

Hoffer drank some beer. He kept his eyes closed and his head tipped back against his easy chair as he did so, as though something—lifting the bottle, the act of drinking, or possibly the story he was about to tell—sapped his strength. When he was done drinking, he rested the bottle between his legs, opened his eyes, blinked rapidly, and slowly pulled in a noisy breath.

"A few years after I moved here, this would have been sixteen or seventeen years ago now, I met a woman by the name of Hedda Fogerty. She was a widow, lived up in Houghton, sold used books by mail out of her home. We became good friends. To this day I think that woman carried on better conversations than anyone else I've ever met. She's dead now, and a day doesn't go by that I don't miss her very badly.

"One morning I get a call from her. She's found a book I've been looking for, she says. It's a first edition of John Crowe Ransom's poems, dust jacket, near mint condition, cheap. Do I want it? You bet your sweet ass I do, I tell her, and I hurry up there, which is no easy task—wasn't even back then, when I was considerably younger. I've got to take my boat over to the mainland, pick up my car where I park it at Seward's, and drive all the way up to Houghton, which is a good forty-five miles.

"So I get up there, but before she can show me the Ransom book, I notice these boxes sitting in her front hall—four of them, I think—all filled with books by some fellow named Alexander Bassett. The name's familiar in a foggy sort of way. Do you know what I mean? It was like hearing the name of a town someone mentioned to you years ago. You know you've heard it before, but you can't put your finger on where. As I told you, I'm not as sharp on literature as you'd think from looking at my shelves. But my curiosity's piqued. I know Hedda's got great taste. I trust her judgment. I figure there must be something to this Bassett person if she's put her hands on four big boxes of his books. Either he's very commercial or very collectable or he's a helluva writer, maybe all three. So I ask, and she tells me all about him. You can imagine my surprise when I found out he was born in Rock Creek."

"So you began collecting," Ginnie said.

"Not exactly." The old man took another swallow of beer and immediately began to cough and choke. The first few throaty hacks worsened, his face reddened, and his gnarled hands clutched for the armrests of the easy chair. Andy leapt up and hurried to his side, but Hoffer shook his head vigorously, waving him away as the fit slowly began to subside. "I'm...I'm all right... thank you, but I'm fine." He swallowed hard, coughed a final time, and sighed, wiping a single tear from his right eye. "The juice found the wrong tube, as my mother used to say." He nodded at Andy and smiled. "I'm fine now."

When they were settled again, Hoffer composed himself and picked up where he had left off. "As I was saying, I didn't exactly collect Bassett's books. I bought two of them from Hedda that day—*Doctor Howell*, I believe, and *The Pharisee*. He was a powerful writer, but frankly his politics left me ice cold. When I discovered his poetry, though, I was enchanted. I got every collection Hedda could lay her hands on. I thought *The Voice of the Storm* was wonderful."

Ginnie grinned. "The storm awakes and drives its dulling din/Upon the land./Women walk the shore by night/Seeking children murdered/By the wind."

Hoffer leaned forward suddenly, staring at her with what Andy took to be a combination of wonder and admiration. "How did you know that?"

"I'm a fan," she said with a shrug.

"Yes," Hoffer said slowly. He studied each of them for several silent moments. "I believe *The Voice of the Storm* was the man's last book."

"That's right," Andy said. "1961."

"Have either of you any idea why he stopped writing after that? It seems he was going great guns up until then, and if I'm not mistaken, he lived a few years longer. Why no more books, no stories or poems?" He gave Andy a close, scrutinizing stare. "Why?"

"I know what you're asking, but you're wrong—or at least you're not exactly right. Bassett had slowed down a lot earlier than 1961. Did you know he was investigated by HUAC?" The old man made a slight head gesture that might have been a nod. "That was in 1952, about a year after *The Pharisee* was published. The common academic wisdom is that *The Pharisee* was the man's magnum opus, that he poured into it a whole lifetime of experience and thought. One critical study I've read said the process burned him out, left him drained. And then McCarthy came along and drained him even more."

Hoffer smiled faintly. "Interesting. But he *did* write more after that."

"Yes, but not at his usual pace. Instead of a book or two a year, he didn't publish another novel until 1958—that was *Let Darkness Fall*. Then he did *Peter Wept* a year or so later, but both of those books were disasters. They weren't nearly up to his old standards. The critics ripped them apart. The sales were horrible. He never wrote another novel, and even *Voice of the Storm* was more of a reprint collection. It only had three or four new poems in it; the rest were early things he'd published in magazines back in the forties."

"And that was it?"

"That was it," Andy said. "He lived until 1969, but he never published another thing. Whether or not he was working on anything, some great unfinished novel or story collection or something, no one knows. They didn't find anything in his papers after he was gone, but a couple of experts don't put much stock in that. See, he'd been in failing health for a long time—bad heart. The theory is that he knew he was dying and destroyed his unpublished papers before the end."

"I suppose one of your missions is to find out whether or not that's true," Hoffer said.

"I'd sure like to. There's so much about the man no one seems to know—where his socialist politics came from; why he was so reclusive, even at the height of his success; why—" he glanced at Ginnie with a tiny smile "—he only wrote one stage adaptation of his work, even though that one was such a big hit that the public was clamoring for more; why he suddenly refused to see or talk to Jackson Kretchmer, his lawyer and one of his best friends, after 1954; why he was on the road in Ohio when he died in '69. So many things to look for, so many answers to find."

"And yet you've found nothing," Hoffer said very softly.

"Almost nothing."

"So essentially what you're doing is chasing a mystery."

"Yes," Andy said. He hesitated and frowned, disturbed by the aptness of the phrase. "I'm afraid chasing a mystery is exactly what I'm doing."

6

TWO THINGS HAPPENED before they left the island that afternoon. Both were mysterious and confusing; even later that day Andy only understood one of them.

They talked for more than an hour, but Alexander Bassett soon became a side issue, the lack of information about the man forcing them down different avenues of conversation—other poets and novelists, book collecting, wilderness living. Finally, Ed Hoffer asked them if they would like to take a closer look at what he called his "treasure vault," and proceeded to show them around the cabin's main room while he described the various minerals and gems, the acquisition and restoration of the old Victrola, the widow woman in Calumet who had sold him that ancient bicycle with the towering front wheel.

They were being led, Andy realized, artfully guided toward the door and hence out of the cabin and off the island. A burst of momentary anger at this silent deceit faded when he took a close look at the old man's face. There was weariness etched there in lines so stark he couldn't believe he had missed it before. Hoffer was not used to entertaining—that was obvious—and their surprise visit was wearing him thin. Even as he took them from shelf to shelf, his shuffling gait became more pronounced and his back bowed farther than before, as though invisible weights were being piled on his shoulders one at a time.

When they paused before a section of books containing first editions of *Seascape*, *Fields of Fire*, *The Biggest Angel*, *Traveler's Light*, and *The Voice of the Storm*, Andy noticed for the first time that Ginnie wasn't with them.

ALEXANDER'S SONG

He looked around and saw her standing on the far side of the cabin, next to one of the closed doors, in front of a small, freestanding knickknack shelf piled with yellowed newspapers and faded magazines. Hoffer's back was to both of them as he described one of his favorite poems in the *Fields of Fire* collection, and Andy waved to Ginnie, motioning her over, like a child on a museum tour afraid that one of his wandering pals will be caught by the curator touching the dinosaur bones.

Ginnie didn't seem to notice. He frowned, waved again, and finally saw that she was looking right past him, staring at their host's back with an expression that contained so many different elements it was impossible to decipher. When at last she snapped out of whatever was bothering her and returned to Andy's side, Hoffer had gone on to talk about another poet, one he admired much more than Alexander Bassett, although Andy missed the name and Hoffer's point about different political philosophies addressing the same theme in similar ways.

"What's wrong?" he whispered to her while the old man talked on. "What were you doing—"

She shot him another baffling look and shook her head. Andy opened his mouth again but didn't have a chance to ask another question.

"Don't you agree?" Hoffer said, turning back to them.

Andy nodded quickly. "I think so...of course...yes."

That was the first strange thing that happened. The second came a few moments later, when they stopped in front of a box containing fifteen or twenty pieces of odd-looking rock. It turned out not to be rock at all but petrified wood, and as Hoffer launched into a detailed description of the geological process that turned wood to stone, Andy's attention wandered, first to Ginnie and her distant, troubled expression, then to an old roll-top desk pushed against the wall to his right.

The top of the desk was open, revealing a great accumulation of papers and notes. Andy stared down at it, bothered by something he couldn't recognize. There didn't seem to be anything out of the ordinary. There were bills (from Seward's Outdoor Adventures for gas and oil; from Copper

Country Services for bottled propane; from Good Folks Rexall for various prescriptions). There were check stubs. There were bank statements. There were scribbled notes, reminders from Hoffer to himself to complete various projects or to pick up milk the next time he journeyed into town. There was junk mail, a lot of it. There was a nice-looking volume of Carl Sandburg's verse.

Hoffer was saying, "I found this particular sample on a trip to New Mexico years and years ago..." but Andy barely heard him. There was something, he knew, something there on the desk, something that...what? Something that wasn't right? Something that didn't belong there? He bit the inside of his cheek, told himself quite firmly that he was thinking pure nonsense, but nevertheless felt his chest tighten, as though something were squeezing or pressing down on his heart. For an instant he was afraid that he wouldn't be able to draw a breath, but then the moment was past and he was fine.

Second world, he thought again, but the words meant nothing more than they had the first time. He scanned the drifts of paperwork again, but felt only that impossible pair of impressions: one, that everything there was ordinary and dull, and two, that *something* there was not ordinary at all.

"...nature's real miracles," Hoffer was saying, and Andy glanced at the old man, glanced at Ginnie, glanced at the door, and suddenly found himself wanting quite badly to leave the cabin. It seemed they had been in there too long. The crisp clarity of the spring day outside felt irrationally like something greater than it was, something somehow perfect yet too far away to touch.

Ginnie was standing a few paces behind them, staring at the floor, her arms folded over each other, hugging her midsection as though she were cold. Andy got her attention and raised his eyebrows, motioning at the door. She looked relieved, and Andy couldn't help being glad that she agreed with him. He didn't understand it at all, but he thought that even five more minutes in Ed Hoffer's cabin would be five minutes too long.

ALEXANDER'S SONG

7

AN UNCANNY CONFIRMATION: he felt better as soon as they descended the steps and started back down the path to the cliff. Although those two nagging words—*second world*—still drifted aimlessly through his mind, they no longer seemed as mysteriously important as they had before. Ginnie's behavior still puzzled him, and he wasn't sure he'd be able to stop thinking about whatever it was (or wasn't) he had (or hadn't) seen on the roll-top desk, but for a short time, anyway, he was able to enjoy the walk through the woods to the water.

"I'm sorry I couldn't tell you anything," Ed Hoffer said as he shuffled along beside them. "I shouldn't have let my loneliness and curiosity get in the way of your business. I'm sure you have plenty more important stops to make. But still, I hope you don't think your time was entirely wasted."

"Not at all," Andy said, glancing at Ginnie. "We had a very nice visit."

"You'll send me a copy of your first article when it appears?"

"Uh...sure, of course."

"Good, good. I'll be looking forward to it."

Andy sighed. Something more seemed to be required. The old man had, after all, indulged their curiosity as much as he was able, and had shared with them his remarkable collection of antiques. Whether their time was wasted or not (Andy's opinion was that it certainly had been) was really beside the point.

"You have a very beautiful island here," he said, pausing and looking up at the trees. The late afternoon sun filtering down through the evergreens cast a soft, magically pretty greenish light over everything. "It's so isolated. With the wind blocked out and the sun coming down, you could almost forget that it's only forty-five degrees. It's like summer in the middle of the cold. It's hard to believe there are still big chunks of ice floating around in the lake."

Hoffer looked back at him. "And Winter slumbering in the open air, wears on his smiling face a dream of Spring."

Andy started. "That's—"

"Coleridge."

"Yes," Andy said, and felt uneasy again, as though he were looking at a mathematical equation that didn't properly add up. "The poet laureate of the bucolic homesteader, I suppose?"

Hoffer's smile was thin but genuine. He planted his walking stick, started forward again, and didn't say another word the rest of the way to the cliff.

8

ANDY TRIED TO get an answer out of Ginnie as they climbed into the boat and drifted away from the dock, but she shook her head and refused to speak.

"Come on," he said, "what happened to you back there? You were fine before you wandered off to the other side of the cabin. What was it? Did you see something? You know, toward the end there, I didn't think—"

"Not now," she said, her voice low and harsh. She cast a look upward, where the old man was still watching them from the top of the stairs.

Halfway back to the outfitter at Harker's Landing, however, she became a different person. She turned around on her bow seat and gestured wildly for Andy to cut the throttle. The sullen, worried expression she had been wearing for the last half hour fell away. Her look was the one Andy was more accustomed to seeing—bright eyes, quirky grin, quick and energetic movements.

He twisted the throttle to idle and allowed the boat to drift on the gentle swells. "What's going on?"

"What the hell do you think *this* means?" she said. He was confused until she reached up inside her windbreaker, underneath her sweatshirt, and pulled out what at first he thought was a large piece of thick cardboard. When he took a closer look he realized she was holding an old-fashioned photograph, the image a little fuzzy, a little faded, but still easy to make out.

ALEXANDER'S SONG

He was amazed, too much so to be genuinely angry. "Did you steal that?" She nodded. "What, are you crazy? You actually *stole* that from his cabin?"

"Take a look at it."

"I don't want to take a look at it! Ginnie, Christ, what if he finds—"

"Just take a look."

"Goddammit, I don't even want to touch it. I—"

"Andy..."

Her eyes were still glittering, but now they shone with much more than intelligence or excitement. He had a hard time deciding just what emotion he saw there, and reluctantly leaned forward, reaching as far as he could without getting up and rocking the boat. She held the photograph out to him. He closed his fingers around it, looked, and understood immediately why she was so agitated.

The picture was even older than he had originally thought. He guessed that the clothing, hair styles, and overall *look* of the three young men standing with their arms around each other's shoulders pegged the date at some time in the 1920s, although it might have been even earlier than that. The men were somewhere between eighteen and twenty-five, he thought; it was difficult to tell. They were clean-shaven, nicely dressed, standing in front of a huge tree that spread its branches high above their heads like a canopy. The one on the right wore a cap at a rakish angle. The one on the left had spectacles. The one in the middle was Alexander Bassett.

"Do you see?"

He nodded wordlessly. He had seen several other pictures of Bassett as a young man, none as early as this, but close enough that the identity was unmistakable. Even then, in his late teens or early twenties, Bassett's eyes had been dark, his expression piercing, slightly disturbing, outwardly questing and inwardly withdrawn at the same time.

"Hoffer actually had this in his—"

"Turn it over."

He looked up at her, too startled by the photo to understand.

"Turn it over."

There was a newspaper clipping fixed to the back of the photograph with several strips of dry, cracked transparent tape. The clipping was brittle, aged to an overall brown with several reddish spots of foxing scattered across the body of the article. A headline—CONSTABLE ADMITS FRUSTRATION ON TRAIL OF MADMAN—was laid out above two columns of tiny type, or what remained of two columns. The first half-paragraph of each was intact. Below that, the remainder of the story had been torn off or had simply fallen away. When Andy touched the jagged bottom edge, a piece of newsprint disintegrated beneath his finger.

> Rock Creek Constable Elwood McFarren said yesterday that clues to the identity of the man responsible for the gruesome slaying of local youths Francis Belknap Hale and Charles Grant McCready have been, in his words, "difficult to come by." McFarren, speaking to a town meeting, said that despite the assistance of peace officers from as far away as

There was another line or two after that, but Andy stopped reading. His eyes jumped briefly to the remnant of the second column. He saw the words *obviously dealing with an amoral, extremely dangerous lunatic* in quotation marks, and looked up at Ginnie.

"Francis Hale," he said, shaking his head slowly.

"Yeah, Frank Hale. And Charlie McCready, too."

"I never dreamed they might be real. Did you—"

"Never. How do you think Hoffer got hold of this? What do you think it means?"

Andy shrugged, shook his head again, and finally turned the picture over. "Gruesome slaying," he murmured, so softly that he might as well have thought the words instead of spoken them.

Across a gulf of nearly seventy years, the faces of three happy young men flashed him an ageless smile.

THREE

THE BONEYARD

1

That night, as the clock crept past ten-thirty and headed for eleven, there was a knock on Andy's door. He marked his place in the book he was reading—an old, dog-eared Bantam edition of *To Raise Brave Men*—and went over to answer it. Ginnie was standing in the corridor, dressed in blue sweatpants and a Rock Creek Voyagers tee-shirt, holding something by her side; the hallway was too dark for him to see what it was.

"I've been waiting for you to come back downstairs ever since dinner."

He shrugged absently. "Busy."

"Let me take a shot—reading *Brave Men*, right?"

"Good guess."

"Anything?"

"I don't know. I don't think so. Maybe, if I knew what I was looking for. All I see is the same book I always saw. It's still a great work, but I can't spot anything strange or unusual about it."

"Just one of those things, then," she said. "He needed names for his main characters and used a couple of guys he used to know."

"Probably."

He searched for something else to say and discovered that he didn't really want to say anything at all. His two-mindeness about Ginnie—admiration and gratitude for her help on one hand versus the selfish need he felt to keep his project to himself on the other—was slowly resolving itself. He had felt it on the trip back from Green Lake to town, had been aware of it strengthening as he sat across from her at dinner, and had felt it really kick in as his solitary evening of reading wore on. He wouldn't necessarily say she was a liability, but the stunt she had pulled that afternoon made his selfishness seem like a fair, good thing.

"I thought you might want to take a look at this," she said, temporarily removing the burden of inventing small talk. She held up the object she was carrying—a book, trade paperback size, maybe two hundred pages, black cover made of thick, cheap stock. In red against the black was a simple drawing of the State of Michigan, the long horizontal mass of the Upper Peninsula separated from the Lower Peninsula mitten by the Straits of Mackinac. The title, also in red: *Michigan Mayhem*, and below that: *An Examination of Death and Mystery in the Midwest by David F. Kumlien*.

"It's my mom's copy," Ginnie said. "I swiped it out of the living room bookcase."

Andy was interested in spite of himself. "Anything about McCready and Hale?"

"Uh-uh, just the Haag story, but I figured you'd want to check it out anyway. There's some stuff in there I'd completely forgotten about. You might get a kick out of it." She paused. "You know, I had a feeling all that stuff in the newspaper clipping, the gruesome slaying, the dangerous lunatic, all of that, was the same thing my mom was talking about this morning. I was going to ask her if she knew anything more about it, but tonight didn't seem like the right time."

He raised his eyebrows. "Oh?"

"She's pissed that I was gone all day. More specifically, she's pissed I was gone all day with *you*. You'll be glad to know she thinks you're a little crazy."

ALEXANDER'S SONG

"Maybe she's right," Andy said, with just a trace of a smile.

"Hey, don't worry about it. It's just that she could never stand Bassett's books. She thinks he was a subversive or something. I guess that makes you subversive too, by association. She'd prefer it if I didn't hang around with you."

Andy swallowed hard. "It seems to me...." He hesitated, uncertain, unaccountably shy. Say it, he thought, get it over with, spit it out. "I'm not sure we ought to keep working together, either."

Ginnie's brow furrowed. Her mouth opened, but like a movie print with a mismatched soundtrack, several seconds went by before any sound came out. "I don't understand."

"Well, really...you see, I think...the problem is what...what you did this afternoon."

"Oh, that." She seemed relieved. "You mean you're still worried about that picture? That's ridiculous."

"No, what's ridiculous is that you took it in the first place." He felt the shyness drop away like a cloak slipping to the floor. Anger replaced it, and looking at her smiling, smug expression didn't make things any better. "Don't you understand what you did today? Don't you get it? You took something that didn't belong to you."

"A picture. A stupid picture."

"That doesn't matter. Jesus Christ, Ginnie, for starters it's an antique. With Bassett in it, it's probably worth money—good money. Even without him, it'd probably be worth something. And even that's beside the point. It wouldn't matter if it was an Instamatic snapshot taken last week. It wasn't yours. That's the only thing that counts."

She pulled a pouting frown. He saw that she was upset, but only because he was, not because of any sudden remorse over her actions. "I thought the Hale and McCready thing, and the fact that Bassett was in it, well, you know, I thought that was important."

"It is, or it might be. But you could have just told me about it. Forget that it's stealing, that it's wrong. What about me? I'm trying to find information in

89

this town. I need people to open up, but they've got to trust me before they'll do that. What's going to happen if word gets out that I rob every house I visit?"

Ginnie laughed, annoying him even more. "Are you kidding? You really think he's going to miss that one picture? You really believe he's going to notice it's gone? In that room full of junk he's going to spot one thing out of place?"

"I don't know," Andy said, wanting the conversation to end, wishing it had never begun. "I really don't know. All I know is I've been waiting all night for the phone to ring, for Hoffer to call up and accuse us of being thieves." He sighed. "Whatever we learn from that picture, if anything, it's not worth that."

"So what do you want me to do? You want me to take it back? Is that it? You want me to rent another boat at Seward's and trek all the way out there and confess? Because I don't think I can do that, and besides, I don't think Hoffer's worth it."

"I don't understand."

"Oh, I think you do. He lied to us today. You know that as well as I do. What was he doing with the picture in the first place? Where'd he get it? Is it just a collectable he picked up from that book lady in Houghton, or what? And why didn't he tell us about it? Why'd he say he didn't know anything about Bassett when a few feet away he had an original photo of the guy?"

Andy had no answer to that. The question had bothered him all evening—that one along with many others, some simply pesky nuisances, others genuinely, deeply disturbing: Was Bassett connected to the so-called gruesome slaying of Frank Hale and Charlie McCready, or was it merely incidental that the newspaper clipping was taped to the back of that particular photo? What exactly *was* Bassett's connection to the two young men? And how had they become, in name at least, the main characters of both the novel and stage version of *To Raise Brave Men*?

He reached no meeting of the minds with Ginnie that night. He could not shake his anger at her, or his fear that Hoffer would discover his missing treasure and call them to account. She steadfastly refused to admit that

ALEXANDER'S SONG

taking the photograph had been anything more than a petty wrong. When she left his room it was with the understanding that they would talk more the next day, decide where they stood and what exactly was their future together as a research team. As for the questions concerning Frank Hale and Charlie McCready, Andy told her that he needed some time to think, at least the night and the following morning alone to ponder how to follow up on the new information, if indeed he decided it was worth following up at all.

That last was not precisely true. Even before Ginnie had paid her visit he had decided to nose around the matter, to see what could be uncovered without digging too far. His problem then became how—and how to do it without Ginnie finding out.

The next morning he arose early, when no one in the house would be awake. He dressed quickly, tiptoed through the corridor, down the three flights of stairs, and across the living room. He slipped outside into chilly, foggy air just as it was getting light. His pickup grumbled when he started it, as though it wanted more time to rest and warm up before being put to work, but he didn't care if anyone inside heard him now. He was away, rattling off on what he had to admit was probably a fool's errand.

2

IT TOOK HIM the better part of the morning, but eventually he found them both, buried less than a hundred feet apart in the same graveyard.

On a hunch, he had skipped the Catholic cemetery adjacent to St. Anne's on Ontonagon Street and had tried Holy Faith Methodist first. Two hours of walking up and down among the markers had turned up nothing. He backtracked to St. Anne's and wasted another ninety minutes there. He was tempted to surrender after that, but instead he drove to Houghton Street and went into a grungy little diner called The Place. He asked a few questions of a young man who was seated at the horseshoe-shaped counter, shoveling in a breakfast of scrambled eggs, hash browns, and steak. The young man stopped eating, took off his Berkley

PAUL F. OLSON

Fishing Line cap, ran a hand through his mop of brown hair, gave Andy a dark, questioning expression, but finally told him what he wanted to know.

Oak Hill was the community cemetery, open to all faiths. It was situated, appropriately enough, on Oak Hill Road, about five miles away, midway between the town and Lake Manabozho. By the time Andy got there it was after ten o' clock, but the fog was still holding, keeping the world wrapped in a blanket of gray, absorbing light and sound, lending an eerie, dripping, junglelike atmosphere to the northern forest of hardwood and pine.

He parked the truck as far over on the shoulder as he could and climbed out, staring at the white picket fence that surrounded the graves, the little turnstile entrance beneath an arch of wooden letters spelling O K HILL. The cemetery was laid out across a series of three rolling hills, each a little larger than the one before. He guessed that by the time he had walked from the gate to the far back wall he would have climbed forty or fifty feet.

Once inside he could see that the place was maintained, though not perhaps with the same sense of community pride lavished on the signposts and sodium lamps back on Michigan Street or the sidewalks in the residential district. The grass had missed its last few fall cuttings; even dead, even matted down by a winter of heavy snow, it looked wild and deep. Old autumn leaves had windrowed against the fence on the eastern boundary. Tree limbs that had fallen in long-ago storms were scattered about. Gravesite flowers had rotted to stems. Tiny American flags had faded to white and been tattered by the wind.

There was something about the place—its general appearance combined with the isolated location, the forest on all sides, and the fog—that sparked something deep in Andy's chest. It felt starkly romantic, and he had a sense of death as something both lovely and lonely. He stood just inside the turnstile for almost five minutes, breathing deeply, taking it all in, before he began his search.

The going here was slower than at Holy Faith and St. Anne's. There, given the space limitations imposed by the streets and buildings in town, the graves had been laid in neat and orderly rows, like recruits lined up for inspection. Here there were no restraints, and nothing at all resembling order. There were graves everywhere, on the hilltops, on the sides of the hills, in the little valleys *between* the hills. Some of the family plots were enclosed in rings of shrubbery or behind low fences of wood or iron. Others had nothing to set them apart, as when he came to the Trelawneys—eleven graves in all, scattered amidst the Stuarts and the McBargles. He even saw a few newer stones outside the main fence, two rows a few yards to the south—forerunners in a slowly-progressing cemetery expansion.

It was twelve-thirty and he was gradually working his way up the last hill, losing hope, when he finally found what he was looking for:

FRANCIS BELKNAP HALE

Our Beloved Frank

1909 - 1927

Snatched from our arms,

He sleeps now with angels.

Andy did the math and shuddered. "Our beloved Frank," he murmured. The sound of his voice was swallowed by the fog.

The next one was back about thirty feet and well off to the right, part of a family plot laid beneath the limbs of a tall white birch.

CHARLES GRANT McCREADY

Loving Son of Matthew and Nora

Devoted brother to David, Elizabeth and Daniel

Born April 3, 1911

Cruelly murdered August 10, 1927

There is peace in heaven and glory in eternity.

Andy stepped back, shaken. He tried, but couldn't drag his gaze away from that line, that one line in particular: *Cruelly murdered August 10, 1927.*

One eighteen, the other sixteen, he thought, and was stunned by the clarity and power of an image that overtook him. He saw a day in August more than sixty years ago. He saw rain, morning mist, row upon row of black umbrellas. Two open graves, two closed caskets. He heard tears and mumbled prayers, a solemn minister performing two separate services, the same pointless, hollow words meant to sooth, failing twice. He could smell the wet roots and mud in each grave. He could actually feel the unutterable pain of a small town as they tried to cope with these deaths, the mystery of them, the raw sorrow, the knife-edged anger, the religious awe.

Cruelly murdered...

Snatched from our arms...

Cruelly murdered...

He sleeps now with angels.

He closed his eyes and clenched his fists, reaching for reality, willing the picture back into whatever black, swampy pit it had climbed out of.

"Not a relative of yours, is he?"

To his credit, Andy didn't scream. He did, however, nearly jump out of his skin, and he spun around so quickly that he almost lost his balance and fell.

At first glance he thought it was Ed Hoffer, and he thought crazily, *Jesus, he's here for the picture! He tracked me all the way out here because of what Ginnie did!* Then he realized it was just another old man, not as old as Hoffer, perhaps seventy, perhaps less than that. He was a little shorter than Hoffer but carried himself straighter, giving the impression that he was the same height. His face was weathered but not too wrinkled. He was nicely dressed—brown corduroy slacks, a woolen overcoat, a knit scarf, a cap.

"No," Andy said, trying to smile and calm his wildly jittering nerves at the same time. "I'm just visiting, looking around." He gazed past the man's shoulders, past the lower hills and the gravestones and the gate to Oak Hill

Road. The only vehicle out there was his own truck.

The man nodded. "Quite a story there. Goddamned shame what happened to that kid."

"You know about it?"

"As much as anyone."

Andy couldn't believe his ears. This morning jaunt had been more emotional than intellectual, an action he undertook because he felt the need to do something and didn't know where else to start. He hadn't necessarily expected to find the graves, but he had allowed himself to hope. Never, though, had he dreamed that he might hear the story behind them, not so soon.

The old man seemed to be studying Andy's face with unusual interest. "I wasn't here back then," he said, "but you know how it is in towns like this. Stories find their way around, especially juicy ones. They get passed along like old clothes." He grinned, showing white, perfect dentures. "I suppose you wouldn't mind if this particular piece of clothing got passed along to you."

"Well...no."

"It was something, all right. McCready here was fifteen-sixteen years old when he and a friend—Frank Hale, he was maybe eighteen, he's buried right over there—went out in the woods one day and never came back. You know about that part?"

Andy shook his head.

"Well, that's the way it was. They just vanished. I guess there was a search, but this is big country around here. Unless you know where your people started, or where someone saw them last, what chance do twenty or thirty or even a hundred fellows in a search party have of finding them?"

"But they were found," Andy said. He glanced at Charlie McCready's gravestone. "Weren't they?"

"They were, but it was an accident, just one of those things. Maybe a week later, some fisherman was taking a shortcut through the woods and stumbled over them. They were lying in a clearing about fifty feet off the footpath that leads from Green Meadow Trail to Preston Lake." The old man paused, coughed, rubbed the back of his hand across his mouth, and offered Andy an expression that was a frown in name only; deep down it had the sly look of someone who secretly relished his grisly tale. "It was awfully bad."

"Really," Andy said noncommittally. He flashed briefly on the story Ginnie had told him the day before, the account of Royal Haag's murder. He didn't think anything could be quite as bad as that.

"Yessir. I'm talking really, truly bad, first-class bad, just about as bad as it gets."

Now Andy took an uneasy step backward. His image of the castrated, disemboweled union organizer came again, stronger than before, and as he mentally pushed it away he found himself looking out at Oak Hill Road again, searching for any sign of a vehicle, even a bicycle. His own truck looked very lonely pulled over on the shoulder, resting in the weeds.

"Somebody had been all over those boys. They'd been hacked to ribbons, chopped right up in little pieces." Another insincere frown. Or perhaps, Andy thought, this one was more genuine; he couldn't say for sure, and he doubted it even mattered. "It was a real sight, I heard. An arm here, its hand over there. A leg on one side of the clearing, the other leg somewhere else."

"Jesus," Andy said weakly. In a distant way, he became aware that the fog was lifting at last. The visibility was better, the light stronger. A tiny segment of rainbow shimmered in the droplets of mist hanging over the entryway arch.

"A real sight," the old man repeated. "The elderly gent who first passed this on to me said that whoever did it must have been big and strong. Crazy, probably. Or awfully mad about something. Either way, the result was the same. Those boys were seriously butchered."

The rainbow was gone. There was just a shaft of sunlight there now, angling down to the ground like the beam of a diffused stage spot. Andy felt his stomach clench and loosen, and he realized for the first time how bizarre this situation was, how unbelievably absurd. It didn't seem right

ALEXANDER'S SONG

that he was hearing this tale. Even assuming the old man was lonely and normally talkative, as old men often were, it seemed impossible that he should be relating such a story as one total stranger to another on the basis of a three-minute acquaintanceship. What was more, he seemed to be *enjoying* it, taking pleasure from the expression on Andy's face and the way he fidgeted.

The image of Royal Haag had left Andy's mind. Even the similarities in the violence of the two cases were not enough to keep it there. Instead he saw the picture Ginnie had stolen, three happy young men with their arms around each other. Frank Hale, dead. Charlie McCready, dead. And Alexander Bassett, not dead, at least not in 1927. Bassett had lived forty-two years past that fateful August day, and what in God's name did *that* mean? he wondered.

"It had been almost seven days," the old man said, "and it had rained a lot that week. You can imagine what five or six days of warm summer rain and animals and bugs and whatnot might do to a scene that was such a Christ-awful mess to begin with." Another frown-smile, or smile-frown. "Just imagine it, sir. Just close your eyes and imagine it."

"No, thank you," Andy managed to say. He swallowed, tasting bile on his tongue. "Did they ever find out who—"

"Don't know. If I heard that part, I've forgotten now. I do remember they had one suspect right off the bat, some young fellow who was always chumming around with those two. They had some club—the Dublin Society? Something like that. I suppose the law figured this boy was always with them but didn't seem to be anywhere around on the day they got killed. He seemed like a natural suspect. But they questioned him for three days and finally cleared him."

"Do you remember his name?" Andy asked. His voice seemed to come from somewhere else, miles away.

The old man shook his head. "Bucket, Backer, Backus, Barrett, something like that. It doesn't matter. He was cleared, and I don't recall hearing they ever found the murderer."

Bucket, Andy thought, Backus, Barrett—he was cleared. He felt a sense of giddy relief out of all proportion to the decades that had gone by since the crime. Cruelly murdered. Snatched from our arms. But Alexander Bassett had been exonerated.

Something else occurred to him, and he was about to ask the old man if he knew anything about the Royal Haag affair, but the man cut him short by squinting at the dial of his watch.

"I have to get back to town," he said. "I'm already well past the time I allow for my daily walks."

"You...you *walked*? All the way out here?"

"Oh, sure. Fast walk, too—out and back, ten miles, hour and a half. Keeps the juice flowing." The old man paused, smiled, and gave Andy a broad, stagy wink. "If I were you, I wouldn't stick around this boneyard too long."

Andy was still dealing with the idea of a walk from and to town, feeling ashamed as he realized that he himself couldn't hope to complete such a venture in less than half a day. He didn't immediately catch the implication of the man's last statement. "Why's that?"

"Oh, well, you just never know." His smile broadened. "You stay here long enough and McCready's vengeful spirit might decide to pay you a visit. I've heard he likes to do the jitterbug on people's bones."

"Are you—"

"Have yourself a nice day." The old man pivoted sharply and strode downhill toward the turnstile.

"Hey, wait a minute!" Andy called. "What's your name?"

The old man raised a hand in a jaunty little wave, but he never looked back.

"Jesus Christ," Andy murmured. He considered running after the man, perhaps catching him, pushing him up against the picket fence, demanding to know his name, but the stupid and ultimately meaningless melodrama in such a gesture stopped him in time. It didn't matter what his name was. It didn't matter why he had stopped to talk to Andy when

ALEXANDER'S SONG

he was supposedly in the middle of a routine, brisk fitness walk. None of it mattered. His story of the Hale and McCready murders probably didn't even matter—although on that point he was less sure.

He thought he was beginning to see some connections, although *see* really wasn't the right word. It was more a matter of *feeling* something, *sensing* something was there, if he could only zero in on it, tune out the interference and concentrate for a while. Bassett's apparent friendship with the murdered young men was most likely a part of it. He was beginning to think that the novel in which characters named Frank Hale and Charlie McCready starred was a part of it, too.

At the very least, he thought, there were new things to look at. He had chased down Rock Creek's blind alleys for more than a week. Ed Hoffer, the antique photograph, Hale and McCready, and *To Raise Brave Men* gave him new territory to wander. Even if they, too, turned out to lead nowhere, at least it would be a *new* nowhere. Better still, tomorrow morning he could expect the express shipment from New York. What had Joanne told him? The Bassett journal was dated 1926 or '27? He didn't need to glance at the date on McCready's tombstone to know what a remarkable stroke of Providence that was.

Things are speeding up, he thought, but that reminded him a little too much of the foolish optimism with which he'd arrived in Rock Creek. Better to say nothing. Better just to plug ahead, follow what random clues there might be, and leave it at that.

3

HE GOT BACK to Turner's at two-fifteen, intent on beginning a new reading of *Brave Men*—not a general reading but a thorough examination with a fine-tooth comb. Instead he found Ginnie waiting for him outside his room, sitting on the floor, her back against the wall. She was idly flipping through a thick stack of white paper.

On his way back into town he had kept an eye out for the old man, intending to stop, talk him out of his walk, give him a ride, ask him for more information. Either he had been slower leaving the cemetery than he thought or the old man was a much faster walker than he had admitted—maybe both. He didn't spot him until he was just over a mile from the town limits, at the point where Oak Hill Road split, the left-hand branch leading eventually to Ontonagon and Michigan Streets, the right meandering along the woods until it finally linked up with the highway on the far side of town. The old man was taking the scenic route, for Andy's purposes the wrong way.

He stopped at the junction, debated the wisdom of following, and finally decided there wasn't any. Catching up with the old man along the way was one thing. Chasing him down when it meant taking a detour seemed pointless and maybe even obsessive. He sat there for a moment anyway, leaning forward against the steering wheel as he watched the old man stride briskly around the bend, probably heading for the scattering of homes along the eastern edge of town. Then he sighed, lit a cigarette, and turned toward the bed and breakfast.

"Standing guard?" he said now to Ginnie.

She looked up from her papers, startled. "It's about time. You really outsmarted me, didn't you?" He raised his eyebrows. "You know what I mean. 'Oh, we'll talk tomorrow, Ginnie. We'll iron all of this out in the morning.' Then you get up and sneak out before dawn."

"That's not true."

"Oh?"

He smiled weakly. "The sun was already up when I left."

"Ha-ha." She stood. "You'll be glad to know that while you were running around God knows where, I was finding things out."

"I wasn't just running around, Ginnie. I was working, too."

"Hmm. I thought maybe you ditched me, hoping I'd use all my free time to run out to Wolf Island and return a certain picture. But I didn't. I went and saw my old friend Connie LeMay instead."

ALEXANDER'S SONG

For a moment the name meant nothing to Andy. It was just a nugget of information, covered by a layer of memory too thick to unwrap. Then it came to him. "I thought the library was closed on Sundays."

"It is. I went over to her house. I told her I was starting school tomorrow—true—and that I needed to look up some things for one of my new classes—not true. She didn't have anything better going on, so she took me down to the library and let me in." For the first time since he'd gotten there, she smiled. "They have a little newspaper morgue in the basement. I'll bet you didn't get down there, did you?"

He shook his head.

"It's not much, really. A few years' worth of the Houghton paper, some issues from L'Anse and Marquette and Iron Mountain, and about seventy-five years' worth of the Rock Creek *Record-Journal*. You know what that means. Seventy-five years of a weekly small-town paper. Seventy-five years of the high school honor roll and who married who and who wants to be mayor and whose cousin is visiting from Chicago for a few days. Junk, mostly. But in between—" she held up the stack of paper "—there's a bit of real news once in a while."

For the first time he saw what she had—photocopies of newspaper articles, old ones judging from what he could see of the typeface and the rather poor way they had reproduced. On the first one, he saw the headline TRAGIC FIRE CLAIMS LOCAL MILL OWNER, 58, and below that: *Friends and Foes Alike Mourn theLoss. He Helped Bring Prosperity to Our Corner of the World, Says Mayor Heikka.*

"May I?"

She handed him the sheets. He thumbed through them quickly, disturbed at the way certain words jumped out over and over again: "death" and "murders" and "tragedy" and "Constable McFarren"—he saw each of those at least ten times. He also saw the phrase "dangerous lunatic" and the names "Francis Hale" and "Charles McCready" more often than he could count. "Blood" was there, and "grisly discovery," and "funeral" and "burial." Some of the reports had the typeset date above them, most

101

from the *Record-Journal* dated Wednesday, August 17, 1927. Next to those on which no date appeared, Ginnie had scribbled down the issue in which she'd found them. The latest he saw was Wednesday, January 25, 1928.

"The reporting stinks," Ginnie said as he rifled through the pages. "Maybe that was just typical for the time, I don't know. My guess is, they just weren't used to having to practice real journalism around here. That August seventeenth issue alone—every article in the paper that week was about McCready and Hale. It must have knocked them for a loop, having something like that to deal with."

Andy nodded. "This local millowner business—what's all that about?"

"Ah, I thought you'd be interested in that. That's Bassett's father, William. Do you know how he died?" Andy shook his head. "He was killed in a fire on March sixth that same year, 1927."

"You don't think—"

"That there was a connection with the murders? No chance. The fire started in his office at the mill. The paper said some kerosene leaked out of a storage drum, Bassett lit a match, and boom. Completely accidental. But I thought you'd want to see it."

Andy was impressed with the amount of information she had ferreted out in a short time, and with the fact that she would even bother, given the way he had treated her yesterday. He also felt slightly weak, overwhelmed at the way he had gone from no information to too much information in only twenty-four hours. Whether or not the death of William Bassett and the murders of Alexander's friends had anything to do with his later literary career still remained to be seen, but that was not the point right now. He still had to sort through all of it, study all the data, make the appropriate notes, and then decide what he had.

"I appreciate your help," he said. "You did a good job. It's going to be fascinating going over this, even though I already know the story of the murders."

ALEXANDER'S SONG

She looked surprised, then a little disappointed. "The way they disappeared? The fisherman who found them? The way they were chopped up? Questioning Bassett? Everything?"

"Not the details, but the rough outline." He told her about his visit to Oak Hill. Oddly enough, the only thing she seized on was what the old man had said to him at the very end.

"He really told you that? I mean the part about not sticking around the boneyard too long?"

"Yeah, why?"

"Give me those." Before he even knew what she was talking about, she had torn the stack of photocopies out of his hands. She raced through them, top to bottom, grunted a curse when she didn't find what she wanted, and went through them again. "Here," she said at last, pulling out a sheet and thrusting it in Andy's face. "Read that."

The two column article was headlined CONSTABLE BEGS COOPERATION. He skimmed through it and caught the general drift. Two weeks after Hale and McCready's deaths, the forest clearing where they'd been found was still a disaster area. Physical clean-up had taken longer than anyone had hoped, and even with the help of state authorities, the Baraga County Sheriff, and policemen from nearby towns, the search for clues was painstakingly slow. The unseasonably rainy weather was a factor, but so was the endless stream of curiosity seekers who tramped into the woods to see the gruesome scene. They came from Rock Creek. They came from Alberta. They came from Covington. They came from L'Anse and Baraga. They came from Houghton, Hancock, Calumet, and even as far away as Iron River and Crystal Falls. Four policemen were assigned full-time to barricade both ends of Green Meadow Trail, but even at that, reporters and gawkers found ways to sneak through the forest for pictures or a peak, trampling possible physical evidence, hampering the investigation.

The part of the article Ginnie wanted him to see came midway down the second column, where Elwood McFarren made his plea for the understanding and aid of the locals. "Please, please," McFarren was quoted, "try to see it from our point of view. I know human nature, believe me. Everyone wants a look at the boneyard. But if we're going to stand a snowball's chance of catching this madman, we need everyone to just stay away and let us do our job."

"So what's the big deal?" Andy said when he was done reading. "You mean the fact that he used the word 'boneyard'?"

"Well, yeah. Don't you think it's odd?"

"Odd? No. A coincidence, maybe." He shrugged. "It's not as if nobody's ever used the word before."

She shook her head fiercely. "I'll admit it's not an original noun, but it's not exactly common either. It's not one of those words you hear every day, or even every month. I just think it's...I think it's odd that we'd run across it twice in one day, not about the same place, but about the same event."

"So what are you saying, Ginnie? Do you think that was McFarren I ran into out there? I guess it could have been; he was maybe old enough."

Ginnie laughed. "You'd better hope it wasn't. If it was, you had yourself a *real* ghostly encounter, even without McCready's vengeful spirit. Elwood McFarren died when I was a little kid, maybe seven or eight. I remember—it was a huge deal. He was like a hundred and ten years old and he'd been constable here since the dawn of time. It was a real occasion. There was a cortege right down the middle of Michigan Street, all the shops closed, all the kids got out of school. I mean, Jesus, it was like the president had died or something. They even did away with the title of constable in his honor. Ever since then we've just had plain old police chiefs."

"Then it *was* just a coincidence," Andy said.

"Maybe," she said, sounding unconvinced. "Either that, or...."

"Or what?"

"Or maybe you met someone who was around back then and remembered McFarren using that phrase. And if that's the case, he was probably lying to you. He probably knew more than the bits and pieces he said got passed along."

ALEXANDER'S SONG

Andy sighed. "That's a lot of maybes and probablys. If you don't mind, I'll stick to the coincidence theory. I've got enough loose ends to keep me busy, without chasing around after someone's vocabulary. Do you mind if I borrow—"

He stopped, turning toward the stairway. They heard the sound of footsteps, and through the balustrade they saw rising black hair, the top of a head, a face, and finally the rest of Max Turner as she reached the top step. She turned toward them, her gaze sharp even from the other end of the corridor. She looked at Andy first, then turned and studied her daughter. After a second or two, she looked at Andy again. He felt the sensation of water dripping down his spine and turning to ice.

Don't look at dat witch woman, he thought nonsensically. *Don't look in dem eyes when she pissed. Turn you to stone, dat's what she do.*

"Virginia," Max said coolly, "I'm going to need your help fixing dinner. We got two new overnights in a little while ago; it's going to be a full table."

"Sure, mom, I'll be down in—"

"And, Mr. Gillespie, there's a phone call for you downstairs. You can take it in the living room."

He tried to thank her, but she pivoted smoothly and started back downstairs. "Please come now, Virginia," she said as she disappeared. "There're a million things to get ready."

"Nabbed by the cops," Ginnie said under her breath. "Jesus, you'd think we were having an affair or something."

They looked at each other. Neither of them spoke. Neither of them laughed.

"Virginia!" Max snapped, her voice fading as she passed the second floor and headed for the first. "Now!"

"Yes, mom!" Ginnie called back, and murmured: "The life of the mind loses out again."

A moment later, they were following Max downstairs.

105

4

THAT NIGHT ANDY dreamed again—dreamed awake this time. It happened late, as he was sprawled on the bed in his room, surrounded by the news clippings, his notebooks, a copy of *To Raise Brave Men*, and the copy of David Kumlien's *Michigan Mayhem*. He began to drift, his tired eyes glazing over, his pencil slipping from his hand, rolling off the mattress, falling to the floor. He knew where he was, but he felt himself moving, leaving the world of the bed and breakfast and entering a world of half-sleep, half-dream, floating, sailing along to another place. He saw himself climbing the steps on Wolf Island, going up to the top of the cliff where people were waiting for him. Faces, each one fuzzy and blurred by distance, peered over the edge. He heard muttering voices, muted laughter. *Going up*, his mind said lazily, *gonna climb all the way until I find the answers.*

It was strange that he would feel such things in a dream, even a waking dream like this, but he began to tire. Much as they had when he and Ginnie had climbed the steps in real life, his legs began to stiffen and ache, his lungs began to burn. Like a child just beginning to understand the mechanics of running or throwing a ball, it occurred to him that he was climbing inefficiently, but with all the topsy-turvy logic of dreams, it took him a while to understand why. His hands, he finally realized. He wasn't using his hands. If he put them on the railing and used his arms to help haul himself up, the climb would become considerably easier. But when he looked down at his right hand he saw for the first time that he was holding the copy of the Kumlien book, his index finger marking the chapter called *Halvard Borg, The Lumber Town Butcher: Rock Creek, 1908-1909.*

"Lumber Town Butcher," he mumbled. "Yellow journalism. Sensational pulp crap nonsense."

He had read the chapter earlier in the evening, going over the story of how Royal Haag had been killed by Borg, a local bum who two months later wrote a confession note and splattered his brains over the walls of his cabin. The useful facts had been few and far between, the gory descriptions of both

ALEXANDER'S SONG

Haag's body and Borg's suicide painted in minute, breathless detail. He had been reminded of his student, Kevin Caspian, enthusiastically describing to his friends the decapitation scene in some new underground music video, and had immediately written off his chances of finding anything remotely useful in either the Haag murder or the entire Kumlien book. Which left him wondering why he was carrying the book now, why he was marking that particular chapter, why he didn't just throw the damn thing over his shoulder and into the lake below—which is precisely what he did a moment later.

When he reached the last step, he found that the entire clearing at the top of the cliff had been transformed from a rocky, barren patch of open ground to a festive party site. There were round tables with colorful striped umbrellas, cedar poles topped with Japanese lanterns, a metal tub filled with ice and bottled beer, a mahogany bar where bottles stood in neat rows and glasses were stacked in two impressive pyramids.

For all of that, there were only a handful of people there. He saw Ginnie and Max Turner, Connie LeMay from the library, old Toivo Lammi and his wife, Jeanette. Near the bar, standing with his back to Andy, peering over the edge of the cliff, was the old man who had approached him in the cemetery. He saw Albert Anson, the owner of Allie's Bar and one of his first interview subjects. Next to him was the man named Sheridan, the salesman who had been staying at Turner's and who (Andy was sure) had left Rock Creek for Duluth more than a day earlier.

Andy stood at the top of the staircase for almost a minute, like a guest waiting to be formally announced. He was well aware how absurd the situation was. He knew that he was dreaming, floating on mental images while treading on the line between sleeping and wakefulness. He realized that if he opened his eyes right now he would find himself right where he'd started, lying on his bed, surrounded by the tools of research. But he wasn't sure he wanted to open his eyes. The dream was giving him a slightly uncomfortable feeling, and perhaps if it became *actively* uncomfortable he would opt to escape, but for now he wanted to go with it, ride along, and see where it took him.

A hand fell on his shoulder. He turned, recoiled, and then brought himself under control. The man standing there was Charlie McCready, not more than a kid really, sixteen years old, dressed the way he had been in Ed Hoffer's picture. He grinned at Andy and jerked a thumb toward the opposite side of the clearing. There, just emerging from the woods, came Ed Hoffer himself. He shuffled into the light, supporting himself on one side with his walking stick, on the other by leaning on the shoulder of someone Andy at first thought was a young Alexander Bassett. He frowned, blinked, and realized he was wrong. It wasn't Bassett but Frank Hale, youthful and vigorous, doubtless capable of carrying Hoffer on his shoulders if need be.

Hoffer and Hale stopped, and the old man raised his gaze, his pale, watery eyes looking across at Andy. Everything in the clearing came to a standstill. The sound of waves and wind stopped. The conversations between Ginnie and her mother, Toivo Lammi and his wife, the salesman Sheridan and Connie LeMay, all hesitated long enough for Hoffer to speak to him.

"Come," he said in his thin, frail voice.

Andy looked at Charlie McCready. McCready nodded. "Go on, it's all right. He's got something he wants to show you."

Andy shrugged and walked toward the old man, threading his way through the obstacle course of umbrella-topped tables. To get there he had to pass by Ginnie and Max, and as he did so he was aware of Ginnie silently urging him onward, Max trying to carve out his heart with the burning heat of her eyes.

"Welcome to the second world," Hoffer said.

"What?"

"The second world...my world...sometimes called the world of secrets...sometimes called the boneyard." He slowly lifted the hand with the walking stick and gestured around the clearing. "My place. My party. Welcome."

Andy didn't know what to say. He wasn't sure he wanted to say anything, or even if he was supposed to. He checked behind him and saw

ALEXANDER'S SONG

everyone staring at him now, mouths open but no sound emerging, drinks in hand but untasted.

"Come with me," Hoffer said, and before Andy had a chance to agree or not, he was grasped by Hale and McCready, propelled along after the old man, out of the clearing and into the woods.

"Go for it!" Ginnie shouted, and someone—Sheridan?—echoed, "Go for it, Gillespie!"

There was no path. The only path, the one that led to Hoffer's cabin, was a hundred yards behind him. Here there was just muddy, rolling ground blanketed with pine needles, an occasional fallen tree, a few stumps, some rocks. It might have been a difficult walk if they'd had very far to go, but after less than a minute Hoffer stopped and rapped his walking stick on something entirely out of place in that setting, something that not only didn't belong there but could not even have gotten there in real life. It took magic to get an object like that out into the middle of the woods, silly, twisted, illogical dream-magic.

"Well, I gather this is what you want," the old man said. "Feel free to take a look."

Andy laughed. "This is a joke, right?"

"Oh, no. Indeed no." Hoffer shook his head solemnly. Hale and McCready shook theirs, too. "I thought I explained it to you. This is no joke. It's the second world, the place where the answers are."

Andy stared at the roll-top desk. He felt different, *changed*. Where before he had been floating along on the sharp senses, quick reflexes, and able wits of his dream buzz, now he felt muddy and thick, dumb, slow. He had the vague sense that Hoffer was right. The desk was what he wanted, sure enough. The desk was important, vital in some way. He just didn't understand how, or why, or what he was supposed to do next.

"Our time's running short," Hoffer said. "If you want a look, you'd better be quick about it."

Andy frowned and stepped forward, hoping something would come to him. He reached out and touched the fine, smooth wood. It was cool and slick beneath his fingers. He stared at the miniature mountain range of papers piled there, ordinary papers, the records of Hoffer's personal business, notes and checks and bills.

"Of course," he murmured, beginning to remember. There was something he needed to see here, something he had looked for when he'd visited the old man's cabin. He had almost seen it then, or perhaps he *had* seen it, spotted it without recognizing it. He was beginning to see it again, or at least he was starting to feel it. It was here somewhere, in that envelope addressed to Seward's Outdoor Adventures, for instance, or in this note Hoffer had written for himself: *See K. Oppenheimer—ask if he'll split f.wood again this summer.*

He had almost picked up that note to study it more closely when a thunderous crack echoed through the woods. He threw himself to the ground. His right shoulder struck the sharp edge of a rock, sending an arrow of pain down his arm, but at least he hadn't been shot. Jesus, he thought, if that goddamned bullet had gotten me, I—

The crack came again, thin and clear and hard. He waited for the sound to die away, then raised his head and saw that he was alone. Hoffer, Hale, and McCready were gone. The desk was gone. There was another crack, and then another, until he understood that what he was hearing wasn't the sound of gunshots but someone pounding, hammering on wood, driving a nail or... or...or knocking...

His eyes snapped open and he bolted up, sending *To Raise Brave Men* and several of the photocopied news stories to the floor. He almost tipped his ashtray over too, but caught it just before it slipped off the bed. After a second or two of dazed confusion, he realized that somewhere along the way he had crossed the black line, passing from the world of drifting awake into full sleep. The dream he'd been having had gone with him, or maybe *he* had gone with *it*. That was a crazy damn thing to be thinking, but—

The person outside the room knocked again. "Mr. Gillespie? You in there?"

"Oh, shit," Andy said, as he finally realized what it was that had pulled him back across the line.

The man in the corridor was young, nineteen, twenty at the outside. He had curly blond hair and a peach-fuzz mustache. He wore jeans, a flannel shirt, and a bright green down vest that was open to reveal a gun belt with a service revolver in the holster.

He grinned. "Andrew Gillespie, right?"

"Yes." Andy felt himself trembling. "Do I—"

"Jeff Lamoreaux, Rock Creek Police. You got a couple minutes?"

5

"SORRY TO BE buggin' you so late," Lamoreaux said as he settled himself on the bed. "We got a little temporary manpower shortage. Chief's on vacation, Betty Rhodes is sick, and the other two're coppin' speeders up by 41. That leaves me to take this case alone." He grinned again, saying, Andy supposed, something along the lines of *You know how it is.* "I understand you almost got your head blown off today."

"Well, that's a crude way of putting it, but yes, I guess it was pretty close."

Lamoreaux laughed. He reached into his vest pocket and pulled out a Ziploc Baggie containing something that looked like a shiny mangled marble. "Dug it outta Max's livin' room bookshelf. It's from a .22. Ain't no bazooka, but if it'd hit you in the right place, it woulda done its job. If that ain't crude, I don't know what is."

Andy lit a cigarette and shivered.

"I pretty much got things figured out," Lamoreaux said, "but I'm gonna need your side for the record." He took out a spiral notebook, flipped it open, and poised the tip of his pen on the top line. "Lemme have it."

Andy closed his eyes and tried to compose himself. He still felt groggy from his short sleep, and dream residue clung to his mind like flakes of old paint—Hoffer, McCready, Hale, an impossible party in an impossible place, that goddamn desk again. He pushed as much of it away as he could and thought back to what had happened to him that afternoon.

They had gone downstairs, the three of them. Or rather, Max had gone first, storming into the kitchen where she immediately began slamming cupboards and rattling pots, while he and Ginnie had followed sheepishly behind.

"I'll see you at dinner," Ginnie had said, going after her mother. Andy had nodded. He had wanted to thank her for the news clippings, but she was already gone.

He took the call in the living room, the same place he'd spoken to Joanne on Friday night. The phone line sounded strange when he picked it up. There was none of the open, hollow silence of someone waiting on the other end. This silence was heavy, thick, solid, dead.

"Hello?" He waited, thinking that it was Joanne again and that they had another bad connection, but that idea blew up a moment later. "Hello? This is Andrew Gillespie...hello."

He grunted, hung up, and started toward the kitchen. He didn't especially relish talking to Max in her current mood, but he had to ask if she'd gotten the name of the caller. He took a step, perhaps as much as a step and a half away from the telephone. What happened then happened too fast to describe it in orderly, linear fashion.

"The window near the couch exploded," he told Lamoreaux. "I don't mean it broke or cracked, I mean it actually.... Well, you must've seen it. I jumped, or at least I think that's what I did. Maybe I tripped on that throw rug Max has in front of the bookcase; it wouldn't be the first time. Maybe I did both—jumped first, then tripped. I really don't remember. All I'm sure of is that shattering noise, and hearing something next to me that sounded like someone putting his fist through a wall. Max and Ginnie came running in from the kitchen and found me sprawled there on the floor." He paused. "And that's the story."

"That's it?" Despite his smile, Lamoreaux looked disappointed. "From the way Max described it, you were almost hysterical, like maybe you'd seen Charlie Manson out there pointin' an Uzi at you."

ALEXANDER'S SONG

"Well, I was shook up, sure. At first we didn't know *what* had happened. We thought someone might've thrown a rock through the window, something like that. We didn't see that bullet you found—none of us thought to check the walls and furniture—but when we didn't find a brick or anything lying on the floor, we figured it out; it had to be a gunshot. After that, it's fair to say I was a little upset."

"A little upset—hey, that's good." Lamoreaux jotted one final thing in his notebook, then closed the cover and slipped the book back into his vest. "I guess I'd be shook if I'd come as close as you did, even if it was just Nellie Ecklar firin' off his birthday present."

Andy frowned. "I'm sorry?"

"Nellie Ecklar. See, that's what I figured out. The shot came from the east side of the house, right? Carl and Sue Ecklar live over there, with their boy Nelson. After I talked to Max and found the slug, I went next door and checked it out. Sure enough, Nellie got a .22 for his fifteenth birthday last week."

"Oh," Andy said. He knew he should feel calmed by the explanation, but he didn't. "What happens in a case like this? I suppose he won't go to jail, but does he at least get hauled up in front of a judge or something?"

"Well, we got a problem there." Lamoreaux rubbed the back of his neck. "Nellie denies firin' the gun. He said he was gonna go out yesterday, plunk cans down at the dump, but he's takin' this weekend remedial math class over to the school and it ran long. He wanted to go out today, but he hadda help his dad clean out the garage. His folks back him up. They say the gun ain't been shot since they bought it."

"But—"

"Look here. You don't want to make a stink about this, do you? I can't do nothin' about it, really, not unless you press charges, and to tell you the God's honest, I'm not even sure you can. You just happened to be in the way. If anyone wanted to press, it'd hafta be Max—it's her house—and she don't want to. If Nellie would confess, I s'pose I could haul him in, lock him up for an hour or so, make a big stink, terrify him, let him go. But so long as the kid and his parents deny it, my hands're tied."

"Can't you confiscate the gun?" Andy said. "Couldn't you run some tests to find out if it had really been fired?"

Lamoreaux considered that. "I could. I never thought of it till just now, but you're right. The question is, why bother? The kid probably feels bad enough—bad enough, anyway, that he's gonna be a lot more careful in the future. That's all that matters. The case is solved. I know he did it, Max knows it, and you know it, too. I don't see no point in wastin' a buncha time and money provin' what everyone already knows."

Andy frowned.

"Aw, Jesus," Lamoreaux said. "You *do* know it, don't you?" Andy didn't answer. "C'mon now, mister, I see that look on your face. It means one of two things. Either you wanna be a sonuvabitch about this and make as much trouble as you can for a poor, careless kid or...or you buy Nellie's story and you think someone else did it. Is that the deal? Are we back to Manson with a machine gun? You think someone wanted to kill you?"

"I'm not sure what I think," Andy said truthfully. "It's just that it seems you're being awfully dismissive about the whole thing."

"I don't know what that means."

"It means you're writing it off pretty quickly. Property was damaged today; I was almost killed. It might have been the boy, but maybe not. I would think you'd want to find the truth."

Lamoreaux shook his head. "Maybe I gotta cut you some slack. You're pissed. You got good reason to be. I guess I'd be a little pissed too, maybe royally pissed. And you ain't from around here. Max says you're from Chicago. Well, all right, when guns go off in Chicago it probably means business, I can understand that. In a town like this, though...Jesus H. Christ, mister, guns go off around here all the time. Just about everyone hunts, and that means they gotta practice, usually by shootin' out beer bottles in their back yard. Once or twice a year a slug goes astray, you know what I mean? Houses get hit, cars get dented, a window gets broke. It happens. It don't

ALEXANDER'S SONG

mean the guy—who's usually either sloppy or drunk, sometimes both—was tryin' to kill you."

"I guess not," Andy said. He tried to say it with an apologetic smile on his face, but he must have failed, because the police officer swore again.

"I'll make you a deal, Mr. Gillespie. You give me somethin' to go on. You tell me who might've been tryin' to kill you. You give me a reason anyone, anyone at all, might *want* to kill you. You show me why Nellie Ecklar or anybody else has it in for you. You do that, I won't be so…*dismissive*. Otherwise, let's leave this damn thing alone and let me get back to checkin' shop doors on Michigan Street. Fair enough?"

Andy swallowed. His face was hot; he could actually feel the color creeping into his cheeks. "Fair enough," he said.

Lamoreaux stood. He walked to the door, opened it, and paused. "With the manpower shortage, I'll be workin' all tonight and tomorrow afternoon till five. You gimme a call if you crack this big case, all right?" He laughed. "I won't be holdin' my breath." The door rattled in its frame when he shut it behind him.

Well, Andy thought, point made. Lamoreaux had wanted to make him feel small, and he had—about two and a half inches tall, to be precise. Somebody trying to kill him? Sure, of course. Maybe it was Ed Hoffer, getting revenge for the stolen picture: *I want my property back or I'll turn your brains to hash, Gillespie!* Or it might have been the local John Birch Society, upset that he was writing about a dead commie. Was the John Birch Society still around these days? Maybe…probably…if it was anywhere, it would be in Rock Creek.

He walked to the window and pulled the drapes back, gazing into the yard below. A thin sliver of moonlight sailed behind the clouds, not enough to illuminate anything.

He felt overwhelmed again, pushed under by new information, useless information that did nothing, really, but distract him from his real work; by old photos and old gravestones; by desks and dreams; by gunshots and cops. He almost hoped ….No. He *did* hope. He hoped that when the journal Jo was sending showed up tomorrow, it would contain nothing he could use. After that, he would be perfectly justified in leaving Rock Creek and moving on to New York, or even in going back to Chicago for a spring of relaxation, a summer of hot sun and long days, before he had to return to work.

"Hey," he said, his hand tightening on the drapes, his voice a husky whisper.

There was someone standing in the back yard, near the trees at the far edge of the property. Someone tall and slim. He saw a face turned up toward the top story of the house, looking at his window, at his room, at him.

Andy didn't move. The person staring at him didn't move. Nearly a minute went by before he realized that he was holding his breath, and then he let it out in a long, gusty, rustling sigh.

Who are you? he thought. On the heels of that came another, stranger, almost ludicrous question: *Why do you want to kill me?*

Like a man awakening from a deep sleep, he reached up and rubbed his eyes with the backs of his hands. When he looked again, he realized that what he had thought was someone watching him was really just an illusion, an optical trick caused by darkness. Still, he stayed there at the window for a very long time, not wanting to move.

FOUR

AIRBORNE LIT 101

1

Monday morning dragged.

After Ginnie went off to school Andy stationed himself in the living room, wanting to be nearby when the package from New York arrived. As one hour dragged by, then two, he paced around the room, picking up fashion and decorating magazines and putting them back down, staring out the unbroken window on the north side of the house, studying the collection of books on Max's shelves (not as eclectic as Ed Hoffer's library, but impressive in its own way: Harlequin and Silhouette Romances in proper numerical order, books on the early Michigan fur trade, Stephen Hawking's *A Brief History of Time*, and many good mysteries by the likes of Jim Thompson, Fredric Brown, Elmore Leonard, and Tony Hillerman). While he browsed, he avoided looking at the damaged spot where Jeff Lamoreaux had dug the .22 slug out of the wood.

At five minutes to ten, a man by the name of Buddy LaChance showed up from the Rock Creek True Value, carrying a tool box, some putty, and a large pane of glass already cut to the measurements Max had given him on the phone. "You the fella almost got his ass blown away?" LaChance asked him.

"Almost," Andy said.

"Guess an air conditioned head's one of them things you could do without, huh?"

"I don't—"

But LaChance had already gotten to work, chuckling softly to himself and acting as though Andy were no longer there.

Andy tried to stay seated on the couch, with only a few quick, nervous pacing trips around the room and out into the front hall, but when the package had not arrived by ten-thirty, Max had had enough.

"I want you out of here," she told Andy. "You're driving me crazy, and you're in Buddy's way."

"Don't mind me," LaChance said, wiping his putty knife on the leg of his jeans. "Just about done here, anyhow."

"You're in *my* way, then," Max said. "What you pay a day for room and board gets you just that, room and board. It doesn't give you the right to wander around my house all day, getting on my nerves."

"What do you want me to do, Max? The package—"

"I don't give a damn about your precious package. It'll get here when it gets here. As for what you can do—go sit on the porch, go up to your room, take a walk around the block. I don't care. I'm going to start house cleaning as soon as Buddy's finished. If you're not out of here by then, I'm going to vacuum right over you." He tried obeying her order, or as he preferred to think of it, taking her advice. But the day, though sunny and stunningly clear, was too cold for porch sitting, and twenty minutes in his room, looking out the window, listening for the sound of a delivery van, took his nerves past fraying to the point where they actually snapped.

Maybe Jo was right after all, he thought dismally. Maybe they *don't* have express deliveries to Rock Creek. But that, of course, was absurd. Since he'd come to town, he'd already seen a Federal Express truck in front of the drug store and a Purolator van cruising down Michigan Street. The package would be here. They had express service everywhere these days; some places just took a little longer than others.

At a few minutes past eleven he decided the waiting wasn't doing him any good. He was too jumpy, running to the window every time a car drove down Victory Street, and in the meantime other business was being ignored. He had promised Ginnie that he would complete the last in the round of interviews they had started on Saturday, and now was probably as good a time as any. If the package came while he was out, so be it, it would be waiting for him when he got back. And if it didn't come, then at least he would have kept his commitment and another name could be scratched off the list.

2

THE SIGN WAS still up in the window of the Trading Post—GONE TO WHOLESALE GIFT SHOW!! BACK ON MONDAY!! SORRY WE MISSED YOU!!—but this time Andy saw a car parked out front and lights on inside. The door was open. When he went through, bells strung from the pneumatic closer announced his presence, although no one came forward to greet him.

He walked past the empty counter up front, where an electronic cash register was almost lost among racks of postcards and bumper stickers that said things like THE QUAD LAKES ARE WALLEYE HEAVEN! and A BAD DAY FISHING IS STILL BETTER THAN A GOOD DAY AT WORK! He heard a radio playing in the back of the store, and he followed the sound down aisles of souvenirs that were mostly gaudy, mostly plastic or rubber, mostly cheap. They were the kind of items that twenty-five or thirty years earlier would have been derided as "Made in Japan" or "Imported from Taiwan." These days, Andy was willing to bet that the fancy cash register came from Japan while most of the tacky souvenirs sported red, white, and blue "Manufactured in the USA" labels.

PAUL F. OLSON

The storage room door was ajar, held open with a large cardboard carton. The radio was louder back there. He heard an announcer talking about the stupendous values on spring jackets to be found at some clothing store in Houghton's Copper Country Mall. The commercial ended, the weather report came on—continued clear and cold through tomorrow morning, then colder still, and rain. Andy waited, but no one emerged to help him.

"Hello?" he said, but there was still no answer. Apparently customer service didn't count for much in the off-season, not in junky gift shops that probably did ninety-five percent of their business between Memorial Day and Labor Day. He decided it was either go in or go home, waited a moment longer, considering, then sighed and went in.

There was someone sitting at a big metal desk just around the corner. Andy saw a gray head bent over what appeared to be an old-fashioned ledger book. Next to the ledger was a calculator, its window showing a row of green numbers. The radio was on a shelf to the right of the desk, wedged between stacks of files and boxes of envelopes, rubber bands, paper clips, rolls of price labels, and a rack of rubber stamps.

"Mr. Visnaw?"

"Yes, sir. Just a moment, please."

Andy leaned in the doorway, pretending to be interested in the shelves of extra merchandise and boxes marked <u>Quad T-shirts XL</u> or <u>C.skin hats all sizes.</u> He was beginning to wish he had stayed and waited for Jo's package after all, when the man at the desk finally closed his ledger and turned around.

"What can I help you—"

They stared at each other like characters in a sitcom, mouths hanging open, eyes wide. Andy shook his head and began to laugh. He didn't think the situation was exactly funny, but after the confusion of the last few days, he was glad to see his sense of the ridiculous was still intact.

"Well, my graveyard loving friend," Martin Visnaw said with a faint smile. "What brings you to my humble shop?"

3

THEY DIDN'T STAY at the Trading Post very long. Once Andy had told him why he was there, Visnaw became too excited to sit still. He paced around the back room, smiling, laughing, offering enthusiastic exclamations while Andy explained the purpose behind his research, the difficulties he'd encountered, his connection with Ginnie ("You know Miss Turner?" Visnaw said. "What a pleasure it was to meet her all those years ago—so bright, so energetic!"), and what he had been doing at Oak Hill the day before.

"A biography," Visnaw said when he was finished. "Good God Almighty, I've been waiting for something like this for years! I once thought I might write it myself. It's unbelievable." He stopped pacing and stared at Andy with bright, glittering eyes. "You're a brave, lucky man."

Andy shrugged, a little surprised at Visnaw's restless, electric energy. "'Foolish' is the adjective that seems more appropriate. I'd feel luckier if I didn't keep running into brick walls every time I turned around."

"Ah, but that's the nature of the game. Isn't a little mystery and frustration what it's all about? Isn't it all part of the adventure?"

"I guess so," Andy said.

"Well, of course it is! I don't ….Look, why don't we get out of here? I know the perfect place to talk."

Andy was startled again. He looked around at the boxes and racks, out the door at the empty aisles. As far as he could tell, the back room was the perfect spot for a conversation, and it didn't appear they were going to be disturbed. "Didn't you just open? I thought you were out of town for the last—"

"The Grand Rapids Gift Show, yes." Visnaw shook his head. "That was a waste of time, but no bigger waste than sitting here all day waiting to sell one sweatshirt. The truth is, when it's not the peak of summer, I pretty much open and close when I want. Business at this time of year isn't what you'd call steady."

"But—"

"Let's go to the airport."

Andy thought he must have heard wrong. "There's no airport in Rock Creek."

"Of course there is."

"But there can't be. When I first knew I'd be coming here, I planned to take a plane. I made some calls, but the travel agent told me the best I could do is fly into Houghton or Marquette and rent a car."

Visnaw was laughing before he even finished. "Mr. Gillespie, this isn't the kind of airport you fly into. Well, of course it is, yes—but not on any airline. You'll see."

Andy was hopelessly confused. Why would they go to an airport to discuss Alexander Bassett? He had an image of the two of them sitting in those big pay-as-you-watch television chairs, and then an even more ridiculous picture: sitting next to Visnaw on an empty luggage carousel, going around and around while debating the merits of *Seascape* as opposed to *A Daughter's Song*.

"I'm expecting a package to show up back at Turner's," he said, spreading his hands apologetically. "Maybe we could talk over dinner some night, or—"

"Oh, come on." Visnaw grew serious and studied Andy closely. "You really *don't* have a sense of adventure, do you?"

"What do you mean?"

"I mean you, hesitating like a kid on his first date. Jesus Christ, let go a little. What's wrong with you?"

Andy stepped backwards. "I don't think that's any of your—"

"It'll be fun. You'll see things you've never seen." Visnaw laughed yet again, his eyes glittering brightly—but glittering with something sharper and a bit harder than simple good humor. "If you come with me, I'll tell you secrets. I'll tell you things about Mr. Bassett you never dreamed."

It was like being back in the cemetery, caught off guard by this man appearing out of nowhere, listening to his strange story and watching him vanish like a ghost. He suspected there was no good argument to anything

ALEXANDER'S SONG

Martin Visnaw might say, and more than that, he didn't think he should be arguing.

I'll tell you things about Mr. Bassett you never dreamed.

Well, really. What was he supposed to say to that?

4

HE WAS GLAD he'd kept his image of luggage carousels and modern amenities to himself. Even still, he felt foolish. It wasn't that he had doubted the existence of places like the Rock Creek Area Airport; it was just that he'd never expected to actually see one.

The airport was located three miles northwest of town, off a county road that meandered through the wilderness and eventually, Visnaw told him, crossed the Sturgeon and Silver Rivers before meeting up with Highway 38 near Alston. When they eased off the access drive and into a parking area of thinly-scattered gravel, Andy looked around and for no apparent reason thought of the first edition Laura Ingalls Wilder books Joanne collected. He was puzzled until he realized why the thought had come to him, and then he bit his cheek to keep from laughing: *The Little Landing Strip in the Big Woods.*

The single runway was short, narrow, and had a roll to it that might have been pretty in a meadow but looked bluntly frightening here. Its surface was grass, worn down in most places to the dirt beneath, and it was surrounded by weeds and scrub, beyond which the forest reared up, ready to catch any aircraft that had too long a takeoff run or veered too far one way or the other on approach.

The only building on the property was a windowless tin shack next to the parking area. A cheap padlock kept the door closed, and a tattered windsock, its original bright orange faded almost to white, fluttered from a pole on the roof. A few feet away was an old fuel pump overgrown with weeds, the hose and nozzle lying on the ground beside it, the numbers reading $21.00 for 35 gallons from some long-ago sale.

Martin Visnaw saw Andy's expression and smiled. "The place doesn't look like much, I know, but it's quite serviceable. Actually, the only pilots in town are myself and Anna Grosskopf, whose husband owns Good Folks Rexall. It's like having a private airport, except for a few high-rolling tourists who fly in during the season. I don't even have to maintain it. The town and county need to have it available for emergency ambulance flights, so they keep the grass cut and the snow plowed. I pay a modest fifty dollars a month for a tie-down fee, and the place is virtually mine. What more could I ask?"

"You're a pilot?"

"Didn't I make that clear?" Visnaw pointed to a little red and white plane parked a hundred yards away, ropes running from its wings and tail to iron rings in the ground. "Piper Tri-Pacer Niner-Double Four-Six-Alpha. Your ticket to the skies high over beautiful Rock Creek."

"Oh," Andy said. "No, I don't think so. My package—"

"With all due respect, Mr. Gillespie, why don't you shove that package up your ass?" Visnaw's smile indicated that he probably didn't mean that the way it sounded. "I haven't been up in over a month. I need to scrape some of the rust off my wings, so to speak. You need to talk about Alexander Bassett. What better place to have a nice, private conversation?"

Like the smile, the tone of the old man's voice was pleasant enough, but it carried something else, the same trace of snide or mildly mean-spirited humor Andy had heard the day before, when Visnaw had said that thing about Charlie McCready's spirit doing the jitterbug on his bones.

Andy didn't want to fly. Andy *hated* flying. He flew commercially only when necessary, and the thought of going up now in that tiny old plane with this eccentric man was enough to make his heart thunder. Yet he didn't see any way out of it. They were three miles from town, sitting not in his own pickup but in Visnaw's Buick. And Visnaw was right, of course. He did need to talk about Bassett. *I'll tell you secrets,* the old man had said.

Andy sighed. "One hour, no more," he said, but even as the words came out of his mouth, he knew he sounded like a man who compromises because he has nothing to bargain with.

ALEXANDER'S SONG

Visnaw led him to the plane. It was a short, squat little thing that looked extremely unairworthy, like an old cookstove with bumblebee wings. Andy touched the fuselage near the ID numbers—N9446A—and was unsettled to find that it was not covered with a skin of metal but with fabric, something he had assumed gone with the era of Lindbergh and the barnstormers.

"Safe as a house," Visnaw said absently, lifting the engine cowling and pulling the dipstick. "She's a 1954. Sounds old, I know, but not for a light plane. Twenty years on a bird like this is the equivalent of six months on a car. After thirty-five years she's just getting broken in."

Andy nodded doubtfully and watched as Visnaw ran through his preflight, inspecting the propeller and spinner, the nose gear, the main wheels, the wing struts and the control surfaces, which he named off like an instructor: ailerons, flaps, rudder, elevator. The last step came when he took an empty baby food jar out of his jacket pocket and filled it with reddish fuel that he drained from a tiny spigot on the starboard wing. He held the jar up to the sun, squinted, and gave a satisfied nod.

"Not a drop of water in the tanks. We're all set."

"I want to ask you something," Andy said. A disturbing question had been playing at the edges of his mind, but he wondered if he was truly curious or only hoping that the old man would give him a cockeyed answer, anything for an excuse to write him off and avoid going up.

"Fire away," Visnaw said cheerfully, climbing in the right-hand door and sliding across to the pilot's seat.

Andy swallowed. "Yesterday, at Oak Hill, when we were talking about McCready and Hale...."

"Courage, man," Visnaw laughed. He was studying a laminated preflight card, checking gauges, flipping switches. "Spit it out."

"You said that Hale and McCready...that they had a friend. But you pretended not to know his name. Why'd you do that? You knew who Bassett was. I assume you also knew he was the friend. Why'd you play dumb?"

Visnaw smiled. "I didn't know who *you* were."

PAUL F. OLSON

"I'm sorry?"

"Just as I said—I didn't know you from Adam." He put down the checklist. "When I moved here twenty years ago, I was naive. I'll wager I was much the way you were when you arrived to do your research. I was ecstatic about living in the town where my literary hero grew up. Naturally, I expected the locals to understand and share my excitement. I asked about Bassett at every chance. I ran from the grocery store to the drugstore to the restaurants and bars, blabbering away about him. But I learned quickly enough that most people didn't want to talk about him, or even hear someone else do the talking. You said you've encountered problems. Imagine what I faced back then, during the height of the Cold War. Mentioning Bassett was a good way to have your loyalty, your patriotism, even your manhood called into question. Say you liked Bassett and they called you a traitor. After a while you learned to keep your mouth shut."

Andy shrugged. He didn't know what he'd wanted to hear, but the answer sounded like the most reasonable one he could expect. After all, hadn't he kept quiet himself, standing right there in front of McCready's grave and not saying a thing?

"So hop in," Visnaw said with a grin, motioning to the seat beside him. "Let's do some flying."

5

THEY BOUNCED TO the end of the runway, where Visnaw swung the airplane's nose into the wind and held it there with the hand brake that hung down below the control panel. Pushing in the throttle, he ran the engine up until Andy thought the noise was going to blow his head apart. Then he began turning the ignition key back and forth. Each time he clicked the key to the left, the engine RPMs dropped noticeably, only to rise again when the key returned to the rightmost position. Two clicks left, two right; One click left, one right. When he was done with that, Visnaw pulled out a black knob labeled CARB HEAT, and once again the engine roar diminished. Knob in; RPMs up.

Andy was alarmed. "Everything okay?"

"Right as rain," Visnaw said. He swept his gaze from left to right, taking in the instruments one at a time, before lifting the radio microphone from its clip near his left hand. "Rock Creek traffic, Tri-Pacer four-six-Alpha's departing two-six. We'll be in the area."

Before Andy knew what was going to happen, Visnaw pulled the control wheel all the way back into his belly, causing its twin in front of the passenger seat to pin Andy in place like a rude hand. Visnaw pushed the throttle in completely. The noise of full power made the earlier roar seem like a mild cough. A moment went by while the plane shivered and rocked, then Visnaw released the brake. They lurched forward. The nose came up immediately and they rumbled down the grass strip, gathering speed, like a three-legged animal staggering along on its hind legs alone.

"Going up!"

Andy had just been getting used to the sight of trees moving past either wingtip, disappearing behind them with gradually increasing speed, not turning into a flashing blur as they might from a commercial jet, but coming and going too fast to really notice size or detail. He clutched the seat with both hands. The bottom dropped out as they rose into the air. The wheel in front of him went forward, giving him breathing space as their steep, nose-high attitude vanished, along with the uncomfortable bouncing of the wheels and that frightening, drunken sensation that they might topple over on their back any moment. When he oriented himself to the new sights and feelings, he saw that they were climbing, rising safely above the forest at the end of the runway, clearing the rolling hills as they gained altitude.

"Sorry about that," Visnaw said over the engine roar. "I know it's a little uncomfortable taking off snout-up like that, but it's the way you do it on a short, soft field—takes the stress off the nose gear and gets you up faster." Before Andy could respond, he tapped an instrument that showed a needle pointing midway between the numbers 5 and 10. "Climbing seven-hundred feet a minute. We'll level out at two-thousand."

"Two-thousand *feet?*" Andy supposed it wasn't a lot, compared to 35,000 feet or so on a cross-country flight, but in this airborne bank vault it sounded like half the distance to the moon.

"You want to go higher?" Visnaw's eyes were twinkling again.

Andy recoiled. "I want to go down."

"Now, now. You gave me an hour. Relax and enjoy yourself."

Andy desperately wanted a cigarette, but he was afraid the small plane would explode the minute he lit up. The automobile-style ashtray and lighter on the control panel did nothing to ease his fears, so he simply maintained his death grip on the seat while watching the view of the wilderness turn into a vista resembling that from the top of Silver Mountain, then drop still farther below, becoming a smooth blanket of springtime gray and brown. The shadow of the plane tracked across that blanket like a swift, dark bird.

Visnaw said, "You have a favorite?"

"Favorite what?"

"Book, what else? A favorite novel? Poetry collection?"

"Oh. Yeah, I guess I do. For myself it would be *The Pharisee*. As a teacher, I'd have to say *Brave Men*."

"Ah, the Hale and McCready story."

Andy nodded. "Except it's not, not really, is it? I mean, the characters have the same names, but the story doesn't have anything to do with…with the murders…does it?"

"That depends on your viewpoint, I guess."

"What does that mean?"

"Watch," Visnaw said. He eased back on the throttle and pushed the control wheel forward, bringing the nose down a few degrees below the horizon. He pointed out the altimeter reading—2100 feet—and reached up to turn a crank on the cabin ceiling. "Trim," he said. "It lets you fly hands-off, keeps you straight-and-level if the thermals aren't kicking up."

ALEXANDER'S SONG

He demonstrated by removing his hands from the wheel and pointing to the instruments, every one of which held steady. Andy gripped the seat a little harder, his fingers beginning to throb.

"What did you mean about *Brave Men?*" he asked, curious, but also desperate for anything to keep his mind off where he was.

Visnaw rested one hand lightly on the wheel. "Do you know why Bassett left Rock Creek?"

The change of direction made Andy frown. "You mean originally? Sure. He went off to college—University of Wisconsin. That would have been shortly after the murders."

"Two weeks after, to be precise," Visnaw said. "He took a train out of town less than three days after the police cleared him of any wrongdoing. But I'm talking about the next time, the last time. He spent four years in Madison, came back home with his degree, and stayed in the Creek almost eight years. Do you know why he finally left?"

Andy shook his head, then said, "He'd sold a couple of stories by the time he moved to New York. One to *The American Mercury* and one to *Blue Ribbon*. I always assumed he left because his career was starting to take off and New York was the place to be." He hesitated, thinking. "As a matter of fact, I think he'd sold *A Daughter's Song* to Lippincott by that time. It didn't come out until '41, of course, but he'd made the sale. Right?"

"What do you make of that book?"

"I don't—" Andy stopped, rubbing his eyes. Visnaw's constant shifts in topic were leaving him a little woozy. He looked down, calling on all his patience (no use snapping at the man who held your life in his hands) and trying to bring his thoughts into order. He saw the ground moving at an odd angle below and realized that Visnaw had initiated a slow, shallow turn back toward the east.

"It's a wonderful book," he finally answered. "For a first novel, I'd say it ranks right up there with some of the greats."

"Do you notice a connection with Hale and McCready?"

"No. I mean…no. It's not even close, at least from the little bit you told me, the little bit I know." He sighed. "What does this have to do with why Bassett moved to New York?"

Visnaw chuckled, though it was soft and the sound was swallowed by the constant roar of the engine. "Mr. Gillespie, you surprise me. Surely you of all people must know that everything in literature relates to everything else. An author's work is directly connected to every work before it, and to everything in the author's life. Isn't that what you tell your students?"

It was, Andy thought, and more than that, the better students usually figured it out for themselves. But he didn't want to answer out loud, for fear Visnaw would use what he said as a launching point for yet another digression.

"What *is* the connection with Hale and McCready?" he asked.

"Why do you want to know? I thought you were curious about why Bassett left town."

Andy's head spun. He stared at the old man's smiling face and felt an overpowering urge to crush it with a punch. But he spared some of his anger for Ginnie, too. *This* was the man she insisted he talk to? *This* was the man who held keys to hidden secrets? *This* was why he had given up the chance to tear open his package the second it arrived? He tried to see what was ticking in Visnaw's brain, but couldn't. Perhaps he had a hidden agenda. Andy himself had been known to use roundabout discussions to lead his students toward a particular truth. He suspected, though, that something else was at work—a lonely old man eager for any conversation, no matter how maddening, or maybe just a perverse sense of humor.

"You've asked a lot of questions," he said slowly, determined to stay calm. "I'd sure be grateful if you gave me just one answer."

Visnaw pointed below. They were over the town now, the streets and shops and houses crawling past, the forest coming up again. To the right, the Quad Lakes sparkled. To the left, in the distance, Keweenaw Bay on Lake Superior was like an endless plate of gray steel.

ALEXANDER'S SONG

"You do have answers, don't you?" Andy said. He decided to turn one of the old man's tricks back on him. "Good teachers don't ask what they don't know."

"Point well taken," Visnaw said, and Andy wondered if the man's smile ever disappeared completely. Even when he was being serious he wasn't serious, not entirely. "I can tell you one thing I know. I talked about everything Bassett did being connected. Nothing so unusual there. It's what the connection is that makes it noteworthy."

Andy waited for the rest, but it didn't follow right away. Visnaw banked the plane to the right, toward the lakes.

"One of the universal themes of literature is love, am I right?"

"Of course," Andy said. "Do you mean Bassett was in love when he—"

"What would some other ones be? Growing up? Maturation? Loss? Fear? Longing? Sacrifice?"

Andy nodded. "Some of those can be the same thing, depending on how they're used. Loss and longing, sacrifice and growing up, they go together."

"What about death?"

"What?"

"Death, Mr. Gillespie. Would that be one of the universal themes?"

"Yes. Obviously."

"And death…it can also go together with other things? Death and loss? Death and longing? Death and sacrifice? Death and fear?"

Andy nodded again. He saw that the ground was closer, assumed it was an illusion, looked again, and understood that he was wrong. The nose of the Tri-Pacer was farther below the horizon. They were descending. Lake Manabozho was directly ahead of them, but it was swinging off to the left as he watched. They were angling westward. There was the thin dark line of the Chippewa River's east branch curving through the trees, connecting Manabozho to Green Lake.

"Wolf Island," Visnaw said suddenly. "Ever been there?"

"I—"

Visnaw chopped the power. "Let's go take a look."

6

IT WAS LIKE a dream of falling, the plane dropping, the ground rising dramatically, alarmingly. Andy felt himself floating up to the limits of his seatbelt, and he had a terrifying image of his body tearing through the top of the cabin and hurtling toward earth. The propeller on the nose windmilled. Below it, the brown forest became a field of dazzling blue. He saw a miniature boat drifting on Green Lake and imagined the face of the fisherman in it turned upward with concern.

"The Tri-Pacer has its defenders," Visnaw remarked casually, "folks like me who have learned to love it. But many pilots consider it a bit of a joke."

"Good God, you don't—"

"They call it a 'bug smasher' or a 'flying milk stool' or 'the Piper Tri-Crasher.'" He added cheerily: "They're really not far off the mark."

Andy screamed—or thought he did. A split second later he realized the sound was the rushing wind combined with the clatter of panic in his own head.

"In this bird, Mr. Gillespie, a power-off descent is a bit like cranking a piano up into the air and cutting the rope."

The water was closer, the tiny boat now a medium-sized boat, getting to be a big boat. Andy tore his gaze away from what he was sure was his impending death, but what he saw in the cabin—Visnaw's wild grin, the altimeter needle unwinding crazily—was almost worse.

At what must have been the last possible moment, Visnaw added power and eased the wheel back. Uncounted G-forces shoved Andy down against the seat, and the sudden change of attitude rocked his brain, but he managed to catch a glimpse of the fisherman throwing himself to the bottom of his boat as they roared past, less than fifty feet above the water.

"You're fucking insane," Andy said.

ALEXANDER'S SONG

"Ah, no, I'm fucking *good*. Learned to fly from a retired fighter pilot right after the second war. You talk about death. There was plenty of that around in those days."

Andy didn't care anymore. He ripped his pack of cigarettes out of his pocket and lit one, not willing to wait for the onboard lighter but using his own. He took three long, deep drags and tried to relax, but the sight of the water ripping past, almost close enough to touch, made it difficult to quell the tension boiling away inside, threatening to blow him apart.

"Death," Visnaw said. "That's why Bassett moved to New York. It didn't have anything to do with stories and novels. It was because his lover was murdered."

Andy almost dropped the cigarette. He thought he'd heard Visnaw correctly, but it was hard to be sure. Too much was happening too fast. The plane banked to the right, giving him a much, much closer view of Green Lake than he wanted, and when they leveled off again, Wolf Island was in the middle of the windscreen.

"His lover was murdered," Visnaw said as the sheer rock cliff rushed to meet them. "And he fled the Creek like a dog, just the way he'd fled earlier, after the deaths of his best friends."

He's saying Bassett was guilty of something, Andy realized, but the thought was almost lost as they raced toward the cliff, overwhelmed by the certainty that Visnaw was going to pilot them directly into it. What would that be like, a plane hitting a rock wall at 120 miles per hour? What would it look like? What would it *feel* like?

He squeezed his eyes shut and scrunched himself down farther in the seat. For an unknowable span of time—it couldn't have been more than twenty seconds, possibly even less than that—the deafening roar of the engine became his entire world. He wasn't thinking about Alexander Bassett, or Frank Hale and Charlie McCready, or why Ginnie had sent him to see this certifiable lunatic. He wasn't even thinking about death. He was just there, held by a lap belt in a cocoon of impossible noise, wrapped in thunder.

Something changed again, a new set of forces pushed against him, and when he opened his eyes he saw Wolf Island's trees whizzing by a handful of feet below. He thought he saw the winding trail that led from the top of the cliff to the cabin, and he thought he saw the cabin too, a momentary blur of brown in the middle of the forest.

7

HE STILL REMEMBERED a flight he had been on as a boy of ten or eleven—Chicago's Midway Airport to Logan in Boston, accompanying his father on one of his many business trips. The weather in the Midwest had been no great shakes, but New England was another story altogether. Fierce thunderstorms had been moving through the region all day, complete with lightning and heavy rain and hail and winds occasionally gusting to fifty miles an hour. The landing in Boston had been a true white-knuckles experience of rocking and bouncing, overhead compartments popping open and spilling their contents of pillows and blankets, whining engines, moaning passengers. He couldn't say for sure if that's where his discomfort with flying came from, but it was certainly where he formed his opinion that landing was the worst part of the trip—without exception, the absolute worst.

When they'd taken off from the Rock Creek grass strip, Andy had already been dreading the return. Anticipating the approach over towering trees, thinking about the small plane shooting into the narrow alley carved out for the runway with so little margin for error had been almost more than he could handle. Ironically, he virtually missed the experience.

After the overflight of Wolf Island he blanked out, not physically but mentally. Sky and woods and water were all around him, the engine bellowed on, but Andy was aware of it distantly at best. He didn't know where they went after passing the island, if anywhere. He didn't know if Martin Visnaw spoke to him again. He had no idea how much longer they were up. It was as though he saw Ed Hoffer's cabin one second and the next was standing on the ground, a good distance away from the Tri-Pacer, while Visnaw rigged the tie-down ropes and secured the cabin.

"I ought to call the police when we get back to town," he heard himself saying. Visnaw glanced over at him and laughed. "The cops, the FAA, somebody. You should be—"

"Spare me, please," Visnaw said. His voice was heavy with disdain, but his face was still alight with wry good humor. "I said you had no sense of adventure; I was definitely right."

"But you're crazy, you—"

"I gave you everything I promised, didn't I? A nice flight, a little fun, and conversation. I told you about Alexander Bassett. We talked about literature."

"We didn't talk about shit. You spun a bunch of ridiculous riddles, that's all."

"Life is a riddle, Mr. Gillespie. Think about that one."

"But nothing you said made the least bit of sense!"

"Excuse me, but I think it did. I painted the picture. The lines are all there. Now it's up to you to interpret them."

"More bullshit," Andy muttered. The old man was walking away, but he didn't follow immediately. "Ginnie was crazy to think you could help."

"You want help?" Visnaw said. He was halfway to the car. He stopped and turned back, shaking his head. "Here it is. Death. We talked about death. That's the connection you're hunting for. Bassett's life was founded on death. Look to his lover. Her name was Grace Mahler, by the way, if that helps. Look back farther than that. Look to Royal Haag. They're the only clues you need." He pulled back the sleeve of his jacket and checked his watch. "I'm running late for an appointment," he said. "It's been a pleasure."

"What does Royal Haag have to do—"

"Death," Visnaw repeated, and laughed, and got into his car and drove away.

Andy stared after him, his mind bogged down with things that seemed like nonsense, unconnected threads that couldn't be sewn together. Royal

Haag, he thought. What in the name of God does *he* have to do with it? And this lover—

He stopped and looked around, understanding for the first time exactly where he was, realizing what had just happened. He stared at the tie-down row, the Tri-Pacer next to Anna Grosskopf's newer Beechcraft. He turned, taking in the overgrown fuel pump, the abandoned tin shack with its ancient windsock on top. He pivoted back and looked at the empty access road.

"Shit!"

He started jogging, but Visnaw's car was lost in a cloud of dust as it turned onto the county road heading back into town.

8

MAX WAS ON the living room phone when he walked in. She waved him over. "Hold on a minute, he just came in."

The road between Alston and Rock Creek was better traveled than he had a right to hope, but even still he'd only been able to get a ride as far as the town hall on Ontonagon Street and had to walk the last seven blocks to the bed and breakfast. It was 3:20 when he arrived.

"Hello?"

"Did it come?"

Joanne.

"I'm not sure." He covered the mouthpiece. "Max, my package…?" She gave a single, disinterested shake of her head and went upstairs. Andy raised the receiver back to his mouth. "Not yet, Jo. When did you send it?"

"Are you implying I'm not true to my word? When did I say I'd send it? Saturday, right? Isn't that what I said? It went off Saturday morning. And while we're on the subject, you owe me a hundred dollars."

"*What?*" He was sure he must have heard wrong. "I thought it was thirty-five. That's what you said, you told me—"

ALEXANDER'S SONG

"It *was* thirty-five, Andrew dear. But there was another little goodie I found when I went back to buy it. Actually, I didn't find it; the store owner pointed it out. He said if you were a Bassett nut—his words, by the way, not mine—you'd want this, too."

"What is it?"

"That cost another thirty dollars. That's sixty-five. And the package was so heavy, the express fee came to $32.50. The last two-fifty's for my time and effort."

"The other book," Andy said. "What was it?"

"I accept personal checks, cashier's checks, or money orders. No credit cards. And just send it to the Orlando address; I'm going to be back there by the end of the week."

"Jo, the other book—"

"You'll want to check this store out when you finally leave the sticks and head to New York. The owner really knows his stuff. He met Bassett once, at some theater opening. He's hot to talk to you."

"Jo—"

"His card's in the package—name, address, hours, phone number, the whole thing."

Andy couldn't help smiling. "You're being pretty damn helpful for someone who thinks I'm an idiot."

"I explained that last time," she said. He heard her laugh, sounding sharp and tinny over the phone line. "And besides, I suppose if you get enough rope, you'll just hang yourself, won't you? Bassett's your hobby. Fine. I had trouble with that when we were married, I admit. But there were so many things I had trouble with. Bassett was just a tiny part of it. Now it doesn't matter anymore. In fact, I find it kind of amusing."

"But don't you think—"

"I'll be glad to hand you all the rope I can find. It's the least I can do. If you were a cliff diver, I'd be right there behind you, ready to give you a push."

"Gee, thanks."

137

"Don't mention it." He heard a man's voice in the background, and Joanne's muffled response: *I said I'd be ready, I will. Stop worrying, for Chrissakes.*

The man said something else, followed by silence. Andy waited, and finally jumped in. "You still there, Jo?"

"I'm here, but not for long. We're going out. Remember, now. One hundred dollars, not a penny less. Check. Orlando. I'll expect it to be waiting there for me when I get back."

The line went dead.

Andy hung up and looked helplessly at the empty living room. He wondered when Ginnie would be home from school. No package, no Ginnie, no answers, and nothing to do, nowhere to go. He crossed to the couch on the opposite side of the room and sat down. His legs were still wobbly—nervous air legs, not sure if they were down safely yet or not. He took the big glass ashtray off the end table and lit a cigarette. He looked out the newly-installed window and tried to remember just which quadrant the bullet had come through yesterday.

Jesus, he thought, this whole thing is getting ridiculous. He felt wobbly all over now, loose, confused, out of control.

Death, Martin Visnaw had said. Death. And the hell of it was, there really seemed to be something to it. It was amazing, he thought, how looking into a writer's early days, his boyhood and adolescence, could center so much around death. Frank Hale and Charlie McCready. This new figure, Grace Mahler, Bassett's lover. And, for some reason, Royal Haag.

He drew on his cigarette and used his free hand to hold on to the arm of the couch, as though he needed that stability to keep himself from being swept away.

He heard the sound of a small plane circling the bed and breakfast, going around and around, getting lower with each pass, lower and closer. He looked wide-eyed toward the ceiling, and only then realized there was no plane at all. The sound was just the ghost-roar of Martin Visnaw's engine, the echo of the Tri-Pacer trapped in his own brain.

9

THE PACKAGE, DELIVERED by an overworked express driver, showed up just before five.

Ginnie, however, didn't turn up at all that night.

FIVE

YESTERDAY'S VOICES

1

By eight-thirty that night Max had worked herself into a frenzy. Not long after that the police arrived. At quarter to ten, Andy was summoned from his room and treated to another interview with Jeff Lamoreaux, this time in the company of a woman officer named Elizabeth Rhodes. The three of them sat around the kitchen table drinking coffee, while Max alternately paced to the front door to look out at an empty Victory Street and used the phone to call everyone in town who had ever known or heard of her daughter.

"I told Betty about your little bout of excitement yesterday," Lamoreaux said. "Just for the record, she agrees with me. Right, Bets?"

Rhodes lit a cigarette, dropped the match into an ashtray already filled with seven or eight butts, and nodded. "Kids and guns," she said, grinning at Andy. "You know how it is."

"Well, I didn't," Andy said dryly. "But thanks to your friend here, I've been enlightened."

Lamoreaux took out his notebook. "You saw Virginia Turner this morning?"

"At breakfast, yes."

"You been seein' a lotta her, I guess."

"What does that mean?"

Lamoreaux shrugged. "Max said you two'd been workin' together for a while. That right?"

"'A while' is a relative term," Andy said. "She just got into town last... Thursday, I guess it was. I met her at dinner that night, but I didn't really get to know her until Friday."

"What were you up to?" Rhodes asked.

Andy sighed, lit his own cigarette, and told them about his project. When he mentioned Alexander Bassett, the officers exchanged confused glances; it turned out that neither had ever heard of the man. They seemed about as interested in the whole thing as they would have been had he and Ginnie been studying the growth patterns of native lichens.

"So this book you were waiting for, this diary or whatever it was, she was going to come right home after school and take a look at it?"

"That's what I thought. This morning she said she'd rather start class tomorrow, just so she could be here when it arrived. She was as excited as I was to see it."

"Yeah, right," Lamoreaux said. "Apparently somethin' come along that excited her more."

"Like what?"

"An old friend, maybe. Max's already been in touch with a couple of kids in Virginia's class. Seems there's this boy, Mike Volkman. They get along pretty good every summer, when Virginia comes back from Utah. She talk to you about that?"

Andy shook his head. "That doesn't mean anything, though. We've been pretty busy."

"Right," Lamoreaux said again. "But here's the scoop. These kids Max talked to, they saw Virginia leavin' school with Volkman at about ten to three. That's the last anyone caught sight of 'em. Now we ain't followed up yet, but Max said she's been tryin' to call Volkman's house all night. No answer. Which is about what you'd expect. Lee Volkman works nights at the Michigan Tech Forestry Center in Alberta, and Penny—that's Mike's mom—spends a lot of time over at her sister's place."

"I don't get it," Andy said. "The parents are gone, fine. But what's that got to do with Ginnie and her friend?"

"Oh, they probably just headed out somewhere," Rhodes said. "Maybe went to a movie in L'Anse, or went bumming around up in Houghton."

"Or maybe," Lamoreaux put in, "they're out by one of the lakes, gettin' to know each other after a long winter apart." He laughed. "If you know what I mean."

Andy stubbed out his cigarette, surprised that he could find himself angry at this man twice in the span of twenty-four hours. "If you're so sure that's it, what are you doing here?"

"Oh...well...that's just public relations. Max called us up three times already, and every time she was shakier than before. Betty and me talked about it, right, Bets? We figured we'd come over, make a show, nose around a little, and hope the kid walks in while we're here."

"And if she doesn't?"

"There's not much we can do," Rhodes said. "We can follow up on a couple of Max's phone calls, take a few notes, keep our eye out for Turner and Volkman while we cruise around town. But it's all unofficial. We'll have to wait till at least tomorrow afternoon before we jump in with both feet."

Back upstairs, Andy thought that everything he'd ever seen in bad movies and read in second-rate detective novels about small town cops was true—at least in effect, if not cause. Their incompetence stemmed not from ignorance or malice, but from a frustrating kind of naivete. Used to handing out speeding tickets and dealing with alcohol-related incidents—traffic accidents and domestic disputes, after-work arguments and barroom brawls—they came to believe that nothing seriously bad ever happened on their watches. A shooting? Just a kid goofing around with his first gun. A disappearance? Horny teens getting away from the grown-ups.

It wasn't so much that he doubted either of those scenarios. They seemed reasonable enough on the surface. Certainly nobody had been trying to kill him by firing through Max's living room window, and Rock Creek *did* seem like an unlikely place for an abduction of a sharp, capable seventeen-year-old girl. But that didn't mean he wanted to write off either incident as lightly as did Lamoreaux and Rhodes.

In particular, he was more bothered than he cared to admit by Ginnie's failure to come home. He remembered exactly what she'd said that morning before heading off to school: *I'll be home by three-thirty at the latest. Try to be done with the journal by then, so I can take a crack at it.*

Of course both of them had expected the parcel to be delivered first thing in the morning, not at the end of the day. And more importantly, Ginnie taking a crack at it hinged on Ginnie being home. Three-thirty at the latest, he thought. Was she so enamored of this Mike Volkman character that she would have forgotten all about her promise? He found that hard to believe, given the excitement he'd seen in her eyes every time Bassett's name was even mentioned.

He smoked two cigarettes back-to-back and waited for the sound of Lamoreaux and Rhodes driving away. Five minutes after that he left his room and tiptoed down the corridor, went down the stairs to the second floor, and crept like a thief to Ginnie's room at the end of the hall. Just to be sure (if nothing else Max might be in there, checking for the third or fourth time, trying to find a clue to her daughter's whereabouts), he tapped on the door. There was no answer, so he drew a deep breath and went in.

It took him a moment to find the light switch, which was inconveniently located on a side wall. He flicked it on, blinked, and studied the drawing taped next to the switch—a stick-figure girl riding a gigantic stick-figure horse. In the sky, a bright green sun beamed down on mount and rider, and next to that, scrawled in the shaky hand of a first- or second-grader, was her name: Virginia E. Turner.

The rest of the room was surprisingly spartan. He pondered that for a moment, then realized that she probably moved most of her personal items back and forth between Utah and Michigan. This year, with her father's unexpected job transfer catching everyone off guard, she had obviously just packed the bare essentials. There was a poster of the rock band Great White over the bed and another of a leering Axl Rose on the closet door. Last year's Audubon desk calendar sat on the nightstand, open to the month of August. There were a few textbooks and a copy of *Cat's Cradle* by Vonnegut. A dusty sailboat suncatcher dangled in the window. That was all. As far as he could tell, there was no sign Ginnie had been in the room for months, let alone that very morning.

What are you looking for? he wondered. What are you trying to prove by sneaking down here? That Ginnie's all right? Or that Lamoreaux's an asshole and she's not all right at all? Three-thirty at the latest, she had said, and now it's ten-thirty and maybe she's out with Mike Volkman but maybe she's not and why the hell are you thinking the things you're thinking?

That last part irritated him, because the sad truth was he didn't really have any idea *what* he was thinking. Brief, baffling, encoded messages were skipping through his brain like AM radio signals on a stormy night. Bits and pieces of things he didn't want to consider flitted past, and even if he was able to connect them he wasn't sure he wanted to, because the picture they would make was large and unbelievably strange and terribly ugly and probably, bottom line, not much more than a tired man's crazy fantasy.

Second world, he thought, and he wondered if that recurrent phrase was really just a way of referring to the place where the mysteries were. The second world was where Alexander Bassett's past was hidden. The second world was where that gunshot came from, the place where last night's strange dream had originated, the place where an old, dangerous pilot filed his flight plan, and the place where Ginnie was now.

There was a rattling burst at the window, and Andy threw himself against the door jamb, his heart leaping into his throat. When he could breathe again, he understood that it had only been the wind driving a nighttime rain against the glass. He could hear it coming down steadily now, spattering the outside of the house, drumming in the gutters.

He shut off Ginnie's light and left her room in a hurry.

2

HE FELT BETTER with his books. They were piled everywhere on the desk now—his complete Bassett collection, his notebooks, the stacks of newspaper clippings, the two items Jo had sent him—forming a miniature mountain range with sharp peaks and shallow valleys.

Up until Lamoreaux's visit, he had been spending the evening with Bassett's journal. As Jo had hinted on the phone, the time frame could scarcely have been better. It covered everything from March 18, 1926, through September of 1927, Bassett's seventeenth birthday through his journey to the University of Wisconsin. It had been difficult, but Andy had resisted the urge to jump straight to the end. It would be far too easy, he knew, to get sidetracked by the murders of Charlie McCready and Frank Hale. But in reading from the beginning, he found himself facing another difficulty.

Bassett's life through his seventeenth year had been one of almost spectacular ordinariness. He went to school, he studied, he read (favoring not political fiction but potboilers and pulp magazines), and he enjoyed discussing the things he read. He worked evenings and weekends stocking the shelves and running deliveries for the Rock Creek Apothecary. He played baseball (shortstop and second base, mostly), and avidly followed the Chicago Cubs.

Given the fact that his later life had been spent in virtual monastic solitude, the most unusual thing about his teenage years had been his level of sexual activity. By Andy's rough count, young Alex Bassett had slept with seven different women by the time he came of age. One of these conquests, he was ironically pleased to note, was Jeanette Comstock, soon to become the wife of Mr. Toivo Lammi, he who fretted over speaking Russian and dreaded the heathen Chinee.

ALEXANDER'S SONG

Nowhere could Andy find evidence of a budding leftist or literary radical. There were no comments about the high-living greed of Americans in the twenties, no polemical rants against the abuse of the working class, no indictments of imperialism. No etiology for the man's later work at all, even, as Andy had always suspected, in Alex's relationship with his wealthy and successful father. Instead, long passages of the journal praised William Bassett as a hardworking, loving, caring, devoted family man.

Somehow papa always manages to escape that busy prison of a workplace long enough to attend our ballgames, and his cheering is always loudest of all. His voice rises above the thunder of the crowd, thrilling me when we're ahead, boosting me when the other team is having its way with us.

That was one typical entry. Another had Alex musing for almost a full page on how such a busy man could always find the time to lavish attention on his family. *I know it's difficult for him, for few are the successful men who can serve two masters,* that passage concluded. *Papa does it, and we are all the richer for it.*

And still another entry, with what Andy was learning was typical modesty for the young man, spoke of William Bassett as a role model:

I'm certain that I'll never be like papa. I lack all of his burning drive and much of his intelligence. Yet nothing will ever stop me from being proud of him, and nothing will limit my fervent attempts to follow his lead. If I could become half, or even one-fourth, of the man papa is, I would surely be satisfied.

Hardly the stuff of an angry youth pushed into rebellion, Andy thought. Could Bassett have been afraid that his father might someday find and read the journals? That didn't seem likely, not when he was constantly stumbling across poetic descriptions of *Eleanor's soft mounds of passion* or *Jeanette's lovely pink bud, soft, scented, delicate, the gateway to her soul.*

Likewise, he was unable to see any early traces of the writer's later reclusive lifestyle or depression. The man who by mid-career was, according to one editor Andy had seen quoted years ago, "A walking shell, a soul who has forever lost his grip on happiness" had been a staggeringly busy, productive, and outgoing youth. In the few snatches of early poetry and prose Bassett had jotted down in the journal there were clear hints of a deep thinker, a gifted writer, a sometimes bleakly poetic mind at work. But cynicism and misery…he couldn't find so much as a whisper of those things.

There were missing portions, too. Here and there a page had been torn from the journal, leaving a narrative gap of a day or two, sometimes leaving behind a jagged edge of paper and a handful of words clinging to the binding.

Frustrated, Andy wondered who had removed the pages. Bassett himself? Some collector? A bookstore vandal? It was pointless to speculate. These things happened. They went with the territory in the used and rare book trade. He had once paid a healthy sum for a first edition of Hemingway's *Torrents of Spring* after carefully checking the binding, cover, dust jacket, and copyright page. Later, after getting the book home, he had discovered three chapters in the middle of the novel that had been mercilessly highlighted and underlined in ink by some long-ago student.

The thing that ultimately made him take a break from the journal, however, wasn't the bother of missing pages or the chipping-at-stone-with-a-butter-knife process of trying to find clues where none were present. It was his discovery of a small passage dated December 14, 1926, the day before Christmas break in Bassett's senior year of high school:

Today in English, Mr. Duggan had us put away our texts. With the holiday and the promise of the New Year just around the corner, he wanted we seniors to forget about sentence diagrams and gerunds for a while. He asked us to stand in turn and speak of things seldom mentioned aloud. He wanted to hear our hopes and dreams for the future.

Without exception, the members of our class are brimming with desire and fired by ambition. Sully is going to graduate top of his class from the University of Michigan, attend an Ivy League law school, and one day become the Chief Justice of the Supreme Court. Frank wants to be a captain of industry. "What industry?" Duggan asked, to which Frank replied with a laugh: "Any industry!" Davey wants to become Rock Creek's mayor. Carl St. Onge said that he plans to control the mining business from one end of the Upper Peninsula to the other. Sam Gustafson (that's right, sad little Sam) is going to become the most famous naturalist who ever lived, turning out photographs of birds in their environs that will forever change the science of ornithology.

Even the girls, like shy Beverly LeMarque, have big dreams. Beverly said she plans to enter politics and become a member of the House of Representatives. Before the laughter died away, she amended that, saying she would run for the Senate instead. And she was serious!

Of course I am like all my classmates and friends. I plan to take up my pen and change the world.

Andy sighed when he read that, saddened not so much by the fact that Bassett had made a good run at his heart's desire but ultimately failed (after all, he must have learned that even the best and luckiest writers must settle for altering the lives of their readers; changing the world was out of the question) as by the quality of lost innocence in that passage. He thought of the kids he had been teaching for the last eight years. Did any of them really graduate from high school believing they could change the course of history or alter the planet in some appreciable way? A few, maybe. A precious few. The rest seemed to know exactly what they would be getting into after school, which made them creatures of realism but not, Andy thought, creatures of happiness or hope.

When he came back from his talk with Lamoreaux and Rhodes, he put the journal aside for a time and turned to the other book Jo had sent. When he'd first pulled it out of the red, white, and blue express envelope, he had been startled, surprised to have such a treat dropped into his lap. He'd been intrigued. It didn't cover the period he was interested in now, but it was a period he was almost certainly going to have to research heavily if he ever hoped to write even one publishable article.

The book was thick, three times the size of Bassett's journal. The handwriting inside was small, cramped, filling margin to margin on both sides of more than six-hundred pages. The legend on the dirty gray cover, printed in bold letters that had faded only a little over the years, read *Jackson Willoughby Kretchmer 1950-1959.*

It was late, already after eleven, when Andy began to read.

PAUL F. OLSON

3

EXCERPTS FROM THE *journal of Jackson Kretchmer:*

July 11, 1952

    I told the fucker! God damn it. but I told the man he needed help! Of course I'm talking about Alex again. who else? He came to my office this afternoon (one of the first times I've seen him since those damned Congressional hearings last year) waving manuscript pages in my face. Or at least I thought they were manuscript pages. I was on the phone with Lou Bettelheim at Doubleday. important business. but of course it's always important with Lou. I hung up. though. God save my black soul. I actually put the receiver down on the Great and Mighty Bettleheim.

    Alex was wild. The last time I'd seen him that way was right after that nonsense with Mark Langdon/Jerome Wandry Jesus Fucking Christ climbing Mount Rushmore. has it really been five years? Five years gone by since whatever happened that night in the theater? It has. And that means it's been five years since I've seen Alex pale and shaking and spewing ridiculous bullshit about his past and refusing to answer my questions or make any kind of sense.

    "Relax. boy." I tell him. "Have a couple of shots while I read over your manuscript. Then we'll talk about whatever's got you in a whirl."

    "It's not a manuscript." he says. "These are letters. Take a look."

    So he drinks his scotch. two of them in about the space of time it's taking me to write this sentence. and I look over the crap he threw down on my desk. and I'd tell you about it in detail but it's just more of the same. the same utter shit he tried forcing on me last year. Letters. He claims they're letters from this ghost. this demon that has been clanking chains in the dark for more than ten years now. Once he confided to me that it was a man named Jens Carlson. the one who murdered his boyhood chums. Now he says he doubts that. but insists it *is* the same monster who killed his betrothed. Mailer. Mahler. whatever her name was. who killed poor Calvert Drummond and also

ALEXANDER'S SONG

Oglebay, the two-bit poet. That's what he says, but I, having plodded over this nonsensical horseshit several times, say the writer <u>must</u> be some kind of subconscious part of Alex's mind.

It <u>had</u> to have been Alex himself who wrote that gibberish, spelling it out in neat schoolboy print. Whether he writes the letters in some sort of hypnotic trance and doesn't realize it later, or whether he is playing some demented game with me, surely there can be no other explanation. I will believe in a fucking ghost or maniacal killer when I believe that the earth is flat and that the moon is made out of balls of cotton.

But of course getting Alex to see that, getting the poor troubled boy to admit he needs help immediately, is something I do not think I'll ever be able to do. I can hint. I can suggest. I can try to point him in the right direction. But dear God, how can I ever tell him outright? He thinks I am his dearest friend in the whole wide world.

February 3, 1953

At last I've seen bits and pieces of Alex's new book. The working title is ECLIPSE, though he says he may change it to LET DARKNESS FALL.

I'm not sure what I expected from the work. After waiting so long, I suppose I expected the follow-up to THE PHARISEE to be a real barn-burner. Wouldn't you? If a great writer writes his greatest book and then takes more than three years to produce the first seventy pages or so of his next project, wouldn't you be excited? Wouldn't you be expecting one of the mightiest, most earth-shattering novels the literary world has ever seen?

Alex sat across my desk from me, steadily chugging booze while I read the sample chapters. It's a God damned lousy thing to say, I know, but I can only hope my severe disappointment didn't show on my face. The book is a piece of year-old dog shit, and that's as much charity as this old son can muster....

May 17, 1953

Caroline Friedman's party last night. Jesus Christ riding an elephant, does she get more beautiful every fucking day? She's done something with her hair.

151

don't ask me what, but just looking at her made me stiff as steel, and knowing she was nearby fucked up my conversational abilities most of the night.

The usual crowd was there. Caroline gets an entertaining group together, though she's never been known for finding the very best people. Steinbeck came and left early. Philip Wylie was up from sunny Florida and had some interesting things to say about Ike. Bill Faulkner dropped by before leaving on a European speaking tour. Edward Hopper (I hear he's a friend of a friend of Caroline's husband) gave us all an impromptu lecture on art history. Hem was rumored to be in town but didn't show. Neither did Alex, even though the son of a bitch has been feeling a little better lately and told me he'd try to make it.

I probably would have skipped the joint by ten, but as I was snatching a last drink from the bar, someone with as rich a baritone voice as I've ever heard came up behind me and said, "You're Jackson Kretchmer, aren't you?"

"Jack," I said, not turning around.

"You're Alexander Bassett's business manager?"

"Lawyer," I said. "And friend."

Then I turned around and saw him. It was Jerome Wandry, that actor who uses the stage name Langdon, the one who had the run-in with Alex during rehearsals for BRAVE MEN. He looked a little older than when I'd seen him last (or maybe it was simply seeing him close up, without makeup), and I could tell right away that he was three sheets to the wind. He was swaying slowly from side to side. His hair was uncombed, his tie pulled down, his shirt out of the back of his pants and hanging down below his jacket.

"The stupid shit hasn't published anything in a while," Wandry said. "What's the matter? He drink himself into an early grave?"

"Perhaps you missed what I said, Mr. Wandry. I told you Alex Bassett was my friend."

"I heard you as clear as a bell, Kretchmer. He's still a stupid shit, and as far as I can see, you're one too. Only turds stick to other turds."

I grabbed my drink and shrugged past him, figuring I'd gulp the whiskey on the way to the door and be outside before Wandry even noticed I was gone. I could see Caroline later in the week and make apologies for my quick exit—give me an excuse to be near her again. But the actor was quicker than I thought. He caught up with me as I was getting my coat.

"If you see the stinking bastard, be sure to give him my best," Wandry said. "Tell him his favorite star of the Great White Way said we'll meet again in hell."

Even after that I almost walked out. It would have been easy enough to do, for the man was an idiot at best and so drunk that he was babbling. But, damn it, my curiosity rose up and got the better of me.

"What the hell happened between you two?" I asked.

Wandry seemed startled "You mean your dear friend didn't tell you?"

"Not for lack of trying on my part," I said. "He's always refused to talk about it."

He didn't believe me, or looked as though he didn't _want_ to believe me. Then that piss-wobbly drunkenness left his features, and he said, "I guess you two aren't as good friends as I thought."

I was going to protest that, but he didn't give me the chance. He put a hand on my chest and backed me into the corner near Caroline's coat rack. I didn't know what the fucker was going to do—tell me a secret, curse me, or beat the living shit out of me. He looked capable of doing any one of those, or for all I knew, all three. In the end, he told me a helluva secret.

I didn't get back home until I don't know when. I suppose it was close to two in the morning. It doesn't matter very much, because I haven't had a God damned wink of sleep since then. That might be the norm after one of Caroline's bashes, since I'm usually so blessedly under the spell of her beauty, but this time I've hardly thought of the wench at all. It's good old Jerome Wandry I've been thinking about. Jerome. Jerry. Mark Langdon. Oh yeah, and Alex too, poor Alex, so confused and troubled. Did I really think his problems started around the time of the House hearings? Jesus Christ taking a bubble bath, I was wrong. I was wrong. The boy has been fucked up for years....

4

ANDY READ UNTIL almost dawn.

That Jack Kretchmer had been in the center of an almost permanent artistic whirl was a part of his fascination, of course. That the man had known and rubbed elbows with Hemingway and Faulkner, Ralph Ellison and Duke Ellington, James Cabell and James Cagney, Edward Hopper, Gwendolyn Brooks, James Baldwin, Edith Hamilton, Lillian Hellman, Charles Lindbergh, Walter Lippmann, John Marin, Gary Cooper, Robert Penn Warren, John Crowe Ransom, Maxfield Parrish, Cole Porter, Ayn Rand, Joe DiMaggio, Carl Sandburg, Arthur Miller, Mack Sennett, John Steinbeck, Robert Frost, Deems Taylor, Harold Vanderbilt, Marilyn Monroe, Wallace Stevens, Eugene O'Neill, Paddy Chayefsky, and John Dos Passos—that he had known all those people and literally three or four dozen more, that alone made the journal difficult to put aside.

But it was the mystery of Alexander Bassett, a dark puzzle that simultaneously became clearer and more baffling, that really kept him at it. Once Andy fell into that particular hole, he knew in his heart that he wouldn't be climbing out for the rest of the night.

5

EXCERPTS FROM THE *journal of Jackson Kretchmer:*

August 7, 1953

The oddest damn thing happened today. Had a lunch meeting with Harrison Kellogg, otherwise known as Kellogg the Wonder Pony, the co-counsel in the RCA negotiation. Since it was too fucking hot to even think of sitting in some noisy restaurant, we agreed to talk over franks and soda in Central Park. Meeting lousy, but that's not what this is about. You can find the particulars of that fiasco in my office notebooks.

ALEXANDER'S SONG

After the Pony and I had our harsh words, I was walking back toward Fifth Avenue when I passed two men hurrying along. The one in the lead was of medium height, thin, and damned handsome. The one behind—well, I didn't see anything unusual about him at first, other than he seemed to be tailing the other fellow. Now you're not going to catch me joining that parade that seems to get bigger every day, the one where certain shitheads just can't find enough bad things to say about New York. But I'll have to admit that I didn't think a helluva lot about this little bit of tracking, or stalking, or whatever in God's name it was, until that second man glanced in my direction, stumbled, stopped, and stared at me. He ducked his head and shuffled his feet, which was as good as giving up the chase, as the lead man was already disappearing around the next bend. We looked at each other for maybe ten seconds before I cleared the God damn wires in my brain and found my voice.

"Alex," I said, for certainly it was him. Dark glasses and a scruffy beard, a wide-brimmed hat tipped down to his eyebrows, couldn't disguise that familiar face for long.

He shuffled his feet. I took a step in his direction. "Jesus Christ, Alex," I said to him, "What're you up to now, boy? Are you—"

He broke like a frightened rabbit and ran. I considered going after him, but knew I didn't stand a hope in hell of catching him. I remember several years ago, back in what I'm going to have to start calling the good old days, I used to call Alex "Mr. Famous Author." I joshed the boy about giving in to the high life and growing soft. But Christ, the way he lit out of there this afternoon, I'm going to have to take back all that spoofing. He didn't run like any 44-year-old I've ever seen. He put my 41-year-old bones to shame.

I stood there in the middle of the path, my meeting with the Pony forgotten, trying to understand why my friend would run away from me like that. It must have been ten or twenty seconds later when I turned around and caught sight of that first fellow again. He'd come back. He was standing at the bend he'd already disappeared around once, staring past me at Alex's vanishing back. There was a big, bright smile on that handsome face.

"Hey!" I called to him. "Hey, you—"

PAUL F. OLSON

Maybe I've got the God-fucking plague, because that bastard fled too. I had time to call after him once, "Hey, damn you, mister—" before he was out of sight and I was all alone on that path in the middle of the park....

August 9, 1953

Finally. Finally God damn it. Finally I got through to him. Two days on the phone since that episode in Central Park, and when I wasn't keeping my fucking ear glued to the fucking receiver listening to the endless fucking ringing of his unanswered fucking phone, I was traipsing back and forth between my office and his apartment. And after all of that, I finally reached the son of a bitch this afternoon. He had the gall to pick up the phone after only one ring. And what did he say to me? Did he listen to me? Did he answer one fucking question? Did he allow me to vent my concern or frustration or confusion?

No.

The bastard said one thing: "I almost had him," he said. "I almost had him. Two weeks I've been chasing him, and today I almost had him."

That's all he said: "I almost had him, Jack. I almost had him, but he got away."

August 29, 1953

Jesus jumping fucking Christ flying a red balloon, I think I know what madness feels like. Of course there are plenty of people who would happily testify to the fact that I've always been crazy. Didn't Hem say that to me last summer? Didn't he say, "Christ, Jackie, you're a definite case," and didn't he call me "the King of the Loons?" But after having Alex over to the house today (the first time I've been able to nail him for a long sit-down since THE PHARISEE came out) I'm starting to understand what real madness—true, undiluted madness—is all about. Alex's, yes, but mine too.

"How long have we been friends?" I asked him.

He pulled a snotty little brat's frown on me, as though the question wasn't fair. I asked him the same question again, and he said, "Years and years, Jack."

"That's no answer. How long?"

"Ten years?" he said with a shrug.

"Longer than that, Alex. Try twelve. We hooked up the same month A DAUGHTER'S SONG came out. I've been with you since the start, my boy. We've been together from the very beginning."

"So?"

"So I've been there with you through everything, the good times and the times shit was falling on you. I helped you with your contracts. I took you around and introduced you to other writers and editors. I smoothed things over when you were having trouble with whatisname, Bernstein, that featherhead at Simon and Schuster. I celebrated with you when the critics were kind, and I held your God damn hand when they raked you through the slime."

He raised his drink, took a long swallow, and slammed the glass back down on the coffee table. "What's your point, Jackie?"

"Damn it all, you know what the point is. Look at me." He kept his eyes turned down. "Look at me, you son of a bitch! There's shit falling again, a ton of it, and I want to help you with it. I need to help you with it. But you won't let me!"

"It doesn't matter," he said, and for the first time that day I heard some kindness in his voice. "You can't help me. Nobody can." He laughed. "I'm beyond help."

"No one's beyond help, not if they'll ask for it, or at least accept it when it's offered. Jesus Christ, boy, look at yourself! You're drinking far too much, you're not getting a lick of sleep—anyone who looks at you can see that. You're not writing a God damned tenth as much as you used to, and frankly, the stuff you're cranking out is about as fresh as those old stories you showed me, the ones you used to write in college. You won't answer calls from Random House. I've got Washburn calling me, wanting to know what's wrong with you. Dollars to doughnuts you pissed that contract away. You've got promises for stories and poems stretching back three years—all unfulfilled. You could've bounced back after HUAC, I know it. If anyone could, you're the one. But you stopped cold, you busted your chance. You made worldwide news by telling the committee to take a flying fuck at the moon, and then you run away and hide. You wrote THE PHARISEE, the strongest book you ever did, you won awards, you made the newsreels, your face was on television, you had critics calling you more than a great writer, you had them saying you were probably the best of the century—and then you shut off the tap."

"Stop it, Jack."

"No. God damn you, I won't stop. I can't."

"I don't have to answer to you for my writing habits." He laughed again. "Or lack of them."

I nodded. "You're right, you don't. But way down deep, I'm not talking about your writing, and I think you know it. I'm not talking about that piss-poor excuse for a novel opening you showed me last winter. I'm not even talking about your drinking. Or your depressions. Or the sixty cigarets you're puffing away every day. Or the fact that half the time you stay holed-up in that apartment of yours, withering away for lack of sunshine and fresh air. I'm talking about the other thing. The thing underneath everything else. The cause."

"My monster," he said, looking into my eyes for the first time.

"Yes. Jens Carlson. I—"

"There is no Jens Carlson, Jack."

I didn't know what to say. It had been a while, I admit, but at one time I'd heard so much about that man (or his ghost) that hearing Alex now say those six fucking words was the equivalent of finding out that Alex himself did not exist, or that *I* didn't. Could it be that he had finally realized the truth? Was he ready to admit that he'd been fearing a memory all these years? That his dread of a dead man was just dementia? Did he know that he had written all those letters himself? Did he understand at last what his mind had been doing to him?

"There *was* a Carlson, of course." He took another drink, lighted another cigaret. "He was Hal Borg's illegitimate son. He killed Charlie and Frank. But he's dead now. He drowned in Green Lake twenty-six years ago."

ALEXANDER'S SONG

"But, Alex, you always claimed his ghost—"

"There're no such things as ghosts. Don't you know that? When you think you see a ghost, it's really just Boris Karloff hiding behind a lot of funny make-up."

My relief to hear him say those things was cooled by my fear of what he might say next. I didn't dare jump in. Shit, I didn't even want to move. I sat on my hands, waiting for him to continue.

"No ghosts," he said again, his voice barely above a whisper. "I thought I'd made that clear the last time we spoke of these things. No ghosts, Jack. It's the living. It's the people who live and breathe. That's who we have to fear. The quick, Jack, not the dead."

"Aw, Jesus, Alex."

"My father killed two men."

"Yes, but—"

"And the sons of one of those men killed Frank and Charlie. And I killed him."

"You don't know that, Alex." My head was spinning. I didn't know if we were making progress or not. I was afraid to breathe. "You said Carlson fell in the lake when you hit him. But you didn't see him drown. For years you told me you never saw the corpse."

"Death, Jack. Do you understand? My life is death. It was predestined. It was set deep in my blood when my father killed for the first time. The son of a bitch had everything, Jack! He had close to a million dollars in a time when his workers were glad to have sixty cents. He could have gone anywhere, bought anything. He didn't have to kill."

The boy began to weep. Writing now, remembering it, makes me want to cry, too. The tears burst from his eyes and his body shuddered with one deep God damn sob after another. The cigaret between his fingers fell to the floor, and I snatched it off the carpet and dropped it into the ashtray without thinking about it.

"Frank..." he murmured. "Oh, God, Frank, and Charlie, and my mother...my... my muh...muh...my mother, oh, shit...and Grace...Cal...Henry...death, Jack, it's everywhere, it's followed me, and I can't get rid of it. I can't."

159

The sobs became too much for him, completely choking off his power of speech. I sat there helplessly, watching, wishing I were more of a man so that I could hold him tightly, ease his pain, at least <u>say</u> something.

"I don't know who," he managed to say after several horrible minutes. "Damn it, Jack, I don't know who it is! It's not Jens Carlson. I knew that years ago, after the theater. In some ways I always knew it. Blaming it on the man, or his ghost, or whatever—that was too easy, and I knew it was a fantasy. It's someone else, some maniac. Jens Carlson is dead."

Too bad you weren't sure of that five years ago, I thought, not after the theater but <u>before</u>. Five years ago you thought the actor cast as Charlie McCready in BRAVE MEN bore too much of a resemblance to that God damned Carlson. You studied him for weeks. You started watching him and following him. And then you attacked him. Two days before fucking opening night, for Christ sakes, you attacked the man, almost killed him. Too bad you didn't realize Carlson was gone back then. It would have saved a lot of pain for you, boy, and me, and everyone involved with the show, and maybe most for Jerome Wandry who spent two weeks in the hospital and didn't work again for more than three years. You were the one who flipped, Alex, but everyone thought it was Wandry, the flaky actor. It couldn't have been the famous writer who flipped, oh no. He was just under a strain, a little nervous, a little distraught. The blame was all Wandry's, they said, and Wandry almost lost his career because of it.

I was ashamed of every one of those thoughts even as they occurred to me. Alex needed me, God damn him, and all I could do was sit there, being an utterly despicable asshole, condemning him in my mind.

"I almost caught him," Alex was muttering. "About a month ago, I guess it was. I saw him watching my apartment, the first time I'd spotted him in over a year. I started following. I chased him for two weeks. He never slept, I never slept. It was a hunt." His eyes were red, bulging with excitement. "Hotels, restaurants, streets and alleys. Do you realize what I'm saying, Jack? For the first time I was stalking the stalker."

"Jesus Christ in a taxicab," I murmured. "Central Park."

ALEXANDER'S SONG

"Yes. The Park. I was following him there. You cut the hunt short that day, but I found him again an hour or two later. In the end it was all for nothing. He got away. I lost him in Macy's one afternoon and never found him again. He hasn't been outside my apartment since. But I was close. So many times I was so close."

I still had not the slightest clue what to say. I was thinking about the handsome man moving quickly ahead of Alex in Central Park. A lunatic? Was it really possible? Or was *I* the lunatic for being pulled into my friend's long mental nightmare?

"He kills everyone. Not just a few people, Jack. Everyone. Everyone I've ever been close to. My parents, my friends, even my fiancé." He put his hands up to his eyes, rubbing hard. "Everyone who's ever meant anything to me, that maniac finds them and kills them. It's my destiny." He dropped his hands and stared at me. He said it again. "Everyone."

"No," I shot back, "that's not true. You have lots of friends, you have business associates. Jesus Christ, Alex, you know more people than—"

"Acquaintances," he said, as though the word were profane. "Not friends, not *real* friends. The acquaintances, the work faces, they come and go, they survive. The real friends die. All of them."

Well, what in the name of God was my answer supposed to be? Did I want to admit that I saw the bits of truth in what he said? It was damned odd the way Calvert Drummond and Henry Oglebay had both been brutally murdered, the editor and the poet, the two associates that had become more than associates, that had turned into Alex's close friends. Drummond had been tortured, died slowly. Oglebay's throat had been cut. Even I had seen the strange connection between Alex and his friends—and hadn't I had several dark wolf's hour thoughts, moments when I dared to think the coincidence was too much, that maybe Alex himself had wielded the knife?

One more thing forced its way into my mind. I didn't want it to. Shit no. It was one of those thoughts too crazy or frightening to deal with but too damnably powerful to keep away.

PAUL F. OLSON

If everyone that ever grew truly close to Mr. Alexander Bassett finished his existence with a gruesome, untimely demise...if that was true, what did that mean for me?

6

THREE-THIRTY A.M.

Andy's stomach was churning.

His head throbbed.

The implications of Kretchmer's journal were like a powerful wave, sucking him out to sea no matter how hard he tried to keep his feet planted on the beach. The things he was reading were like a dreadful undertow, drowning him.

He looked up, pale and frightened, when he heard the sound of something out in the corridor. His first thought was that it was someone moving like a phantom down the hall. Then he imagined that someone was hesitating outside his door, touching it. Finally he understood that it was only his own exhaustion working, building intruders out of the brick and mortar of the rainstorm outside.

The open journal called him back like a siren.

7

EXCERPTS FROM THE *journal of Jackson Kretchmer:*

April 20, 1954

The first words I heard were "Well, look who's decided to join the living," spoken in a sexy, throaty female voice. My vision swam and I caught small, misty images of red hair, a white uniform, teeth, a hand holding a bag connected to a long tube. I wasn't able to piece any of it together before I returned to the darkness.

I've learned now that all of that happened early yesterday morning, around breakfast time. Six A.M. on April 19th, almost forty-eight hours after I was attacked and nearly killed on the street outside my office.

Why don't I remember the attack?

ALEXANDER'S SONG

April 22, 1954

 Feeling better today, a thousand percent better. Asked about going home, but the doc only laughed. At least another two weeks, the bastard said. Seems they have shitty, stinking rules like that for patients who have been stabbed seven times....

April 23, 1954

 The parade never seems to end—one fucking cop after another, assistant D.A.'s, and worst of all, reporters. The papers are having a field day. They call me "The Man Who Cheated Death" or "Kretchmer the Unkillable." I've tried to decide which one I like better, but can't.
 I keep telling them, everyone from the cops on down, that I can't remember anything. Left for the office early, I say. Things to do. I turned onto the street. I saw the office door. I reached for it. And then I was here in the hospital, waking up in front of a bombshell of a nurse who I was too fogged-over to fully appreciate. That's all. I can't tell them anything else, but they keep coming, the same ones over and over, everyone in the world that I would never ever want to see, including the so-called friends and well-wishers—while the one man I would very much like to talk to refuses to show his God damn face....

April 25, 1954

 Blondie, the new morning nurse, came in a little while ago and handed me a folded three-page note. She didn't know a damn thing about it, just that some man had dropped it off at the desk a few hours ago, while I was sleeping. I asked what his name was, but she didn't know. I asked what he looked like, ditto. The night duty nurse hadn't paid attention, or hadn't said. Then Blondie laughed, which is always nice, because a man in the state I'm in needs to see some jiggling tits once in a while, especially early in the morning.
 "You want to know who it's from, Jackie, why don't you just read it?"

PAUL F. OLSON

Jack,

I could say many things here at the start of this letter, including how sorry I am for what happened to you and how deeply I pray for your recovery. I could say those things, and I would, except for the fact that I believe you know how I feel. Also, I know you too well, we've been through too much. If anyone would be driven batty by essentially meaningless expressions of sympathy, it would be you.

Of all the things I have ever written, this note is one of the most difficult. No, scratch that. It's not one of the most difficult: it is beyond doubt the hardest thing I've ever attempted to put down on paper.

I love you, Jackson Willoughby Kretchmer.

You have stood by me since the beginning (as I suppose you would be the first to point out). I'm not sure what you remember about those times, but I recall them as hectic, productive, exciting, and often filled with joy. You understood my periodic depressions and helped me move beyond them. As things have grown more strained in my life these last few years, you alone have tried to understand my terrible destiny. That's why I'm saying goodbye, why I must sever all ties, personal and professional, for now and all time. It is the only way I can properly express my thanks to you for all you've done. It is but a small sign of my great affection.

I know what you're thinking. I must have known such an attack could happen to you. We discussed, after all, the fate of those who dare to be my friends, and how could I not anticipate that you might be next? Or perhaps your thoughts are grayer than that. You might be doubting my sanity and thinking it was me who caught you outside your office a week ago.

I cannot respond to that second charge. It is up to you to look into your heart and see the truth, to study everything you've learned of me over the years and draw your own conclusions. As to the first charge, that I suspected something

ALEXANDER'S SONG

might happen to you and allowed our friendship to continue anyway. I can give you some answers. I don't like them, but they are as honest as I can be:

1) I valued our friendship too much to let you go. I allowed my selfish need to have your stability in my life to cloud my better judgment. (And yes, I did crave your companionship and strength; even over these last years, when it must have seemed to you that our relationship had deteriorated and that I had grown to hate you, it hadn't, and I didn't.)

2) You were my last anchor to the past. With my family gone and most friends vanished or dead, with Rock Creek a distant memory and the first days in New York a hazy bit of nostalgia, you were the last one left from the early days. No man relinquishes the past easily.

3) This is the hardest to write; it pains me even to think it, let alone say it to you. I believe I was experimenting with you, as ghoulish as that may sound. You were a safety net of sorts. As long as I kept you in my life and nothing happened to you, then maybe the last twenty-six years could be dismissed as a bad dream. I gambled with you, Jack. I rolled the dice with your well-being. Although I knew something could happen at any time, I didn't let you go, just in case something <u>didn't</u> happen. It was a crap shoot, and I knew better, but I couldn't help myself. Selfishness, again.

So I am bringing our friendship to an end. I already visited your office and had Bernadette return all my files, contracts, letters, income tax forms, ledgers, the works. Do not try to see me. I have moved, leasing a new place under an assumed name. My telephone number will not be listed in any directory. Any future dealings with magazines or book publishers (in the event I ever finish and sell <u>Eclipse</u>, or another story, or another poem) will be handled in such a way that you will not be able to discern my whereabouts from them. I may even leave the city. I'm not sure of that yet, but it remains a possibility.

> *This is as it must be, Jack. I hope you see that. Recover swiftly, my friend. Go in peace. And I hope with every ounce of strength in my body and mind that you can still find it in your heart to think well of me, to remember the good times, not the bad, to absolve me from blame, to understand what happened, and why, and how. I hope you will always carry a flicker of our friendship with you (as I will!), and that you will take it to your grave after a long, happy, and healthy life.*
> *A.B.*

I admit it. I admit it. I admit it.

Only now, almost two God damn hours later, have I been able to stop crying.

July 19, 1954

Damn the man. God damn him. God damn his black, shriveled soul to hell. I've been looking and looking, calling, using an army of private dicks and even a few actual cops. How could he have covered his tracks so well? Did he drop off the face of the earth? He seems to be nowhere. Absolutely nowhere. I can't find him, and I'm beginning to wonder if I'll ever see him again.

My friend. Oh, my poor lost friend....

8

HE READ UNTIL the very first streaks of gray light were in the sky. He was only up through the end of 1955, but the references to Bassett had almost stopped by then, and his eyes couldn't take any more. There were still almost four years to go, several hundred pages of the cramped, tight writing, virtually the last record of a vital man who had died of lung cancer in 1960.

To the sounds of wind singing under the eaves and rain drumming on the roof, Andy put the journal aside and went quietly out into the corridor. He needed coffee to clear away the cobwebs of sleeplessness, to chase the

ALEXANDER'S SONG

demons of murder and mystery and old darkness. He was betting that he could get in and out of the kitchen before Max woke up, if she had slept at all with her daughter missing.

He was shutting the door behind him when he saw the envelope. It was held under the brass room number by a strip of transparent tape. Written on the envelope was the single word GILLESPIE.

He pulled the envelope down, tore open the flap, and tipped it over. A photograph, a Polaroid, fluttered out and fell to the floor. He picked it up, turned it over, and stared at it, shaking his head in confusion.

The picture was of three grave markers situated under a tree, the branches bare of leaves. The stone in the center was a tall family plot marker. It had a name engraved on it in deep letters:

GULLIVER

To the left was a smaller stone:

DWIGHT JASON GULLIVER
Attorney   Town Councilman   Friend to Many
May 9, 1935 - July 4, 1987

The stone to the right, identical but for the lettering, bore the inscription:

LENORE SCOTT GULLIVER
"Lonnie"
September 30, 1938 - July 4, 1987

Andy frowned, trying to pretend he didn't feel a chill running relays up and down his spine. He looked down the corridor, as though expecting someone to be watching him. He remembered phantom footsteps in the hall several hours before, sounds he had told himself were created by the storm.

There was a single slip of paper still inside the envelope. There was printing on it—the same straight, block letters in which his name was written, impossible to analyze and, he supposed, impossible to trace.

**WHEN FLOWERS GROW TOO CLOSE TO THE TREE THEY MUST BE TRIMMED
SO SAITH THE POET SO SAITH ME
I AM THE GARDENER I PRUNE
WHEN NECESSARY
STUDY TOMBSTONES AND ASK YOURSELF
WHY
I HAVE HER**

He read the note three times, then had to race back into his room, into the bathroom, where he vomited violently, as though his insides were being ripped apart by a cold, murderous hand.

The Gardener, he thought, and *I have her* and *second world* and *my poor lost friend*—those thoughts and a hundred, a thousand, a hundred-thousand others tore through his mind in the scant space of seconds.

Dawn crept onward and the rain continued to fall.

PART TWO

INTO THE SECOND WORLD

Frank Hale often thought about courage. The sweltering tropical nights were made for such useless ruminations. He wondered where courage came from, why some men had plenty of it while others seemed completely unacquainted with the concept. He thought about what it took to find courage and use it. The courage to help your friends; the courage to *make* a friend; the courage to live life and face death; the courage to step out of the light and onto the vast, dark plain beyond. Each morning these nocturnal thoughts would flee, but in the hours between darkness and dawn they were all he could hold onto, the only things he had to keep him going.

Alexander Bassett
from *To Raise Brave Men* (Novel, 1945)

SIX

DREAMS AND SECRETS

1

When it came to dreams, Andy had become a soiled virgin. Their weird, energizing shine and dark glamour had faded away. Their presence did not excite or surprise him. Their content (when he could remember it) no longer stimulated him in ways either good or bad. Nothing at all about the dreams moved him anymore.

Study tombstones and ask yourself why, the Gardener's note had said, but Andy had learned that asking *anything* was less than worthless. There weren't any answers. There was only the ongoing mystery, dark, shadowy, folded in upon itself, unreadable, indecipherable, taunting him every time he slept.

In the most recent dream (one of the approximately ten percent he could recall with any accuracy upon awakening), he had found himself once again on Wolf Island, this time in Ed Hoffer's cabin. It was a rainy day. Martin Visnaw was there. So was Ginnie Turner. So was Joanne, and a man he didn't recognize but whom he was quite sure was Jackson Kretchmer. Ed Hoffer was also there, of course, leaning forward on his walking stick, acting the perfect host while the six of them animatedly discussed literature. There was a lot of strange, angrily literate, Edward Albeeish conversation in that dream, but the only part that really mattered was a frenzied moment near the end, just before waking. Andy was standing at Hoffer's roll-top desk, rummaging through the papers, scattering them like dead leaves, crying, "Of course Walt Whitman was a goddamned transcendentalist! Everybody knows he was a goddamned transcendentalist! I know it, you know it, Jo knows it—and she's not even a scholar! The greenest college freshman in the world knows that Whitman was a goddamned transcendentalist! What I want to know is: *What in the name of Christ bugs me about this desk?*"

That was the way it always went, he thought groggily as he lay in bed afterwards and smoked. The dreams were five percent incongruous casting, five percent unusual location, ten percent honest questions, and eighty percent babble. In sum, a hundred percent horseshit.

He stumbled out of bed, crushed his cigarette in the ashtray on the desk, and tugged the drapery cord. He peered owlishly at the rain pounding downward, the trees doing their endless windblown dance, and sighed. It had been pouring ceaselessly since Monday night. Now it was Thursday, another day when he knew he should pack up and get out of town, and another day when he knew he wouldn't.

There were two official cars in the bed and breakfast parking lot, one a Rock Creek Police Department vehicle, one from the Baraga County Sheriff's office. He felt a lump rising in his throat but swallowed it quickly. He was getting used to seeing cars like that.

By his rough count, the search for Ginnie involved better than sixty people. Most of those were volunteers, but there were plenty of area and state cops, two K9 teams—one with a regular search dog, the other with a specially trained cadaver-sniffing dog that everyone in town knew about but no one acknowledged out loud— a Coast Guard helicopter that came and went as weather conditions allowed, police from the Keweenaw Bay Indian Community, state conservation officers, and even one FBI agent who went by the somewhat unsettling name of Coffin. Coffin was in his mid-twenties, short, thin to the point of emaciation, and seemed a great deal of the time to be sleepwalking. He frowned a lot, as though he resented the fact that a federal case was being made out of one missing girl. He loved to talk about baseball, but the subject of Ginnie Turner brought back the frown and made him zip up tight.

For his part, Andy had joined the search yesterday. His group of six, which included Officer Betty Rhodes and local volunteers, had systematically moved through their designated grid, which cover part of a large meadow outside of town, near the old Manitou Pulp Mill. They were looking for a footprint, a candy wrapper, a cigarette butt, a shoe or other article of clothing, anything at all that could be classified as out of the ordinary.

Although the entire town and miles of surrounding wilderness were subject to search, the Manitou Meadow was the focus of special attention. At least one team concentrated its efforts there each day, because it was there that Ginnie's on-again, off-again boyfriend Mike Volkman claimed to have seen her last.

Volkman's version of events went like this: he and Ginnie had walked to the meadow after school on Monday. They had each drunk a can of pop, Mike a Mountain Dew, Ginnie a Diet Coke. They had talked about things—what they had been up to for the last seven months, their plans for the summer, what was new in Rock Creek, what teacher had gone off the deep end and become a religious fanatic, who was dating whom, who had scored (and with whom, and how many times) after the last weekend dance, why Mike, a football star, continued to get shitty grades in all his math classes despite constant special tutoring.

Ultimately, a disagreement had reared its ugly head. Mike seemed hazy on the exact cause, but he was pretty sure it had begun because he was eager to continue the conversation while Ginnie had suddenly become agitated. She told him she had to leave, go home, see someone or something. (The police, of course, eventually pieced together that the someone in question was Andy and the something the journal from New York.)

After a brief but apparently bitter quarrel, during which Mike had accused Ginnie of turning "tight-assed" on him over the winter, he had left her standing there as he stormed out of the meadow.

"You wanna go home? Then go home! Walk yourself home, you stupid bitch! I don't care!"

Those had been his parting words, uttered sometime between four and four-thirty. From there he had picked up his car and gone to visit his sister's husband in L'Anse, a relative whose main purpose in Mike's life seemed to be the fact that he sometimes bought beer for Mike and his friends.

Andy had been surprised that the boy would admit a legal violation of that nature, but he came to understand why when the brother-in-law reluctantly corroborated the story and Mike dropped down a few notches on the list of suspects.

In hiking through the meadow, crisscrossing back and forth in heavy rain and ankle-deep mud, Andy had gradually come to realize that Coffin's lack of enthusiasm was the rule, not the exception. The entire search seemed to be a mere formality, something that had to be done because it was the custom—or at least the *decent* thing to do.

The police officers and most of the volunteers were in agreement that of the dozen or so possible causes for Ginnie's vanishing act, foul play was at the bottom of the list. With murder or kidnapping all but ruled out, no one really expected to find Ginnie's blood-soaked blouse or the crushed Marlboro butts left behind by her killer.

"Kids run off," was the opinion of Carrie Ives, the grocery store clerk putting in a few hours on Andy's search team. "They get pissed off at their folks, they fight with their boyfriends, they start feelin' all grown-up, they go. Happens all the time."

"That's right," said Jack Seely, an unemployed logger who sometimes drove a county snowplow in the winter. "Once they hit sixteen-seventeen, you can't keep 'em around. An' not only that," he added in a low, confidential tone, "Ginnie never liked her mama very much. Carla Knudson over to the post office, she tol' me they fight all the time. Betcha twenty bucks she's thumbin' her way down to wherever it is her daddy's workin'. She'll turn up with him in a couple-three days, you wait an' see."

Andy, who thought he knew a Ginnie Turner who was quite different than the one imagined by the townspeople, kept his mouth shut. Ginnie had been eager to get away from Mike Volkman because she wanted to go see *him*. That was a given, and it had made Andy himself a prime suspect for much of the day on Tuesday. Even now, his airplane ride with Martin Visnaw and his return to the bed and breakfast to wait for his package established as positive alibis, he was still the stranger in town, essentially an unknown quantity. Although he pretended not to notice, it was hard to miss the suspicious looks people cast his way, or those folks who turned their backs every time he opened his mouth to speak.

At other times, doubt crept into his mind. At those times, he thought that Ives, Seely, and all the others were probably right. Ginnie's above-average intelligence and the fact that she was more intense, more driven than most kids her age didn't necessarily preclude an irrational act of running away. If anything, he supposed, it might enhance the prospect.

Although she had seemed fine Sunday night, anything at all could have happened in school on Monday—a fight with a friend (as she had quarreled later with Volkman) or an argument with a teacher, perhaps. Though it seemed unlikely, she might have forgotten all about the Bassett journal. She might have been seized by a sudden urge to run, to get away, an urge that would seem intelligent enough to a girl unaccustomed to having stupid thoughts, an imperative that a driven person would find difficult to ignore.

"We appreciate the help," Betty Rhodes had told him at the end of Wednesday's search. "You want go out again tomorrow, we'll be meeting outside the town hall at first light. We can use you. Every day this drags on, we're going to be getting fewer volunteers. Folks tend to wise up after a couple of days and realize they're just goose-chasing their own tails."

But standing at the window and gazing out at the rain, Andy thought he would just as soon pass up the opportunity to wade through weeds and muck for another eight hours. If he thought he could help Ginnie by going out, he wouldn't have hesitated. But he had serious doubts that one more drenched rat in the Manitou Meadow would turn up what two days of constant searching had failed to find.

He thought again about leaving. It would be so easy. With a quick packing job, he could be on the road and free of Rock Creek in less than half an hour. He had certainly established precedent for such an action. Too much trouble with a student—transfer him to another section. Tough sledding in his marriage—let his fingers do the walking through the "Attorneys" listings in the Yellow Pages.

But there were just too many reasons to stay, not least of which was self-preservation.

Although the Rock Creek cops, the state police, and even dour Coffin had assured him repeatedly that he was no longer under suspicion for anything, he didn't think it would take them long to change their minds should he suddenly take a powder and vanish from town.

And of course there was the simple but unavoidable matter of Ginnie herself. Her intelligence had startled him. The way she had insinuated herself into his project (and his life) had unnerved him. Her rash behavior had infuriated him. But all that aside, and as much as its essential altruism shocked him, he knew he would be unable to live with himself if he left Rock Creek before she was found.

And, oh yes, there was another reason too. It might not be the biggest reason, but it was important.

He was, of course, thinking about the thing that had brought him to town in the first place.

He turned and studied the books and papers on his desk, that small, irregular mountain range that served as a reminder (as though he needed one!) that the clock was still ticking. As he had already told himself a hundred times over, he had spent more time in Rock Creek and had found much less than he had ever expected. Now he had to knuckle down, buckle down and make a dedicated, honest effort to fit Jackson Kretchmer's

ALEXANDER'S SONG

journal into the scheme of things. Only then could he find the truth. Only then could he decide whether A) he now had countless new and surprising avenues to explore, or B) he now should throw everything in the trash bin and give up.

The week had been a disaster all around, and his research had suffered as much as anything. Tuesday's police interviews and Wednesday's search team had precluded not only honest to God work, they had virtually stolen all his opportunity to *think*. The time had come, he knew, to get back to some real labor, to decide the future of the project, to fish or cut bait, to shit or git, as Kevin Caspian (or Ginnie herself) would have said.

A man he didn't recognize, dressed in a dirty yellow slicker over faded jeans, came out of the front door, hopped in the Baraga County Sheriff's car, and drove off. The Rock Creek police had remained behind, most likely fulfilling what seemed to be their main task in this long official dance: comforting Max. He wondered who had pulled that duty this morning. Betty Rhodes? Good old lovable Jeff Lamoreaux? One of the others?

For perhaps the tenth time in the last three days, Andy thought about going downstairs and having a talk with them. For the tenth time in the last three days, he honestly considered the idea and rejected it. And for the tenth time in the last three days he felt guilty and miserable for doing so.

He tried to convince himself that he was keeping quiet for reasons of self-preservation again. He had, after all, gone through a brief period of intense official scrutiny. It was true that they had cleared him in the end, but he was afraid that if he came forward with what was essentially a crazy, half-baked, virtually unimaginable story, they would begin to suspect him all over again, convinced that he was inventing wildly implausible scenarios to keep the spotlight off himself. *Hey, Bets!* Jeff Lamoreaux would say. *You remember Sam Sheppard's one-armed man? Wait'll you get a load of what this Gillespie clown cooked up!*

But that was too easy, and Andy knew it. It was that realization that made him feel so awful. He *knew* the real reason he wasn't stepping forward.

It was self-preservation of a sort, he supposed, but an ugly kind, a vile kind, the lowest kind.

"I don't want to look like a fool."

There. It was out. Spoken aloud.

Andy Gillespie didn't want to look silly.

The idea *was* crazy. He understood that. It was an idea that would make people laugh at him—and didn't enough folks around town already think his interest in Bassett-the-commie was funny enough? It was an idea that would make all those who thought kids ran off as routinely as they washed their hair give a knowing sigh, cock their heads, and twirl their index fingers around their ears. It was an idea that would make Carrie Ives snort with laughter and Jack Seely slap his knee. It was an idea that would make Coffin the FBI man frown and turn his thoughts to long balls and double plays.

It made Andy want to do the same.

I have her, the note on his door—the note no one but him knew about—had said.

And, of course, Andy's dark and horrible secret was that he thought the note writer was talking about Ginnie.

2

FOR REASONS HE was helpless to decipher, his dreams often involved stairs. More often than not, they involved these *particular* stairs, the ones leading from the waterfront to the top of the cliff on Wolf Island. Climbing them on that rainy Thursday, he had to pause halfway up, look around, and clench his hands into tight, painful fists. Only when he was convinced that he was climbing in real life and not in the world of sleep was he able to resume, reaching the top breathless and achy.

He had spent the morning going over his notes, then tracking down two grave markers in the newer section of Oak Hill. Studying the stones closely (*just doing what the Gardener told me to,* he had thought a little crazily), he was unable to find any clue to the identities of Dwight Gulliver and his wife, Lenore.

July 4, 1987.

Recent enough, no doubt, for just about everyone in town to remember. He could walk into the grocery store or the Rexall, into one of the outfitter's stores, into any restaurant or gift shop, ask the question, and probably get an answer. But like so many other things, he was afraid that asking about the Gullivers would make brows furrow even deeper at the very mention of his name. He could hear them now, just the way he had imagined Jeff Lamoreaux talking about Sam Sheppard. They would be gathered on their barstools or in their fishing boats or around Carla Knudson's window at the post office, and one of them would say, *Yeah, I'm talkin' 'bout that Gillespie fella. First he's got his nose to the ground 'bout the commie, then he's hooked up to Max's kid, and now he's askin' 'bout Dwight and Lonnie. What the hell's goin' on with him, anyway?*

Before he left the cemetery, he glanced toward the last hill at the back, toying with the idea of returning to see the graves of Hale and McCready. But the memory of being there once was strong enough, and that phrase from Hale's marker—*Snatched from our arms, he sleeps now with angels*—sent a chill wriggling down his spine.

He had hurried out of Oak Hill, stopping just long enough to put bold question marks next to the Gullivers' names in his notebook. Then, gunning the engine, the back tires of the truck spitting chunks of gravel, he was off to the next stops on his list: Seward's Outdoor Adventures, Green Lake, Wolf Island.

He was entertaining several possibilities about the outcome of this visit, ranging from the fruitless (Ed Hoffer turned out to be nothing but the frail, harmless old man he had seemed last time) to the unthinkable (Hoffer was the Gardener, the man who had sent the note, the man who perhaps had Ginnie, possibly even the man who had taken the shot at Max's window, that shot the police were ready to blame on Nelson Ecklar next door).

That last version also branched off down varying paths of possibility: Hoffer had Ginnie but Andy was able to rescue her; Hoffer captured him and held him prisoner along with Ginnie; Hoffer killed him and Ginnie during their attempted escape; Hoffer took a shot at him right now, from the top of the cliff, scoring a direct hit between Andy's eyes and sending his lifeless body tumbling ass over teakettle to the lake below.

Realistically, he knew that he was getting carried away. Without even breathing hard or breaking a sweat, his mind had switched itself on, kicked the imagination into overdrive, and created a lurid plot. Gunshots and kidnapping indeed. The truth was, the odds against Ed Hoffer being the Gardener were at least ten million to one. As they said on television cop shows, what was his motivation? There was only one that Andy could see, but even that bordered on the absurd. The man had an antique photograph. Ginnie stole that photograph. So what? He became a gun-toting kidnapper?

The odds that the Gardener's note meant anything at all weren't much better. To overlook the evidence against the Ecklar boy and find dark intent in a stray gunshot was foolish. To feel so certain that the line *I have her* referred to Ginnie was even worse. And to put those two things together...well, there was a name for that kind of thinking. Psychiatrists used it all the time.

The most likely explanation was that Hoffer was just a quiet old man, a former insurance broker from Detroit; the gunshot was an accident; Ginnie had run off to see her father; the Gardener's note was some kind of dumb prank played by a bored teenager, someone looking for a laugh by teasing the new man in town.

Sure. Probably.

But he had to know. He had to find out for sure.

And even more than that, he wanted to know about Hoffer's desk.

ALEXANDER'S SONG

3

HIS LUNGS BARELY recovered from the climb, Andy lit a cigarette as he walked through the woods to the cabin. He felt threatened, exhausted, buried, broken, stimulated, and beguiled— all because of the recent bombardment of strange information he had received. Although the comparison was not a comfortable one, he was beginning to understand how conspiracy buffs could manufacture plots and intrigue and hidden gangs of terrorists out of nothing but an echo and a shadow.

His earlier thought, that the events of the week thus far had prevented him from working, had been disingenuous. He had actually managed to squeeze in several hours of desk work each evening, even last night when his bones and muscles were crying wearily from his day on the search team, when, even after a warm bath and a change of clothes, he felt as though he would never again be truly warm and dry.

Some of that work had been further reading in the Bassett journal. Much more of it had involved his new list of names.

He had started the list after studying the Kretchmer journal, beginning by writing down the names of everyone who seemed to fit directly into the story, later adding those he suspected were marginal players. Neat, orderly, and precise at first, the list had gradually taken on a life of its own, turning into a complicated chart complete with bold lines drawn between names and notes crammed into the margins. Looking at it now was like studying an extremely twisted family tree, perhaps one assembled by a genealogist with a heavy drinking problem.

The fact that Andy had no idea who some of the people were didn't help. This Jens Carlson, for instance. Or Oglebay, the one Kretchmer had called a two-bit poet. Who were they? Trying to establish and then understand what were at best cloudy and at worst non-existent connections made him feel as though he were back in college, searching for the similarities between *Hedda Gabbler* and *Catcher in the Rye*.

The margin notes only served to highlight his confusion.

Visnaw mentioned the union man, Haag. How can that possibly fit? That was one of them.

Another read: *Did A.B. really kill Jens Carlson?*

Another: *Who did William Bassett kill? A.B. said two, but did he? Might be only A.B.'s delusion????*

Must learn more about the lover, Mahler! read a fourth.

And a fifth: *Don't forget, this is a very small town! Halvard Borg (Carlson's father??) maybe related to M. Borg, Marilyn, Myrna, whatever her name was. That old troll lady was certainly the right age. Maybe even H's daughter?!?!*

Despite the tantalizing possibilities (The Haag-Borg-Carlson thing, for example), Andy wasn't even sure if this was a genuine puzzle, or if he was simply getting mired down in lots of ordinary facts, the meaningless hash that makes up the histories of peoples' lives. Certainly Alexander Bassett's life had turned out to be a great deal darker than he had ever thought, but that wasn't necessarily headline news: FAMOUS AUTHOR DRINKS! FAMOUS AUTHOR WALKS FINE LINE OF MENTAL ILLNESS! FAMOUS AUTHOR MAY HAVE BEEN VIOLENT!

Deep down he knew he would be a lot happier if he could simply dismiss the whole knotty tangle and walk away. But the names kept calling him back. Bassett, Kretchmer, Carlson, Haag, Borg, Wandry, Hale and McCready, Henry Oglebay, Calvert Drummond, Grace Mahler—there were so many of them! The faint connections, or lack of them, plagued his thoughts until he could no more escape them than he could understand them. Forget the college analogy. In college, no matter how infuriating the work, there was always a getaway: a party, a lit students' bull session, a girl, a quick game of three-on-three basketball.

What he actually felt like was a man trying to complete a vital but murderously complicated job of electrical wiring in total darkness. The darkness could be dispelled, but only when he finally managed to get all the proper lines together, find the right switch, flick it, and flood the scene with light.

4

HE PAUSED ON the edge of the clearing, looking through the constant curtain of rain at the cabin. Unlike his dreams, where this place was populated by all manner of unlikely people, Hoffer was there alone, sitting on his porch, a long stick of ash across his lap and a pocketknife clenched in his clawlike right hand.

Andy's first call failed to penetrate the old man's hearing. He tried again. This time Hoffer looked up, frowned, and finally raised a hand in a feeble wave.

"Mr. Gillespie, isn't it?"

"Andy."

"Yes, of course." He put the whittling stick aside, laying it down next to an impressive pile of curled shavings, and invited Andy up. "You picked a helluva day for wilderness exploring. You want to hang your jacket on the doorknob, it'll dry faster. Or better yet, we can go inside by the fire. Your call."

"I'm fine out here." Andy knew it was wrong. How was he going to get another look at the roll-top desk while sitting on the porch? "This shouldn't take very long."

Hoffer grunted. "I imagine not. You asked all your questions the other day—and went away disappointed, if memory serves." He patted his shirt pocket as though looking for cigarettes. "You thought of something else?"

"I did...that is...oh, Jesus...what the hell?"

It was like a low budget ghostly special effect when the old man began to fade. Too smooth, too perfect. Andy thought of a light on a rheostat being dialed lower and lower until bright was dim, until dim was just a flicker.

He rubbed his eyes, snapping back from wherever he had been, looking around stupidly, realizing that he was even more tense about this visit than he had admitted to himself. There was no other explanation for it, the way his mind had gotten away from him there for a minute or two. It was almost like another dream.

The reality was that he was still standing on the edge of the clearing, the rain still slanting down. There was no one on the cabin's front porch, no lights burning inside, no ribbon of smoke curling from the chimney. He studied the two Adirondack chairs placed side by side to the right of the front door, shaking his head as though helpless to understand why he wasn't sitting there with Ed Hoffer. The wind gusted at his back and the trees whispered their secret messages above his head.

He went up on the porch and knocked, but the unmistakably empty look of the cabin was no illusion. He felt like a bungling burglar as he paced the length of the porch, peering into windows. He caught glimpses of a bookshelf, a table full of mineral samples. He could see part of the roll-top desk—the back and one side, mostly—but couldn't get the right angle to see the paperwork piled there.

He sank down in the first Adirondack, mulling over his choices. Both the boat and the canoe had been tied to the dock. That meant Hoffer was somewhere on the island. He might be out walking in the woods, or gathering firewood, or fishing, or bird-watching—whatever he did to get him through the long, lonely days. It would be simple enough to wait for him to return, but Andy didn't like that. It would make him look too eager, sitting outside the door, waiting to pounce on the man as soon as he came back.

Unfortunately, his other option was equally bad. If he went back to the mainland now, completely empty-handed, without even trying, then why in the hell had he trekked all the way out here in the first place?

He lit a cigarette. Suddenly his eyes opened wide and he sat up straighter as a question lurched into his head: *What would Ginnie do?* It would have been hilarious if the search now going on back in town didn't make it so poignant.

There wasn't really any doubt. He knew very well what Ginnie would do. If she were here, she would bring it up, he would unsuccessfully try to stop her, and she would laugh and toss her hair and say something blunt, something along the lines of, "Jesus, Andy. We're here, aren't we? So why not?"

ALEXANDER'S SONG

He took a long, slow pull on the cigarette and stared at the cabin door. What if Ginnie *is* here? he thought. There was a dark question. What if the place she was in such a hurry to go Monday afternoon wasn't back to the B&B but here, to Wolf Island? What if she'd finally seen his side of things? What if the guilt finally caught up with her and she decided to return the picture before another day went by? What if she rented a boat and came out here and confessed, but what if Ed Hoffer flew into an insane rage and—

I HAVE HER.

He pitched the cigarette, half-smoked, over the railing. It landed in the mud and sizzled out. The crazy idea continued to form in his mind.

If Hoffer really was on the island, would he lock his front door? Unlikely; who was going to break in? The flip-side, of course, was that if Hoffer was on the island he could return any minute. Andy didn't relish the idea of being caught snooping around the old man's desk. The police were tired enough of him as it was. A trespassing complaint wouldn't smooth the waters at all.

Theoretically, though, the same thing could happen if Hoffer came back and found Andy sitting on his front porch, littering his yard with cigarette butts. After all, wasn't he the same man who had cried "Halt and identify!" on Andy's first visit?

It could be a sticky situation either way, and the sad truth was that he probably shouldn't have come to the island at all. At the very least, he should have spared the visit a little more thought, considered this contingency and been prepared for it. But he hadn't. He was here. It was too late now. So what?

He turned in the chair and looked through the nearest window. The corner of the roll-top mocked him. He imagined it with a high, taunting voice. *What about me, Andy? Don't you want to know what it was you saw here last time? Don't you want to figure out what you've been dreaming about? C'mon, boy, don't you want to know? Don't you want to understaaaaaaaaaand?*

He stood and stretched lazily, pretending to study the trees on the south side of the cabin, turning with painstaking slowness and taking in the woodpile, the clearing, the path back to the lake. He held his breath for a second, listening, but he didn't hear the sound of approaching footsteps mingled with the patter of rain.

The doorknob was cold, slicked with mist. It turned easily beneath his fingers, too easily. Amazed, slightly confused, feeling daring and irresponsible and utterly, hopelessly damned, he pushed open the door.

His last thought before he went inside was to wonder if Ginnie would be proud of him.

5

THE DREAMS WERE a lot like this, this sensation of being somewhere he didn't want to be and would never belong.

"Mr. Hoffer? Hello, Ed? I knocked—maybe you didn't hear me. It's Andy Gillespie. Remember? I was out here last weekend with—"

The words died on his lips. The interior of the cabin was cold and dim. Unless Ed Hoffer was lying dead in one of the side rooms (another happy thought!) Andy was as alone in this cabin as if it were his own. The desk was just three feet away, within easy reach now. As hard as he tried to come up with something, there was no longer any reason not to go the rest of the way. He walked over to it and rested a hand on the polished wood side. The slatted top was rolled down, covering the interior of notes and papers he wanted to see. He grabbed the tiny brass knob, tugged, and felt his heart turn into a cold lead ball. He tried again. The top teased him by rattling in its tracks. He was about to give it everything he had when he noticed the tiny keyhole above the knob. The lead ball grew heavier.

It wasn't stuck. Of course not. It couldn't be anything as simple as that. The damn thing was locked.

The absurdity of the situation was impossible to miss. He ground his teeth together but couldn't stop a grim laugh from escaping. Here was another contingency he hadn't foreseen. Jesus, they were piling up like cordwood. He felt like the explorer who sailed from home without charts, the climber who departed base camp without ropes and pitons. He wondered bitterly just what he'd come to the island for, anyway. Was he really looking for something, or just trying to prove what a damned fool he was?

There was no need to ask what Ginnie would do this time. There was no doubt she was bold, but he didn't think she would resort to smashing her way into the desk. Not even she would go *that* far.

He took a long, slow look around the cluttered main room, as though the answer he was seeking might be found elsewhere. Forgetting that Hoffer could return at any time (or, for that matter, that he might be a blue and stiffening corpse behind any of the several closed doors), he crossed to the bookcase and stopped in front of the shelf containing *Seascape, The Biggest Angel,* and the other Bassett books.

For no apparent reason, he remembered Hoffer saying *Bassett was a powerful writer, but his politics always left me ice cold.* On the heels of that came the memory of Ginnie quoting from "The Voice of the Storm," and something else—the way her brief recital had seemed to please Hoffer in a quiet, rather mysterious way.

So what did that prove? That the old man knew more about Bassett than he'd let on? That was obvious, anyway. The photograph Ginnie had snatched told him that. Andy couldn't imagine any possible connection between a Lower Michigan insurance broker and a twentieth century literary giant, but then again this room, this strange hodgepodge that resembled nothing so much as the fruits accumulated by an eccentric, bookish scholar…this room made it difficult to think of Hoffer as just a garden variety whole life huckster.

Could he be the Gardener? Almost certainly not. The key to the puzzle? Old photos aside, it didn't seem likely. But Andy was growing edgier with every second. He was feeling that sensation of something important, the same feeling that had previously beckoned to him from the roll-top desk, now coming at him like radio signals from all around the cabin.

PAUL F. OLSON

Turning to go, he noticed something he had missed before. There was a small wooden trunk stored beneath the desk, neatly tucked between the legs, mostly hidden behind the stool where Hoffer sat to pay his bills or whatever it was he did there.

He knelt in front of it and did a double take when he saw the decoupage picture on top—a faded portrait of Edgar Allan Poe, permanently fixed to the lid by countless layers of yellowing shellac. On the front of the trunk, below the hasp and padlock, the legend ANNALS OF THE DUPIN SOCIETY was carved in crude, shaky letters. His first impression was of a child's hand, a third-grader's declaration of SUSIE LOVES JOHNNY.

Dupin? he thought. *Auguste* Dupin, Poe's great detective? The forerunner of Sherlock Holmes? The fictional grandfather of Poirot and Lord Peter Wimsey and Philo Vance? Of Maigret and Sam Spade and Travis McGee and Lew Archer and V.I. Warshawsky and Joe Leaphorn and all the rest? *That* Dupin?

Something about that detective, or perhaps the name itself—The Dupin Society—bounced off a fragment of memory in the back of his mind and produced a soft, hollow clang. He tried helplessly to understand it. His gaze was drawn back to the picture of Poe, but the man's piercing, edge-of-madness eyes gave no answers, no clues.

"I suppose I should call the police, but that'd be a trick. Had my phone taken out last year, and the nearest booth's almost three miles away on the mainland."

The cry that escaped Andy's throat was truncated, pathetic, the sound of a small dog being run over by a truck. He scrambled away from the desk and saw Ed Hoffer standing in an open doorway across the room. Behind him, Andy caught a glimpse of another desk, a wooden filing cabinet, and piled reams of paper. Then the door was shut and the old man was shuffling toward him.

"Jesus," Andy murmured. It had the ring of a confession, but he guessed that didn't matter much when he had already been caught red-handed.

ALEXANDER'S SONG

Hoffer smiled. Andy wished he knew the man better. He thought the smile had a hint of malice in it, but it was hard to be sure. It might have been a simple grin of genuine amusement. At least he *hoped* that's all it was.

"Let me guess," Hoffer said. He hobbled to the couch in the center of the room and lowered himself slowly, like a marionette being controlled by an arthritic puppeteer. "You thought I was gone. You wanted to wait for me, but the rain made it uncomfortable, so you came inside to get dry. How's that? Or this one: You were just coming up the porch steps when you thought you smelled smoke inside. Thinking I might be trapped by fire, you abandoned all thoughts of your personal well-being and gallantly rushed in to save me, not knowing that I was safely locked away in another room and that the last fire around here was in the woodstove last night. Close?"

"Nothing as noble as that, I'm afraid."

Hoffer glared at him, gripping his walking stick so tightly that the thick blue veins on the backs of his hands stood out like ropes.

"I'm sorry," Andy said. "I called for you…I knocked…but you didn't answer and…and I didn't think you were around, so…" He shrugged, flashing a weak smile, knowing that whatever he said wouldn't be enough.

Hoffer patted his shirt pocket, just as he had done in Andy's daydream, and grimaced. "Things have reached a damn pretty pass when a man can't spend a few hours in his study without having his privacy violated."

"Look," Andy said. "I was wrong. I admit it. I told you I was sorry."

"Sorry. Hmm. I wonder." His gaze continued to bore holes into Andy's skull. "Just what can I do for you, Mr. Gillespie? While I decide how to handle this intrusion, I might as well find out what you're doing here."

Andy didn't know what to say. What came next when explanations were out of the question and apologies fell on deaf ears? He glanced at the trunk under the desk, eyeing the somber portrait of Poe.

"What's the Dupin Society?"

Hoffer uttered a sharp laugh. "Are you telling me you came all the way out here in this miserable weather to ask about that damned box?"

"Not exactly, no. I didn't even notice it the last time we were here. I just spotted it today, before you walked in."

"Ah, so you're here on other business. Well, at least that makes more sense. For what it's worth, the Dupin Society was an old Yale organization. It's probably still in existence, though on what level I couldn't say. You've heard of Skull and Bones?"

"Of course."

"The Dupin Society was a cut-rate version of that, popular for a time, though not nearly as ancient or prestigious. I doubt any Dupins ever went on to become leaders in world finance or ambassadors or presidents or anything of that sort. As I understand it, though, the basic premise was the same. They had a windowless house—a tomb—where they held meetings, secret goings-on, oaths of silence, spooky and complicated induction ceremonies, all that fuss and nonsense."

"So you went to Yale."

"Hardly. My father did. He was one of the founding Dupins. Somehow that box escaped New Haven with him, and when he died, it passed to me—lucky soul. Like most old things that get handed down, it came incomplete. There's no key. I haven't the slightest idea what's in there. It might be old bones and ledgers written in blood. But then again, it could be an empty whiskey bottle and a photograph of some naked 1895 sorority queen."

Andy nodded, though he thought it was odd that Hoffer had never been tempted to break open the trunk and look. It would be an easy job; a file, or even a screwdriver and a hammer would do the trick. He studied Poe's picture and the poorly-carved lettering.

ANNALS OF THE DUPIN SOCIETY.

He wished he knew what it was about that name that kept tickling the back of his brain. Had he run across another Dupin Society somewhere? Maybe that was it. The Dupins, probably a group of fanatics, the Poe version of the Baker Street Irregulars or the Sons of the Desert or the Trekkies.

"You've certainly accumulated some interesting things over the years."

ALEXANDER'S SONG

Hoffer straightened slowly, his rheumy eyes narrowing and sharpening again, his hands still throttling the walking stick. "I doubt you came here just to compliment me on my collection. Why don't you stop playing games and tell me what's really on your mind?"

Andy shifted, absently laying a hand on the side of the desk. When he realized what he'd done, he jerked away as though scalded. His lack of planning, the impulsive nature of this trip, was suddenly like a great gray blanket pressing down on him, smothering him beneath its weight.

It would have been so much easier if the desk had just been open. All he'd needed was a quick glimpse, a tiny little peek. Into the cabin, take a look, gone again. It could have been so simple. But now...it almost seemed as though it had been open on his first visit to tease him, locked today to frustrate him further. Of course he didn't really believe that—among other things, it was a ridiculously paranoid thought—but true or not, the basic facts remained the same: he wanted to know about the desk, and now he had to decide whether or not to ask Hoffer about it.

But when he finally opened his mouth a few seconds later, what came out didn't have anything at all to do with the desk. It was the other thing that had been on his mind so much recently. Obviously, without his knowing it, it had become the *major* thing, because the question slipped out without consideration, naturally, almost instinctively.

"Does the name 'the Gardener' mean anything to you?" he asked.

6

SAFELY AWAY FROM the dock, he throttled the motor back to neutral and allowed the boat to drift, ignoring the rain, the wind, and the restless swells of the lake, as he looked back at the rugged cliff of Wolf Island.

The feeling he'd had inside the cabin, that weird sensation of confusion and incompetence, of being so blind that he was missing something of paramount importance, was so strong now that it was with him even here. It radiated off that cliff a quarter of a mile away, from the rock itself and the high stairway that he could just make out as a dark, zigzagging line scaling the heights. It came from the woods and from the cabin hidden in those woods. It had changed slightly, in some ways becoming even worse than what it had been originally—no longer a true feeling of missing something, but a feeling of actually *seeing* it yet being unable to comprehend.

When Andy had asked about the Gardener, Ed Hoffer had leaned forward at an alarming angle. His mouth dropped open, his eyes bulged, the walking stick clattered to the floor. For a single long, gut-twisting moment Andy had thought the old man was having a heart attack. Even when Hoffer recovered, Andy knew that something—maybe everything—had changed. He just didn't know how. He couldn't understand why that feeling of significance missed had doubled, or why the air in the cabin suddenly seemed so thick and heavy that he could almost see it.

His own heart began to pound. This is it, he thought wildly. I'm here. I'm right in the middle of the second world. And despite the fact that the thought seemed random, almost completely without sense, he knew that it was vital.

"This is bullshit," Hoffer had said then. "You're just wasting my time. Why don't you go away and leave me alone?"

Andy shook his head. "The Gardener," he pressed, not quite believing that he was doing it but helplessly charged by the electricity of the moment. "Who is he?"

Hoffer's hands fluttered down like crippled birds. He pressed them against the cushions of the couch and pushed himself to a standing position.

"I don't have to answer any of your questions. You break into my home while I'm otherwise occupied, you snoop like a spy and a thief, you paw over my possessions. I have a gun here, you know. Homeowners have shot trespassers for less."

He took two steps in Andy's direction, and Andy temporarily forgot that he was dealing with an old and infirm man. He backed up defensively and banged against the roll-top desk. The desk shifted, bumping against the wall behind, and when Andy turned, distracted, he saw something there, dangling from the kind of screw-in hooks people buy to hang their coffee mugs.

He was struck once again by what a grand farce this trip had become. It was like wandering into a surrealistic movie, waking up and finding himself in a Gary Larson panel or part of a Matt Groening cartoon.

The key. It had been there all along. If he only would have opened his eyes he would have seen it. He could have gotten into the desk, seen whatever there was to see, and been gone before Hoffer even knew he was there. He felt thick, dull, stupid, and was sure that Ginnie would have noticed the key immediately. Ginnie would never have been so blind.

He wished Ginnie was with him now. Perhaps she would have a rational response to everything.

"I wish you'd tell me about the Gardener," he heard himself say. Movies again. This time he was watching himself, as if from a distance, forcing issues that were pointless to force, asking questions when he really ought to be sitting in a boat heading back to Harker's Landing. "Who is he? What does he have to do with some people named Gulliver?"

He was probably imagining it, but for a fraction of a second he thought Hoffer's eyes bulged again at the mention of that name.

"Gulliver?" the old man said, his voice a husky whisper. *"Dwight and Lonnie* Gulliver?"

"Yes! Who were they? Who's the Gardener?"

"I...I don't...."

"Mr. Hoffer, please, listen to me. I'm sorry I broke in here. I'm sorry I disturbed you. But this is important. I have to know."

"I. Don't. Have. Any. Idea. Who. You're. Talking. About."

"But you do! You just mentioned them by name! Who *were* they?"

Hoffer didn't respond. His age-dimmed eyes were not bulging anymore. Now they were sparkling brightly—with anger, with tears, with fear, Andy couldn't tell. A nerve in his wattled neck twitched madly. The crippled birds fluttered at his sides.

"You have to leave," he said at last. "You must leave now. This isn't a joke, Mr. Gillespie. I want you off my island."

Andy looked helplessly from Hoffer to the door and back again.

"I'm not joking either," he said. "This is important. It sounds ridiculous—hell, I know that. It sounds *crazy*. But somebody's life might depend on this. You know something, I can tell, I can see it in your face. You have to tell me. Who's the Gardener? Did he kill the Gullivers?"

"I can't help you."

"But—"

"For Christ's sake, man, I can't help you! Don't you understand that?"

Andy thought he might be sick. His head was spinning in wide, lazy circles and his stomach churned with sour bile. He did not consciously start to move, yet found himself walking toward the door. He stumbled, put a hand out to steady himself, and caught the edge of the desk. Something rattled inside, a locked secret he would apparently never find.

Was he quitting? he wondered. Could he quit? He didn't want to, but the look on the old man's face was suddenly too much for him, too baffling, too strange. It filled him with a nameless, crawling fear. It made him feel disoriented, lost, as though he were slipping from dream to reality and back into dream, following the curves of an endless maddening circle.

"You're the Gardener," Andy said, hand now on the doorknob. "Jesus, you're him, aren't you?"

Hoffer's mouth opened in an O of genuine amazement. After a moment he shook his head. It was a very small movement, just a quick left-to-right, a gesture that started and ended so rapidly it might have been a trick of light and shadow.

"Go now, Mr. Gillespie, before we're both sorry."

"Can't you tell me anything? Anything at all? If you know …if you could answer…you…you've got to…."

He trailed away, shaking his head in frustration. The old man's look was still eerily strange, but now it was stony and cold as well. Wordlessly, it told Andy the end had come. There had been precious little so far, but there would be even less now. All conversation was finished.

"You're just hurting a young woman!" Andy barked as he tore open the door. "I want you to understand that. If you know something and you won't share it with me, you're just hurting an innocent girl."

Hoffer stared at him, face a granite mask.

Andy floundered for one final second. Then he slipped outside. "It's on your conscience," he said, slamming the door behind him and stomping off the porch.

Now he drifted and stared back at the dark bulk of the island, the rain sharp and chilling as it soaked through his clothes. A distant loon called twice and was silent. The boat bobbed up and down, up and down.

"Not the Gardener," he muttered. "Nope." And that was undoubtedly true. But the impression of feeling something, seeing it, almost touching it, refused to leave. What did Hoffer know? What knowledge was he hiding, denying? The identities of the Gullivers? The Gardener?

It was too much like the stone walls he had run into when asking around town about Bassett. Cold looks, cold shoulders. Did all of Rock Creek know the answers to the questions he was asking? Did everyone know, and would they all refuse to talk?

When he throttled up a few minutes later, bringing the bow around and pointing it toward Harker's Landing, he felt that a half-dozen puzzle pieces had been snapped into place. The problem was, four or five dozen *new* pieces had simultaneously been dropped into his lap.

Let's try this, he thought absently. Alex Basset's father, William, the rich mill owner, kills the union organizer Royal Haag. Then he frames that old backwoods badman, Halvard Borg, and kills him too. Now according to the Kretchmer journal, Borg had a bastard son. Carlson. Jens Carlson. So how does he fit? Was he another killer, one who perhaps had a son of his own, a son named Ed Hoffer? And what if Hoffer—

No.

It was no good. Just like his virtually incomprehensible notes back home, each question, each hypothetical link, just raised more questions.

For instance: Why did Bassett think Jens Carlson was following him for so many years, when apparently he knew that Carlson had drowned in this very lake decades before? Was he really being followed? By someone who perhaps *looked* like Carlson, say Carlson's son, Hoffer again?

But why would Hoffer (or anyone else) follow Bassett? And who was killing those who grew close to the author—the editor, the poet, Grace Mahler? Who attacked Jack Kretchmer? And why? It seemed almost impossible that so many things could stem from the murder of Royal Haag by William Bassett, even granting that such a murder had occurred in the first place.

And the Gullivers...damn it, did they even fit? Or were they some sort of distracting side issue, relentlessly dragging him off track? They had died in 1987, almost twenty years after Bassett's death, more than eighty after the murder of Royal Haag. Surely they couldn't be connected.

Could they?

"I'm sorry, Ginnie," he whispered, his voice swallowed by the clatter of the engine. "I'm lost. I can't make sense of anything."

Suddenly, above the engine noise, he heard a single gunshot from somewhere along the western shore. His heart fluttered. There was a second shot, a pause, and then a third. He flinched each time and almost threw himself to the bottom of the boat before remembering where he was. This was the north country. As Jeff Lamoreaux had told him, guns went off around here all the time. For all he knew, it was the Ecklar kid, finally progressing from shooting at neighbors' windows to taking a pop at some birds or squirrels.

But that thought didn't do a great deal to comfort him. He turned the tiller, taking the boat a little farther away from shore, more toward the center of the lake. Only when he was straight out from the dock at Seward's Outdoor Adventures did he turn in. And even then he gave the motor everything it had as he raced for the safety of dry land.

ALEXANDER'S SONG

7

HE TOOK THE long way home, circling back into town from the east and north. His intentions were simple enough: stop by the Manitou Meadow to check on the progress of Betty Rhodes and that day's search team. But before he even came to the abandoned mill and that huge expanse of muddy field, he slammed on the brakes of the truck, brought up short by something along the side of the road.

It was a big house, set back at the end of a long driveway. Both the drive and the yard around it were overgrown with brown weeds and dead witch grass and scrubby, tangled thickets of tag alders. The house itself was long abandoned, shutters dangling, windows broken out, porch sagging, a large portion of the roof close to collapse.

Andy stared at the building and the yard, unable to say what had made him stop, why one abandoned dwelling in a town that had more than its fair share of them should have made him slam on the brakes in such an abrupt, almost panicky way.

From the back of his mind, a mist of half-formed images floated up. He saw (or at least *thought* he saw) piles of books, a long staircase, an old-fashioned lantern casting its warm glow through a circular lens.

Stairs again.

He let out his breath in a long sigh. The meaningless images scattered back to wherever they had come from, leaving him with nothing.

He concentrated. He frowned. But the house refused to yield whatever secrets it possessed.

Eventually he gunned the engine and pulled away, convinced that his frustrating search for facts was making him chase shadows everywhere, in even the most unlikely places. Graveyards and islands and abandoned houses, all in one day. It was a far cry from the libraries and university archives he had envisioned when he started out, so far that it should have been laughable. But he didn't feel like laughing.

A few seconds later, when he rounded the bend by the mill and meadow, his answers were there. The cars parked on the side of the road and the slicker-clad volunteers moving in a slow line told him everything he needed to know. There had been no progress. Ginnie was still missing.

His hands trembled almost imperceptibly on the steering wheel, but he barely slowed down as he went past.

SEVEN

REACHING FOR THE GREAT BEYOND

1

The phone at the bed and breakfast had been ringing off the hook all week. Turner relatives from as far away as Europe (a distant cousin of Ginnie's serving with the Air Force in West Germany) and family friends from all over the Upper Peninsula kept calling and calling. The police, when they weren't actually there, called. The editor of the local weekly paper called. A radio station in Ginnie's winter home of Provo called twice.

But on Thursday things were different. That night all the phone calls were for Andy.

The first one came in just after seven. He was in his room with the Bassett journal and his growing pile of notes when he was summoned downstairs by one of the other guests, another traveling sales rep, this one a computer systems man from somewhere in southern Ohio.

Max was in the kitchen with her ex-husband. Gil Turner had arrived from Louisiana that afternoon. He was a big man with a *huge* voice, and he was using every decibel of that voice now to lecture Coffin, the FBI agent, and Norman Paquin, the local police chief, on the subject of incompetence in the ranks of law enforcement. Andy picked up the phone in the living room and kept his voice low.

"Hello?"

"Hey, you, where's my check?"

Coming back from his private world of depthless mystery and mounting frustration, recognition was slow in coming. He stared at the endless variety of patterns made by the rain trickling down the living room window (the same window through which the bullet had entered on Sunday, he thought uneasily), and finally succeeded in pinning down the voice.

"Back home in Orlando, Jo?"

"We just got back this afternoon. Where's my check?"

"I haven't had a chance to mail it yet." He took a deep breath and briefly sketched in the story of Ginnie's disappearance. "If I hadn't been so damn busy, I would've—"

"Never mind, just send it when you can. You know, it's funny. Bob said something like this would happen. He said you'd dodge payment as long as you could, especially when the bill got up to a hundred dollars."

"Tell Bob I love him, too." He fumbled for his cigarettes. "Is that all you called for? To dun me for cash?"

"Actually, no. I wanted to tell you I stopped in to see Fishbein one more time before we left New York."

"Fish Find?"

"Fish*bein*, Andy. Jesus, you know, the book dealer. His card was in with the journals?"

"Ah, right. Mervyn Fishbein, a classic bookseller's name if I ever heard one. What'd you go over there for?"

"Not for my health, that's for damn sure. The last time I was there he'd said something about combing his stock for more crap by your pet writer. It's quite a store, you know. Not all that big, but one of those cramped, dusty places with books floor to ceiling, aisles so narrow you can't squeeze through them. And more books packed away in the attic, apparently—boxes and boxes of them. He said he might be able to track something down if he really looked, so I thought I'd drop by to see what he turned up."

"And?"

"He didn't find any books, or so he said. But he found something."

"What?"

"That's why I'm calling. He didn't say. What he did was tell *me* to tell *you* to call *him*. Tonight was what he said, but it's probably a little late for that now. Tomorrow then, first thing."

"You mean it can't wait until I get to New York…*if* I get to New York?"

"Isn't that what I just said? Or am I starting to imagine things?"

Andy frowned, watching the rain and slowly drawing on his cigarette. From the kitchen came the sound of Gil Turner calling Paquin "an asshole, a disgrace to your fucking badge!"

"I don't get it," he said to Jo. "Was it a book? A magazine? Another journal? What?"

"It was *nothing*. Good God, aren't you listening to me at all? It was information, just something he thought you'd want to know."

"Oh."

He leaned against the bookcase, sighing. He supposed it had been foolish to hope things wouldn't get any worse, but this crossed the line into the realm of absurdity. It was like something out of a Robert Ludlum novel. *Pssst. There's a book dealer in Manhattan, name of Fishbein. He's got something important to tell you, something he thinks you should know.*

"Andy, are you all right?"

"I'm fine. Why?"

"You sound different tonight…I don't know…odd."

"Oh, well, I'm tired. Exhausted really. It's been a hell of a week, what with this search and everything."

"The search isn't your responsibility."

"Jo—"

"No, hear me out. I don't want to tell you what to do. I didn't know this girl, after all."

PAUL F. OLSON

"I did."

"Yeah, so you said. But, Andy, you've only been in that town a couple of weeks. How involved can you get?"

Funny you should ask, Jo. You can get real involved around here. Too involved. By the way, did I happen to mention that I'm already so involved the cops questioned me for five hours the other day? What do you think of that?

"In my humble opinion, you're acting flaky," Jo said. Andy was listening closely, but for the first time in the three years since their divorce her voice was serious, devoid of any cynical undertones or her usually wry sense of humor. "You've been awfully cryptic since you got to that place. Trying to get anything more than a syllable or two out of you has been like...well, you've been acting like a character in a goddamn spy novel or something."

Andy actually jumped. Hearing his own thoughts echoed like that was more than strange. It was positively eerie.

"Andy?"

"Yes?"

"We're friends, aren't we? I mean even after all the shit, we're still friends?"

"Of a sort," he said, thinking about some of the things she had said to him in the last few years, particularly when she had moved in with Bob Jackowicz, the man she liked to call "my current lover," the man she had always been more than happy to point out was more successful, wealthier, more adventurous, more mentally grounded and emotionally open, and yes, even handsomer than Andy himself would ever be. "I guess in a world where anything's possible, yeah, we're still friends."

"Then why won't you talk to me? I'm worried about you."

"Oh, now that's just ridiculous. I'm fine, Jo. Really. Fine and dandy."

"Hmm."

"And what does *that* mean?"

"I guess it means I'm baffled. You've always been locked inside yourself. You've always been too tight, too private. You've always been afraid to open up and—"

ALEXANDER'S SONG

"Water under the bridge, Jo. We covered all this in marriage counseling. A long time ago. Ancient history."

"—but you're worse than ever lately," she went on, as though he hadn't spoken. "These phone calls, Jesus, it's like trying to hold a conversation with a stone. I'm trying to be helpful, I'm trying to show concern, but you just pull your little clamming-up act and get weirder by the minute."

He sighed again. "Is that so?"

"Andy, what the hell's going on?"

Well, you see, Jo, this whole thing turned out to be a lot more complicated than I ever expected. Bassett was a bizarre guy. There was a lot of death in his past and a lot of suffering and enough strange behavior for ten Hitchcock movies. And now there's an old man here who knows more than he's telling me, and another old man who knows a lot too, but all he wants to do is kill me in his airplane. You ought to be here, Jo, you'd love it. There are gunshots and cops and missing girls and psychotic notes from some wallbanger who calls himself the Gardener. To top it off, I'm having vivid, crazy dreams like you wouldn't believe. Shit, you think our phone calls are weird? You ought to be here in Rock Creek.

But he didn't say any of that. What he said was, "I've got to run, Jo. The police are here about Ginnie—you know, the missing girl. They want to use the phone."

"Andy—"

"I'll give Fishbein a call in the morning. And I'll get your check off tomorrow, too."

"Andy, dammit—"

"I'll be in touch."

He put the receiver down and gripped the edge of the table as he began to shake. The rain danced on the windows. Outside on Victory Street a pickup rumbled by, tires hissing. From the kitchen he could hear Paquin trying to reason with Gil Turner. "We've done our level best," the police chief was saying. "We've done everything humanly possible up to this point. Didn't I come back early from my vacation? Didn't I get every agency here as quickly as I could? Didn't I organize a thorough search, and haven't I been out there with them every day, tramping through the woods?"

Andy was gripped by an odd sense of vertigo, as though he and the table he was holding on to were perched on a narrow ledge, high above the rest of the living room. The floor with its thick carpet looked yards below him, and it seemed to turn around an invisible axis, moving in large, lazy circles.

He thought about his flight with Visnaw, how Visnaw had flown him over Wolf Island—almost directly *into* the island—saying in response to his questions about Bassett: *Death. That's the connection you're hunting for.* He thought about his visit with Ed Hoffer that afternoon, and the way Hoffer knew more about Bassett than he had said. He thought about the way the old man had recognized the names of Dwight and Lenore Gulliver, even going so far as to use Lenore's nickname, Lonnie. He thought about the Gardener's note, the picture of the tombstones, and that damned single line at the end—*I have her.*

He almost ran into the kitchen to tell them everything. It was gibberish, most of it, and no matter how he tried to order it, it would *sound* like gibberish when he spilled it out. It wouldn't make sense, trying to connect Bassett and Hoffer and Ginnie. It wouldn't lead to anything. But at least he would know he'd tried, he had done his job, done his best.

Later, he was almost able to convince himself that he actually would have done it, if only the phone hadn't rung again at that very moment. The electronic bray was loud and jarring, banishing the adrenaline that had been surging through him and chasing the vertigo away. He snatched the receiver off the hook and barked into it, momentarily forgetting where he was.

"Yes?"

"I'm sorry, I must have the wrong number. I was trying to reach Turner's."

"Oh...that's my fault. You've got the right place. Would you like to speak to Mrs.—"

"I'm trying to get in touch with a guest. Andrew Gillespie."

ALEXANDER'S SONG

Andy stiffened. He was sure that synchronicity was supposed to be a happy thing, so he couldn't imagine why the sound of his own name coming through the receiver made his stomach do a slow roll.

"Speaking."

"Andy? Is that you? You sound…different."

Yeah, well, stand in line, buddy. My ex-wife already told me that.

"Who is this, please?"

"It's your old pilot buddy, Martin Visnaw."

Now there was no question about it. *This* synchronicity definitely disturbed him. He thought again about the plane ride, Ed Hoffer, the note. He had checked out Hoffer's reaction to the Gardener's name. Now he felt a nasty but compulsive urge to see Visnaw face to face and do the same with him.

"What do you want?"

"I've got some information for you."

Andy didn't know what he was going to say until the words spilled out of his mouth: "Frankly, I'm not interested."

"Oh, come on. You're not actually holding a grudge from the other day, are you?"

"Actually? Actually, Mr. Visnaw, yes. Yes, I am."

"But—"

"No, hold on. You take me up in that Revell model airplane of yours and almost kill me. You make lots of tantalizing promises, but then don't tell me a damn thing I can use. Then you leave me stranded miles from town, in the middle of nowhere. And now you want to talk to me again? Let me guess. This time you want to take me out in a boat and push me overboard, is that it?"

There was a long pause. Wishful thinking got the better of him; he actually thought the man had hung up. But then Visnaw spoke again, and suddenly his voice was softer, humbler, apparently apologetic.

"I'm very sorry about that. I'll admit I got carried away. I'll admit my pride sometimes gets out of hand. I don't fly nearly as much as I'd like, and when I do it's usually alone. When I get the chance to go up with someone, it's easy to start showing off. But if you truly thought you were in danger, you're wrong. I've been flying for years. I'm a *good* pilot. You were never in jeopardy. And as for the other things, the way I teased you...well, after my pride, my sense of humor is my biggest enemy. I think you saw some flashes of that the first time we met, out at Oak Hill."

"Get to the point," Andy said, sounding more controlled than he felt.

"The point, yes. The point is, I've thought about you a lot since Monday. Your project excites me, and I feel bad about the way we parted. I ought to be helping you, not turning you into an enemy. But to tell you the truth, Andy, there's really not a lot I could have told you about Bassett the writer. I might be the expert in this backward town, but you...you're right up with me on that score, probably even *ahead* of me. But then that's not why you're here, is it? You're looking for earlier data. You want to know about his childhood, am I right?"

"You are," Andy said softly.

"Of course I am. So I started thinking. I realized I upset you the other day. I was ashamed of it. I asked myself how I could make it up to you. I wondered, do I have any information Andy can use? I was quite sure I did, but it took me some time to find it. It was well buried in my files, and I wasn't able to put it all together until a few hours ago."

Andy closed his eyes. Two images were running through his mind simultaneously, like different movies being shown on a split screen. One was an undeniably attractive picture of Visnaw handing him stacks of paper on which he would find what he needed to organize his clutter of random information and solve the puzzle. In that picture, all the answers suddenly became obvious. Visnaw's tidbits weren't like the Kretchmer journal (or the Bassett journal itself, for that matter), which only tempted and tantalized but then left him more confused than ever. Visnaw's tidbits were clear. Visnaw's tidbits were logical and sensible. Visnaw's tidbits were keys that opened all the right locks.

ALEXANDER'S SONG

The other image wasn't nearly so comforting. It was an image of Wolf Island's precipitous rock wall rising suddenly in the windshield of Visnaw's airplane, getting closer and closer until there was no way—

"Still there, Andy?"

"I'm here."

"You interested in what I have?"

"I...I don't...." He closed his eyes again. "Yes. I guess I am."

"Then jot down these directions to my house. You can come over and have a drink while I lay out what I've got."

"I don't think—"

"You got a pen?"

"Mr. Visnaw, I—"

"Get this down. It's kind of tricky."

Andy's jaw clenched. He didn't like this. Things were moving too fast. A nagging voice was yammering away in the back of his mind, warning him of something, telling him to watch out, be careful, be wary. But when Visnaw began rattling off street names, right turns and left turns, he did as he was ordered and reluctantly searched through the drawers of the living room table for something to write with.

2

WHEN HE WAS back in his room, buried again in his notes, Andy couldn't say what it was that had ultimately made him turn down the invitation. There was no one good answer. Or, more truthfully, there were *too many* good answers—the memory of Visnaw mildly poking fun at him in the cemetery; the more-serious "jokes" on the plane ride; the dark; the ongoing rainstorm; the time, relatively late already and getting later by the minute.

The best answer of all was one he didn't want to admit. It had to do with notes on his door and photographs and coded messages. He might have been willing to risk a trip to Wolf Island, because he had never believed, not really, not truly, that frail old, pale old, limping and shuffling and wheezing old Ed Hoffer could be the Gardener. He had allowed the possibility, he had toyed with the idea, but he had never taken it seriously. He had gone to see the desk. Yes. That goddamned roll-top desk.

But Visnaw...Visnaw was much heartier, stronger, more fit. And it was night, and it was raining, and he couldn't get that picture out of his mind, that bold Kodacolor snapshot of Wolf Island's cliff rushing closer at well over a hundred miles per hour.

In the end, he had agreed to get together with Visnaw the next day, on neutral territory when the sun was high. They were going to meet for breakfast at The Place, that little diner on Houghton Street around the corner from Good Folks Rexall.

Neutral territory, he thought, almost laughing out loud. It had that espionage novel ring to it again, but the sad truth of the matter was that he was turning into a babyish coward. He no more believed Martin Visnaw was the Gardener than he believed it of Ed Hoffer. He might as well say Max was the Gardener, or Coffin of the FBI, or Carrie Ives at the post office, or Jack Seely the snowplow driver, or Ginnie herself. But it was too dark outside and too wet. Too much had been happening. He was spooked. He had turned into a seven-year-old again, irrationally afraid of what might lurk on quiet, rainy streets after the sun went down. That was it. On the bottom line, that was the only true answer.

"Neutral territory," he muttered, the words dropping into the silent bedroom like a protective charm that had lost its power eons ago.

He finally turned back to his work, but he was interrupted again and again, disturbed by imagined sounds, phantom noises, disturbances that weren't there, false tappings on the window, impossible footsteps moving quietly down the hallway outside his room.

He made very little progress on his notes.

ALEXANDER'S SONG

3

WHEN HE HAD finally gotten back to Alexander Bassett's journal late Tuesday night, after his day of questioning by the police, Andy had been startled, angered, almost outraged to find that the crucial pages were missing. Apparently, the same untraceable vandal who had removed earlier sections of the work had done his damage here as well. This time, instead of just a page here or two pages there, a great chunk of nearly thirty sheets had been torn out. The entries covered Bassett's high school graduation in June of 1927 and his train ride in September down to Madison, Wisconsin, where he was going to attend the university. But everything in between those two events was gone, all of July and August vanished. That included, of course, the all-important period around August 10, when Frank Hale and Charlie McCready had been murdered.

The last entry in the book read:

As the woods flash by the windows of my compartment, an endless rushing curtain of gray and green and brown, I can only swallow my tears as I think about all that I have lost, all that I surrendered. Nothing will ever be the same, and now, at the time of greatest hope and optimism for most boys, on the very threshold of my life as a man, I must accept the fact that my world has been irrevocably altered and that a shadow will follow me all the rest of my days.

Certainly tantalizing, but light years away from providing the kind of answers Andy needed.

Now, as the rain continued its relentless fall, he tried to stop jumping at the noises of his imagination long enough to determine who could have removed the journal's missing pages. It was pointless now to think that such a thing could have been done by some thoughtless bookstore clerk or selfish collector. The only person who would do such a thing had to be the journal's author himself.

Apparently, Bassett had written things in there that he was later... what? Too upset to ever read again? Too *embarrassed* to read? It was possible. Who knew what horrible emotions he might have spilled across

209

those pages in the wake of his friends' deaths? Heartfelt sorrow. Bitter anger. Rage at a world or even a God that could have allowed the murders to happen.

But what about the rest of it? What about the month of July, the first days of August? If he was embarrassed or otherwise unsettled by what he'd written after the deaths, what was going on *before?*

"Oh god," Andy said, darting a glance toward the door, where once again he thought he'd heard a noise. "It couldn't...shit...could it?"

He stared for a long time at the gap of missing pages, the ragged remains jutting out from the binding like broken teeth. He plucked at one of the bits and it came away easily, then crumbled in his fingers, done in by its lifespan of more than sixty years.

He didn't like what he was thinking. Realistically, he knew it shouldn't bother him. The man was dead. What possible difference could it make? He was a grown man, after all, and he should have been perfectly capable of dealing with tarnished idols. Only little children were upset when they found out their favorite homerun slugger snorted coke. Only kids like Kevin Caspian grumbled when learning that the leather-and-studs heavy metal star they listened to drank milk and gave money to orphans. He pulled another tatter of paper away from the binding. He dropped the crumbled remnants on the desk and put a hand over his eyes.

If anything, the very possibility that such a scenario might be true should have excited him. With a little more research he might be able to uncover something resembling proof, and that was all he would need—not absolute, legal, beyond-a-reasonable-doubt proof, just the right clues suggesting the right things. And then what? Why, it was obvious. He could forget the series of intellectual, foot-noted, literary articles and instead churn out a blockbuster book. *Murder on the Best Seller Lists. Death Among the Literati.*

But when he looked into his soul and asked himself if the prospect truly stimulated him at all, he felt sickened, weakened, diminished. He didn't want a tarnished idol. He didn't even want to toy with the possibility of one. He didn't want to push the Bassett journal aside and pick up his notebooks. He didn't want to jot down these most recent speculations.

But he did.

4

FROM THE RESEARCH notebooks of Andy Gillespie:

Okay, Mr. Chickenshit, let's deal with this. You want to disprove it? Great! But you can't do anything one way or the other until you deal with it.

Hypothesis: A.B. killed F. Hale and C. McCready.

Sure, that day in the cemetery, Visnaw said they questioned A.B. and cleared him. The old articles Ginnie found said it too. But what does that prove? Would that be the first time the cops had their hands on the right man and let him go? Hardly.

So okay. A.B. killed his best friends. Brutally. Why? Beats me, but obviously something was going on for some time before 8/10/27, at least through the month of July—hence the missing journal pages. Fighting about something? Maybe so. Kind of hard to work backwards with so little to go on, but come to think of it, working forward is harder still. Without the pages, and with all three main characters dead, it's going to be almost impossible to find any kind of cause or starting point.

But let's run with something else a minute. Jens Carlson. Maybe Carlson witnessed murders. Maybe confronted A.B. afterward. Did A.B. kill him too (see Kretchmer journal "Jens Carlson drowned in Green Lake.")? That would explain, sort of, that craziness about A.B. swearing that the ghost of Carlson was following him around New York for years. A guilt thing. A.B. imagines Carlson in Manhattan because he's never forgotten or gotten over what he did to his friends. See, they're all tied together, McCready, Hale, Carlson. He writes Hale and McCready in as the main characters of To Raise Brave Men, like some kind of weird penance thing, a kind of twisted tribute. At the same time he conjures up Carlson's ghost. Hell, it almost makes sense.

But wait. Also see Kretchmer journal for this: Jens Carlson was the bastard son of Halvard Borg. A circle again. Everything keeps coming back to the Haag murder, even though it happened before A.B. was born. How long before? Let's see, it was in 1908, so almost a full year, and nineteen years before the Hale and McCready business.

Thoughts in the boat this afternoon, coming back from W. Island (backed up again by Kretchmer): A.B.'s father kills Royal Haag. It's nasty but makes sense. William Bassett was a powerful mill owner, and stood to suffer a lot if Haag's unionizing attempts went through. Maybe the heat was on. Maybe he was about to be caught. So he picks out a scapegoat, the bum named Halvard Borg. Frames Borg. Kills him. Makes it look like a suicide. But there's a catch. No perfect crimes, right? You bet. Even if it takes a lot of years (nineteen years, for example) the truth always comes out.

Borg had an illegitimate son. The illegitimate son knows the whole story. How? Doesn't matter, at least not now. The illegitimate son decides to clear his dead father's name, or how about this? He decides to use it for his profit. Yeah. So he blackmails the eighteen-year-old A.B.—I'll tell everyone your father killed my old man, etc., etc., blah, blah, blah. William Bassett had been dead a few months at that time, fried in the mill fire, but A.B. loved his father, didn't he? Look at all those journal entries. A.B. thought his father walked with the gods. He would have been pretty damn susceptible to a blackmail attempt. He would have done anything to protect dear old dad's name.

Anything? Like murder? Sure, maybe.

So how do Hale and McCready fit in? Could it be Carlson went to them first? Could it be they were working with Carlson against A.B.? Maybe they weren't such dear friends after all. Maybe they'd had some kind of falling out (something back in that missing month of July, for instance), and they were striking back at A.B. by helping in the blackmail attempt. That way, if he was pressed enough, A.B. would have to remove all three and—

ALEXANDER'S SONG

Christ almighty, this gets darker by the minute!

Questions: None of this fits with the A.B. quotes in Kretchmer's journal. Not even close. Those quotes said William Bassett killed a couple guys (supposedly Haag and Borg). Said the son of one of those men (supposedly Carlson) killed Hale and McCready. Said A.B. himself only killed Carlson, or at least hit him and knocked him into the lake (quote: "Never saw the corpse."). So that kind of throws the whole blackmail thing out the window, doesn't it?

But if A.B. knew who killed his friends, and if knocking Carlson into the lake was a kind of accident (a fight or something), why didn't he tell police? Why did he remove the journal pages? Why did he feel guilty for so many years? Or did he feel guilty?

And more questions: What about all the murders in New York, apparently all A.B.'s close friends? What about the attack on Kretchmer? Unless A.B. really did kill Hale, McCready, and Carlson—unless he was killing all his friends in New York too—unless he attacked Kretchmer—if he didn't do it, who did?

The Gardener. The goddamned Gardener again.

Could it be?

Could the Gardener have been alive back then, stalking A.B.'s friends?

Could the Gardener still be alive today, still going after anyone who gets close to A.B., or A.B.'s memory—people like Ginnie? And me?

Guess that's really stretching things to make that particular connection. Neither journal ever mentioned the Gardener, not by that name, not even in all A.B.'s crazy rambling about death, etc., in the Kretchmer volume.

Confession: As sick as it is, I'd almost rather A.B. was the killer. At least he's dead and gone—more than twenty years dead and gone. The Gardener, on the other hand, appears to still be alive and kicking.

Yeah.

Alive and kicking.

And here in Rock Creek.

5

HE MIGHT HAVE kept going. He wanted to. Despite the fear conjured by those last several lines and the revulsion he admittedly still felt at the whole idea of Bassett being some sort of psychopathic killer, he was getting excited. None of the theories came together, and there remained a disturbing wealth of questions and holes, blank spots and discrepancies, gaps and improbabilities...and yet Andy helplessly felt a tingle at the back of his neck, a stirring deep in his chest.

Gaps and holes, yes, but for the first time he was making connections. Right or wrong, links were being forged.

He paused to light a cigarette and glance yet again at the rain-streaked window. Then, pencil in hand, he looked down at his notes, poised for the stream-of-consciousness flow of ideas to begin anew. He was about to write something—he wasn't exactly sure what—when someone knocked on his door.

He jumped.

"Phone call. Hurry it up. You've tied up the line enough tonight."

It was Max's voice, sounding just as tense and edgy as it had all week, except that now Andy thought he detected other notes there as well. Weariness, perhaps, which would be understandable enough for someone who had slept only a few fitful hours in the last four days. Weariness. And also the first faint traces of defeat and resignation.

"Coming," he said, quickly stubbing out his cigarette.

Max was already nearing the stairs by the time he got out in the hall. He called after her—"Any idea who it is?"—but she kept walking, head down, ignoring him.

"Max, I asked—"

"I'm nobody's goddamned secretary," she snapped without looking back. "Just keep your business short. In case you hadn't noticed, we have an emergency on our hands around here."

"Max, Jesus—" He caught up to her halfway down to the second floor, considered putting a comforting hand on her shoulder, but thought better

ALEXANDER'S SONG

of it. "I'm sorry, Max. I didn't ask these people to call. I know you want to keep your line open, and I know—"

"You don't know anything!"

He pulled away from her, from the sudden fierce fire of her gaze. Did she still blame him for something? For all or part of Ginnie's disappearance? Even after the police had exonerated him? Even after he'd spent all day yesterday searching the Manitou Meadow?

"I want Ginnie back as badly as you do," he said, knowing immediately that it was wrong, shallow, callous. He had known Ginnie only a few days, and even at that had never been quite sure whether he genuinely liked her or only grudgingly admired her.

His own words reminded him of something that had happened at work the year before. One of his fellow teachers, Elaine Reisner, a Spanish instructor, had lost her nine-year-old son in a car accident. Elaine had been out of school for almost three weeks, and on the day she'd returned, everyone in the faculty lounge had crowded around her, offering the usual empty words of sympathy: *I'm so sorry...God works in mysterious ways...a horrible thing, just horrible...if there's ever anything I can do* ....And then, in the middle of that, Howard Tyler from the phys ed department had said, "I know how you feel. Lost my dog to cancer last year," doubtless meaning well, for Howard generally did, but nevertheless shocking the lounge into silence and sending Elaine running from the room, sobbing.

Andy felt his cheeks grow hot, and in the rush of the moment tried to decide if he should apologize to Max or if that would only make things worse. He opened his mouth, but Max snarled at him and cut him off.

"I'm giving you five minutes on the phone. No more."

And with that she was gone, racing ahead of him down the stairs, leaving him behind.

This time he didn't bother trying to catch up.

6

"DON'T TALK, MR. Gillespie. Just listen."

The connection wasn't the best—there was a constant crackling noise coming through the receiver, and beneath that was a low, windy kind of hum—but there was something peculiar about the voice, too. It seemed weak, fragile, and was muffled as if by great distance, or as though whoever it was spoke into the end of a long cotton-wrapped tube.

"Who is this?"

"You're in danger, Mr. Gillespie."

"Visnaw? Is that you? What's wrong with your voice? It sounds like—"

"Listen to me! You're in danger. I don't know what to tell you beyond that. Don't ask how or why, or even what you should do. The only answer I have is to tell you to leave town. If you go…I'm not certain, but if you leave, everything will probably be all right."

"Who the hell is this?"

There was a drawn-out pause, filled with nothing but that awful crackle, that distracting hum. Andy was about to bark out his question again when the muffled voice finally spoke. "I'm a friend. Whatever you might think, whatever else you might want to believe, I mean no harm—not to you or anyone else. You've been asking questions about someone called the Gardener. I'm telling you to stop. The Gardener is dangerous. He'll kill you."

Andy's mouth opened, but all he managed was a perplexed little squeak. Without being aware of it, he had grasped the edge of the phone table; his grip was tight, his knuckles bloodless. With his other hand he had twisted the cord of the receiver into a knotty jumble of wire. He could hear the sound of his heart, a ghost-echo pounding in his ears.

He thought he recognized the voice, although that wasn't exactly it. It wasn't so much the voice itself that seemed familiar. It was far too muffled and cloaked by the noise on the line to be completely recognizable. What rang the bell were the speech patterns, the inflections, the hesitant pauses between words.

ALEXANDER'S SONG

"This man called the Gardener," the voice went on before Andy could speak, "this man murdered Dwight and Lenore Gulliver, and he killed many others, too. Now there's a missing girl. I don't know her name, but I have my suspicions. If it's her, if it's the Turner girl, the one who was working with you…if he took her, then you're most likely next, Mr. Gillespie. It fits his pattern. He'll want you next."

Andy finally forced it out: "Hoffer? Is that you?"

"There's no explaining what the Gardener does, but he works in patterns. Once you've seen them—the patterns, I mean—you'll never mistake them again. You…you're part of the pattern now."

"Goddammit, answer me!" Andy cried. "Is that you, Hoffer? I thought you said you didn't have a phone. Where are you? How do you know about the Gardener?"

Again there was no reply for a very long time. Uneasily, Andy realized that Max was watching him from the kitchen doorway, her ex-husband and the local police chief standing just behind her. He flashed them an embarrassed smile and tried to bring himself under control.

"Hoffer?" he said, so softly now that his voice was just above a whisper. "I know it's you."

The line crackled and hummed. Then, unmuffled at last, Ed Hoffer said, "Yes, it's me."

"Where are you? You told me you had your phone taken out."

"I'm on the mainland."

"But how—"

"By boat. A very difficult journey, late at night, in this weather…and at my age."

Suddenly the whole picture came into focus. The hum and clatter was the sound of wind and rain and waves rolling up on the Green Lake shoreline. The muffled quality to Hoffer's voice had been the old man's poor attempt to disguise his identity. He had covered the receiver with a handkerchief or a towel, perhaps a cap or the sleeve of his jacket. It was ludicrous, maybe even humorous, but Andy was rapidly losing whatever low-level sense of amusement all this continuing spy novel business had initially brought him.

He could see the whole thing: the wide gravel parking lot; the concrete apron where a small mountain range of overturned canoes awaited rental; the long, low, log building with the dirty plate glass window; the Michigan Bell pay phone hung beneath a blue plastic hood on the side.

"You're at Seward's, aren't you?"

"No."

"Yes, you are. I know it. I can hear the lake in the background."

"And so what if I am?" Even without the baffle covering the receiver, Hoffer's voice was soft and distant. "Where I am is irrelevant. It's what I'm trying to tell you—that's what's important."

"I know that. I understand. But this is no way to talk. I've got questions and...okay look, do you have a car there? Or better yet, just wait. I'll come get you. I can be there in twenty minutes."

"No, Mr. Gillespie."

"What?"

"I said no. Don't come out here. It would be a complete waste of time. I'll be long gone before you can even get in your car."

"But I have to talk to you."

"No! Don't you understand? I'm telling you everything I know right now. The Gardener is after you, or if not, he will be soon. You've brought it on yourself. Not that it's your fault. You didn't know. But the reason you're in Rock Creek, it's that very reason that makes the Gardener want you. The missing girl you mentioned...is it who I think it is?"

Andy looked around. The spectators had vanished back into the kitchen. "Yes," he said hoarsely. "Virginia Turner, the one who was with me last weekend."

"Then that proves it. The Gardener will want you next. And he's very dangerous. The best thing you can do, the only chance you've got, is to get out of here now, go home, back to wherever you came from, and forget about your little project."

ALEXANDER'S SONG

"But who is he?" Andy said. There was a note of desperation in his voice; he was helpless to change it. He could tell that Hoffer was getting ready to hang up on him. "Who the hell is the Gardener?"

"I don't know who he is. I don't know why he does what he does. I only know what I'm telling you. You came here looking into the past, reaching for the great beyond. The Gardener doesn't like that."

"I don't understand."

"I can't be any more plain," Hoffer said, and Andy thought he heard him sigh deeply as he did so. "He doesn't like what you're doing."

"You mean my research? Alexander Bassett?"

"He doesn't like people to get too close to Bassett. He never did."

Andy felt the muscles of his chest tighten. "When flowers grow too close to the tree they must be trimmed," he murmured.

"What?"

"The note..." he paused, glancing toward the kitchen again. "The night Ginnie vanished, I found a note on my door. Among other things, that's what it said. 'When flowers grow too close to the tree they must be trimmed.' It also said 'I have her.'"

Andy waited, but the old man didn't say anything.

"Hoffer?"

Nothing.

"Mr. Hoffer? Are you still there? Please, you must see now. You've got to understand why I need to talk to you. You're the only one who might—"

"I have nothing else to say."

"But Christ—"

"Christ has nothing to do with this."

"Mr. Hoffer—"

"Just do what I said."

"But—"

"Don't come to Seward's. Don't come back to my island. Don't try to see me, and don't talk to anyone else about this either. Just leave. Forget about Rock Creek. Forget about Alexander Bassett."

219

Andy was almost ridiculously close to tears. "Please..." he said, as if in prayer.

But the line had gone dead.

He stared at the receiver, hung up a moment later, and allowed his gaze to drift toward the window. He told himself that he wasn't going crazy, that his mind wasn't shattering into a thousand pieces. He might feel that way. He might even be tempted to believe it. But it wasn't true. He wasn't losing his mind. His honest and humble dreams had not led him into this. Ginnie's chance early arrival in Rock Creek had not doomed her. The Gardener was not real. *Nothing* Ed Hoffer had just said was true. And there was not a dark figure moving stealthily out there, just beyond the glass, sneaking through the trees at the edge of the yard.

The non-existent figure stopped and turned its non-existent head toward him. Its non-existent face looked very white in the darkness, a shapeless blob of gleaming lamp light.

Andy swallowed hard.

A non-existent hand floated up and gave him a short, non-existent wave.

Andy shut his eyes hard, squeezing the lids down until they hurt.

When he looked again, the non-existent figure was gone and Max Turner was standing next to him, telling him shortly that she needed to use the phone.

7

HE THOUGHT HE knew what had happened.

The Gardener had snuck into the bed and breakfast while he was busy on the phone and the Turners were occupied with the police. Perhaps he had used the front door, but more likely it had been the back. A quick trip up the rear stairs, all the way to the third floor, down the corridor to Andy's room, another note on the door, and then gone, back into the rainy, windy night with only a pause to give Andy a short, meaningful salute.

He was sure of it.

ALEXANDER'S SONG

But there was no note on his door when he got there. His room was just as he had left it—no note anywhere in there, either. Not on the bed. Not on the dresser. Not on the desk with all his paperwork.

Well, maybe he was losing his mind after all. Either there was no one outside and he had imagined the whole thing, or there had been someone there (a neighborhood kid, an old lady looking for her lost cat, a drunk relieving himself in the bushes) and Andy just assumed it was the Gardener. Either way it wasn't pretty. He supposed he'd had a right to feel a little upset. Hoffer's call had hardly been the most soothing, reassuring conversation of his life. But to create monsters out of shadows, or even worse, to create the shadows themselves ....

He opened the desk drawer and pulled out the envelope he'd tucked in there on Monday night, the one with his last name printed across it in bold block letters. He opened it, extracted the photograph, set that aside without looking at it, and gently unfolded the note.

He began to read.

Immediately his heart froze in his chest. His throat constricted. A single breath forced its way out painfully, whistling, and it seemed as though he could not draw another to replace it. A high, harsh ringing started in the center of his brain and rushed outward, filling his ears, deafening him.

A GARDENER'S JOB IS NEVER DONE

HE CAN PRUNE AND PRUNE YET NEW FLOWERS ALWAYS REPLACE THE OLD GROWING TOO CLOSE TO THE TREE

BUGS TOO

PAUL F. OLSON

BUGS MAKE A GARDENER'S LIFE DIFFICULT

SOMETIMES IT IS FUN TO WATCH THE BUGS SCURRY FOR A WHILE BEFORE KILLING THEM

He looked at the photograph lying on his desk. It too had been replaced. In this picture, an old black and white that had grown brittle around the edges, a single tombstone sat beneath a winter-bare tree. The grave was covered with the remains of many flowers. The legend on the stone was stark, simple, utterly unhelpful:

CALVERT JULES DRUMMOND
1894 – 1943

He turned the photograph over. There was nothing on the back but a few dirt smudges and the faint ring from a water glass someone had set there many years before. He dropped the picture, which fluttered lazily to the floor, and put his hands up to his temples. It didn't stop the ringing.

"Cal Drummond," he said softly, his breath still rasping in his throat. He remembered that name from the Kretchmer journal.

It had been one of many names, many victims—Cal Drummond, Grace Mahler, Henry Oglebay.

He looked at the new note that had magically replaced the old. From there he looked down at the photograph on the floor. He did that for several seconds, glancing from note to photograph, photograph to note, and back again. Then he saw the footprints that he had missed before, impressions left in the carpet by a pair of large boots. The impressions came through the door, crossed the room to the desk, and headed back out again. Not all of them were clear. In places the carpet nap had already sprung back up. In other spots, the prints of his own sneakers had crossed over the boot prints, mostly obliterating them. But he didn't need flawlessly undisturbed tracks to tell him what had happened in here while he was on the phone with Hoffer.

He got out of the chair and knelt on the floor, putting his hand on one of the prints. It was still damp.

He no longer thought that he might be losing his mind. Instead he felt sane to an almost frightening degree, his mind clogged with nightmares but still sharp and clear, functioning perfectly. Too perfectly.

He wanted to throw his head back and scream.

8

"SOMETIMES IT IS fun to watch the bugs scurry for a while before killing them," Norman Paquin read slowly. He was sitting across from Andy at the bed and breakfast's kitchen table, his police chief's hat and rain slicker on the counter behind him. He lit a cigarette and tipped his chair back on two legs. "What do you suppose that means, Mr. Gillespie?"

"I have no idea," Andy said, shaking his head and apologetically spreading his hands. "But surely you can see it's important."

"Well now, maybe." Paquin leaned back even more, until it seemed he was in danger of toppling over. Then, suddenly, he brought the chair forward again with a bang. "Some might say that. But frankly, I've got to tell you I think it's a crock of shit."

"I beg—"

"Look here. You come in here, wasting my time with some bullshit about killing and kidnapping, and when I ask for something…well, you know, something concrete, you hand me this note. You tell me it's important, but it looks to me like a hint from Heloise or something. Flowers, pruning, bugs—what the hell is that? Something off of that *Victory Garden* show on public TV?"

Andy sighed. It brought a strange look from the chief, but he didn't care. He felt as though the world was slowly collapsing around him. He looked toward the window above the sink. The gray morning light looked pathetic, sick. The glass was streaked with rivulets of water, and he wondered if maybe it was going to rain forever in Rock Creek, if the rain was just going to keep falling and falling until the land was flooded and they all washed away into the Quad Lakes.

"Got anything else to say?" Paquin asked.

Andy sighed again. He had hoped the chief would be different, but it was the same old story. Norman Paquin was just Officer Jeff Lamoreaux with a longer job description.

"You've got to believe me," he said.

Paquin scowled. "I don't have to do anything, Mr. Gillespie. Now you tell me: where's this first note? The one that said 'I have her'?"

"I explained that," Andy said, struggling mightily to keep the emotion out of his voice, to keep from crying, to keep from yelling in anger. "It's gone. The Gardener obviously sneaked into my room last night and switched it for this note."

"Uh-huh. And you got that first note when?"

"Monday. Monday night. Or early Tuesday morning, I guess, after midnight."

"Is that so?"

"Yes. Dammit, I told you that."

"So why didn't you come forward then? Care to tell me that? You supposedly had this note that supposedly figures into the Virginia Turner case somehow. Why'd you keep it to yourself all week?"

Andy floundered. "I...I don't...I wasn't sure, or rather I didn't want to..."

"Amazing," Paquin said, shaking his head in disgust. "You're one of those nuts who's got to feel important. We get them every time there's a major case, which isn't too often around here, but all the same we get them. These folks always have to get involved. They've got to stick their fingers in. Sometimes they even confess to things they didn't do. But you're different, Gillespie. You're so messed up, you can't even cook up a decent story. You write a note, wave it under my nose, and can't even back it up with any halfway decent lies."

"They're not lies!"

Paquin waved his hand dismissively. "Save it. Get out of here. And while you're at it, be glad I don't run you in and file charges."

"Charges? You're kidding! Your men questioned me for five hours on Tuesday! You questioned me yourself! There couldn't possibly be any—"

"I'm not talking about those charges. See, here's how I figure it. If you really got this note Monday night and kept it to yourself all week, then what we'd have is obstruction of justice. And if you're just making the notes up, which is what I'd swear on my mother's grave you're doing, then you're wasting my time, keeping me from doing my job, slowing me down. That could be obstruction of justice too, by the way. Or maybe interfering in the course of an official investigation, something like that. Either way, I'm sure the prosecutor could find two or three different things to charge you with, and at the very least we could lock you up for about forty-eight hours, which is what your kind of bullshit deserves."

"But Ed Hoffer told me the Gardener is dangerous. He said my research would make the Gardener want to—"

"Shut up!"

Andy pulled back, eyes wide, hands clenching and unclenching fitfully.

"I'm not listening to you anymore, Gillespie. Don't you get that yet? You're a crackpot. But I did my part. I took down your report. I've got your information, and I know how to contact you if we need to follow up later, which I doubt we will, but you never know. Stranger things have happened, I suppose. In the meantime, I'm finished with you and I've got real work to do."

Andy wanted to say more. He needed to say more. But there just didn't seem to be anything he could say.

The rain rattled the kitchen windows and Andy hung his head in defeat.

9

BUT NOTHING LIKE that actually happened. It was just another one of his vivid and colorful dreams, one that somehow got sandwiched into the two hours of sleep he got that night, just before dawn.

When he opened his eyes he saw that it was not, in fact, raining anymore. The morning was bright, sun-washed, and the air had a clarity that told him the storm front had moved beyond them at last. He thought that should have lifted his spirits a little, but somehow they did not feel lifted at all. If anything they felt lower than ever before.

The dream had told him. The dream had confirmed what he had suspected last night. The dream had proved it.

He could not go to anyone for help.

There was some kind of madman loose in Rock Creek, at the very least a kidnapper, and very possibly something even worse, something darker. The madman might well be after him. Surely the notes indicated as much, and Ed Hoffer's phone call backed it up.

The Gardener was after him. And Andy could not go to the police. He had only Hoffer's black riddles and Martin Visnaw's prankish sense of humor to fall back on. In other words, he had nothing.

He was in trouble.

He was badly frightened.

And he was utterly alone.

EIGHT

OVERLOAD

1

This is easy, or at least it's easier than you thought it would be. You thought it would be tough, leaving with the job half-done, or one-quarter done, or one-tenth done. But it's not hard at all. Amazing what you can do when those...ahem...outside influences push you in the right direction. Just get that suitcase out from under the bed, books and notes on the bottom, shaving kit next, then those last few packs of cigarettes, and top it all off with the clothes. Jesus, it's a piece of cake. A quick breakfast, a stop for gas at the Shell station out near the highway, and you're on your way. Easy as pie. And you do not feel like a shit for running away, do you? Of course not. You're not a piece of shit. You're not a coward. Even someone as tough as Ginnie would be hard-pressed to blame you.

Ginnie.

But Christ, don't think about her. Don't let something that simple keep you from the job at hand. She's beyond help now, certainly beyond any help you could give. Don't think about her. Just move. Move.

2

LATER HE THOUGHT it was almost funny, the way his undoubtedly good intentions were undone by something as pedestrian, as mundane, as stupidly boring as breakfast. He supposed that old saying was right after all. For want of a nail...

There had been no meals served at the bed and breakfast all week. Some mornings Max had put on a pot of coffee and left a plate of doughnuts on the kitchen table, other mornings the guests had been invited to kindly take their breakfasts elsewhere and keep their mouths shut about the inconvenience. Nobody who knew the current situation in the Turner family—and that included, of course, all paying guests—dared to question or complain.

Andy had known all that, of course. In the heady rush of packing to leave, he had simply forgotten.

He settled his bill with Max, who seemed more than happy to be rid of him. He tried to tell himself that she felt that way about all the guests, and had she not needed the money, she would have preferred to shut the bed and breakfast down altogether. But in his rattled state of mind, he couldn't help thinking that the ease with which she dismissed him was directly related to him, an outgrowth of his connection to her daughter, his nosy questions about the Rock Creek Commie, his bothersome phone calls, and maybe a few other side issues—the "coincidence" of the broken living room window, for example.

Don't feel guilty. You haven't done anything wrong. Just get in the truck and drive.

But as he coasted through town, planning to pick up a prefab, plastic-wrapped Danish when he stopped for gas, he remembered his appointment with Martin Visnaw. He faltered, foot coming off the accelerator and angling toward the brake. That voice in the back of his head ordered him to keep going, and it was right, but suddenly there were several other considerations.

First, Visnaw had said he had some new information. Maybe that didn't matter, since he had decided to abandon his project anyway. But it couldn't hurt to at least listen to what the man had discovered.

Second, Andy was a breakfast eater. He had an ungodly long drive ahead of him back to Chicago, and even on lazy, do-nothing days, his body demanded at least a little caloric tribute before it would begin functioning properly.

Third, and perhaps most unavoidable, Andy had been raised to be polite. The fact that he was usually private, almost always coldly dedicated to his own needs and desires, had nothing to do with it. It was a matter of manners. When you made an appointment for breakfast (or dinner, or a game of golf, or whatever), you either kept that appointment or phoned well in advance to cancel it.

And so he decided to postpone his departure from town long enough to stop at The Place on Houghton Street. He didn't have to listen to whatever it was Visnaw wanted to tell him, but he could at least drop by long enough to explain his new lack of interest and have some bacon and eggs in the process.

Undone by breakfast. That's what he realized later. He had been undone by an urge for toast. He wasn't sure why that struck him as especially odd. It was just another strange joke in the long line of strange jokes that had begun with his arrival in Rock Creek.

Although this particular joke, he found out much later still, was perhaps the most dangerous one of all.

3

ALTHOUGH IT WAS almost mid-morning and a weekday to boot, The Place was busy. Or perhaps it only seemed that way, due to the cramped, claustrophobic quarters the restaurant occupied. The customers sat knee to knee, shoulder to shoulder, on stools around a long, narrow, horseshoe-shaped counter. Each place setting was its own little universe, complete with ashtray, menu, napkin dispenser, salt and pepper shakers, bottle of ketchup, and plastic bottle of French's mustard. Inside the horseshoe, the two overworked waitresses bustled back and forth, barely squeezing past each other when they had to, often disappearing through a swinging door at the open end, where evidently they traded order slips for meals in what appeared to be a very tiny kitchen.

Andy paused just inside, slightly stunned by the overpowering aroma of the restaurant, a blend of old grease, new grease, good food and bad, tobacco, the fainter smells of gasoline and sweat that clung to customers' clothes. Next to the door was a bulletin board covered with three-by-five cards that advertised a wide variety of available goods and services (Firewood 4 sale - split and stacked; Babysitting in my home, very reasonable; 1976 Impala, runs good, $250 or will trade for boat and trailer), and next to that was a Rock Creek Voyagers calendar, with the dates of all varsity athletic events printed in red. Andy stared at the calendar for a moment while allowing his eyes to adjust to the bright fluorescent light and the burning pall of smoke, which was thick enough to bother even him, who could smoke up a room with the best of them.

When he turned at last to face the horseshoe, Martin Visnaw wasn't there. He checked his watch. It was nine-twenty. Their meeting had been set for nine. He didn't think twenty minutes was enough to make the man give up on him, but then again, nothing he'd seen from Visnaw yet fit into the realm of perfectly normal behavior.

There was one open seat on the far side, and he worked his way over there, murmuring apologies to those whose backs he bumped while squeezing along between the stools and the wall. The older of the two waitresses showed up almost immediately. Andy found that missing out on the meeting made him more eager than ever to be on the road; much of his appetite had fled.

"Just coffee and toast, please."

"Cinnamon, raisin, white, or wheat?"

"Wheat."

ALEXANDER'S SONG

"You got it." She was back with the coffee in less than thirty seconds. "You're Gillespie, right?"

"Yes, but how—"

"I'm Jean Brackett. I was on the east-side search team the other day."

Andy nodded, remembering her from the general gathering on the town hall steps, one of the volunteers huddling in the doorway to get out of the rain, smoking and drinking coffee, waiting for her assignment.

"That fella from the Trading Post was in here a while ago."

"Martin Visnaw?"

"That's him. Left something for you." She pulled a white envelope from behind the order pad in her apron pocket. "Said he had to run, but he'd be back to you later."

She was gone again before Andy could ask any questions, leaving him to open the envelope and unfold the piece of paper inside. At first he thought it was one of his own photocopied newspaper articles, one of the many Ginnie had found for him at the library on the death of William Bassett or the murders of McCready and Hale. But then he saw that there were two articles on this page, both from the Rock Creek *Record-Journal* dated Wednesday, April 26, 1939, almost twelve years after the others. The reproduction was poor, the chillingly brief story and its sidebar companion next to impossible to read.

LOCAL WOMAN STRUCK BY TRAIN

The body of Miss Grace Annabelle Mahler, age 27, of Rock Creek, was found alongside the Wisconsin and Lake Superior Railroad tracks Tuesday morning. It was discovered in the weeds approximately one-half mile west of the Iron Street crossing by two local youths (see next story). When contacted, Constable Elwood McFarren issued the following statement: "We believe the young lady came to grief sometime late Monday night, when she was hit by either the 11:27 to Ashland, Wisconsin, or by the

11:42 to Duluth. We'd like to find out if she was walking along the tracks when hit, or if she was crossing at Iron Street and got dragged to where we found the body. That's one of those things we'll probably never know. We'll probably also never find out how she missed seeing the train, or why a pretty young unmarried girl like her was out walking alone at that time of night in the first place. It's a tragedy, plain and simple. A real sad case."

Miss Mahler, a 1930 graduate of Marquette High School, had moved to our town two years ago and was employed by the Watt brothers as a secretary in their offices at the Watt and Mellon Timber Corporation. She is mourned by her mother and father, both of Marquette, and an older brother residing in Michigamme.

Andy read the article twice before going on to the sidebar, which didn't illuminate a thing. It was headlined YOUNGSTERS HAPPEN UPON GRUESOME DISCOVERY and told the story of Lester Cressey, 9, and his brother Luke, 7, who had found Grace Mahler's body while walking along the railroad tracks looking for lost coins and old bottles. Nevertheless, Andy read this story twice as well, wondering how all of this fit into the things Visnaw had been saying on their plane ride, that seeming nonsense about Mahler and Bassett and love as one of the enduring themes of literature. If nothing else, it disproved what the man had said about Mahler being murdered, didn't it?

He lit a cigarette, but it smoldered away unsmoked as he read and pondered.

His lover was murdered, Visnaw had said. And Bassett fled the Creek like a dog, just the way he'd fled earlier, after the deaths of his best friends.

There were questions there. How did Visnaw know that Bassett and Mahler were lovers, or that the death had not been accidental? The article hadn't mentioned it; Andy had never seen it mentioned anywhere. But even taking Visnaw at his word, there was a larger issue: What precisely had the man been telling him? What conclusion did he want Andy to draw? That Bassett had fled because the love of his life had died under tragic circumstances? Or...

Or what?

Or, perhaps, that Bassett had killed Grace Mahler and run before anyone learned the truth.

We'll probably also never find out how she missed seeing the train, or why a pretty young unmarried girl like her was out walking alone at that time of night in the first place.

But what if she wasn't walking alone? Andy thought. What if she was out for a moonlight stroll with her lover? And what if she didn't miss seeing the train? What if she saw it perfectly well, right before she was pushed in front of it?

His thoughts tumbled on, freefalling.

Suppose Bassett really had murdered Frank Hale and Charlie McCready. Forget the whys and hows for a moment, just suppose. He kills his friends and within weeks leaves town, hightailing it down to south-central Wisconsin and the university there. Then suppose that twelve years later he shoves Grace Mahler in front of the 11:42 to Duluth and weeks after that leaves town again, this time for the bright lights of Manhattan. Kill and run, kill and run. As Visnaw had suggested, it was a link. An echo. A pattern.

Jean Brackett brought his toast and topped off his coffee, but even the little appetite Andy still had was suddenly dulled, blunted by the pain of a headache that pulsed steadily behind his eyes.

He didn't think that anything had changed. In fact he knew it hadn't. The questions were still unanswerable. It was all well and good to say, suppose Bassett killed his friends, suppose Bassett murdered his own lover. But when you finished with all that supposing, you had to ask why. And then you had to go looking for proof that was either non-existent or, at the very least, extremely well hidden.

And on top of everything, towering over it like a great black cloud that darkens the entire sky, there was the Gardener.

Andy sighed. The headache backed off a notch, then slammed home again even harder than before. He took a bite of his toast and felt it stick in his throat like glass. No, nothing had changed. There were still the questions and the Gardener, the mystery and the danger. Grace Mahler's rather interesting death was not enough to keep him in Rock Creek in the face of all that.

What was enough was something Jean Brackett said when she brought him his check a few minutes later.

"Y'know, I almost forgot. There was someone else in here askin' about you."

Andy looked up, surprised. "Really?"

"Yeah. Not this mornin'. This woulda been...Jesus, it musta been dinner on Wednesday, after we were out searchin'. Yeah. Wednesday. I remember, cause she asked about you, and that day was the first I ever heard of you. Lyle Leveille was on my east-side team that day, and he told me all about you, the way you're from Chicago and been hangin' around askin' about that old writer and all."

Andy nodded impatiently. "This person who was asking—"

"She wanted to know if I knew you, and I said I knew who you were but we weren't friends or nothin'. She asked if I knew where you were stayin'. I said no. Lyle didn't tell me that part, though he probably knew. He knows all the scoops on everyone."

"Excuse me...who was it? Who was looking for me?"

She looked surprised. "Didn't I say that?" She laughed, as though amazed by her own forgetfulness. "It was Marilyn, Marilyn Borg, from over to the hotel."

Andy frowned. "Marilyn Borg?"

"Yeah. She said if I ever saw you, I oughta send you over her way. She said she had some things you might wanna hear."

ALEXANDER'S SONG

4

THE LOBBY OF the Sleep-Tite was exactly as it had been on Andy's first day in town, dark, empty, dusty-looking, filled with the specters of a hundred old smells. This time, though, he didn't have to ring the bell and wait. This time Marilyn Borg was coming out from behind the desk just as he was coming in. She stopped as though surprised by the presence of a burglar, stared at him for several long seconds, coughed, and then broke into a wide grin.

"Well, look what the effing cat dragged in." She issued one of the sharp laughs Andy remembered from their first meeting. "I guess you must've found yourself a cheaper room somewhere. I waited that whole afternoon for you to come back. Just about broke my heart."

"I ended up staying at Turner's," Andy said. "You wanted to talk to me?"

"You must've been visiting the Ptomaine Palace."

"I'm sorry?"

"The Place. Rock Creek's solution to world starvation—poison all the hungry people. You were talking to Jeannie Brackett."

"That's right. She said—"

"Come on in the back and sit down. I just made a fresh pot of coffee. Strong enough to make you grow tits...well, that's for girls. For you, I guess it'd just put some hair on your chest."

Andy wanted to decline. He was supposed to be on the road by now, well beyond the town limits and leaving the Upper Peninsula behind. But he had a sinking feeling that he wasn't going to be leaving, not today anyway. It was late, getting later by the minute, and the prospect of an eight-hour drive back to Illinois was looking less attractive all the time. Even the thought of going as far as Green Bay, or less than that, only to the Wisconsin border...even that was beginning to seem like too much to handle, with his headache throbbing the way it was.

And worse, he had to admit that he was getting caught up again. Grace Mahler, Marilyn Borg...his interest was piqued. Visnaw had said he had no sense of adventure, but that was wrong. He had one, all right. He tried to stifle it, but it kept coming back.

The rooms behind the front desk had been furnished as a small apartment. There was a kitchen, a bedroom, a bathroom, and a room that served as an office of sorts, with a desk and a file cabinet, an ancient Smith-Corona typewriter, and several extra chairs. Marilyn led him past all that to a living room that held an easy chair and a couch. There was a small color TV on a table in the corner. The sound was turned down, but Andy recognized Bob Barker supervising the spinning of the big wheel on *The Price is Right*.

"Plant your ass," the old woman said. She pointed to the couch and disappeared into the kitchen, presumably for some of her tit-growing coffee.

Watching her come back with the mugs, Andy was struck by how apt his original impression had been. She really was a troll. Impossibly tiny. Leathery skin. Beady eyes. And that head full of bristling white hair. There was something about being in her presence, especially here in her living quarters, that put him on alert but relaxed him, too. He thought that here at last was someone who wouldn't pull any punches. He didn't know what she was about to tell him, but he felt sure that it would be the truth.

"I've seen you around," she said, handing him his mug and lowering herself into the easy chair. "That first day...what was that? Three weeks ago? I figured then you were just another effing flake. We get them, you know. Three or four times a summer some asshole pops into the lobby and wants to know about that commie writer. I tell him the same thing I told you. I don't know a goddamned thing about the writer, except that his daddy was richer than God. They go away and I never see them again.

"But you...Jesus, hon, you didn't quit. Every few days I'd see you again, going up and down the effing street, talking to people. Finally, I had to say it. I didn't know what you were, but you sure as hell weren't a flake. You're serious-minded. I like that. And I figured we ought to talk again."

He started to say something, but she held up a wrinkled hand. "I didn't know where you were staying, but I mentioned you to that bitch Brackett.

ALEXANDER'S SONG

Sooner or later everyone in town goes into that dump to eat. I gambled you'd get the message, and I was right. Here you are."

Andy sipped his coffee. She was right. Besides being incredibly hot, it was strong enough to make him grimace and force his eyes wide open.

Marilyn saw his reaction and laughed. "Sorry about that. But when you get to be my age—which is eighty-three, by the way—you need something to keep you going."

Andy nodded and set his mug down warily on the end table next to the couch. "So what did you want to tell me?"

"Oh, just a few things. Could be you already know them. Like I said, you're a hell of a lot more serious-minded than those other commie-fans who waltz through town. If you've been looking as hard as I think you've been, you might know this. How you'd find out is beyond me—it's not like it's written down somewhere—but what do I know? Maybe you guessed the right things. Maybe you asked the right questions. Christ knows there's a few folks left around who were here back then. Sometimes I think this whole effing town is made up of old farts like me. Maybe you found the right one."

"Well, I talked to Albert Anson and Evelyn Van Wyck, the Lammis, a couple of others. Either they didn't want to say much or they didn't have much to say."

"Not surprised," she said, taking what seemed to Andy a fantastically huge swallow of coffee. "It could be I'm the last one left who knows. Shit, for that matter, maybe I'm the only one who *ever* knew."

"Knew what?"

"About Bill Bassett and a man named Halvard Borg."

Andy sat up straight. "You know, I wondered about that. The Borg connection. Was he your grandfather?"

"Grandfather!" This time her laugh wasn't sharp but full of great humor. In contrast to her age and appearance, it was almost a schoolgirl's giggle. "You know how to spread the horseshit, don't you? Grandfather. Christ. Didn't I just tell you I was eighty-three-effing-years-old? Hal Borg was my brother."

237

"Your brother?"

"Older brother, you can give me that much. I was a late one. My mama was close to forty when she spit me out. You have any idea what that means? How old forty was for childbearing back then? Hal was already twenty-eight when I was born. He died when I was two. I guess you could say we weren't especially close as brothers and sisters go."

Andy nodded. "Your brother...he had a son?"

"Ah, you see? You *have* been digging around. He had lots of kids, almost more than I could keep track of. He was awfully goddamned busy for a man who never took a wife."

"His children were illegitimate?"

"I guess that's what I just said, wasn't it? I don't think the old tosspot ever fathered more than one with the same woman. Nor did he take any hand in raising them. A real fuck-em-and-leave-em man, that was Hal. Shit, if I'd ever had a family reunion, I would've been there by my lonesome. And all the while these woods were crawling with my nieces and nephews, or half-nephews, or whatever the hell you'd call them. And if you think that's a laugh, think of this: every last goddamned one of them was older than me! Older than their own aunt!"

"One of his sons was named Carlson, wasn't he? Jens Carlson?"

Marilyn nodded. "You know that much, then I guess you've heard what my brother did. You must've picked up the story, how he killed a man and then took his own life in shame."

"I heard."

"Well then, let's get down to where the cheese binds. You heard it. You probably read it in the town records. I'm betting you also saw it in the paper and in that book, the one that pussy of a professor from downstate churned out a few years back."

"Hal Borg, the Lumber Town Butcher," Andy said softly.

"Yeah, you read it. Goddamn, I knew you'd been digging. But here's the story. My brother Hal was a lot of things—a layabout, a drunk, a thief, a brawler, a gambler, maybe most of all a man with his brain in his cock. He never held a job for more than a week or two at a time. He was never sober for more than ten minutes. He'd rob you blind if you blinked. The way I've heard it, he even managed to steal the first car that came into this town. Belonged to one of those asshole lumber barons, I forget which one. The fool used to drive down the middle of Michigan Street, spooking horses left and right. And Hal stole that car, wrecked it out on King Oak Road. Rock Creek's first case of grand theft auto, though of course they didn't call it that back then, and it was my own older brother who did it. How's that for an effing family history?

"But the thing is, for all of that, for all the shit he was, Hal was no killer. He no more murdered Royal Haag than I did—and just in case you're wondering, you've got to remember I was barely one at the time."

"If he didn't..." Andy said, and paused. He knew what she would say if he asked the question. In a crazy way, it was inevitable. He'd been toying with the same possibility himself less than twenty-four hours ago.

"It's not *if* he didn't. He didn't. I can't be any plainer than that. He was no killer. For all his fighting—and yeah, the man was a hell of a street-and-saloon fighter—he didn't have it in him to kill. He didn't even hunt and trap. He would've starved before he took a life, and he probably came close to doing just that more than a few times. He'd work, take the few pennies he earned, and spend them on booze. He'd beg venison and squirrel and what-not from his drinking buddies, but he wouldn't ever go out and bag a deer himself."

"It was William Bassett, wasn't it?"

Marilyn studied him closely with her tiny, dark eyes. He thought it was an appraising look that held a hint of pride, as though her description of him as serious-minded had just been tested and proven.

"Bill Bassett, the commie's daddy. You're absolutely right. It was Bassett who killed that Royal Haag—and don't ask why; I couldn't tell you. All I know is, he thought he could get away with it. And why not? This town was full of rich men in those days. You lived here then, you were one thing or another. You were either stinking rich or dirt-eating poor. But of all those wealthy bastards, Bill Bassett was the wealthiest of all. He owned two lumber mills here in the Creek. He had an interest in a copper mine up in the Keweenaw and an iron mine or two over near Ishpeming and Negaunee. He had money dripping out of his ears. Money corrupts people even today, am I right? It buys you out of just about any pissy trouble you stumble into. Back then it was even better. Money made you an effing king. I said he was richer than God. It's true. But there's more. A fellow with Bassett's moolah in Rock Creek back in oh-eight wasn't just richer than God. He *was* God."

"So Bassett killed Royal Haag," Andy said. "Probably because Haag was trying to unionize the loggers and millworkers, which would mean money out of Bassett's pocket. Money for higher wages. Money for safety improvements."

"Could be. And he thought he'd get away with it, because the rich sons of bitches in Rock Creek always did. But he didn't figure things right. He didn't know just how popular Haag had gotten in these parts. It wasn't like he'd killed the president, but maybe in some ways it was worse than if he had. Haag was big shit. The workers loved him. They rallied around him. And when he was dead, they turned him into an effing legend."

"He became a martyr."

"That's it!" Marilyn cried, nodding eagerly. "Haag became a martyr. Maybe if Bassett had bumped him off a few years earlier, when he'd first come to town, it would've been different. But he'd allowed too much time for the man to build himself up. Suddenly he was dead and there were meetings. The workers got together in the taverns. They gathered in the streets. Whatever passed for law around here wanted to brush the whole thing off, but pretty soon there were torchlight parades past the town hall, demanding an investigation, demanding an effing murderer so they could string him up in the middle of the street."

Andy nodded. He could imagine the mob scenes perfectly, could almost see the marching throngs, the flaming brands, the symbolic nooses clenched in bloodless fists. He could hear the voices raised in chants of anger.

ALEXANDER'S SONG

Marilyn swallowed some more coffee and went on: "So Bassett got scared. He realized two things. One, they were going to find out that he did the deed, and two, once he was caught, all the money in the world wasn't going to buy his way out of it. So he looked for a scapegoat and he found my brother, a loser, a drunk, a man nobody much liked or cared about, and who had a reputation as a real asshole's asshole, the kind of effing idiot who'd torn up men's faces over something stupid like who paid for the last beer."

"Excuse me? Marilyn? This is all very interesting, it really is. To tell you the truth, I'd thought about some of these same things myself. But you sound so sure of yourself. If you were only one or two when this happened—"

"How could I know it's gospel?"

"Something like that, yes."

"I know because I got it from the horse's mouth."

"But—"

"Hold on, hon, hold on. I'm not talking about my no-account brother. I picked it up...oh, I figure it would have to be fifteen or sixteen years later, from one of Hal's boys, one of those bastard nephews who happened to be about ten years older than his ever-loving auntie."

Andy swallowed. "Jens Carlson?"

Marilyn frowned, regarding him cautiously, suspiciously. "I told you Hal had lots of offspring, didn't I? How would you know I was talking about Jens?"

"Just a guess," Andy said weakly, feeling alternately amazed and heartsick at how perfectly everything came together. Last night it had just been rambling speculation: William Bassett killed Royal Haag and Hal Borg; Hal's son knew the truth; eighteen or nineteen years later he approached William's son with what he knew. Speculation, nothing more. And yet now that speculation was being backed up with solid evidence, proof from the horse's mouth, who claimed to have it from the horse's mouth herself.

He leaned back on the couch and lit a cigarette, not asking for permission to smoke, but Marilyn seemed relieved to see him do it. She produced her own pack of cigarettes, lit one, blew out smoke, and coughed. They stared at each other silently for almost thirty seconds.

"Seems you might know more than I thought," she said at last. "Either that, or you're one hell of a goddamned guess-maker. But anyway, you're right. Jens was his daddy's favorite, his first kid and the only one he ever paid the least bit of attention to. He was born in '97, when Hal was just eighteen, so he was close to twelve years old when this murder shit all blew up—old enough to know things and understand.

"So one day around Christmas of 1908, Jens is sitting with his daddy in his daddy's cabin outside of town. I'm sure his mama, Bessie Carlson, didn't want him going over there as much as he did, but he managed to sneak away from time to time. So there he was. It's cold out, snowing. Hal's drunker than Billy Hell, just like usual, and he's showing Jens how to make little wooden boats by whittling stove lengths, working for a while, tossing back more whiskey, working, tossing, working, tossing, just like that. And pretty soon he's so addle-brained he just starts talking. He tells Jens how he had a visit from the richest man in town. He tells Jens how the richest man offered him a goddamned sled full of money if only Hal would step forward and take the blame for something bad this rich son of a bitch had done.

"'What's that, daddy?' Jens asks.

"'Nothin' you need to know about, boy,' Hal says back to him.

"'But daddy—'

"'You hush. You wanna know, you can pro'bly figger it out for your own self. Think back a month or so. Think back on somethin' awful, awful bad that happened in town. You'll get it.'

"Well, Jens didn't get it, not then. But he listened good while Hal told him about the fight he'd had with this rich man, how Hal said he wouldn't take all the money in the world to confess to what this rich man did. What good would money do him when the street mobs hung him from the town hall flagpole? What good would money do him in hell? Jens listened, and a week later, when his daddy was dead, called a suicide, and everyone in town was talking about the confession note he left behind, he started putting two and two together.

"See, Bill Bassett had a goddamned low opinion of my brother. He knew the man was one step above pond algae in brains and balls and ambition, so he figured he could be bought. But he couldn't. So Bassett still needed his damn scapegoat, and now he had new trouble. It wasn't just him anymore. Now there was someone else floating around who knew the truth, someone he figured was unreliable. So Bassett came back a few days later and killed him, shot him up close, in the temple, and left the confession note there to close the whole damn Royal Haag story once and for all."

"You're sure he wrote—"

"Oh, I'm sure all right. It had to be Bassett. Only Jens knew it; it was another thing Hal had spilled out in a drunken ramble. My brother was illiterate. You understand? He had the writing and reading skills of a dead stump. He couldn't have written that note. He couldn't have written SOS if his ship was sinking."

"Jesus," Andy said.

"Yeah, Jesus. Jesus Effing Christ."

"So Jens knew the truth, once he pieced it all together. Did he ever do anything about it?"

"What, and maybe be killed himself? No, he held the secret inside. Stewed over it the rest of his life, I suppose. And one day about 1925 he shared it with me. Funny thing, that. We were drinking ourselves at the time. My mama had died a few months before and I was living alone for the first time in my life. Once in a while Jens brought over some game he'd trapped or fish he'd caught. I think it was walleye that day, a nice stringer he pulled out of Preston Lake. I offered him a drink, had one myself, though I was still mostly a girl. We talked, and after some time, the story came out."

Andy didn't want to ask the next question, but he knew he had no choice. "What happened to Jens?"

Marilyn didn't answer immediately. She drained her coffee, started a fresh cigarette, and wet her lips with the tip of her tongue. "Not sure," she said then. "His friends said he left late one afternoon to go fishing on Green Lake. Never came back. They found his boat bumping against an old dock all the local men used to use. It was out near Harker's Landing, not far from where Josh Seward has his outfitter's place now. Probably fell overboard. Probably drowned. That's the way it was, and that's the way it still is now. You live off the land, hunting and trapping and fishing, you spend all your time outdoors, every day of every year, and eventually the woods or water'll get you."

"When was that?"

"1927, I think. Summertime. July, August. Yeah. Summertime of '27."

Andy's throat was dry, his stomach was grumbling uneasily, but at least his headache was gone.

"Do you know if Jens ever met the other Bassett? The one I'm interested in? Alexander?"

"The commie?" Marilyn gave one of her trollish shrugs. "Couldn't say. I'm sure he knew who he was. Everyone in a town this size knows everyone else. That's always the way of it. But a woodsman and a smarty-ass rich man's son...I hardly think they would've been friends, if that's what you mean."

"It might have been an interesting meeting," Andy said softly. "If, that is, they ever actually met."

Marilyn gave him another scrutinizing stare. Then her beady eyes lit up and she laughed. "Interesting. Hell yes. I guess it would've been. I guess it would've been damn interesting."

5

ANDY LAY BACK on the bed in his new room on the Sleep-Tite's dingy third floor. He closed his eyes. It was just after two-thirty in the afternoon, but he had only finished his conversation with Marilyn twenty minutes before. Almost four hours of conversation, more than four cups of that toe-curling coffee, and here he was, his good intentions shattered, staying in Rock Creek despite all reason and logic.

ALEXANDER'S SONG

It was difficult to remember with precision everything they had talked about. They had discussed the William Bassett-Halvard Borg story, of course, and the tantalizing possibility that Jens Carlson might have actually met William's son, Alex. Somewhere along the line, Andy had run down a list of names for her, asking for anything she might know about any of them.

Frank Hale and Charlie McCready? She knew about the old murders, of course ("Biggest effing story of the century around here," she said), but nothing more.

Grace Mahler? She drew a blank on that name. When reminded that Mahler was the young woman who had been struck by a train in the thirties, Marilyn frowned and said, "I guess I might remember that. We're no different than anywhere else. We've had a few cars and people run down by trains over the years."

Ed Hoffer? Sure, she told him. Of course she knew that hermit out there on his island. Nice man, from what she could tell, though she'd only spoken to him once in the grocery store, and that had been all of seven or eight years ago.

And finally Andy had taken the plunge. It wasn't something he had consciously planned to do. It was more of an accident, really, a question that flowed naturally out of the current discussion, a path he followed only because he had been feeling more and more relaxed in the company of Marilyn Borg. Her style was straight from the hip, but there was very little malice in her. She dealt from the top of the deck, utterly open, as guileless as anyone Andy had ever met.

"What about the Gardener?" he asked.

Marilyn's expression was blank. "What gardener? You mean that idiot Joe Allenbach from J&B Landscaping?"

"No," Andy said, unable to restrain a small smile. "Or at least I don't think so. The man I'm talking about...well, as far as I know, he's not a *real* gardener. It's what he calls himself, like a nickname or a codename or something. The Gardener."

She shook her head. "I wouldn't know about that. Sounds awful strange to me."

"Strange," Andy agreed. "Yes."

She rose slowly and came over to sit down next to him on the couch. "You're a man with a hell of a lot of questions," she said. "Old murders, old train wrecks, hermits, men with silly names. You trying to tell me that all of that horseshit is what you've been digging for? I thought you were looking into a dead writer."

"So did I. I came here thinking I'd find out what Alexander Bassett was like as a boy, you know, what kind of grades he got in school, what kind of clothes he wore, what sports he played, if he had friends or kept to himself, that kind of thing."

"So?"

"So it's not turning out that way. I'm learning more than I ever thought I would. It's certainly a lot more than I *wanted* to learn. Everything's coming in so fast. At first no one would talk to me at all. They said, 'What do you want to know about a dead commie for?' or 'He hasn't lived here for fifty years, he's ancient history.' But lately I'm getting all these bits and pieces. They keep dropping on me from everywhere. They keep piling up. My brain's having a little trouble holding it all. It's like overload."

"You want to talk about it?"

"I'm not sure."

"Well, shit, hon, you listened to my tale. Least I could do is listen to yours."

"But I'm not sure there even is a tale!" Andy said. His voice had gone up half an octave, becoming plaintive, almost whiny. He didn't care and did nothing to stop it. "I don't even know where to begin, Marilyn. Every name I mentioned to you—Ed Hoffer, Hale and McCready, Mahler, the Gardener—they're all tied somehow to Alex Bassett. There's a link there, and it goes beyond Rock Creek to something that followed Bassett the rest of his life, all the years in New York right up to the end, when he died

ALEXANDER'S SONG

in '69. And it goes backwards, too. It goes back to your nephew, Carlson, and to your brother, and to William Bassett. Whatever happened to Alex started when his father killed Royal Haag. I just don't know what it is, or why it happened, or how."

Marilyn didn't respond. She was looking away from him, eyes on the television, where someone's soap opera tragedies were spinning out in silence. She lit a cigarette and drew on it slowly, holding the smoke in for a very long time before letting it out.

Andy could guess what she was thinking. She was thinking he was crazy, which was probably fairly close to the mark. Right at the moment, he *felt* crazy. He had said too much, and now she was doubtless cursing her decision to talk to him. Serious-minded? she was thinking. The man's an effing loon!

"You need comfort," she said after another minute had gone by, startling him not only by speaking but by what she said. "I wish it was mine to give, but it's not."

"Marilyn—"

"No, hon, hear me out. All I can tell you is this: you've got to be right. It's got to be whatever you called it—linked, connected, tied together. If I've learned anything in the last eighty-three years, that's it. Everything's connected. Everything's all knotted up together. No matter how much you want it to, the past doesn't go away. Jesus Christ, it just won't.

"I don't really understand what you're looking for. You tell me my brother and his kid, who died a coon's age ago, are connected to some commie writer who died in '69. I don't get it. I'm not sure I *want* to get it. But I believe you. You want me to put your mind at rest, I can't do that. But I can help you, maybe. I'll do that, if I can. You just tell me how, just say the word."

Andy leaned forward and put his head in his hands. "I don't think anyone can help me, Marilyn."

"Well, you go back to Turner's and think about it. Give me a call if you hit on something I can do. We'll talk again later."

"Turner's," Andy said, suddenly remembering his decision to leave. He looked at his watch. It was close to two. "Oh, shit. I'm not staying at Turner's anymore. When I stopped in at The Place this morning, I was on my way out of town."

"But you can't do that."

"I can't?"

"No! Jesus, why do you think I wanted to talk to you?"

"I don't—"

"I want your help. Hell, I thought that was plain as day. I'll help you if I can. I said that and I meant it. But I want your help, too."

"I don't know what you mean."

She sighed. "I guess you're not as serious-minded as I thought. No, no, don't give me that look, I didn't mean it. Maybe I didn't make myself as clear as I wanted, but that crap with Bill Bassett and my brother...that's been weighing on my heart for years. After Jens drowned, or whatever in God's name happened to him, I was the only one who knew, and I kept the secret the way he did, carrying it around for years. But shit, hon, I'm tired of it. I want to clear my soul before I die. I want the truth to come out."

"You want to go public?"

"Of course! But only with proof. A lot of babble from a wrinkled old broad like me wouldn't mean anything to anyone. They'd think I'd gone over the edge—senility, that Alzheimer's, whatever. I want some absolute proof that Bassett murdered Haag and killed my brother."

"Proof?" Andy repeated, as though the word were foreign. "I doubt there is any proof. Nothing that could still be uncovered today."

"Maybe not, but if it's there, you could find it. You *are* serious-minded. I knew that when I saw you trotting around town, asking your questions. That's why I came to you. To make a trade-off. I give you information on your commie-writer's daddy, you help me find proof that my brother was innocent."

"Oh, I don't know. It seems—"

"I'm not fooling myself," Marilyn said. "I know there isn't a soul left in this town who really cares. Me. Just me. I'm the last effing one. If we found something, I'll lay a hundred dollars we couldn't even get that pissant newspaper to print the story. But maybe we could find enough to at least call up that pussy professor and cram his 'Lumber Town Butcher' bullshit down his throat. That would be more than enough for me. Since that book came out, dragging my family name through the mud, dredging up shit that'd been buried for Christ knows how many years…ever since then, I've wanted to do it. But I'm too old and probably too stupid to do it by myself. With your help? Who knows?"

"You're not stupid," he said, meaning it.

"Flattery again. You're a goddamned master."

"But, Marilyn, I don't even have a place to stay. I checked out of Turner's hours ago, and with her daughter missing, Max wouldn't exactly appreciate the trouble of checking me back in."

"Then you'll stay here."

"I couldn't."

"If it's still the rates bothering you, forget it. You'll stay free, a guest of the house. In return for finding the proof, of course."

"And if it turns out there's no proof to find?"

"You just do your best. You try, and I'll be satisfied."

Andy sighed. "I don't know."

"Christ Almighty, hon, you're digging this ground yourself. What in the hell have you got to lose? You can clear Hal's name and find that connection you've been looking for all in one stroke!"

He thought about it. She was right, of course. No matter which way he looked at it, starting from the present and working back to the Royal Haag murder, or beginning with Haag and advancing, the result would be the same. And it would really just mean spending more time in the areas he'd already covered, retracing his steps, following and refollowing the same lines until, with any luck at all, something would finally become clear. Perhaps he wouldn't be able to establish the necessary links. Perhaps Marilyn would never see her brother's name made blameless. But perhaps… perhaps he could…perhaps she would.

"There's one more thing you ought to know," he said. "It doesn't make any more sense than the other things I've been talking about, but it's important enough that you should hear it. Once you do, you might not want me staying here."

"I doubt it would come to that," she said. "But go ahead, shoot."

He took in a deep breath and held it, as though trying to gather the emotional strength to continue. His stomach was still bubbling away, churning with acid, and his thoughts were all across the board, scattered across the landscape of the past in every possible direction. Maybe he shouldn't have brought it up. But it was too late now. She was waiting for him to go on, waiting to hear it, and damn it, he knew that he owed it to her. She talked about help, both of them giving and receiving it. What help could either of them be to each other if they didn't start from square one, if she wasn't made aware of the truth, the risks involved?

At last he released the breath he was holding, pushed back the fearful uncertainty as best he could, and told her.

Now, as he lay on the bed with his eyes closed, he decided that she'd taken it well, certainly better than he'd had any reason to hope. If she had doubted the truth of what he'd told her about the Gardener, she had done a damn good job of keeping it to herself.

"Who would've thought?" she'd said softly when he was through laying out the story of the notes, the photographs, and Ed Hoffer's strange warnings over the telephone. "You go back in time so many years and find out you've got your hand in a goddamned snake's nest. Seems to me those effing snakes should've been dead long ago."

"I'm going to have to talk to Hoffer again," Andy said. "Whether he wants to or not, I've got to see him one more time. But if what he said was true, that the Gardener goes after people interested in Bassett, then I'm in danger. That's the real reason I was leaving town today. The mystery was part of it, you know, the fact that every direction I turned was just a dead end, lots of tidbits and no proof in sight. That was part of it. But I was running from the Gardener, too."

ALEXANDER'S SONG

"And you figure he'll follow you here."

Andy shrugged. "It's a small town. It won't take him long to find out I'm not at the bed and breakfast anymore."

"And you don't want to go to the police boys, I suppose. No, don't answer that. It's a dumb question. Paquin and his gang have all the smarts of those potted plants out in the lobby."

"So I've gathered," Andy said, and briefly told her about his two encounters with Jeff Lamoreaux.

"Gunshots, too. Jesus Christ. Well, there's nothing to be done about it, I guess. You can either run or stick it out and find the truth. If you've got the balls to go with that serious mind of yours, if you want to stay around and dig some more, then I'm with you."

"Even if the Gardener follows me here? Into your hotel?"

Marilyn laughed. "Hon, by the time you get to be my age, you'll find out that it takes a hell of a lot more than some sissy flower-pruner to throw a scare into you."

Andy thought that was an exaggeration, a kind of bold bluff. It was hard to say just what Marilyn's little troll eyes were telling him, but he thought he saw a trace of fear there. Fear or anxiety. It was a look he recognized from his own recent glimpses into the mirror.

"Let's get you checked in," she'd said then. "No need to put anything in the guest book, not when you're staying free. But you go out and fetch in your things. I'll get you a key. We'll put you up on the third floor and dare old Mr. Gardener to pay you a visit."

So that was it, Andy thought now. Just that morning he had thought he was alone, had been sure that there was no one who could possibly help him, that he had nowhere to go but south. And then he had been undone by breakfast, or to be more exact and more honest, undone by breakfast and a meeting with an incredible old woman.

In the span of just a few hours, things had changed. He was no longer completely alone. He was back in the thick of things. He had almost escaped, and yet found himself once more lost in the second world, the world of buried truths, standing in a tiny open space surrounded by a wall of mystery. There were a few chunks missing from the wall. Some of the chunks he'd slowly chipped away by research. Some had fallen on their own. Marilyn had taken out a few herself, with the eighty-year-old story she had spun for him. But the wall was essentially as tall and strong as it had always been, the second world still large and forbidding and very poorly lit.

He thought about what he had admitted to himself yesterday and had said again to Marilyn, how everything came back to William Bassett and Royal Haag, how it jumped from there to Halvard Borg, from Borg to Jens Carlson, and from Carlson to Hale and McCready. Alex Bassett. Grace Mahler. The Gardener. The victims in New York. Jackson Kretchmer. The Gullivers. Ginnie.

And me? he wondered. But he already knew the answer to that.

He sat up. He felt horrible, his body running on empty after only an hour or two of restless sleep, some of The Place's dry toast, and lots of strong, strong coffee. But there was no sense putting anything off. There was too much to be done, perhaps now more than ever, now that he had an ally. He had to find Visnaw and ask the meaning of the Grace Mahler article. He had to figure out a way to get to Hoffer, and after that find a way to get some answers from the old man. He had a call to make, too, something he'd promised to Jo on the phone last night. He had trouble remembering precisely what it was.

"Fishbein," he said aloud, the name and the promise coming back to him.

He got up and rummaged in his suitcase for the book dealer's business card. Then he went to the phone, punched the button for an outside line, and dialed. As the connection was made and the phone began to ring in distant Manhattan, he tried to brace himself to hear whatever it was the man wanted to tell him. More bits and pieces, no doubt. More questions raised. More mystery. More overload.

"Fishbein's Treasure's," a thickly-accented voice answered.

"Yes, hello. My name's Andy Gillespie. I'm calling from Michigan, trying to reach a Mervyn Fishbein."

The second world closed in on him again.

6

HE DREAMED AGAIN that night. Nothing new there. What was new, or at least a little bit different, was that this dream was not sharp and vivid, stark and clear. He had been getting used to the idea of dreams that were such an incredible approximation of life that they seemed like life itself—life with a few impossible twists, yes, but life all the same. This time, however, his slumbering mind conjured a rushing phantasmagoria of disjointed, impossible images.

He dreamed he was walking down a long, dark stairway that led to an underground library crammed with books. The stairway and the library were a part of the cabin on Wolf Island. The cabin was owned by Ginnie Turner. His ex-wife had rented him the boat he used to get to the island, and halfway across the lake he passed Martin Visnaw, sitting in a rubber raft and attending to four or five fishing rods.

"Hey-hey there!" Visnaw called to him in the voice of the book dealer, Mervyn Fishbein.

"What are you doing out here?" Andy shouted back, but before the words were completely out of his mouth, Visnaw and the raft were gone.

He reached the island. He talked to Ginnie. They spoke about cars and horses and basketball, and then she showed him to the stairway, leaving him there to negotiate the long way down by himself. When he reached the bottom of the steps and entered the library, he found himself surrounded by the people with whom he had searched the Manitou Meadow—Jack Seely, Carrie Ives, Betty Rhodes from the police force. They were each reading paperback copies of *To Raise Brave Men*, the books held open in one hand, their other hands holding aloft pruning shears, such as a gardener might use to trim hedges.

Andy spoke to them—he couldn't recall precisely what he said, or even if he spoke in English—but they kept on reading, ignoring him. The long blades of their shears caught the glow of the green-shaded lamp in the corner of the room, making them gleam like lanterns. Andy spoke again, muttering something very much like gibberish, and then walked toward the nearest bookshelf for his own copy of Alexander Bassett's fourth novel. He pulled out a book. It was small, black, its title stamped in gold on the cover: *The Annals of the Dupin Society*. He dropped the book quickly, as though it were a hot coal, and picked up another. *The Annals of the Dupin Society*. He picked up a third, and a fourth, and a fifth. *The Annals of the Dupin Society* every time.

"That's the way it is in small towns like this," he heard Marilyn Borg say behind him. But when he spun around, startled, it was Ed Hoffer standing there, finishing the statement. "People around here are always getting hit by trains."

There was a set of shears in Hoffer's hands, and as Andy watched they began to change, the blades melting down into the handle, darkening, turning black.

Black.

Hoffer was holding a black book.

Except that it wasn't Hoffer anymore. It was Martin Visnaw again. And then it was Ginnie. And then it was the ghost of Frank Hale standing beside another wraithlike figure, a pretty young woman wearing a name badge that said HI! MY NAME IS GRACE MAHLER!

Then it was Marilyn Borg.

Then it was Joanne.

And every one of them was holding the same small black book.

The Annals of the Dupin Society.

That was when Andy woke up.

7

DESPITE THE DREAM, he felt better that Saturday morning than he had felt in quite a while. For the first time that week he thought that his agenda was clear, that he could at least begin the day operating with a plan, which was a far cry from the dazed and foggy instinct under which he'd been operating lately. Go here, go there. Why? Seems like a good idea, that's why. But maybe not. Maybe...no, don't think about it too much. Just do it. It's better than doing nothing.

The night before, he had shared a few beers with Marilyn in the lounge off the Sleep-Tite's lobby. Andy remembered thinking on his first day in town that the bar in a place called the Sleep-Tite would have an equally ridiculous name—the Drink-A-Lot, perhaps. It turned out to be a bit more subtle than that. It was called the Angler's Rest, and it was decorated with huge deer racks and dusty mounted walleye and muskie. An old black-and-white aerial shot of the Quad Lakes and surrounding woods had been blown up to fill one entire wall.

"You do a good business here," Andy said when they entered.

Marilyn explained that she only rented the space to the Jeffersons, a brother and sister team in their mid-fifties, who ran the lounge independently of the hotel.

"Well, whatever. Somebody does a good business," he said, looking around at what was a very dark and noisy place, busy on that Friday night with loggers and truckers and other assorted workmen drinking away substantial portions of their paychecks to the tunes of George Strait and Reba McEntire on the jukebox.

Over the course of the evening, Andy told Marilyn about his phone call to the bookseller in New York and about his tentative plans for the next day. Marilyn listened carefully, nodded thoughtfully, and said that she agreed with his agenda.

"Just remember, I'm here to help," she said. "You got questions, problems, anything like that, just come to me. I told you I'm old and stupid, but I've probably got a few tricks left in me. You need me, I'll see what I can do."

Andy appreciated the confidence she showed in his ideas and the renewal of her offer for support. Looking out his window at Michigan Street lying silent and empty in the early morning light, he knew that it was that very support that made him feel relatively good about his day's plans.

A phone call to Florida.

A visit to the Trading Post.

If time permitted, another visit to Ed Hoffer.

He dropped the window drapes back in place and headed for the shower, thinking, planning. If someone had actually been sitting in that single car parked at the curb across the street, if someone had actually been gazing up at him as he gazed down, Andy hadn't seen it. And if he had seen it, he surely didn't want to admit it.

A busy day stretched ahead of him, and the last thing he wanted was to start feeling afraid all over again.

NINE

SWALLOWED WHOLE

1

It took Visnaw five minutes to find what he was looking for in the back room of his store. He finally located it behind a towering stack of cartons and wheeled it out into the open. It was a small chalkboard on a rolling stand, not the kind of chalkboard you'd find in a school room or used by a teacher in a lecture hall, but the kind a child might use while *playing* school. Written on it in old ghostly letters was the message ALL MOCCASINS 30% OFF NOW THROUGH OCTOBER 15, and the old man erased those words with a paper towel before taking a brittle piece of chalk from the tray and printing the name ALEXANDER BASSETT at the top of the board.

Andy leaned in the doorway and waited. He had already been in the Trading Post for an hour, and as usual was losing patience with Visnaw's idea of a joke, the old man's evasive, roundabout way of going from Point A to Point B via the rest of the alphabet. In fact, he had begun to wonder if Visnaw had ever reached a Point B at any time in his life. At least, Andy thought, he'd had what seemed a reasonable explanation for missing their breakfast appointment the day before. If it was another joke, at least it didn't *sound* like one, and it was offered with a somber, genuine apology.

"Business," Visnaw had said by way of explaining. "Can you believe that? Except for June, July, and August, being open here is just a formality. I could just as well shutter the place up and winter in Acapulco. And don't think that idea hasn't crossed my mind once or twice. But yesterday, when I was on my way to meet you, I ran into someone special. He's a fellow from Indiana, comes here for a long vacation weekend every year about this time. He's some kind of special ed tutor, and he always buys sweatshirts and souvenirs by the boxload to take to the kids back home. I give him a twenty-percent courtesy discount, and he still manages to spend three or four hundred dollars. I wanted to see you for breakfast, but around here in the off-season, well, you just don't turn your back on that kind of business. I darted into The Place, left those articles with Jean, and hot-footed it back here to open the store as fast as I could."

Mollified, Andy had asked for Visnaw's interpretation of Grace Mahler's death.

"That was really something, wasn't it?" the old man said with a smile. "A young woman comes here from Marquette, gets what was a pretty decent job for those days, takes a young, bright, ambitious lover, has everything in the palm of her hand, and then boom! It all ends under the wheels of a westbound freight."

"That's the second time you've mentioned that," Andy said, "that Bassett and Grace Mahler were lovers. How do you know? It didn't mention that anywhere in the article."

"Patience, patience. I've got some questions for you."

"I wish I could say that surprises me," Andy said with a sigh.

Visnaw chuckled. "When we went flying on Monday, you mentioned that you were waiting for a package from New York. Did it arrive?"

"Yes."

"Bassett's boyhood journal?"

"Yes, and another book. A journal kept by Jack Kretchmer."

"Jack Kretchmer?" Visnaw's eyes were wide. "You mean *Jackson Kretchmer? The attorney?"

ALEXANDER'S SONG

Andy nodded. "Bassett's friend and business manager, at least until 1954."

"My god, what a find! And it's perfect. What I need to know is this: in either of those diaries, did you find anything out of the ordinary? Any evidence that Bassett's life might not be all that it seemed?"

"I might have," Andy said, knowing full well what Visnaw was getting at, but trying to play the old man's dance-around-the-truth game for himself. "I'm not exactly sure what you mean."

Visnaw said, "Anything at all. Any connection to, let's say…violence? Any traces of assaults or murders? Something like that cropping up in Bassett's life?"

For just a moment Andy didn't speak. He was remembering his fears of two nights ago—both of them—the fear that perhaps Alexander Bassett had been a killer, and his other fear, that this man he was talking to now might be the Gardener. Both those ideas seemed suddenly absurd. They had been night thoughts, rain thoughts, easily pushed aside in the light of a bright and sunny morning.

Visnaw's open, grinning face could no more belong to the Gardener than Andy's own. And as for Bassett, he wasn't sure, but he thought he'd come full circle on that possibility, from his initial revulsion with the idea, through his growing excitement that it might be so, and back to revulsion. It had to be faced, he admitted, but he was desperately hoping it could be disproved.

"Actually, there was," he said slowly. "Nothing in Bassett's own journal, but Kretchmer's had some names. It mentioned several people who'd been killed over the years, and a couple of physical attacks. It was all very sketchy and strange, though—hard to understand."

Which had brought them around to where they were now, Andy in the doorway, Visnaw printing the writer's name on top of a child's chalkboard.

"I really don't have time for this," Andy said, glancing at his watch in despair. In some respects it was true. His first three attempts to call Florida had ended with busy signals, and Wolf Island was still waiting. In another respect, however, he knew that he was once again trying to avoid thinking about those dark possibilities.

"No time for new ideas?"

Andy shrugged. "No time for goose-chases."

Visnaw ignored him. "You mentioned names in Kretchmer's journal. You don't happen to have it with you, I suppose."

"Afraid not."

"Well, we'll have to go from memory." He turned back to the board and began a list below the author's name.

WILLIAM BASSETT
FRANK HALE
CHARLIE McCREADY
GRACE MAHLER

"Now it's your turn. Give me the names you can remember."

Andy thought back. "Henry Oglebay," he said. The old man wrote it down. Andy closed his eyes. "Calvert Drummond." Visnaw added Drummond to the list. "I think that was it, but then there were the attacks. One was an actor named Jerome Wandry, stage name Mark Langdon. Bassett had some kind of fight with him, actually put him in the hospital. And Kretchmer himself. He was assaulted by someone in '54, left for dead on the sidewalk. He never saw who did it."

Visnaw completed the list. "That's all?"

"Jesus, isn't that enough?"

"I suppose it is." Visnaw laughed. "I'm not much on official definitions, but I'd say we have enough victims here to call Bassett a bona fide serial killer. It's not much by Ted Bundy standards, but it's pretty impressive all the same. The man was awfully damn good, no denying it."

"I wish you'd stop doing that," Andy said with a shudder.

"Doing what?"

"Making a joke out of everything. It's disgusting. Even if what you're suggesting is true—and all right, I'll admit the same thing's crossed my mind—it's not funny."

ALEXANDER'S SONG

"Mildly amusing, perhaps?"

"Whatever it is, I'm not laughing."

"Ah, no sense of adventure and no sense of humor either. You're a very poor sport, Andy."

"I won't argue with you. I guess I am a poor sport when it comes to something like this. You don't have any proof for what you're saying. There's no documentation at all, unless you've found something that I haven't been able to lay my hands on. Kretchmer's book mentioned names. He even mentioned that he was afraid Bassett might have been the killer. But the key word is afraid. Not certain. He was never anywhere close to being certain. Aside from the attack on the actor, which apparently happened in broad daylight in front of witnesses, there's no proof that Bassett ever laid a hand on anyone."

"All investigations have to begin somewhere," Visnaw said, and laughed yet again. "It's scientific. Begin with a hypothesis, then set about proving or disproving—"

"Oh, come on. William Bassett? Are you seriously saying that Alex murdered his own father?"

"I'm saying it's a possibility. You're familiar with how William Bassett died?"

"Sure, it was a fire. They said—"

"They said there was a kerosene leak and a careless match. At least I think that was it. I'm taxing my memory, after all, going back to some old newspaper story that's been lost in my files for years. But whatever the case, it was a violent death, and I'm quite sure it was in the spring of 1927, just a few months before the next violent deaths."

"Hale and McCready."

Visnaw grinned. "Exactly! I'm merely suggesting that in the spring of that year, our friend Alex might have stepped off some kind of emotional deep end, taking a jump into violence that continued periodically throughout the rest of his life, or at any rate, through whatever period was covered in your Jackson Kretchmer journal."

"And what makes you think he killed Hale and McCready?" Andy asked softly, dreading the response.

"Well, it's nothing concrete, nothing that would satisfy your demand for certainty. But the three of them were good friends."

This time it was Andy who laughed harshly. "To me that sounds like proof that he *didn't* do it."

"Then you're hopelessly naive." The words were sharp but the tone was still gentle, playful, almost teasing. "After all, aren't the worst arguments usually among friends? Don't you see the most anger and hatred between lifelong acquaintances who have fallen out? Between lovers? Between husbands and wives? Friends and family hurt one another, Andy; strangers rarely do."

"I still don't think—"

"Andy, listen to me. All of this is what I was trying to suggest to you in the plane the other day. I'll be the first to admit my style is roundabout, but my points are valid. They're supported by the evidence."

"I disagree," Andy said, still afraid to admit the full extent to which he'd thought the same things. "People don't just kill their best friends."

"And I say they do. I say it happens all the time—either intentionally or accidentally, by acts of brutality or omission, through hatred or cowardice."

"Still..." Andy began uncertainly, confused by exactly what the man was saying.

Visnaw went on: "I know the trail is dim after all these years, but from what I've been able to gather, Bassett, McCready, and Hale were virtually inseparable. I think I told you that the first day we met, out at Oak Hill. The three of them had founded some club together. I always forget the name. The Douglas Society, the Dublin Society, it was along those lines."

Andy gasped.

"What is it?" Visnaw said, leaving the chalkboard and coming over. "Andy? Are you all right? What's wrong?"

"The Dublin Society," Andy croaked, and then, although his mouth continued to open and close, said no more. All that came out was a choppy rush of air.

ALEXANDER'S SONG

Visnaw leaned in close to him, concerned, but Andy only picked up scattered bits and pieces of what the man was saying—*are you...what...didn't...look pale...need anything...glass of water?*—as his mind roared off on its own, racing, tumbling.

The Dublin Society. Of course. *That* was why the legend on the trunk in Hoffer's cabin had seemed familiar. *That* was why he thought he'd heard the name before. It had been Visnaw who had brought it up, as they'd stood side by side in front of Charlie McCready's grave. Of course he hadn't known it was Visnaw then, and the man's sense of humor had been, as always, a touch on the sadistic side, but he had said it, he had mentioned the name: *They had some club—the Dublin Society? Something like that.* Obviously, Andy had stored that away, only to be partially recalled as he looked at the locked wooden box with a picture of Edgar Allan Poe on top and the words ANNALS OF THE DUPIN SOCIETY carved into the front.

He wondered what to make of it. Ed Hoffer, the self-proclaimed bucolic homesteader, professed to know nothing about Alexander Bassett, save for the fact that the man was a pretty good poet. Yet he had owned a photograph of Bassett and two of Bassett's best friends, and apparently he also owned a box that had something to do with a club the three had founded. Did he know that's what the locked trunk contained? It seemed impossible he wouldn't. But then why had he spun that yarn about his father's secret society at Yale? And how, in God's name, had he gotten the trunk in the first place?

"Andy, you better lie down. I'll call over to the clinic and have Doctor Pentland —"

"The Dupin Society," Andy said, voice barely a whisper.

"What?"

"It wasn't the Dublin Society. It wasn't that at all. It was Dupin, as in Poe's Dupin, the detective. The Dupin Society."

"Yes? So?"

"So...nothing." The name didn't matter. Andy knew that. But the thought of that trunk hiding under the roll-top desk in Hoffer's cabin made him more eager than ever to be away from the Trading Post. He wanted to escape from Visnaw's circuitous babble and these new accusations (accusations that were running through his own mind most of the time, anyway) of Bassett's guilt.

"I don't think we're getting anywhere," he said, slowly choosing his words, trying to bring the meeting to a close. "I'm still not sure if you're telling me Bassett was absolutely a murderer, or if you're merely suggesting possibilities."

Visnaw stroked his chin, as though doing a broad parody of a thoughtful scholar. "I'm offering new ways to look at things," he said. "They're things I've discovered and had to come to grips with over the years, and now I'm offering them to you. I think there's a good case to be made for the fact that this writer we both so admire was less a man than he seemed, that he wasn't what he presented himself to be in his work, and that he might have been more than a little bit...well, crazy."

"So basically, you think he killed all those people," Andy said, pointing at the list on the chalkboard. "Alexander Bassett. Nobody else."

"Killed or was otherwise responsible for their deaths—yes. But who knows? If you have another suspect, I'd love to hear it."

"Someone called the Gardener, perhaps?"

Visnaw blinked, but that was all. If Andy was waiting for the same stunned expression he'd gotten from Ed Hoffer (and frankly that's exactly what he was waiting for) he was disappointed.

"I don't know anyone by that name," the old man said. "I'm not even sure what you're talking about. Do you mean a gardener who worked for the Bassetts? One of William Bassett's employees?"

"I wish I knew," Andy said. "I really wish I knew."

Ten minutes later he had left the store, no closer to truth or enlightenment than when he'd gone in. He hadn't mentioned the Gardener's notes and photographs, or Ed Hoffer's warnings on the telephone. Marilyn Borg was one thing. Martin Visnaw was quite another. He also hadn't confessed his own fears of Bassett's guilt, beyond his earlier statement that a few of the same ideas had crossed his mind. He wasn't sure why he'd kept them to himself, but he supposed he didn't want to give Visnaw the satisfaction of knowing they shared the same suspicions.

He didn't like Martin Visnaw. He was sure of that now. The phone call on Thursday night, the sharing of the Grace Mahler article, and their meeting this morning—none of those things had much altered his original impressions of the man, the ones he'd formed while flying high above Rock Creek and Green Lake. He was almost positive Visnaw was harmless, but neither would there be any help from him. Put simply, he was just a Bassett fan, a collector, someone who wanted to know much more than he did and hid his lack of knowledge behind a constant stream of jokes, innuendo, and banter.

Yet one nagging question remained: how close was the man to hitting on the truth? How accurate were his theories? Had Bassett murdered his own father before, as Visnaw had called it, stepping off the deep end?

There was a pay phone on the wall outside Good Folks Rexall; he made that his next stop. There were obviously a few deep ends of one sort or another in Bassett's life, and far away from northern Michigan he hoped to find the bottom of one of them.

He pulled his calling card out of his wallet and dialed.

Florida again.

And this time he prayed he wouldn't get a busy signal.

2

TALKING TO MERVYN Fishbein the night before had been difficult at best. The man's heavy New York accent had been a part of the problem. His habit of racing through what he said, rushing his words, as though in a desperate hurry to finish each sentence, was an even bigger part. Yet the things he had said and the importance of his news had left Andy flushed with excitement.

"As I told your lovely wife yesterday," Fishbein had said without preamble, "I'm not entirely sure what aspect of Bassett's life you're interested in."

For some reason, Andy felt the need to explain that Jo was his *ex*-wife, but Fishbein hurried on, not giving him a chance to say it. "Are your interests strictly literary, I wonder? If they're personal, how personal? Were you as intrigued as I by that fine Jackson Kretchmer item? Or have you not even had a chance to read it, perhaps?"

"I read it," Andy managed to squeeze in. "And yes, I guess you could say I was intrigued."

"Good, good, we're in agreement. A fine item, a very fine item indeed. How could you not be fascinated? Breathes there the man, with soul so dead, who never to himself hath said, a little mystery and mayhem really makes my day!" He laughed, pleased with himself. "Yes, I quote Walter Scott. I quote anyone who serves my purposes—or misquote them, as you noticed."

He went on to say that he'd had the Kretchmer journal in his shop for several years. He had read it eagerly when he'd first acquired it during a Long Island estate sale, studied it and thought about it at length. But in time he'd forgotten it, until he had pried it from the dusty stacks for Andy's "wife."

"It all came back to me then. Incredible business. Imagine it! One of the twentieth century greats snarled in a web of violence. Almost as though Hemingway were suddenly found to have kidnapped the Lindbergh baby, or to have known for certain who did. Of course Hemingway and Lindbergh had higher profiles than Alexander Bassett, Cal Drummond, Jack Kretchmer, and the rest, but I suspect the principle's the same." He took one of his few brief pauses. "That Cal Drummond. You know who he was?"

Andy thought about the Gardener's photograph and sighed. Kretchmer's journal had mentioned "poor Calvert Drummond" and called him "the editor," but beyond that he knew nothing and had to confess his ignorance.

"Ah, I'm not surprised. You're too young, or at least the sound of your voice and the face of your wife says that you are. Drummond was one of those men who shines brightly while alive, so brightly you're sure he'll live forever. And then he's gone, and you're shocked, and time goes by, and you mourn, and the years mount up, and pretty soon you're hard pressed to even put a face to the name, or to remember the list of accomplishments. But he

ALEXANDER'S SONG

was a great man, Mr. Gillespie. A wonderful man. For ten years, the editor of *American Fiction Weekly*. A literary star—that was Cal Drummond."

Now there was a name that Andy knew. *American Fiction Weekly* had been, from the beginning of the depression up until the late 1950s, one of the top outlets available for outstanding writing. During an era when fiction magazines flourished on the newsstands, when the discriminating reader could have his choice of literally hundreds, perhaps even thousands of publications, when you could find anything from trashy war and romance pulps to the works of all the best American writers on a weekly basis…during that time, *AFW* had developed a reputation for publishing the greatest of the greats. Somewhere in his collection, Andy had several yellowed copies of the magazine containing Bassett stories, and he was ashamed of himself for not remembering Drummond's name from the masthead.

"Bassett and Drummond were dear friends," Fishbein said. "But why should that surprise us? It sometimes seemed as though anyone who was anyone eventually became a dear friend of Cal Drummond. You thought Kretchmer rubbed elbows with the elite? Drummond put Kretchmer to shame. He was the kind of editor who took chances on unknown writers, who helped build careers, and who stayed with you no matter what happened—whether you reached the top or crashed back down to the bottom.

"He published some of Bassett's earliest work, the stories that weren't going to *The American Mercury* or *Harper's* or *Blue Ribbon*. As Bassett began to rise, Drummond was right there with him. I think someone once called them a new literary triumvirate. I mean Bassett, Drummond, and Kretchmer. Parties, openings, readings, early demonstrations against the war. They were there, the three of them, inseparable."

"And Drummond was murdered?" Andy asked.

"Oh, yes, most certainly so. Tortured and killed. Found in his summer home in the Hamptons, although as I recall it was early winter when it happened. As I'm sure you learned from Kretchmer's records, it was really just the first of many strange things surrounding Mr. Bassett."

Not quite the first, Andy thought. First there was Hale and McCready, Jens Carlson, Grace Mahler. God only knows who else. His throat was dry when he spoke. "You don't suppose he—"

"Oh, Mr. Gillespie, I suppose nothing. It's not my business to suppose. If Mr. Bassett had a dark life, I ask you, what is that to me? Should I worry? Should I not simply be happy that he left behind so many great works to be read and enjoyed? I can't afford to suppose, not in this line of work. Every great artist is surrounded by clouds and shadows. If I started supposing about those things, poof! All my enjoyment would flutter out the window."

"But you said you wanted to talk to me—"

"Oh, I did. I most assuredly did. But not about Cal Drummond. That's your business. Always assuming that you choose to explore it, of course. If not, that is also your business. There was something, however, one particular thing in Kretchmer's journal that fascinated me. I was helplessly intrigued, all caught up despite myself. Do you by any chance know to what I refer? Can you guess, I wonder?"

"I don't think so," Andy said. "I mean, there was so much."

"Oh, there was, there was. But the thing I'm referring to was Bassett's disappearance. How strange. Exceedingly bizarre. In a book full of things that could only be called unusual, I believe that was the most unusual of all. I tried to put it out of my mind, but couldn't. I was amazed, frankly, that I'd never heard of it before. Of course, the man's career was on the decline by then. By the mid-fifties he was a fading star at best, but still…imagine Faulkner disappearing for the last decade of his life. Imagine Steinbeck hiding away, using some kind of friendly agent to cover his tracks and take care of all his dealings with publishers and the like. That's what it was, you know. Bassett simply vanished, and though he published his last two novels and poetry collection, though he lived almost another fifteen years, no one knew where he was, or what name he lived under, or how to get in touch with him. No one, that is, except one man."

ALEXANDER'S SONG

"Are you telling me you know who that man was?" Andy asked. His heart was pounding. A vein in his neck pulsed. The palms of his hands were cool and moist.

Fishbein told him.

His interest in the matter had led him to contact a friend of his ("Who shall remain nameless," Fishbein said). The friend was a used book dealer in Philadelphia, a twentieth century first-edition specialist with a side interest in the men behind the writers, the business managers and editors who helped establish and maintain careers. Men like Maxwell Perkins. Men like Calvert Drummond. Men Like Jackson Kretchmer.

Fishbein was quite sure that this friend would have in his collection some more of Kretchmer's journals, and as it turned out, he was right. In particular, he had Kretchmer's *last* journal, the one he had kept from August through October of 1960, when he had finally lost his long battle with lung cancer. The friend did some checking, read a few excerpts to Fishbein over the phone, faxed some more from Philly to New York, and supplied the information Fishbein had been wondering about.

The record of those last months had read like a medical textbook. Kretchmer wrote of almost nothing but the endless stream of doctors parading through his life, the tests, the operations, the struggle, the pain. Occasionally, though, he lapsed into memories of his rich and vibrant past. And twice in the final three weeks of his life he wrote about his great obsession.

Although loathe to admit it to any but his very closest associates, he had never given up the search for his lost friend, Alexander Bassett. The trail had been cold from the very start, and after a year or so had gone by the tracks were positively frigid, but still Kretchmer tried. He leaned on any publisher who had ever had a dealing with Bassett (though of course the publishers were as baffled as he was). He exploited his connections in high political circles, tugging the chains of city and state officials, who in turn tugged the chains of police commissioners and district attorneys. He went through an army of private investigators, sometimes hiring and discarding them at the rate of two or three a month. He called in every last old debt gained through a lifetime spent in the world of the arts—all to no avail.

As the cancer ravaged his body and his life began its final ebb, he was still searching. And finally, on October 11 of that year, an answer arrived.

"It came from one of the detectives," Fishbein said. "As I understand it, it wasn't the man he currently had on the payroll, but one of the old ones. The fellow didn't take well to the way he'd been dismissed, so he kept working the case on his own, determined to crack it and carry the answer back to throw in Kretchmer's face."

"And that's what he did?"

"Apparently so, yes indeed. He came to Kretchmer in the hospital and laid it all out. Not Bassett's whereabouts or what name he was living under, not even the details of how he'd been able to stay hidden so long, publishing novels while not even his editors knew where he was. Still, Mr. Gillespie, the detective's information was almost as good as all that. He had the name of the man who had engineered the whole thing, who set up the getaway and helped Bassett establish his new identity, who became Bassett's public front. Do you see? He had the name of the man who invented the whole strange secret and kept that secret so long and well.

"Kretchmer was ecstatic. He wrote in his journal that night. I've seen a fax of the entry. The handwriting is nothing short of pathetic. Can you imagine it, I wonder? You've seen the man's hand when he was at his physical peak. This is the polar opposite. The letters sprawl across the page. They're weak and shaky and faint, simply tragic to look at. But his words were filled with hope and optimism for the first time since he'd entered the final stages of his illness. He knew the name of the secret-keeper. He was convinced he could move from that to actually finding his old crony. He wrote of seeing Alexander again, hugging him, even having him in attendance at the passing. He wrote that he would die with his friend holding his hand. Understand me, please. I don't say he merely hoped for these things. He was completely convinced they would come to pass.

"They didn't, of course. That journal entry was his last. Sometime in the next thirty-six hours, he lapsed into a coma. He was dead within a week."

Andy felt a tightness gathering in his throat and tried to swallow it. He could feel the utter tragedy of the situation, although he wasn't sure why it should strike him so hard. It was just one more mind-boggling bit of horror from Bassett's life. And anyway, what did it matter? Even if found, would the writer have agreed to visit his old friend's deathbed? Almost certainly not. That would have been worse still, for Kretchmer to locate Bassett and be blocked, rejected, shut out again in his last hours on earth.

"You have the name?" he asked hoarsely.

"Oh yes, I have the name. I have quite a few details about this secret-keeper. I know where he lived, what he did to earn money, who his wife was. Kretchmer put it all down at length. But before I tell you, you should understand that I went looking for this information for my own benefit. I wanted to satisfy my nagging curiosity about Bassett's vanishing act. My friends and family tell me I'm a nice man, and probably I am, but it's not my habit to engage in outside investigations for my customers. I sell them fine items at fair prices, and that's usually enough. But as soon as I heard this part, I couldn't help thinking of you. Your wife had told me she'd be stopping back into the shop, and I waited for her. I was eager to see her again, so that I could get in touch with you and pass this along. Given your location, I thought you'd be especially interested in hearing it."

"I'm sorry, I don't know what you mean."

"Well, you see, the first day she was here, the day I showed her the Bassett journal, she mentioned where you were and what you were doing. She said you were in Michigan."

"And?"

"And so is this man. Or at least he was thirty years ago. Right there where you are now. Rock Creek, Michigan. That is where you're calling from, isn't it? You're still there in Rock Creek?"

"Yes," Andy said. His voice seemed to rocket away from him, growing smaller and farther away, dwindling, disappearing. "Rock Creek. That's where I am."

"Well then, you'd better get a pen and write this down. I'll give you everything I have."

And a few moments later, Mervyn Fishbein did just that.

3

IT WASN'T THAT the woman Andy finally reached in Florida denied being Elizabeth Rappala. It was just that she couldn't believe somebody actually wanted to speak with her. You must be looking for some other Rappala, she told him several times; this part of the country's chock-full of retired north-country Finns.

"You're the same Liz Rappala who was the librarian in Rock Creek until last winter?" Andy asked.

"Yes. That's me, all right."

"And your husband is an attorney?"

"Was. Earl passed away in 1973."

"I'm sorry. But he was a lawyer?"

"Yes, sir."

"Then you're the woman I'm looking for."

"I can't imagine why," she said sadly. Her voice was aged but relatively strong. She sounded fit enough, although everything she said was underlaid with the gravel-like rasp of a heavy smoker. "I suppose I'm flattered. At my age, it's seldom anyone even acknowledges you're alive. What can I do for you, Mr...?"

"Gillespie. Andy. I'm calling from Rock Creek. I've just got a few questions. I promise you it won't take long."

"A pity. My son's on the golf course for the day and his wife is out for another seven- or eight-martini lunch with some club friends. I'm all by my lonesome here until at least three o' clock. You can make this last as long as you'd like."

ALEXANDER'S SONG

Andy laughed dutifully and asked his first question: "Is it true you and your husband knew Alexander Bassett?"

"Why, yes." There was a note of surprise in her voice, but pleasant surprise. "Yes, we knew him quite well. Earl grew up just a few doors away from the Bassetts. When he was ten or so, he used to do errands for Willa. Trips to the market, bringing in her winter firewood, odd jobs like that."

"Willa. That was Alexander's mother?"

"That's right. She passed away in…oh, it must have been '31 or '32. Poor thing. She'd been ill for a long time. In her weakened state, the fall wasn't much of a shock."

Andy stiffened. "Fall?"

"Yes. She fell down her cellar stairs. Apparently, she'd been trying to make her way down there for a jar of preserves. Willa was famous in the Creek for her canning. As long as anyone could remember, that's all she did. She was a virtual hermitess—a sad woman with few friends. Never laughed, seldom smiled. But my, was she a wonder in the kitchen. She was a good enough baker, I suppose, but it was pickling and canning that she was truly known for. Her tables at the church bazaars always sold out first. She won every ribbon at every fair. There were enough preserves in her cellar to feed Hannibal's elephants. So, naturally, that was everyone's best guess, that she started down for a jar of peaches or jam, got dizzy, stumbled, and fell."

"Oh," Andy said, and wondered why he hadn't thought to investigate Bassett's mother earlier. A sour taste flooded his mouth, but he tried to ignore it as he jotted down a few lines in his notebook: *Willa Bassett, dead when A.B. was in early twenties, few years after Hale and McC. Good God…again?!?!*

He searched his mind for an appropriate question and finally found one: "So I take it your husband knew Alexander through his work for Mrs. Bassett?"

"We were all acquainted," Liz Rappala said. "My goodness, we lived practically next door to each other. That's how Earl and I met. We were childhood sweethearts, grew up together on the same road outside of town.

PAUL F. OLSON

Alex used to play catch with us sometimes, even though he was a good five or six years older. A delightful boy, he was. Polite. Exceedingly kind. He never treated us as a nuisance. He made us feel important."

Andy nodded to himself and made another note. With the basics established, he didn't see how he could avoid leaping ahead to the vital topic. "Is it correct that your husband did some work for Alexander?"

"I'm not sure what you mean," she said slowly, and for the first time he detected a note of hesitation in her voice. "I mentioned that he ran errands for Willa—"

"No, no, I mean later. After Alexander was a writer. After your husband became an attorney. He did some work for Bassett, didn't he? Important work?"

There was a very long pause. The phone line hissed. Behind him on Michigan Street an empty log truck rolled by, chains rattling.

Finally, Liz Rappala spoke: "That would have been difficult, Mr. Gilstead."

"Gillespie."

"I beg your pardon?"

"My name is Andy Gillespie."

"I...oh...oh, yes, of course."

Andy sighed. He couldn't say for sure, but he thought she knew perfectly well what his name was. A moment ago she had been sharp and quick. Now, it was almost as if she had slipped into a mode called Little-Old-Absent-Minded-Widow-Lady, her own version of Ed Hoffer's bucolic homesteader routine. It was understandable. If he was on the right track here, if Fishbein's information was correct, this would be the kind of thing she had dreaded for years, being confronted with the long-buried secret, having to face that which she and her husband had so artfully concealed.

"As I said, Mr. Gillespie, was it? It would have been quite difficult for my husband to do any work for Alex. Earl and I moved back to Rock Creek after college, and Alex lived on the east coast. A lot of miles between Michigan and New York."

"True," Andy said, "but the kind of work I'm talking about…for that kind of work, it wouldn't matter how far apart they were. Actually, the more miles, the better."

"Mr. Gilliam, I still don't have the slightest idea what you're—"

"It's Gillespie. Andy Gillespie. And I think you do. I think you know exactly what I'm talking about. I've heard from a very good source that your husband is the man who helped Alexander Bassett disappear in the fifties. Earl Rappala was more than a lawyer, wasn't he? He did some low-level work for the OSS during the war. He knew a few things about constructing new identities, starting new lives. And what he didn't know, he could've found out."

"Oh, really now. Please—"

"No, hear me out. Just listen to me. Then if you want to hang up without answering, I guess there's nothing I could do to stop you. I could call you back and you could hang up again. You'd win. Your secret would be safe. But let me at least say what I think."

"No."

"Yes! What difference can it make? Your husband's dead. Alexander Bassett's dead. You've retired and moved away from your lifelong home. Who could possibly be hurt if I discovered the truth?"

She said something very softly, just a few words that Andy at first took to be *We're afraid now*, although he realized later that day that what she'd actually said was *We made a vow*. By that time, though, it didn't matter. By that time he knew.

"I don't even know who you are," she said next. "You could be anyone, any young fool, calling me up this way."

"I'm not," he said quickly. "I'm a school teacher, a writer. I'm working on a series of articles about—"

"Save your breath, please. It doesn't matter. Yes, the man you're interested in took a new identity in the fifties. He disappeared, as you called it. I don't know why. I'm not even sure Earl knew the whole story. An old friend asked a favor and Earl complied. There was an implication of danger, I recall that much. There was mention of lives being at stake. All very theatrical, but also very real. At least that was the way I read things at the time. Our promise of secrecy was of the utmost importance, we were told, and I can only assume that it's as vital now as it was thirty-five years ago."

"But if you were protecting Bassett and Bassett is dead—"

"Dead, alive, I don't care. A promise is a promise, after all. Now, if you've been nosing around Rock Creek for any length of time, I'm sure you've heard that I was the resident expert on Bassett's work. For years I often thought I was the only one in that town keeping the man's name from vanishing completely. Oh, there were a few others, of course, but I was the real keeper of the flame. If you'd like to discuss Bassett's treatment of female characters, or the theme of redemption in *The Biggest Angel*, that's wonderful. I've told you I'm alone today, I'm always eager to discuss literature, and I could chew your ear off. But the subject of Earl is closed. And the subject of disappearances was never open."

Andy swallowed. "The name," he said.

There was more silence on the line. He could barely make out the tobacco-roughened whisper of her breath.

"The name," he repeated. "That's all. What name did Bassett use when he disappeared?"

"Would that help you so much? Would knowing the answer to that so drastically improve your books or essays or whatever they are? Are you so selfish that you need to know, even at the risk of harming someone?"

"There's nobody left to be harmed," Andy said, but he realized that he was speaking to a dead line. Liz Rappala had hung up.

For a moment his mind was an utter blank, and then he felt a wave of self-pity. It was a feeling he'd come to know well during that first long week in town, when one by one everybody had refused to talk to him. It had been lost in the scary blur of events since Ginnie's disappearance, but now it was back, showing its face again, grinning its ugly grin. *I need to know these things!* he thought violently. *Goddammit, why doesn't anyone understand that?*

ALEXANDER'S SONG

A small, frustrated groan escaped from the back of his throat. He put the receiver down and turned to look at Michigan Street, the handful of cars and pickups, the Saturday shoppers heading into the grocery store one and two at a time. Did any of them know the answers he was looking for? Someone among them might, he supposed. It didn't seem likely, but... but the Gardener knew, and the Gardener was undoubtedly here in Rock Creek. Was he over there right now? That man with the three grocery bags climbing into his car? Or that one, the one struggling through the automatic doors with his shopping cart?

"Hey, man, you gonna stand there all day, or what?"

Andy jumped, spun to his left, and came face to face with someone he at first took to be his student, Kevin Caspian. He saw a teenage boy with greasy hair to his shoulders, wearing an open parka, sweatshirt, and jeans. A diamond stud glittered in his earlobe. His hands were shoved deep into his pockets.

Andy said, "Kevin? What the hell are you doing way up here?" Or at least he *almost* said it, thinking it but catching himself in time when he realized it wasn't Kevin at all but just some local kid.

"Car's busted," the kid said. "Gotta use the horn to call my old man."

Andy nodded. "Okay, sure. Sorry." He took one step away from the phone, hesitated, took another step, faltered, and then retreated quickly to the mail dropbox in front of the drugstore, leaning against it for support.

That last idea—that the Gardener could be here right now, only a few feet away—had just slammed into him with the force of a heart attack. It was so simple, so horrible, and somehow he had avoided confronting it until now. What had he been thinking? For godsakes, what? That the Gardener was just a shadow, some kind of mythical thing that only came out at night to leave notes on doors? That he vanished again until the time had come to make the next contact?

The Gardener was a man...or a woman...a real person...a living, breathing human being. And he or she could come up beside him at any time he or she wanted. He could sneak up as easily as the teenager had, coming up behind Andy to say "Boo!" or to—

"You okay, man?" It was the teenager again, at his side without so much as a footstep's notice. "You look kind of fried."

"Fine," Andy said, the word husky and thick on his lips. "I'm...fine."

He pushed away from the mailbox, like a swimmer leaving the wall, and stepped into the street.

"You gotta watch out for that bad stuff!" the teenager called after him. "Get it laced and it'll kill you, man!"

Andy ignored him and took another step. A horn honked. He stumbled backwards as a pickup roared by just a few feet in front of him. Brakes squealed. He heard the driver curse, saw an extended middle finger. Then the engine roared again as the truck sped away, turning the corner and vanishing.

Was that him? he thought crazily. Jesus, was that the Gardener?

There was a yelp of rubber somewhere behind him, but when he turned to look he saw nothing out of the ordinary. There was a car pulling away from the opposite curb, perhaps fifty or sixty yards behind, but nothing closer than that, surely nothing as threatening as another careless pickup driver. He sighed and put his head down and continued across the street, toward the sidewalk.

He tried to get some of his equilibrium back, tried not to think about the prospect of the Gardener being close by. Surely there was safety in numbers, and this Saturday street scene, while a laugh by the standards of a larger city, was relatively congested for Rock Creek. If the Gardener was planning an attack, he would wait for some place quieter, some place lonelier. Besides, like it or not, the Gardener had been nearby all along. The fact that Andy had not thought about it in exactly those terms didn't mean a thing. He had been here. If he had wanted to attack, there had been plenty of opportunities. It didn't—

A panicky voice cried out, sounding small and very far away. Louder and closer was the sudden roar that filled Andy's ears, the dark, flashing movement he saw in his periphery. He froze, but not until he had turned to face the oncoming car head on, until he had seen its broad, primer-streaked hood, its mud-clotted grill, its whirling black-blur tires, its dirty windshield.

It was the car he had noticed leaving the curb, now coming across the street on the diagonal, heading for the other curb, the other side of the street. It was moving fast already, gathering speed, and Andy was directly in its path.

Something struck him on the back of his neck.

He lurched forward and fell to his knees.

Pain arrowed up his thighs to his hips. His breath was knocked from his lungs.

The car was still coming, looming over him like a beast. The tires looked huge. The gap narrowed.

Andy waited for the horn to blare, for the driver to cry out or issue some other kind of warning. He waited for the sound of the brakes locking up the wheels, tires burning on asphalt.

But no warning came. And the car never slowed.

4

HE SHOULDN'T HAVE expected anything else, he realized later. When a car went shooting across the street from one curb to the other at close to forty miles an hour, the chances were good that it was a deliberate, considered action, and that slowing down or attempting to stop were not part of the driver's game plan.

It was one of those situations Andy had read about and seen in movies, but unlike the people in those dramas he had no moment of epiphany, no sudden acknowledgement of his impending death, no roller coaster review of his life and all its sins. He simply didn't have time for any of those things. The entire episode lasted less than two seconds, and Andy spent those seconds in a spiraling whirlwind of images and sound, everything a blur of color, a cacophony.

The thing that had struck the back of his neck hit him again in that heartbeat of time before he was crushed beneath the tires of the car. This time it found the collar of his jacket, the purchase it had been seeking, and it pulled hard, yanking him off his knees and dragging him back to safety.

The car flashed past, all darkness and dirt, bumped up onto the curb, and tipped to one side. It went up on two tires and simultaneously turned, narrowly skidding past the street sign and the corner light pole before thumping back down and zooming back into the street, accelerating and disappearing.

Andy watched it go with a kind of dreamy disbelief before turning to look up into the face of his rescuer. He recognized the earring first, then the hair and the rest of the features. It was the teenager who'd rousted him from the pay phone and who had warned him to use only the purest forms of dope.

"Jesus Christ, man, that was close!" The teenager turned to the crowd that was gathering. "Anyone get the tag number on that fucking lunatic? Anyone see who it was?"

"You..." Andy swallowed and felt a sharp pain in his throat. "You followed me?"

"Yeah." The teenager was pale, breathless. "You were wobbly, y'know? You looked like you were about to take a header. Jesus. I can't believe that guy! You see his face? You recognize the car? Anything like that?"

Andy shook his head and rose shakily to his feet. "You?"

"Uh-uh. But I'll tell you one thing. He had to be drunk out of his mind. He pulled away from the sidewalk over there and came straight at you. Jesus! I've never seen anything like that! He got up speed like a bullet. Un-fucking-believable!"

"Unbelievable," Andy echoed, while one track of his mind took in the excited, worried faces pressed around him and the other track thought back to Max's broken window and the slug Jeff Lamoreaux had dug out of the living room bookshelf.

ALEXANDER'S SONG

It took several minutes to detach himself from the center of the crowd. There were questions and expressions of concern. An elderly man, pointing to Andy's torn jeans and bloody knees, suggested taking him to the clinic on Iron Street. There was talk by more than a few people of trying to follow the wayward car, or in lieu of that, at least reporting the incident to Norman Paquin. This last idea was quickly vetoed. Since nobody had gotten a license number and no one had recognized the dirt-splattered vehicle (*strategically* dirt-splattered, Andy thought), there was basically nothing to report.

Finally, to Andy's relief, the gawkers departed and he was left alone with his young savior. He turned to the boy and stuck out his hand. "You saved my life, you know."

"Aw, I doubt it, man." Despite the modesty, the boy grinned and blushed. "I figure he would of stopped before he got to you. I just didn't want to take any chances."

"Well…thanks."

"No sweat." The boy's grin faded into a frown of concern. "You sure you're okay? You were kind of shaky there for a while, you know, right before it happened."

I'm even shakier now, Andy almost said, but he kept that to himself and lied instead. "I'm all right. I guess it was that breakfast I had."

"You mean, it must have been something you ate."

Andy nodded. They stared at each other for a moment. Then they broke out laughing.

When he was alone again, Andy looked up and down the length of Michigan Street, half-expecting to see the big dirty car waiting up at the next corner, engine idling, biding its time until he dared to cross again.

He's here. He's real. He wants you.

He started walking in the direction of the hotel, his aching knees forcing him into a slow limp. The image of the shattered window was still with him, but it no longer looked out on Max Turner's back yard, grass, trees, and the house next door. This time there was a street out there beyond the broken glass, and he saw huge tires chewing up the pavement, a dirty windshield growing closer and closer.

He could only assume that the gunshot incident had been a deliberate miss, a game of some kind. But what about today? Was the teenager right? Would the car have stopped or swerved in time?

Sometimes it is fun to watch the bugs scurry for a while before killing them.

He wondered if the Gardener had already grown tired of watching, and he wondered if there would be another note waiting for him when he got back to his room.

There wasn't. No note. But there was a new white envelope taped to his door, and as soon as he opened it he knew that the Gardener had been in touch.

5

IT WAS ANOTHER photograph, another faded black and white snapshot, another grave in another graveyard, sheltered by the shade of another tree, surrounded by other stones and the memorials of flowers both old and new.

CONSTANCE EUGENIA WARREN
BORN MARCH 11, 1925
DIED JANUARY 1, 1955

There is no death. What seems so is transition.
This life of mortal breath
Is but a suburb of the life elysian,
Whose portal we call death.

ALEXANDER'S SONG

6

HE STOOD THERE for a long time, looking out the window, the photograph clenched in the fingers of his right hand, his left hand gripping the window sill. Every time he tried to move, his knees threatened to buckle. Every time he removed his hand from the sill, he began to shake uncontrollably.

He was thinking about cars and bullets, serial killers, broken glass, suspicions, and lawyers who helped old friends disappear without a trace. But more than any of those things, he was toying with an absurd image. Absurd but stubborn; it refused to go away.

The time was the future. Three years from now? Five years? It didn't really matter. It was the future, and a young, ambitious scholar had come to Rock Creek, looking for information about his favorite writer. At first things went well enough. Oh, few people remembered Alexander Bassett and fewer still would talk about him, but those were trivial problems compared to what happened when the dedicated scholar finally began to uncover those first few bits of information.

There was a gunshot. There was a racing engine and a blur of tires. One of the young man's friends disappeared into the night. And then the first note arrived, heavy with insinuation. With it was a photograph, a picture of a lonely graveyard and a single stone nestled close on the side of a grassy hill.

ANDREW RICHARD GILLESPIE

He was a good bug

Who scurried with the best of them

Absurd. But oh so stubborn.

The image was finally chased away by movement on the street directly below him. When he looked straight down he could see a car with a dirty windshield pulling into the space in front of the hotel's main entrance. The car was gray. He tried to remember the color of the car that had almost run him down, but couldn't. Gray. Black. Two-tone. Had there been primer streaked across the hood and fenders? There might have been, but everything had happened so fast.

It occurred to him that he should have done something about this much sooner. He should have protected himself—gotten a gun, bought a knife, something. He also should have told Marilyn about the incident in the street, and it would have been wise to show her this latest photo as soon as he'd found it on his door. It wasn't so much that she would be able to protect him, but that she would know what had happened if he suddenly disappeared, or if he was found with a broken neck at the bottom of the stairs leading to the lobby, or if—

The car door swung open and a leg emerged, followed by another, and finally a body unfolded itself from inside. From straight overhead the man who was now standing on the sidewalk looked very tall, quite broad and strong, like an athlete in peak condition.

The man looked left and right, stretched briefly, and turned his attention to the hotel. His gaze wandered across the first floor, drifted slowly up to the second, then scaled the building and came to rest on the third.

Andy's floor.

He felt a mounting pressure in his chest, like a balloon being slowly inflated to maximum size. He felt his heartbeat right there between his lungs, and in his neck, and at his temples. The back of his neck started to itch, the skin crawling, a fine layer of perspiration popping out.

The man's gaze began a lazy crawl along the windows of the third floor, now five rooms away, now four, now three. Andy stood there, knowing he should duck out of sight behind the drapes but as helpless to perform that simple task as if he'd been paralyzed.

Two rooms away.

Andy tried to swallow but couldn't.

One room away.

His brain screamed at him to move. His body simply refused to do it. And then their eyes met.

There was no sign of recognition, none whatsoever. They were like two strangers idly looking at each other across a vast room, not sending any silent greeting, not sizing each other up, merely...staring.

Andy felt a moment of intense disorientation. He was sensing the presence of the second world again. He could feel the place, its pressure, its weight closing in on him, swallowing up the real world, swallowing him. His mind danced giddily around a crucial question. The second world. It was the place where both the mysteries of the past and the answers to everything resided. But had he fallen into that world? Had he been sucked into it? Or had he stepped across its faint border willingly, freely?

That man in the street radiated the power of that world. All the things Andy had been looking for, the things he had been seeking, crossed the three-story gulf between them and filled the tiny hotel room with their darkness. Alexander Bassett, a history of death, vanishing acts, photographs and notes, threats and promises. They were Andy's now, completely and irrevocably. They were Andy's now, and the man below was the conduit by which they had been delivered from yesterday to today.

The man turned away at last and strode toward the front of the hotel. He pulled open the lobby door and disappeared inside. For a few seconds more Andy stood there, rooted. Then he moved. He broke away from the window and ran (scurried) for the door. He raced (scurried) down the corridor to the stairs.

He had actually started down when he realized what he was doing. The stairway ended in the lobby, where the man from the street was right at this moment, where they would meet face to face. He scrambled (scurried) back up and went down the corridor in the other direction, to the fire stairs which led to the hotel's back parking lot.

The metal door clanged shut behind him.

He descended the steps three and four at a time, running.

7

HE WAS HALFWAY to his truck when he saw the man staring at him. It wasn't the man from the street. This man was shorter, and at a quick glance looked harmless. But a closer look showed an angry expression almost hidden behind a thick black beard and eyes that were small and piercingly dark. Even across the lot, Andy sensed the unbridled hatred that radiated from those eyes.

The man was just getting out of his car, which he'd parked at the edge of the Sleep-Tite's lot, near the back entrance of the bank. He paused, turned that glowering scowl on Andy, and opened his mouth as if to speak. His teeth flashed. No words came out.

Andy pivoted awkwardly, almost fell, and sprinted back toward the hotel. But rather than go inside he took the alley that ran along the side of the building, past the dumpsters from the Angler's Rest Lounge, past a side door marked NO ENTRANCE, past an old Ford Pinto that was parked there on three flat tires and a fourth that was dangerously low.

Just before he emerged onto Michigan Street, another man came into the alley. He was old, his back bowed, bending him almost in half. He was wearing dirty overalls and a heavy Mackinaw coat with holes at the sleeves. Slung over his shoulder was a clear plastic garbage bag full of pop and beer cans. He saw Andy hurrying toward him and halted, straightening as much as he could, his toothless mouth dropping open in an astonished O.

"Hidey-howdy!" he said, but Andy edged past him and went on, his heart drumming out a sharp tattoo, certain that he would feel the old man's hand close over his shoulder as he tried to escape, sure that he would be spun around to face that empty grin and a hand holding a gardener's shears.

He reached the street safely but was immediately confronted by them.

A woman he didn't recognize was striding quickly toward him. To his left, a man with a bag from the hardware store stopped and studied him. Farther on, a man barely in his twenties looked up from the job of finding his car keys and gave Andy a cold, blank stare.

ALEXANDER'S SONG

"Heylookout!" a high voice cried, as a boy on a bicycle whizzed past inches away and nearly knocked him sprawling to the ground.

That balloon in his chest finally burst, releasing a flood of cold fire. The world spun wildly around him. There was a noise building in his head, an intense ringing, strong, shrill. In his mind's eye he saw himself staggering helplessly into the street, being struck by yet another car—an accident, a murder, what did it matter? The town was coming for him, a huge, unified, malevolent force, weapons of every size and shape raised to take down the intruder, the interloper, he who dared to look into the past.

Everyone...

8

AND YET EVEN as he imagined that, a tiny voice of reason emerged through the din of panic in his brain, saying it wasn't so. There were people on his side. Yes, of course there were. He had to concentrate on that. To lose sight of it and think anything else was to slide down the slope of legitimate fear and tumble headlong into absolute gibbering lunacy.

There was no grand plan against him.

There simply wasn't.

He had to force the paranoia from his mind. At the very least, he had to push it back to what it had been before the incident with the dirt-streaked car, back to a level that had kept him wary but also had allowed him to function as a thinking, rational being.

He took a slow, deep breath and thought about...Ginnie. That thought was a good one. Ginnie had been helping him. And then there was Marilyn. And the long-haired teenager who looked like Kevin Caspian and had pulled him back from the brink.

I figure he would of stopped before he got to you. I just didn't want to take any chances.

That half-frightened, half-amused voice in his memory helped calm him down. It soothed him to the point where he was able to slow his ragged breathing and steady the trembling of his limbs. He pulled himself a little straighter and forced himself to study his surroundings.

The kid on the bike was long gone. The man from the hardware store had vanished. The young man who had been fishing his car keys out his pocket had driven away. The woman who had been hurrying toward him had gone into the bank.

He nodded to himself and turned around.

The old man in the alley was bent over the dumpsters, searching for stray empties with which to fill his sack.

If he tried hard enough, he could almost laugh. The Gardener was real. There didn't seem to be any doubt about that. But the rest of it...it was almost funny, now that the threat was gone, or rather now that his reason had returned.

"They've got plenty of rooms, hon. I got us a double, with a rollaway for Amy."

Andy looked and saw the man he'd noticed from his room. He was coming back out of the hotel, bouncing his keys in the palm of his hand. From here he didn't look tall and broad at all, nor did he seem to be in especially good condition. Actually, he looked small and thin, a little jittery, a little road-weary, like an accountant or some other low-level executive at the start of a long-overdue and much-needed vacation.

As Andy watched, this man from whom he had sensed such a threat walked over to his car, opened the door, and helped his family pile out—a pretty young wife, a small baby in her arms, a cute little girl of about nine or ten who had been riding in the back seat. The woman pointed at Andy and said something too soft for him to hear. No doubt she was describing the way he'd come racing out of the alley looking foolishly terrified. The man glanced at Andy with utter disinterest, said something back to his wife, chuckled, and went around his car to get the suitcases from the trunk.

Andy turned away, too embarrassed to go into the hotel. He started walking in the other direction, suddenly sure that everyone on the street was looking at him, pointing and laughing like that man and his wife...

but no. That was more paranoia. Apparently, even chagrin could be dangerous. In his present state of mind, who knew where it could lead? Admit that he'd been terrified. Admit that he had overreacted. Admit that he felt a little weak when he thought about the full extent of that overreaction. But don't worry about what others were thinking, especially when they weren't thinking a damn thing.

Passing the grocery store, he looked up just in time to avoid running into a middle-aged woman dressed in white slacks and a jacket of hunter's orange. She was coming through the automatic doors, a week's worth of groceries crammed into a battered old cart with squeaky wheels. It was the noise of the wheels that first alerted him; he heard them, noticed the impending collision, and stepped to one side, up against the plate glass window that looked into the store.

"Excuse me," he said as the woman passed by. "I didn't mean— "

The words died in his throat with the unexpectedness of breaking glass. Inside the store, first in line at the first of two checkout lanes, was someone he had never expected to see. He was bent over an open checkbook, laboriously filling out the blanks while the fat young woman on the register rang up his purchases and the acne-riddled box boy placed them carefully, one at a time, into large, strong cardboard cartons.

The woman in her orange jacket went past with an audible huff, but Andy didn't notice. His head, barely recovered from the panic of a few minutes ago, still susceptible to just about anything, had filled to overflowing with a dozen swirling images and the jumbled, tattered fragments of certain phrases: the Gardener, an old photograph, the Dupin Society. They blurred and blended into a powerful eagerness that bordered on anxiety, an excitement tinged with nervous fear.

He went for the entrance, but caught himself before going in. He grasped the low metal handrail that separated the IN and OUT doors, held it tightly for a moment, and told himself to calm down. He was just coming off an extremely upsetting experience. Never mind that it was also an *imaginary* experience. It was the intensity of the thing, justified or not, that mattered. Surely he couldn't have seen who he thought he'd seen, and did he really want to barge into the store and make a fool of himself all over again?

But when he gazed through the glass doors, the man was still there, and from this improved angle there was no mistake.

"Christ," he said, slightly awed at the synchronicity, the dark serendipity of accidentally stumbling across a man who earlier had been on his list of planned visits. The visit had been forgotten after the near-miss in the street, but now here he was, against all odds, virtually dropped into Andy's lap.

Then the sense of coincidence was swept away, along with all his earlier fear, by a swift and vicious anger. Everything that was happening could be laid at the doorstep of that man inside the store. Not that he was directly responsible—although Andy had yet to rule that out completely—but he certainly shared the blame. His refusal to talk was keeping Andy in the dark. And being kept in the dark was keeping him in danger, a helpless victim to something he couldn't comprehend.

The anger blossomed into righteous indignation. Just a few simple answers might have spared him that incident of thoughtless fright back at the hotel, and that realization alone was enough to push him through the door into the grocery.

He strode over to the checkout lane, stepped around the four cartons the box boy had already filled, and moved up next to the man.

"Excuse me," he said, his voice as cold as midnight ice. "I want to talk to you right now."

9

ED HOFFER LOOKED up and let out a pathetic, startled squawk. His creased and wrinkled face drained of all color. The pen fell from his hand and dropped to the floor. The hand flew up to his chest, as though he were a bad actor miming a heart attack.

ALEXANDER'S SONG

"I've had it with everyone dodging me," Andy said. "As soon as you're done here, we're going to go someplace, sit down, and talk. You're going to tell me everything you know."

Hoffer said something, but it came out as a string of garbled sound, incomprehensible. His hand was still clutching the cloth of his heavy checked jacket.

"Hey now, I don't know who you think you are—"

Andy rounded on the cashier, cutting off her words with one shriveling glance.

"Do you hear me, Hoffer? Finish your business. Now. Then we're going to talk."

"I don't..." Hoffer rasped. "I told you...I can't...."

"You can."

"Please, Mr. Gillespie, don't make me—"

And that was when it happened.

Actually, in that moment many things happened. The cashier turned and fled, going to tell the manager about the strange man who was harassing that nice Mr. Hoffer. The box boy stepped up and tapped Andy's shoulder, trying to intervene. The customers waiting in line behind Hoffer grew restless. One of them pushed his cart a little too far forward, knocking Hoffer against Andy's side. Another said something about "speeding it up, for God's sake."

But Andy didn't notice any one of those things. Not the absence of the cashier. Not the tap on his shoulder. Not Hoffer being pushed rudely against him.

He didn't noticed because his gaze had fallen on the old man's open checkbook.

The effect was not a lightning stroke from the blue. It was worse than that, much worse. A hundred times more powerful. A thousand times more violent.

Later, he was sure that he had never been closer to death than he had been right at that moment. Forget the bullet through Max's window or the car in the street. In that instant, when he saw the checkbook, his heart actually stopped beating. His lungs actually seized up in mid-breath. He was never sure how many seconds elapsed before things returned to normal—and the fact of the matter was that, in many ways, nothing was ever normal again after that.

He suddenly knew what it was that he had almost seen and come so close to understanding that first day on Wolf Island, when he'd been looking at Ed Hoffer's desk. It was so plain now. It seemed unthinkable he hadn't picked up on it immediately. But now he had. It was preposterous, incredible, flatly impossible. It was something that could never be, that violated everything he knew today, everything he'd ever known. And yet somehow, against all the odds, it was true. It was real. It was undeniable. And it explained so much.

He stared wide-eyed at the lines of the check Hoffer had already filled out, the date, the pay-to-the-order-of line, the memo space, the signature. The only thing missing was the amount, awaiting the cashier's final total.

Letters arose in his mind, floating up out of the darkness. He saw the flyleaf in his copy of *A Daughter's Song*. He saw the fine handwriting there.

To Danny...Yours for peace and a better world ....

He looked at Hoffer and shook his head.

"My god," he murmured. "Oh, my god."

Hoffer turned away, understanding what Andy had seen, knowing what he knew. There were tears shining on the old man's face, sparkling like glass.

Andy began to cry as well.

He understood that the knowledge had not fully hit him yet. He'd been struck with just enough of it to render him senseless. God only knew what would happen when the rest of it flooded in.

Had he thought just a little while ago that he had been swallowed by the second world? Good God, that was nothing, absolutely nothing.

This time he had been swallowed for real.

This time he had been swallowed whole.

TEN

CONVERSING WITH THE WIND

1

"Even if your Miss Turner is alive, I couldn't help her. And I must tell you: it's very, very unlikely that she's alive."

Alexander Bassett looked sad as he spoke those words, as though each syllable was a knife blade that carved a tiny chunk out of his heart and soul.

"I'm an old man, Mr. Gillespie. I'm eighty-one years old. I've had a lifetime of pain. My heart has been ailing for the last…God, thirty-five or forty years."

"But the Gardener—"

"The Gardener is stronger than I am. He's more determined than I am. And, as always, his identity is a mystery."

That last word—mystery—was punctuated by the explosive crack of a knot in one of the fireplace logs. Andy jumped. Bassett winced. The cabin on Wolf Island became silent but for the gentle crackle of flame and the keening of the night wind around the eaves.

"Please don't think I'm withholding something," Bassett said at last. "Yes, of course, I hid my real name from you. I had to. Since 1954, only a very few people have known who I really am. Earl and Liz Rappala knew. And Hedda Fogerty—do you remember me telling you about her? The book dealer in Houghton? Her name was one of the few true pieces of information I gave you the first time you were here, one of the bits that wasn't fiction.

"I met her in 1969, several months after I'd moved here. We became good friends. She'd come here to the island or I'd trudge up there to the city and we'd talk books for hours on end. She was the first person with whom I'd been able to do that in years. We discussed everyone, including Alexander Bassett. I was still Ed Hoffer to her, of course, so talking to her about my work...well, at the time it seemed like a grand adventure, an enjoyable game, a puzzle, a challenge to say the right things without saying too much. It was just like the day you were here with Miss Turner. If you remember, I discussed *The Voice of the Storm* with her. Same thing, only with Hedda the talks lasted hours, not minutes.

"But one day I made a slip. I don't even recall now what it was, but I said something that tipped her off. Suddenly, she knew I was Bassett, and though I tried to deny it, she wouldn't be satisfied until I admitted the truth. Still, she kept the secret until her death, good friend that she was. And so she was one of the very select few who knew that there was no Edward Hoffer.

"I tell you that so you won't feel too misused, Mr. Gillespie. You're just one among many. One among all but a handful."

Andy shook his head in awed silence. He had been with Hoffer—Bassett—for almost five hours. In that time, they had discussed many things. There was no doubt that he was sitting in the same room with one of the most famous writers of the twentieth century, a man believed dead for twenty-one years. Still, at regular intervals—like right now, for instance—Andy's shock and disbelief became almost too much to handle.

It was akin to finding out that the man you've lived next door to for years was actually Ernest Hemingway in disguise, that the Idaho suicide had been a sham, a magician's disappearing trick. It was overpowering

ALEXANDER'S SONG

information, impossible to adjust to with any kind of ease or speed. You found yourself just getting used to the idea, and then the amazement would come creeping back in, followed by the doubts, followed by the denial.

And yet he was absolutely certain that it *was* Bassett. Now that he knew it, he could see the resemblance and was ashamed that he'd been too blind to notice it earlier. Bassett was there in the old man's eyes, in the slightly upturned nose, in the usually grim set of the mouth. Even the faint remains of his hairline were right, when you looked in the proper way. It was Bassett. Thirty-six years older than the last known photographs of him. The dashing dark mustache of his youth long gone. The teeth replaced with full dentures. The weather lines deepened to valleys. The eyes grown milky with age. But underneath it all, *breaking through* it all...Bassett.

"You don't believe Ginnie's alive?" Andy said. "There's not even a slight possibility?"

"Possibility? There's always a possibility, Mr. Gillespie."

"Andy. Please." It was the third or fourth time he had said the same thing.

Bassett shrugged. "All right, Andy. There's always a possibility. But in all the years I've been stalked by the Gardener, only once did he stage a kidnapping rather than a straightforward murder or attack—and he ended up killing that person three days later."

"That was...?"

"A man by the name of Cal Drummond. Does the name mean anything to you?"

"The editor of *American Fiction Weekly*. A friend of yours."

"They were all friends of mine, Andy. Every last one of them. The Gardener kidnapped Cal, apparently from his apartment in the city. For three days I received taunting notes. No clues in them, nothing to go on, just hints that Cal was still alive. At the end of three days, I received a photograph of his slain body. It was January, very cold, but the Gardener had taken Cal to his summer home in the Hamptons. Held him there. Finally killed him."

Andy shuddered. "The first note *I* got said 'I have her,' not 'I killed her.' You don't think—"

"I don't know what to think. Perhaps he did kidnap her. Perhaps he's holding her somewhere in town. But that was almost a week ago. As I tried to make clear, the bastard's track record doesn't indicate prolonged mercy."

"If I might ask…" Andy began, but then trailed away timidly.

"Ask. By all means, ask. I've told you more in the last few hours than I've ever told anyone. For all his help, even Earl Rappala understood little of the reasons for my disappearance. I gather I'm to have few secrets from you, Andy, whether I want them or not. So ask away."

"You never told me how many there were," Andy said softly. "Over the years, how many altogether?"

"Oh, Christ." Bassett put a gnarled hand up to his eyes and held it there, as though shielding himself from something he did not want to see. "It depends," he said. "Did the Gardener kill my mother? I've often thought so, though he never admitted it and there's never been proof of any kind. If he did, she was the first. If not, then there were seven."

Andy's breath came out in a rush. "Seven!"

"Eight, if you include my mother. Nine if, God forbid, Miss Turner turns out to be his latest victim." He paused. "And there was the attack on Jack Kretchmer. You said you've read his journal from that period. I'm sure, knowing Jack, he understated things drastically. The attack was exceptionally ferocious. It was a miracle he lived."

"And the others?"

Bassett sighed again. As he had done every few minutes throughout their conversation, he patted his shirt pocket, that absent-minded, searching-for-long-abandoned-cigarettes gesture. Then he held up his hand and ticked off the names on his fingers. "Grace Mahler, my fiancé. Cal Drummond next. Henry Oglebay…Hank…a New York poet with whom I'd become quite close. Connie Warren. George O'Callaghan. Dwight Gulliver and his wife, Lonnie, who knew me only as Ed Hoffer. Seven. Seven people whose only crime was to become friends with Alexander Bassett."

"And through all of that, the Gardener never went after you?"

"Never. I wish he had. In many ways, it would have been easier being murdered at his hands than watching all my close friends perish, than getting all those damned notes and pictures. But he never did. He followed me instead. Sometimes I'd see him in the shadows every day for a month, then not at all for two weeks or two years. But never once did he attack me."

"Why?"

Bassett laughed. It was the sound of paper being crunched into a ball, brittle and harsh. "You might as well ask the rain why it falls. You might as well ask the wind why it blows. I have no idea, Mr. Gillespie…Andy. I haven't a notion. Fate, perhaps. Perhaps it's just my fate."

2

TO ANDY'S GREAT surprise, Bassett had brought him to the island without fuss or argument. He hadn't said anything at all, in fact, until they'd gotten clear of the people in the grocery store. He'd merely allowed Andy to follow him, and once outside had turned around with a look that was impossible to interpret, partially amused, a little sad, his sunken mouth twitching with irony, on the verge of laughter or anger or both.

"So, now you know."

Andy had still been in shock. "You can't possibly…I mean how? For godssakes, *how?*"

"All in good time, Mr. Gillespie. I suppose we have a little bit of that. I tried warning you, but you wouldn't listen. Now it appears we're stuck with each other, for whatever amount of time we have left."

He had driven Andy to Seward's, and in the weakening afternoon light they had motored out to the island, side by side with the groceries in Bassett's boat. That trip and the long climb up the stairs to the heights were hazy now in Andy's mind; he doubted he'd ever be able to remember them with clarity.

He could vaguely recall turning in the car to study the old man's face. He remembered stray phrases from Bassett's poems and novels popping into his head, and he remembered wondering: *This man? He's the one? Can he really be the one who wrote that?* He could recall choppy water, the wind singing in the tops of the island trees, the smell of woodsmoke gradually filling the cabin as Bassett expertly built and lit the fire.

But that was all. Scattered images, *fragments* of images. The rest was lost.

It had been his responsibility to speak first. There was no spoken agreement, no command from his host, but Andy sensed that if he were ever going to hear the whole story, then he would be required to tell his side of things first. If nothing else, he had to raise specific questions for Bassett to answer.

He spent a few moments composing himself, deciding where to begin. He took the bottle of beer that Bassett offered. He lit a cigarette and stared at the window across the room, the one near the roll-top desk. Twilight was slipping upon the world, darkness gathering. A hundred, a thousand, a hundred-thousand thoughts were battling for dominion in his mind.

"Tell me what you're thinking," Bassett said at last, gently prompting. "Tell me what you're feeling."

"What I'm feeling. Jesus." He puffed furiously on the cigarette. "I guess I'm feeling...betrayed."

"Because I lied to you, presented myself falsely?"

"Yes. No." He shook his head quickly. "Betrayed by the world, I guess. Everything I knew, everything I *thought* I knew, just got yanked out from under me."

"Is it really as bad as all that?" Bassett seemed genuinely interested in the answer, but amused as well.

"Maybe not," Andy said sourly. "I ought to be happy, right? What a discovery! What a revelation! I should be dancing around the room, bouncing off the walls. And maybe I am—happy, that is, not dancing. Maybe I'm thrilled but just too surprised to realize it."

ALEXANDER'S SONG

They were silent again. Then Andy took the plunge and began to talk. Without preamble and with precious little sense of order, he told Bassett everything about his early research; meeting Ginnie; the photograph she'd stolen from this very cabin; the gunshot; the journals Jo had found for him in New York; Ginnie's disappearance; the search; the Gardener's notes; the reading of the old records; the things he had discovered; the things he had surmised; the things he had feared. He talked about the things he'd learned from Marilyn Borg and the conversation with Fishbein and the phone call to Florida. He spoke quietly of the dark car bearing down on him in the street.

When he was finished, it was like returning to a small island of consciousness after swimming in a sea of mist and fog. He looked up, aware of his surroundings for the first time in over an hour. It had grown full dark outside while he'd been speaking, and the ashtray before him was full of crushed cigarettes.

"Well," Bassett said softly. "You've been a busy man." He smiled, but it seemed an automatic expression, devoid of emotion. "I knew a little of what you'd been up to, of course. You told me some of it on your first visit, and I learned more from your next trip out here and the phone call I made to you that night. Still, you've come a long way in the last week. It *was* just last Saturday, wasn't it? When you and Miss Turner were here, wanting to know what kind of boy Alexander Bassett was and how he grew up to write novels with a socialist sensibility?"

"A week," Andy said wonderingly. He felt drugged, lightheaded. "Yes, I guess that's all it was." He found it difficult to believe that seven short days could feel like months.

"And the truly amazing thing is, so much of what you've discovered in that short time is true."

That piece of information made Andy sit up a little straighter. His distress must have shown on his face, because Bassett smiled again, warmer this time.

"Not that part," the old man said. "You're sitting here across from me, and you've been honest with me, and now I suppose I should be as honest with you as it's possible to be. I'm many things, Mr. Gillespie—"

"Andy," Andy said absently, for the first time.

"Many things, Mr. Gillespie. A writer, a hermit, a liar, a fraud, a coward. Perhaps a coward most of all. I'm a sneak and an outright deceiver. But the one thing I'm not, the one thing I've never been, is a killer."

"Given my current situation, I guess that should be a relief."

Bassett chuckled. "You've a right to be nervous. But you have nothing to fear from me. It's your *association* with me that should have you worried."

Andy waited to hear that line of reasoning expanded. He expected to hear a history of the Gardener's activities, or perhaps an elegant rebuttal of Andy's suspicions that Bassett had murdered his own friends. But the old man brushed right past that and went off in another direction completely.

"As to the other things you've found, well, as I said, much of it is accurate. Maybe that shouldn't surprise me so. You did, after all, have outstanding sources." He closed his rheumy eyes for a moment, and his voice seemed to drift farther away. "Jack Kretchmer. Christ. I never remember a time when the son of a bitch wasn't writing in one of his journals. He was an inveterate observer, a habitual recorder. To have one of his diaries at your disposal—in your own hands!—was a real coup, Mr. Gillespie."

"It helped," Andy admitted. "The problem was, he was just like me. He understood just enough of your past to confuse him and make him jumpy. But he didn't know enough to answer all his questions."

"A polite way of saying even he, my dear friend, suspected me of things." Bassett waved a dismissive hand. "I can only hope that in the end he trusted me."

"He must have. He was certainly glad to have tracked down Earl Rappala."

"Yes. Well, perhaps he finally deduced the things he didn't know." Bassett flexed his fingers with stiff, deliberate movements. "You did a fair job of deduction yourself. Yes, Mr. Gillespie, my father killed Royal Haag. Yes, he killed Halvard Borg too. And then Jens Carlson appeared in my life eighteen years later to take his revenge. He murdered my father, murdered my friends, almost murdered me and—"

ALEXANDER'S SONG

"Wait! Your father? Jens Carlson was responsible for the fire at the mill?"

"Jens Carlson was responsible for many things, among them that fatal fire. After he died, things were peaceful for a while, but then trouble reappeared in my life. It followed me for years, taking my close friends. When I couldn't stand it anymore, when it got so bad that I was afraid to speak to strangers on the street for fear they'd be the next to die, I made a call to an old friend of mine here in Rock Creek. You did a fine job discovering all of that. Earl Rappala, that old OSS dog, helped me disappear. He did his job well. I'm a little startled to learn that Jack was so close to finding me there at the end. I didn't think anyone would find me, ever again. But of course that was wrong, wasn't it? The Gardener found me—three times, actually. But he's always been an exceptional case, someone with almost terrifying powers to hunt and track and stalk. And you found me, too." He sighed wearily. "Undone by my signature in a goddamned nickel and dime checkbook that isn't even worth balancing nine months out of ten. It boggles the mind."

Andy massaged the bridge of his nose. He was just beginning to see those obvious resemblances between the younger Bassett and this one. They were both striking and disturbing to observe. He opened his mouth to ask a question, shut it again when a more appropriate query came to mind, tried again, hesitated again, and finally spoke from despair.

"There's so much I still don't know," he said. "I've got so many questions, I don't think I could ever ask them all."

Bassett, with great effort, pushed himself to a standing position. He shuffled, back bent, into the kitchen to refill his water glass, but this time he took a bottle of Canadian whiskey from the cupboard over the sink and splashed some of that in, too.

"Bad for the ticker," he said, coming back. "But what the hell. The way I see it, this is two occasions rolled into one. The death of Edward Hoffer and the rebirth of my true self—and all for your own private benefit. Drink that beer and help yourself to another. We might as well celebrate while we can."

Andy frowned. "What does that mean?"

Bassett ignored him. "About these questions of yours, you might as well start with whatever bothers you the most."

"But that's just it. I don't know. Lots of things bother me. *Everything* bothers me. Your disappearance—I'd sure like to know more about that. Why'd you do it, and how? And your death. I assume you faked it, since you haven't mentioned being divinely resurrected. Why'd you pull that stunt in Ohio? What made you do it? And what about—"

"Mr. Gillespie, please, rein in those horses! You've asked a great deal right there. If we're ever going to get through this, we might as well do it in some kind of orderly fashion. Start again, please. Slowly, one thing at a time. I'm too damned old to cope with more than that."

And so they spoke of disappearing, and after that they spoke of death, and outside the wind blew harder than before, making the trees around the cabin bend before its will.

3

BASSETT WAS SURPRISINGLY ignorant about the methods used to affect his disappearance. He only knew that once he'd enlisted the help of Earl Rappala, an intricate clockwork mechanism had been put into motion. Three weeks later he was living in a house in Connecticut, two hours outside the city, using the name Karl Hansson and masquerading for the locals as a schoolteacher who had been forced into early retirement for medical reasons.

"I had to do it," Bassett said. "Vanish, I mean. I knew I had to. I'd tried catching and confronting the Gardener several times—hoping to stop him, hoping to kill him, hoping he'd kill me, who knows?—all to no avail. I'd tried the police. I'd tried moving—four new apartments in five years. All of it was a waste of time and effort. Going into hiding was the only way I saw to protect my last few friends, my publishing connections, people like Jack. But once I'd done it…Christ, it was terrifying, one of the most frightening things you could imagine. As far as the world at large was aware, Alexander Bassett was still alive. He'd just become a little more reclusive than normal. But for me, God, I was right at the center of it, and it had me completely fooled. It was the *totality* of the thing that bamboozled me, how completely Rappala and an OSS pal of his named George O'Callaghan had wiped clean the traces of my old life, how totally and realistically they'd established my new one. The world might have thought I still existed, but for my part, I had doubts. Years before the term became popular, I was having one hell of an identity crisis."

Undoubtedly, the system had been complex to set up, but keeping it going was quite simple. Bassett simply mailed all his business papers, correspondence with publishers, and other assorted dealings with the real world to a post office box in Omaha, Nebraska, which as far as he knew (though he was never absolutely certain) was George O'Callaghan's hometown. O'Callaghan, the middle man, then forwarded those papers to the proper places, apparently from a rotating assortment of drop sites around the Midwest.

Mail going *to* Bassett simply followed the chain in reverse. Those who needed to know had the Omaha address and sent their correspondence there, knowing that any response they waited for would take a long time to arrive.

There were no phone calls, in or out. Even the mail was restricted to only the most necessary items. Old cronies like Jack Kretchmer went unanswered. Fans and literary hangers-on were always ignored. And needless to say, all requests for face-to-face meetings, interviews, and personal appearances were turned down without consideration.

It wasn't a foolproof system. The Omaha box was always an iffy proposition. Someone could have staked it out, for weeks at a time if need be, until O'Callaghan arrived to empty it out. Still, it was a necessary evil. A man like Bassett, even with his career on the decline, had to be reachable by at least a few of his closest business connections. And O'Callaghan was smooth. The box *was* staked out more than once by Jack Kretchmer's private detectives and God only knew who else. But O'Callaghan was never discovered. At least not then.

So foolproof or not, the system worked well enough for a while. It probably would have worked even longer still, had not Bassett made one fatal mistake.

It all came down to Constance Eugenia Warren. It all came down to love.

Bassett met Connie Warren the very first month that he was living in Connecticut under his new identity. She was a twenty-nine-year-old kindergarten teacher, stunningly beautiful, active and smart and independent and, Bassett said with a smile, "probably about fifteen years ahead of her time. A feminist. A sort of superwoman."

They fell in love and saw each other almost constantly throughout that summer of 1954, the first summer of Karl Hansson's "life." The problem arose in late July of that year, when Bassett realized that he wanted to marry her.

"I dithered about for weeks, trying to talk myself out of it. I *knew* what a fool's business I was on. Dammit, I *knew*. But we were so wonderful together, and I loved her so…so bright, so strong…there's no way to describe what she meant to me. So I threw all my doubts and caution out the window and asked her."

The old man sighed. "Once I'd done that, how could I possibly keep the secret? How could I be anything less than honest? Could I let her marry a man who wasn't what he seemed to be, what he passed himself off as being? Hell, if nothing else, it would have been too much like my book, *Doctor Howell*."

Andy nodded his understanding. "Eleanor, the poor young thing, marrying the doctor, the man with the nefarious hidden past."

"Exactly. So I dithered some more and finally told her. Not knowing what to expect, I laid my whole life bare for her. Of course I was hoping she'd sweep me into her arms and swear to love me forever. But I must admit there was a small part of me thinking it would be best for her to simply storm out of my life in anger. It would have saved both of us the trouble of dealing with my past and my rather insane situation.

"But she didn't storm out, bless her and damn her. She didn't storm out, and trouble doesn't even begin to describe what we had in store for us."

Connie Warren not only agreed to stay with him and love him forever, she also swore to make his dark secret her own. She promised to carry it with her, protecting it, holding it privately, always.

"Always turned out to be about five months," Bassett said bitterly. "Then in early December, a month before the wedding, some friends of hers threw a bridal shower. One of the friends was the pampered daughter of our local mayor. There was money involved. The shower was a huge, complicated affair. They rented a train—actually rented an entire goddamned train—and rolled into Manhattan, forty people in two private cars. There was champagne and lobster and caviar and I forget what else, and sometime during the giddiness of it all, Connie told one or two of her best friends who it really was that she was marrying.

"It didn't take long after that. The friends told some more friends, and those friends told some more...or at least I'm assuming that's how it went. Isn't that always the way it goes? And the Gardener was still out there, looking for me, searching, keeping his ear to the ground, and on New Year's Day Connie was murdered. Her throat was slashed while she was on her way from her bedroom to the bathroom." He put his head down, and Andy could see the old man begin to tremble, fighting back tears. "One week...one week before our wedding...she was killed just seven goddamned days before we were supposed to be married.

"I got the note and the picture of her body the very next day."

There was almost no time to mourn. As soon as word reached them that Bassett's cover was blown, Rappala and O'Callaghan went into overdrive. They moved Bassett from Connecticut to a tiny town in western New York State. There was a new name—Victor Paasch—and a new background. They established an entirely new system of mail delivery, using a series of three separate post office boxes in Canada. It was complicated, an example of paranoia carried to the extreme, and yet almost assuredly necessary.

For his part, Bassett continued to work. In 1958 he finally published his first novel since the HUAC hearings of the early fifties. *Let Darkness Fall* was released in the fall of that year, a moderate financial success but a critical failure. Two years later he published *Peter Wept*, and this time even the diehard fans turned away. His last book, the mostly-reprint poetry collection *The Voice of the Storm*, came out in early 1961. The critics were kinder this time. They had to be, since they had already heaped praise on most of the poems during their original releases in the forties. But they were savage when it came to discussing the handful of new work in the collection, and when they discussed Bassett the man, it was with the air of someone whispering about a senile old uncle who has lost his purpose, his reason for existence, his very place in the family.

"I'd made a huge mistake," Bassett said wryly. "I'd stayed true to the vision of all my proceeding work, which meant the times had changed around me and I was no longer fashionable. The country was still very much in Eisenhower mode, mainstream, buttoned up, buttoned down, conservative—but standing on the cusp of the New Frontier. They didn't want to hear someone blather on about what appeared to be old-fashioned socialism. I was either too strong, practically a communist, or too weak, an ineffectual mealy-mouthed ghost from the past who didn't understand the current world order. I was old news. I was yesterday's garbage."

"It must have been very hard to take," Andy said.

Bassett nodded once. "I was hurt. I had plenty of moments of doubt when I thought my critics must be exactly right. But I was living in virtual isolation and couldn't seem to find a grip on the world as it was, instead of as it had been. Also, I had trouble shaking my beliefs of the last thirty years—an old dog unable to learn new tricks, you know. So I kept on typing, working on what I assumed would be my last novel, what I hoped would be my magnum opus, a final great work. I convinced myself that if I could finish it and publish it, it would vindicate me and everything I stood for. Working toward that, striving for that vindication, was probably the only thing that kept me going.

"My heart was getting worse, you see. I was still smoking and drinking too much, not eating enough, certainly not eating properly, not resting, getting sicker and weaker. I had palpitations and bouts of angina. I was developing emphysema.

"And worst of all, the loneliness was wearing me down. I didn't dare fall in love with anyone again, not after Grace, a recovery period of fifteen years, and then Connie. And what woman would have me, anyway? I'd fallen too far downhill after Connie's death. I didn't even dare to make a friend. It had been more than five years since we'd heard from the Gardener, and I didn't want to jeopardize that. Frankly, by that point all I wanted to do was finish my novel, find a publisher, have my brief moment in the literary sun, and die."

Nine years went by between the death of Connie Warren and the next incident. In December of 1964, the Gardener finally broke the wall of secrecy surrounding Bassett, tracked down George O'Callaghan in the small town of Mattawa, Ontario, and tortured him until he revealed Bassett's identity as Victor Paasch—and his whereabouts.

"Again, I'm only assuming that's the way it happened," the old man told Andy. "O'Callaghan was found with cigarette burns over most of his body, every fingernail and toenail pulled out, clamp marks on his testicles. The official cause of death was blood loss after multiple knife wounds to the chest. I suppose the Gardener stabbed him after finding out everything he wanted to know."

The notes Bassett had been receiving off and on for more than twenty years resumed again. There probably would have been more murders as well, but the writer had become a complete recluse by that time. Jackson Kretchmer was dead. Bassett had no friends, no casual acquaintances. He had lost all his publishing contracts after the failures of his last three books. He had no lawyer, no agent, no editor, no publisher. He was completely alone.

And so the Gardener contented himself with the notes, with sending photographs of his previous victims' gravesites, with long and rambling dissertations that recounted the past murders in grisly, if cryptic, detail.

Bassett sighed, and his body quaked again. "For all intents and purposes, I was finished. Although I didn't know O'Callaghan at all, his loss totally devastated me. Another innocent victim. Now perhaps he wasn't as innocent as the others. He must have known, after all, that there was an element of danger involved when he agreed to help Earl Rappala. But nevertheless, he was dead because of me. He had been tortured because of me. Because of me and whatever strange connection I had with the Gardener.

"I stopped writing. Utterly blocked. Couldn't put three words together on paper to save my life."

Not that he had been doing a very good job of it for a long time, he admitted. Emotionally and physically drained by the writing of *The Pharisee*, further battered by the HUAC investigation, and worn down as always by the continuing nightmares of his private life, Bassett had turned in the fifties from a speedy, prolific writer into a man who sat in front of his typewriter for hours on end, turning out only a sentence or two, a handful of paragraphs at best. But even that was a staggering output compared to what he produced after O'Callaghan's death—namely, nothing.

He might have lived out the rest of his life that way, the words dried up, the will to survive gone, the drinking and smoking finishing off his heart, lungs, and liver at the relatively tender age of fifty-nine, except for an accidental discovery he made in November of 1968.

He had just received another letter from the Gardener, and as he was tearing open the envelope he noticed something odd about the postmark, something different. His wits dulled by the shots of straight bourbon he had been drinking all day, he had to stare owlishly at the mark for close to five minutes before the truth finally dawned.

The postmark was not from New York City, the way it had always been before. It was from Michigan. *Rock Creek*, Michigan.

ALEXANDER'S SONG

The knowledge electrified him. He immediately went to the box where he kept his communications from the Gardener, removed all the old envelopes, and after placing them in chronological order and going through them one at a time, discovered that his malevolent shadow had apparently moved to Rock Creek a full two years earlier. It was almost impossible to believe, but the evidence was staring him boldly in the face. June of 1966: a letter from New York City. September of 1966: a letter from Rock Creek. And every correspondence after that bore the same northern Michigan postmark.

"A door somewhere in my mind blew open," Bassett said to Andy. "I had grown apathetic after O'Callaghan's death. Not that I didn't have a right. I think I did. It wasn't genuine, self-pitying apathy that came out of the blue. It was self-protective, it came from fear and disgust and helplessness. I had surrendered, I'll admit it. But I almost feel the surrender had been justified.

"Yet suddenly I didn't feel like surrendering. God knows why, but discovering that the bastard was here in my hometown…it opened that long-closed door and brought back so much of what I'd lost. I still couldn't write, but that didn't matter. I'd gained something else instead. My anger was back. I felt sharp and ready and mean. I'd gotten back the will to live.

"So I thought about everything for a few weeks and came to the only conclusion I could. The will to live had returned, so naturally I decided to kill myself."

4

THE DEATH OF Alexander Bassett on January 20, 1969, had been in the planning stages for almost two months. Now that he knew about Earl Rappala and at least a few of the intricacies behind the disappearance in the fifties, Andy was able to surmise much of how they'd gone about it. What was less clear to him was why.

"Two reasons," Bassett told him, after refilling his glass and strengthening the ratio of whiskey to water. "One was to protect Earl. We never knew whether or not the Gardener got Earl's name from O'Callaghan during the torture session. Since Earl was still alive, we assumed not. But perhaps the Gardener was just marking time. And even if he didn't know who Earl was, if I disappeared again, moved and changed names and went back into hiding, there was a damned good chance he'd find out, especially since all three of us were going to be in Rock Creek. On the other hand, if I was supposedly dead, Earl would be safe from discovery.

"The other reason was cover, because along with my will to live I'd regained my desire to fight, to kill the son of a bitch once and for all. I hadn't had feelings like that since the early fifties. Knowing that he was here in Rock Creek made me want to come back here, find out who he was, and finish him. Obviously, that would be easier to do if the Gardener wasn't also looking for me.

"That's really all there was to it. Protection for the both of us. And since I was already dying and was as good as dead when it came to writing and publishing, well, you can see there was nothing to stop us."

"So you faked the car crash and the fire?" Andy said.

"Not exactly. The car crashed, the fire broke out. The difference was that the body in the car wasn't mine. Earl saw to that, unrepentant spook that he was. If you'd do some newspaper research, I believe you'd find several articles about the theft of a cadaver from a Cleveland medical school just two days before my so-called death. Earl said the only thing that could trip us up was a check of dental records, but how closely were they going to look at the body?

"We'd taken all the precautions to make sure they didn't *have* to look. We'd registered the car in my name. We'd filled it with my papers and records and notebooks and clothes, and salted the area around the crash site with more. We made sure that a week before I left for Michigan, a few of my neighbors found out who I really was. We told them that I was planning to go to Manhattan for a few days—which I did—and from there to Rock Creek. We told them what route I was going to take. Everything fit, do you see? We made sure all the pieces were there.

"Even the blizzard worked out, although of course we didn't plan that. That came from someone upstairs, if you'll credit the existence of such a someone. It was providential, at any rate. It made the crash credible and hampered the rescue efforts until the car and the cadaver were thoroughly cooked.

"And while the stolen cadaver burned to nothing but ashes and bits of bone, I was picked up by Earl and we were on our way to Rock Creek. Alexander Bassett was dead and my fourth identity, Ed Hoffer, was born."

"Ingenious," Andy marveled.

"No, not really. At heart it was just a few spy-thriller clichés cobbled together with some B-movie special effects. But functional. It was certainly functional."

"And yet the Gardener *did* find you."

"Oh, yes." Bassett sighed, cleared his throat, closed his eyes, and repeated, "Yes. He found me. Long before I found him, which is a nice way of saying that I haven't found him yet. Not that I didn't look hard in the beginning. I did. I really tried. But there was one consequence of being officially dead that I hadn't foreseen. It kept me safe from that murdering bastard, but it also made him vanish. He thought I was dead. That meant no more letters or notes or pictures. There was nothing at all from him for years and years. It was like a joke. I'd dropped out of sight, but so had he."

"You gave up looking?"

"Eventually. What else was I to do? Looking seemed all but pointless, and I slowly developed other concerns. I found that being home in Michigan helped to revitalize me. It didn't happen immediately, but gradually the desire to write came back, and ultimately I relearned the *ability* to write as well. I did what a doctor had advised me to do. I stopped drinking. I threw the cigarettes out the window. Living out here on this island—this little hideaway that Earl had arranged for Ed Hoffer to buy—naturally forced me to exercise more. And this northern air is remarkably therapeutic, as I'm sure a city man like you noticed your first day here. My health actually improved a little. Not much—I'd abused myself too long for that—but at least it didn't decline any further and I certainly *felt* better.

"So I began to make progress again on my magnum opus. I lost interest in the Gardener. Not that I ever forgot the things he'd done, but the possibility of finding him and exacting my revenge faded into the back of my mind.

"I've lived much longer than I ever dreamed, longer than I had any right to hope. My past tortures me every day. It mystifies and frightens me. But at least for a time I was able to push much of it to a distant corner and become just a writer again. A lonely writer. A skittish, fearful writer. But, damn it, a writer."

Andy swallowed the lump that was rising in his throat. "How did he find you again?"

Bassett made a small groaning sound. "I haven't the slightest idea. All I know is that it took eighteen years. I moved here in 1969. The next deaths came in 1987. Sometimes…sometimes I think he's like a supernatural monster. Sometimes I think he *is* a supernatural monster, something alien, something that never dies and never quits. You can stop him for a while by vanishing, and you can stop him even longer by pretending to die. But ultimately he'll find you again. Inhuman. Unstoppable."

He leaned back and whispered that last word again, as though he were directing it at the ceiling or at something *beyond* the ceiling, outside the cabin in the cold night air.

"Unstoppable."

5

THE HOURS WENT by and the night thickened and the conversation moved on. It radiated outward, came back, doubled in upon itself, and began moving outward again.

The dark wind swept across the island.

The waves pushed against the shore.

The fire crackled and hissed and popped.

Eventually the conversation drifted around to the present day, the subject of Ginnie Turner, and the subject of fate.

ALEXANDER'S SONG

6

"THERE HAS TO be a better answer than that," Andy said now. "There has to be a reason—a *real* reason. Why has he been after you all these years? What triggered it? What made him keep it up? And why did he only kill people close to you? Why didn't he just kill *you*? Fate. It's interesting, it's poetic, but it doesn't help a bit."

Bassett looked at him oddly. "You're right, of course. It doesn't explain a thing. I only meant to say that I don't know the Gardener's mind. I can't imagine what he's doing. And do you think I haven't wondered about it? Do you think I've spent my life running and hiding and dying without trying to get to the root of the problem? Do you think I haven't spent sleepless night upon sleepless night? Do you think I haven't missed meals and missed work and missed heaven only knows what else while asking myself why? I ask constantly, but I don't know. I can't guess. I can't even begin to suppose."

"But surely—"

"Surely nothing, Andy. Surely nothing. Death has followed me seemingly forever. It or its shadow took away everything I ever loved. It forced an early end to my career, almost an early end to my *life*. You'll have to forgive me if it bothers you, what I say about fate. But goddammit, that's what it feels like! It feels huge and irrational and ultimately inexplicable. It's so beyond understanding that I gave up trying long ago."

Andy looked away. He felt shamed by what Bassett had just said, but it made him angry, too. He felt that anger bubbling away inside, the pressure building, and he forced himself to keep it down, keep it hidden. He had to remember who he was talking to. It wasn't an old, maddeningly obtuse bucolic homesteader. Not anymore. This wasn't Ed Hoffer, it was Bassett.

Bassett!

The man had led an unbelievable life, an impossible existence scarred by murder and hiding, black secrets, blacker death. Perhaps he could help Andy, or perhaps Andy could help him. Perhaps. But anger was not going to solve even a minute portion of the problem.

"We'll figure it out," he heard himself say softly. "Somehow we'll get to the bottom of it."

Bassett's milky gaze sharpened. "Excuse me?"

"I said we'll figure—"

"We? What in the hell does that mean?"

"It means...I think it means..."

"Oh, Christ! Is this my fault, because I brought you here, because I opened up to you and spoke honestly? Is that what planted this ridiculous notion in your brain? We? There is no we. This isn't a team sport. I didn't tell you the things I did to enlist your help. I did it to help *you*, to put a little backbone in the warnings I gave you before."

"But if we'd just—"

"We again! Jesus, man, I won't listen to this. I warned you the other night, when I called you on the telephone. I told you the Gardener would come after you. You've seen some of that for yourself already. You'll see more if you stay in Rock Creek. I should think you'd have a grasp on that now, after everything I told you. Your only hope for survival is to leave town now, give up your interest in me. Go home to wherever you're from, burn your notes, sell your copies of my books, start studying Sinclair Lewis instead. That's why I brought you here and told you everything, so that you'd understand the urgency of it. I wasn't trying to create some foolish *we*."

Andy felt a growing panic. He had imagined a bond forming between them, but now it was breaking, slipping away.

"Go home," Bassett said again, his voice thin and rock hard. "Run your ass off, man. Forget about Alexander Bassett, the socialist hack."

"But...but we could help Ginnie if—"

"You haven't listened to anything I've said, have you? We can't help her. She's dead."

"You don't know that. You told me that when Drummond was kidnapped, you got notes telling you about it. Then when he was killed, you got another note and a picture of the body. Well, I got a note after Ginnie disappeared. It said, 'I have her.' And I haven't gotten anything since to tell me otherwise."

Bassett put up his hands. The gesture was stiff and slow, but the meaning was obvious. "Have it your way, then. She's alive. Bully. Now what are you going to do for her? Tear through every house in Rock Creek looking for her? Check every house in every town in the state? Go to the police, perhaps? Now there's a rich one. I told you I'd done that myself. I tried after the death of Cal Drummond and again after Hank Oglebay was killed. I showed them the Gardener's notes. They took statements from me, mumbled things I couldn't make out—probably complaining about 'nutty author types.' They talked about overeager fans and overactive imaginations. And they laughed, sending me on my way. Don't call us, Bassett, we'll be in touch. And they never were. Never."

"But Ginnie—"

"You keep saying that." Bassett's tone grew sour. "'But Ginnie, but Ginnie.' We can't help her. Open your skull and let the truth in. Alive or dead, she's beyond our reach. We can only help ourselves now, and I suggest you start by running away while you still have time. For my part, I'll help myself by pretending I never met you or heard of you, and by praying that I don't see your name in the obituaries any time soon."

"I don't believe this," Andy said.

"Well, I suggest you try."

"Oh, Christ, don't you understand?" He cautioned himself again about losing control of his temper, but it seemed too late for that. It didn't matter anymore who he was talking to. He had reached his limit and taken at least one step beyond. "Ginnie Turner is missing because of you! An innocent girl is missing because she was a fan of your work, because she wanted to know more about you! Doesn't that mean anything to you? All your life you wrote about service to others and giving of yourself. Didn't that mean anything, either?"

"Of course it did."

"Then do something to help her!"

"I...I can't."

"Maybe not," Andy said. "Not you alone. But what about both of us? What if we work together? Can't we even try?"

"The Gardener is better than both of us," Bassett said evenly. "He killed George O'Callaghan—a goddamned government spy. What can an eighty-one-year-old man with a bad heart and a skinny little schoolteacher full of wounding accusations possibly do in the face of that kind of threat? For godssakes, I think you're insane, but I'll give you the courtesy of listening to whatever you tell me. So speak to me, Andy. Go ahead. Tell me from the depths of your wisdom: what in the name of God can the two of us do?"

Andy's mouth was open, his throat straining. His brain whirled, wildly searching. He tried. He struggled. He fought. But the words would not come.

Bassett looked back at him with his hard old man's stare.

"Well?"

7

THEY CAME OUT of the cabin almost an hour later, not friends but not enemies, either. Andy supposed the best thing that could be said was that they weren't total strangers anymore.

The path through the woods was completely dark, like being in the bowels of the earth. Trees swayed around them, felt more than seen, branches almost touching their faces. Gravel and dirt and pine cones and last autumn's leaves crunched underfoot.

"You're absolutely sure I can't persuade you to stay the night?" Bassett said, a ghost beside him in the darkness.

Andy declined. "I'm worried about Marilyn Borg. She hasn't seen me since this morning. It's...what? Almost eleven now? It'll be after midnight by the time I get back. She knows just enough about this to worry her. I'll be lucky if she doesn't have the police, the FBI and the whole damn National Guard combing the town when I show up."

Bassett was silent for a moment. Then: "How much are you going to tell her?"

ALEXANDER'S SONG

"That's really up to you, isn't it?"

The old man sighed, the sound swallowed by the wind. "I can sympathize with her desire to exonerate her brother. I'd like her to at least know that she's right about my father. But the question is: how do we do that without giving away the rest?"

"That's your decision," Andy said. "I won't say anything to her tonight or tomorrow, but when we talk again, you'd better let me know what I can say, how much I can say, and to whom."

They walked the rest of the way to the cliffs in silence. When they broke out at the top of the stairs the wind struck them full in the face. It was lighter here, the moon coyly dancing in and out of the scudding overcast. The steps going down stood out like long black bones.

"Going to be a rough crossing," Bassett said, musing to himself.

Andy nodded. He had offered to take the boat himself and bring it back tomorrow, thus sparing the old man the strain of the trip and its return. Now, feeling the brunt of the wind, he was glad Bassett had said no. Getting used to easy crossings in bright daylight was one thing. Going out like this, testing his novice status in the middle of the night on severely choppy water, was another.

They went down the stairs, Andy first, the old man a few steps behind. Their boots clocked the slow and steady rhythm of the descent, helping them sink into their own worlds, lose themselves in their own private thoughts. Halfway to the bottom, Andy chuckled softly and shook his head.

"What is it?" Bassett asked.

"Nothing really. But I just realized why Liz Rappala wouldn't say anything to me, why she was so protective. She knows you're still alive, doesn't she?"

"I should hope so. I saw her just a few months ago, right before she retired from the library and moved south."

"I guess it also explains why she was the resident expert on your work. She had the inside line on everything."

Bassett nodded slowly. After a few seconds he said, "That goes for you, too. I imagine you're already dreaming of the articles you'll get out of this."

Andy started. "I hadn't thought of it."

He would have been lying if he said the idea didn't interest him in the least, but for the moment the thought of the Gardener was stronger than anything else. After hearing everything Bassett had told him that long night, the Gardener seemed so large, so important, so *elemental*, that such mundane things as reading and writing, sleeping, eating, working, playing, were impossible to consider rationally.

"We can't do this, you know," Bassett said softly from behind.

"Do what?" Andy asked, although he knew full well what the old man was saying.

"The Gardener. We can't fight him."

"That didn't stop you from trying to catch him in New York."

"Ah, but I was younger then. Much younger."

"It didn't stop you from moving back to Rock Creek to try again."

"I was desperate, and until I got here and settled in and found my new life, I thought I was dying anyway. I thought I had only a few months left."

"Desperate," Andy repeated. The word sounded hollow and tasted bitter on his tongue.

He wasn't sure himself why he was determined to go ahead with this. Was it desperation? It had to be something like that, something close to it. It was no secret that he had always run his life on a kind of single-minded track of selfishness. His interests and concerns had always been of prime importance; other people came second—even when he *knew* that's what was happening and even when he *tried* to make it otherwise. He had ruined his marriage that way. He had alienated a good two-thirds of his students that way, and had failed to help others, like Kevin Caspian, fulfill their potential. He wasn't incompetent, nor was he actively hated. But he was never going to poll anywhere near the top for Teacher of the Year.

ALEXANDER'S SONG

"You have too much growing up to do," Jo had said to him during the course of their six-month bout with marriage counseling. "You can't keep living in your own little self-created bubble. You can't take your goddamned books and run off to Academic Land every time someone has a problem and needs your help."

Had the counselor rushed to his defense? Had the counselor called her harsh or unfair? Had the counselor said she was exaggerating or hitting below the belt? Or had the counselor nodded slowly, almost imperceptibly, in agreement?

So all right then, he was selfish, childishly so. But surely he wasn't doing this to save his own life. The easiest way to do that would be to take Bassett's advice and run. He was doing it, he thought, for that one-in-a-thousand chance that Ginnie could be saved. And yet just a few days ago the idea of putting himself in mortal jeopardy to save a teenager he barely knew…just a few days ago that would have been laughable.

He certainly wasn't laughing now.

They reached the bottom of the stairs and stepped off the landing onto the dock. Almost immediately Bassett let out a sharp cry, and Andy spun around to see what was wrong.

The old man's face was pale, and it wasn't just because it was momentarily being washed by unclouded moonlight. His faded eyes were wide. He was pointing down the length of the dock, his index finger crooked arthritically, jabbing emphatically.

Andy looked. "What? What's wrong?"

"What happened to them?" Bassett's voice was thick and rasping. "Goddammit, where are they?"

Andy realized what Bassett was saying and went cold to the bone. He hadn't noticed before, but the boat and the canoe were missing. When he looked down the dock he saw nothing but wet boards and black water pushing endlessly against the pilings.

"I don't get it," he said. "How—"

"He was here. That son of a bitch followed us here. He took them."

"But—"

"What else could it be?" Bassett sounded suddenly winded, as though his throat was tight and he was having difficulty drawing breath. "Did they blow away? I know how to tie my knots, for Christ's sake. No wind like this could carry off those boats. It had to be him."

Andy was going to say something about kids and pranks, but the memory of Jeff Lamoreaux casually dismissing the gunshot through Max's window brought him up short. He felt strangely light, detached from his physical body, as though his real inner self was hovering somewhere nearby and watching the corporeal Andy Gillespie go through the motions of struggling to understand.

The Gardener, he thought sickly. The Gardener was here. He was here while we were sitting by the fire, drinking and talking. Did he come right up to the cabin, maybe? Did he sneak up to the window and put his nose against the glass and actually *stare* at us? Was he out there in the darkness, grinning madly as he watched us go around and around, rehashing the past and trying to solve the future?

Darker thoughts: For all they knew, the Gardener might still be here. What was to stop him from stealing the boats and then coming back? He might be on top of the cliff, coming through the woods, about to start creeping down the stairs. Or maybe he would just stay up there and aim a gun at them from the top. That would be the easiest thing for him, wouldn't it?

He began to realize the full extent of their helplessness, how they were trapped here, alone on the island (or *almost* alone, perhaps), far from shore and even farther from the help of the people in town. It was a horrible, deadening thought, and he was just coming to grips with it when white light filled the night. Less than a split second later there was a tremendous rushing thunderclap of sound, and a concussive blow knocked them to the boards of the dock.

More white light surrounded them and a wall of heat surged past like a hurricane. It seared Andy's lungs. His nose stung. He imagined that he could hear the hair on top of his head crackling in flames. He gasped out a strangled cry, his throat on fire.

He managed to roll over and saw that the top two-thirds of the stairs had been blown completely away. The steps zigzagged upward and then stopped abruptly, leaving a gaping hole where there was nothing but hard, sheer cliff. Ashes and bits of charred wood were drifting downward like the remnants of a fireworks display, pattering into the water around them, sputtering out.

He scrambled over and knelt beside Bassett. The old man wasn't moving. Andy shook him gently, then cradled the old man's head and slowly rolled him over.

Another cry lodged in his throat.

Bassett's eyes were wide, staring sightlessly. His jaw was slack, his mouth an open pit.

"*Help!*" Andy screamed into the night. "*For godssakes, someone help me!*"

A smaller secondary explosion buffeted him as it took away the landing and the bench at the top of the cliff.

"*NOOOOO!*" he shrieked.

He held the old man across his lap and rocked him, while the ashes fell and the wind kept howling its eternally sad and lonely song.

PART THREE

BATTLECRY AND ELEGY

The death of reason is a desperate thing,
But who can say what reason's birth may bring?

Alexander Bassett
from "The Death of Reason"
published in *The Voice of the Storm*
(poetry collection, 1961)

ELEVEN

KEYS IN A DRAWER

1

It was almost noon on Sunday by the time Andy got back to the hotel. To his relief, Marilyn wasn't at the front desk. One of her part-time employees was working instead, a young girl with short black hair and a strikingly pretty face who eyed him with suspicion as he walked through the lobby.

He was too tired and sore to take the stairs, so he rode the rickety elevator to the third floor, went to his room, stared at his door for a minute, as though unable to believe there was no note from the Gardener taped there, and finally went in.

He stood for a while in the bathroom, gazing at his reflection in the mirror—the bright patch of burned flesh across his forehead, the eyebrows that had been singed almost completely away, the brittle and shortened eyelashes, the long scratch that began on his left cheek and ran all the way down to the jaw line— and then held up his hands and stared at those—rough, raw, puffy, the hands of a creature lost somewhere back on the evolutionary chain.

He frowned, trying to convince himself that he wasn't staring into the face of a monster, remembering that the real monster was still *out there*.

"Shit."

His voice was like the rest of him. Rough and weak and exhausted, it was the voice of the victim, the voice of a man who had gotten into things way over his head.

He watched with mild interest as the eyes in the mirror narrowed to slits.

He turned away when a tear trickled down the wounded cheek.

2

ALEXANDER BASSETT WAS all right.

Of course "all right" was a relative term when you were eighty-one years old, in fragile health, and had almost been blown to smithereens in a sudden late-night explosion. What Andy had assumed to be a fatal stroke or massive heart attack had in fact only been a fainting spell. Either that, or Bassett had been knocked unconscious by the force of his fall; he couldn't be sure which.

The old man came around quickly. His breathing was weak and shallow and he claimed that his heart was palpitating, but he was able to stand with Andy's help and cling to one of the pilings while he slowly composed himself. The only real casualty was the upper plate of his dentures, which had been cracked beyond repair.

"An interesting predicament," he said after several very long minutes had gone by. His voice was slow and thick, the words muddied as he struggled to speak through broken teeth. "No way off the island. No way back to the cabin, either. Do you suppose the Gardener wants to test our swimming prowess?"

Andy had stared at the old man, astonished that he could be joking under the circumstances. "He just tried to kill us. He wasn't testing anything. He wanted to blow us to hell."

"Oh, I doubt it. If he'd wanted to do that, he would have blown up this dock while we were standing here, or set the charge on the steps to go off as we were passing by. I didn't know he was an explosives expert, but it wouldn't surprise me. He's a cruelly efficient adversary."

Andy didn't answer. He was looking down at the boards beneath his feet, thinking about what Bassett had said, half expecting another explosion any second.

"This is a new side of the Gardener," Bassett said thoughtfully. "I've never known him to be so...playful. All this striking but not taking. The gunshot you talked about, the car, this business about watching bugs scurry about. It's almost enough to make you hope he's lost some of the urge to kill."

"I'm still not convinced he didn't want to kill us this time," Andy said.

"Perhaps so, but then that would have been yet another side of the bastard. It would have meant he was tired of watching *me* scurry. It would have meant he was trying to murder me at last."

Andy thought about that. "Are you saying I'm safe as long as I'm with you? Because the Gardener lets you live, I'll live too, by association?"

"I wouldn't dare utter such a thing," Bassett said with a slow shake of his head. "That's been the case so far, but he's much too unpredictable to stake your life on his past behavior."

Andy sighed. He supposed they could go around and around like that for hours—he was trying to murder us, he wasn't trying to murder us, he will, he won't—and the issue would never be settled. The real question was: how safe was he? And based on how safe he *felt*, the answer to that was clear: not very.

3

THEIR BIGGEST PROBLEM, getting off the island, was solved a few minutes later when Bassett noticed the bow of the canoe protruding out of the water, nosing above the waves at the end of the dock. The Gardener had not towed away the vessels after all; he had only sunk them, the canoe on one side of the dock, the boat on the other.

Andy lay on his belly on the boards, cold spray on his face, looking into the water and wondering how it had been done. The boat would have been easy, he guessed. All the Gardener had to do was pull the drain plug and let the thing gradually fill up with water, aided by the weight of the big outboard motor. The canoe, on the other hand…that would have been real work. The Old Town was virtually unsinkable, certainly for one man working alone in the dark and the wind.

Bassett came up behind him. "If we can get the boat out, we'll be all right. A few hours for the motor to dry out, that's all. It should run as good as new."

"Is there any possible way to get back to the cabin from here? Maybe if we wait till morning—"

"We'll be waiting here," Bassett said. "There's a low landing spot on the other side of the island. The path through the woods is overgrown and rather rugged, but I suppose we could manage it. Unfortunately, we can't get there from here, not without the boat."

"Could we—"

"What? Wade? It's three-quarters of a mile if it's an inch, through water up to your shoulders, with a rocky bottom and hidden drop-offs. I doubt even you could handle it, Andy, to say nothing of me. Trust me. We need the boat."

Andy looked at the old man beseechingly. He wasn't sure what he wanted to hear, what comfort he expected Bassett to give. Perhaps he was only trying to delay the inevitable.

Bassett flashed him a sour smile. "You're the one who wanted to fight the Gardener. If you've changed your mind, we could always sit here for the rest of the night. We'll probably freeze to death right before dawn—if we're lucky."

Andy got to work.

Standing in water that lapped at his neck, that was so cold he thought more than once that it had stopped his heart, he found the canoe rope and hauled the Old Town to the shallow water at the base of the cliff. In the fickle moonlight, he saw almost immediately how the Gardener had accomplished the job of sinking the unsinkable. No tipping it over, trying to fill the thing with water. He had simply taken a large instrument—a sledgehammer, an axe—and chopped a hole in the bottom.

He abandoned the canoe where it was and went around the dock, terribly afraid of what he'd find if and when he was able to raise the boat.

The water was a little deeper on that side of the dock. He had to hold his breath and plunge beneath the icy waves three times before finally finding and getting a grip on the bow rope. After that it was a test of sheer strength—pull with all his might, feel the heavy boat grudgingly slide toward him an inch, perhaps two, rest a few seconds, adjust his grip on the rope, and pull again. Over and over his feet slipped on the rocky lake bottom. Twice he stumbled and went underwater, fighting back to the surface, gulping and sputtering. The pain of the cold became numbness, at first a welcome relief, then worrisome.

The job was complicated by the outboard motor, which had tipped down a few degrees and kept dragging on the rocks. Andy was worried about damage. He had an image of rowing all the way back to the mainland. But the only thing worse than that was the thought of diving beneath the water again to try raising the outboard, so he allowed it to drag and catch as he kept on pulling.

It took close to half an hour to get the boat into the shallows, and by that time the numbness had turned back to pain and he was seriously worried about hypothermia. His relief at finding the boat undamaged—the Gardener had only pulled the plug, after all—was tempered by the fact that his work wasn't done. He had to struggle to tip the boat up on the gunwale and unship most of the water, then use the bailing cup tied to the transom to remove even more.

Finally there was the long trip around the island. They tried the motor, but the best it could muster was a second or two of phlegmy grumbling before it choked and died away. And so Andy rowed, pulling for warmth, pulling for safety and an end to the endless nightmare, while his hands blistered and bled, until his back screamed its agony and his arms felt broken and dead. Then a walk through the woods, helping the old man along as best he still could, clearing the brush that blocked the unused path, slogging up the steep hill the led all the way to the cabin in the center of the island.

As he warmed himself in front of the fire, bundled in several layers of blankets and drinking some of Bassett's whiskey from a beer mug, the old man disappeared into the bathroom and came out with a spare upper plate cemented in place.

"You did a good job out there," he said, the garbled lisp gone from his voice. "Damn fine work."

Andy just grunted and shivered.

"I'm quite serious. You saved our lives. As I told you, we would have died if we'd waited out there till morning. Another few hours and the temperature will drop to freezing or below. And even if we'd lived, then what? Wait for a fisherman to come along and rescue us? At this time of year we might have been waiting a week. You would have had to pull the boat out, anyway." He gave Andy a surprisingly warm smile. "You really did save our lives."

"Right now, frankly, I'd rather be dead," Andy grumbled.

"Oh, I'm sure you don't mean—"

"No. No, I guess not." He held his hands out toward the fireplace again, rubbing them together furiously. "After all, why would I want to die so easily? I've got to save some fun for the Gardener, don't I?"

It seemed they had nothing left to say to each other. Andy spent the night on Bassett's couch, tossing and turning, ceaselessly restless, getting up every hour or so to restoke the fire or rearrange the logs. He thought about the close call on the stairs, about whether the Gardener had been trying to kill them or was only being, as Bassett had said, playful.

An explosives expert, he thought hazily. A bomber with a sick sense of humor.

He managed to sleep at last and dreamed of being cold, his blood turned to ice, his lungs laboring to breathe air as white as snow and as sharp as a northern wind. Later, just before he awoke, the dreams changed. They were suddenly brighter, hotter, filled with blinding fire and the sound of thunder in the sky.

4

HE SLEPT BETTER in his bed back at the hotel, but was awakened in mid-afternoon by a knock at the door. Before he could claw his way back to full consciousness, he heard a scrabbling at the lock, the sound of a key being inserted and the knob being turned. He blinked furiously, rubbed his eyes, and watched helplessly as the door swung open.

"Well, sweet Jesus Christ," Marilyn Borg said, "you *are* here. I thought you'd decided to run away or —" She stopped when she got a good look at his face. Her expression darkened. "Maybe you *should've* run away. What was it? You finally meet this Gardener fellow face to face?"

"Something like that," Andy said. His voice was hoarse, his throat scratchy and raw. "Actually, I'm not at liberty to say anything about it right now. I'll have to tell you about it later."

She frowned, the wrinkles of her troll face curving down and deepening. "Somebody threatening you?"

"Well, yes, actually somebody is, but not about keeping quiet. I'm sorry. I can't explain any more than that." Her gaze never wavered, but he sensed the hurt. "I'm sorry," he said again, weakly.

She continued staring. "I heard about your little accident in the street."

"Really?"

"It's a small town." She watched him another moment more. The burned flesh above his eyes itched beneath her scrutiny. "You want to talk, you know where to find me."

He nodded.

"You need my help, same thing."

"Thank you."

She frowned again. "Thank you, Marilyn, and good day to your scrawny ass, is that it?"

"Marilyn, please—"

"Forget it." She turned around and slipped out of the room, the door almost, but not quite, slamming behind her.

Andy sighed and got out of bed. He wished he could have told her more, but what would it have been? *You'll never believe who I ran into yesterday, Marilyn.* No, too trite. How about this: *The end is near, I can feel it. What you want, what I want, it's all just around the corner. Trust me.* Too melodramatic. In the end, he supposed he'd said everything he could, and fair to her or not, it would have to do. He had promised Bassett, after all, and he could scarcely imagine a more important promise to keep. If nothing else, the issues of secrecy and safety were involved. If Marilyn found out and breathed a word of it to anyone ….

It was close to three o' clock, and he had promised to be back at Wolf Island by five. There was work to do. The search was about to begin. The very thought of it set his stomach churning and made his skin tingle with nervous anticipation.

He was a long way from what he had imagined starting out. He and Alexander Bassett were working together—unbelievable enough, impossible, beyond imagining. But then it got carried one step further. What were they working on? Writing the story of Bassett's life? Piecing together the sources of his politics? Tracing the roots of his philosophy? No. They were playing detectives, of all things, trying to find a mass murderer who had been active for more than fifty years. They were trying to save the life of a young girl Andy hadn't even known two weeks ago, a young girl who might well be dead already.

Can you believe it? he asked himself. Would *anyone* ever believe it?

He took a long, hot shower, still trying to chase away the implacable chill of Green Lake that was not quite real but stronger than a memory. When he was done he got dressed, lit a cigarette, and set about the task of organizing his notes and papers into a coherent pile.

Twenty minutes later he was on his way. Despite the lingering pain from the night before, he tried his best to hold his head high and his back straight. Confidence. If he couldn't quite lay his hands on it, at least he could pretend.

But as confident as he appeared, he still snuck out of the hotel via the back stairs. For the moment, at least, the thought of facing Marilyn again was nearly as bad as the prospect of whatever the Gardener might have in store for him.

5

ALEXANDER BASSETT WAS smiling at him, and Andy noticed for the first time how his new upper plate was brighter and more even than the lower. As far as he could tell, the old man had suffered few ill effects from the night before—amazingly few. There were the dentures, of course, and a small cut almost lost in the creases on his forehead, but that was all. If his heart was bothering him, he wasn't saying.

"What is it?"

Bassett said, "It's time to strike a deal."

"Uh-oh."

"No, no, it's nothing serious. I only mean to say that I've agreed to work with you on this, going along despite all my better judgment, and I want something in return."

Andy looked around. Their records had taken over the kitchen of the cabin. They were strewn across the table in piles two feet high, covering the counter next to the refrigerator. And now, before they had even set to work, came the demand he had been braced for: I help you, you (fill in the blank with something blatantly unreasonable) for me.

Well, he could at least listen. How bad could it be? What could the old man possibly ask that would inconvenience him so terribly? He wasn't in this for his own benefit and comfort, after all. At least he hoped he wasn't.

"Let's hear it," he said, resigned.

Bassett smiled again. "I help you, then I want unlimited access to those."

Andy blinked, confused, and finally understood that the old man was pointing at his pack of cigarettes. "Wait a minute. Let me get this straight. You want to bum a smoke?"

"Crudely put, but yes. I want a cigarette now and then as we work. Not too difficult a request, is it?"

"I...I don't know. I mean, your heart—"

"Please don't baby me, Andy. Don't be my mother. Even without the Gardener after you, you'll be lucky to live to my age, and in the event you should do so, you'll resent someone telling you what you can and can't do just as much as I."

"But—"

"I've done without for more than twenty years. I doubt very much I have another twenty to go. If we get into this as deeply as you'd like, I may only be alive a few more days—or *hours*, God knows. I don't want to deprive myself of so simple a pleasure when the end is staring me in the face."

Andy picked up the pack from the table, staring at it blankly. "Just my luck," he said. "I discover a great writer alive and then kill him off with nicotine." He laughed. It suddenly seemed so ludicrous, he couldn't help it. He shoved the pack across the table, into the old man's gnarled hands. "Help yourself. Light, puff, and be merry."

They each smoked a long, slow cigarette before getting down to business.

6

THE ANALOGY OF keys in a drawer came to Andy as they were entering their second full hour of work. Trying to find anything useful in the mountains of paper was like being locked in a room with a drawer full of keys. One of the keys might or might not open the door and allow you to escape. Would it? Wouldn't it? There was no way to know without trying every one and hoping. But as time crawled by and each key turned out to be the *wrong* key, you started to think that you would never get the damn door unlocked, never find the way out.

ALEXANDER'S SONG

While Bassett poured over Andy's notes, Andy looked at Bassett's. Most of the man's old journals, notes, and letters had been disposed of (after being strategically edited) following his "death." Earl Rappala, through an unknown intermediary, had seen to that—anything to enhance the illusion they were creating. University libraries had received the letters and original manuscripts, while Bassett kept only copies. The edited journals were sold off at a large estate sale, from there entering the world of the antiquarian book trade.

As a result, the things Andy had to look at consisted mostly of forty-seven years of periodic communications from the man who called himself the Gardener. They ranged from cryptic messages of a few sentences each to letters of eight, ten, even fifteen pages, each as bafflingly strange and dark as the one before.

Bassett had received the first letter on January 16, 1943, the day after the murder of the magazine editor, Calvert Drummond. In almost every way—the blocky printing, the choice of words—it was chillingly similar to Andy's first message.

WHEN FLOWERS GROW TOO CLOSE TO THE TREE
THEY MUST BE TRIMMED

SO SAITH THE POET SO SAITH ME

I AM THE GARDENER I PRUNE WHEN NECESSARY

ANYTHING OR ANYONE THAT HELPS THE TREE

SUCCEED
MUST BE TERMINATED

THE TREE MUST STAND ALONE

ASK YOURSELF WHY

"The guy's a broken record," Andy said when he read it. "But what the hell does it mean?"

Another note from a few weeks later read:

THE GARDENER MUST KEEP THE LAND ALONG THE TRAIN TRACKS CLEAN

ALL THINGS GROWING OR MOVING NEAR THE TRACKS MUST BE REMOVED

THE JOB IS OLD

THE JOB IS NEVER DONE

Grace Mahler, Andy thought as he read it. It was a confession to a four-year-old murder.

It was pointless trying to learn anything from the communications themselves. Even the relatively straightforward ones (like the Mahler confession) were vague and cryptic. Others, such as the one Andy held in his hand from June of 1952, were nothing but incomprehensible gibberish:

THE GARDENER WAS ALONE AMONG THE TREES
CROUCHING WHILE THE LUMBERJACK WORKED

THE TREES SOBBED AS THEY FELL

THE STANDING TREE WAS SPARED

THE NIGHT SEEMED NEAR AS THE SKY WEPT

A TREE WALKED AWAY LIKE A TRAITOR
LOVE BROKEN AND SLASHED

THE GARDENER WATCHED

Even Andy, who considered himself a fair hand at rooting out the sense that lurked within the secret codes of the best poetry, could make nothing of that.

When he had gone through each of the messages and his frustration was reaching its peak, he decided to try a different tack. Feeling a little like an amateur detective in a novel, he took a pen and paper and wrote down the names of each of the Gardener's victims, along with their dates

of death:
> *Willa Bassett 6/7/31 ???*
> *Grace Mahler 4/23/39*
> *Cal Drummond 1/15/43*
> *Henry Oglebay 11/7/45*
> *Jack Kretchmer 4/17/54 (attack)*
> *Connie Warren 1/1/55*
> *George O'Callaghan 12/3/64*
> *D. & L. Gulliver 7/4/87*

But though he studied the list from every conceivable angle, he was unable to find a neat, novelistic connection between the victims—nothing about their initials or the number of letters in their names or backwards, palindromic spellings—which meant that it was just as he'd feared. Their only link was their friendship with Bassett.

He hunted for clues to the Gardener in that list as well, but aside from the fact that two of the killings had taken place in the month of January and the Gullivers had been murdered on Independence Day, there didn't seem to be any seasonal ties, nothing related to holidays or important dates in history or Bassett's birthday in March or anything of the sort. As far as he could tell, the times of the Gardener's violence were chancy, random, and beyond explanation.

"You've tried all this before, haven't you?" Andy asked when he looked up from his work and saw Bassett watching him with a dry smile.

"Oh, yes, all of that and more. I spent a good many years trying to track him down in that Agatha Christie kind of way, which just goes to show you how naive I really was, and for how long. The Gardener is chaos. That's the real truth of the matter. And chaos can't be explained by adding up calendar dates and dividing by the number of months."

"So it all comes back to you again," Andy said, taking a long swallow of beer from the bottle next to him on the table. "If the link can't be found by looking *outside*, then we have to turn things around and look *in*. We have to assume that the Gardener is like these celebrity stalkers that are running everywhere these days. In a way, he was probably one of the first of the breed. But what made him do it? Your work? Something in one of the poems or novels? An essay you wrote? Something you said in an interview?"

The old man was shaking his head before Andy was even done. "I wasn't doing interviews when Grace was pushed in front of that train. I'd only been publishing short stories for two years or so, and all of those were in literary journals, obscure little rags. My first major sale was in February of '39—to *American Mercury*. Grace was killed in April of that year, and the story wasn't actually published until six or seven months later, sometime in the fall. I wasn't offending *anyone* with my work back then, not a soul."

"But the literary journals," Andy said. "Maybe the Gardener happened across something in—"

"Unlikely," Bassett interrupted. "Again, there's never been any proof of this—no confession note or anything of the sort—but I've always assumed that it was the Gardener who pushed my mother down the cellar steps. That was in the summer of 1931, five years before I'd sold anything to anyone. If the bastard killed my mother, he was spurred by something other than my writing."

Andy sighed and thought again about the drawer full of keys. Now, however, he was starting to think it was worse than that. Every time you tried to pick up a particular key to test it, you found that it didn't actually exist. You stuck your hand in the drawer and encountered…nothing. They were illusory keys, pictures of keys, holographic keys, mirages, unreal.

He lifted a sheet at random out of the stack. In Bassett's writing at the top was the following notation: *Rec'd Feb 3 1947.*

YOU THOUGHT YOU FOUND THE GARDENER BUT YOU LOOKED BENEATH THE WRONG TREE

PAUL F. OLSON

THE GARDENER STILL WAITS CROUCHING WATCHING

THERE IS MUCH PRUNING YET TO BE DONE

He thought of the entries in Jackson Kretchmer's journal and the trouble immediately preceding the Broadway opening of *To Raise Brave Men*. Perhaps there were still a few keys left to try, and just possibly one of them might turn out to be real.

He held the note up for Bassett to see. "This is about that actor, isn't it? What was his name? Langdon?"

"Mark Langdon," Bassett said. "But that was just his stage name. His real name was Jerome Wandry—Jerry. And yes, that's what it's about. February third was just a few days after what came to be known in literary circles as 'Bassett's nervous collapse.'"

"You thought this Wandry character was Jens Carlson?"

"Yes. No." He let out a long breath. "I'm honestly not sure anymore *what* I was thinking. I probably didn't know at the time. It was nothing. Just a crazy overreaction by an overworked, frightened, extremely distraught writer."

Andy frowned. "Tell me about it, about Carlson and Hale and McCready—everything."

"I'd really rather not."

"But it's probably important. In fact, it almost *has* to be."

Again, the old man was shaking his head. "I see this same thread when I read over your notes, this feeling of yours that everything in my life goes back to my father's murder of Royal Haag. Well, it doesn't." He hesitated, smiling gently at Andy. "Not that I don't understand how you might think that. Believe me, I do. I thought it myself for a number of years. I thought somehow the ghost of those days, in the form of Jens Carlson or

Jens Carlson's vengeful spirit or some damned thing, was following me, trying to destroy my life. But the incident with Wandry opened my eyes. I understood that Carlson was dead and gone, and so were those days back here in Rock Creek, and so was anyone who knew anything about them. They were different things. My father and Royal Haag and Halvard Borg and that whole despicable mess were in the past. The Gardener and I were in the present and the future."

"And yet they must be related," Andy insisted.

"Must they?" Bassett smiled again. "I think you're trying to find order out of chaos again."

"Tell me."

"No."

"Why? I don't get it. I thought you said you had no secrets, nothing to hide."

"Not quite. I don't have anything I *must* hide, but there are several things I'd *prefer* to hide. They're just too painful to dredge up again. I owed something to those days, and I tried to settle the debt by writing of my friends as soldiers sacrificed in war—Brave Men. It didn't work. I still felt I owed something, or had something I needed to say. So I memorialized Frank and Charlie on stage. But it still wasn't enough. And when I realized that, which was about the same time I stumbled off the deep end and almost killed Jerry Wandry…when all of that happened, I realized that no amount of dues-paying would be enough. I knew I had to bury the memories of those days. They were too much to face, and my plate was full enough with our friend the Gardener. So I dug a hole, and I put Haag and Borg and my father and Carlson and Charlie and Frank and probably a few other things down there. And I shoveled in the dirt. And I piled rocks on top of the dirt. And I've done well enough since then, at least in that regard, so perhaps you'll understand why I don't want to dig it up now."

Andy put his elbows on the table, his head in his hands, his hands over his eyes. Very softly, he said, "I understand your distress, but I honestly think you might be wrong." He looked up. "The other way, it just doesn't make any sense. All the death and violence in your early life, then all the death and violence from the time you were thirty until today, and none of it connected? I have a hard time buying that. You were a privileged kid from a normal Midwestern town. You went on to become a famous writer, a member of a very elite set. Most people in a situation like that would have lived their entire lives and never encountered anything darker than a mugging on the street. But now you're telling me that these two things came out of nowhere and have absolutely no relationship to each other. That's like saying some impossible kind of lightning struck twice where it shouldn't have even hit once."

He stopped abruptly, slightly breathless, and lowered his gaze from the old man's face, certain that he'd said too much, too harshly. Bassett would cancel their working arrangement. Bassett would throw him off the island, banish him forever. Once that happened, Andy knew that it would all be over. He'd have no chance against the Gardener, and any hope he'd had of finding Ginnie alive would be gone.

But the old man surprised him. "A lightning rod," he said, rising from the table and moving slowly across the kitchen. He stopped at the low wooden counter that was full of pots and pans, chipped dishes and ancient glasses marred by cracks of various sizes. He put both hands on the counter top and leaned against it, his back to Andy. "I've thought of myself that way from time to time, that I'm some kind of rod poking into the sky, attracting all kinds of misfortune. It's a terribly childish way to think—the world is picking on me, I'm a victim of all these nasty circumstances beyond my cause or control. But, goddammit, it's true. I have been. I am."

He turned back to face Andy, the movement so horribly slow that it seemed it would never be complete. "I knew as soon as I heard about it that my father's death couldn't have been an accident," he said. "I knew when no one else could have. That was another thing that was like a detective novel; I possessed a clue that no one else could possibly know. And whether it began that day or the day my father murdered Royal Haag doesn't really matter, because for me the *real* beginning was hearing about the explosion and the fire and that electrifying instant when I realized he'd been murdered."

Once the story was begun, the rest of it followed quickly, like a wildfire burning.

7

ANDY'S DREAMS THAT night were scarcely more troubled than they had been recently, but they were different in another regard. That night he walked the dream landscape not as himself or as a dispassionate third-party observer but as Alexander Bassett, a young Bassett just out of high school, a young Bassett who was forced to confide in his two best friends, because he had kept his secret fears to himself from early March until late June and finally could hold them no more.

They were fishing when he told them, the three of them sitting on a rocky outcropping along the southern shore of Preston Lake, smoking cigarettes they'd stolen from Frank Hale's father and drinking wine they'd appropriated from Charlie McCready's house, laughing once in a while at something one or the other said, but mostly just sharing a companionable silence that Bassett finally felt compelled to break.

Frank and Charlie were immediately skeptical, and why not? They knew as well as everyone in town the official verdict on the death of William Bassett—a leaking drum of kerosene sitting in the corner of the office, a match struck to light a cigar—and they thought it was sad, perhaps even a little odd, that their friend could not accept this verdict as easily as everyone else.

But then Bassett told them about his clue:

March sixth, the day of his father's death, had been a Sunday. The mill offices were closed, as they always were on weekends, or at least as they had been for the last ten years or so, the time in which the timber business in and around Rock Creek had begun to dwindle and die. The previous day, Saturday the fifth, William Bassett had dragged Alexander out of bed early, saying he needed his help at the office. Alex, who worshipped his father, was more than happy to comply.

The help consisted of precisely this: moving seven heavy drums of kerosene out of the office to an empty storage shed several hundred yards away. Two of the drums had begun to leak, and, ironically enough, William Bassett was afraid of fire. The reason he was asking Alex's help with the project on a Saturday morning rather than waiting until Monday, when he could easily have had paid laborers do the work, was simple. William had a busy weekend of paperwork planned. He had already worked late in the office Friday night, well after the second shift (currently the *last* shift) of millworkers had left, and the fumes from the leaking fuel had given him a headache, an upset stomach, and toward the end of the evening, blurry vision. With seven or eight more hours of work ahead of him that Saturday and at least that much on Sunday, he wanted the drums out of there immediately.

So Alex and his father spent an hour that Saturday morning moving the drums.

"Larsson and his crew will cry like babies every time they have to haul a drum back over here to fill the stove," William Bassett said with a laugh. "But to hell with them. That's the kind of work I pay them for."

Then, while his father set to work at his desk, Alex spent another twenty-five minutes or so mopping up the spilled kerosene that had puddled in the corner of the office. He followed that with a thorough scrub-down of the floorboards using soap and liquid disinfectant.

"Maybe it was the stove that exploded," Frank said after he'd heard all this, not yet ready to concede Alex's theory of murder.

"It wasn't the stove," Alex said. "Don't you remember the report? They found two drums of kerosene in the wreckage of the office, at least one of which was so badly corroded that it had definitely been leaking. But I remember that corroded drum; it was the first one my father and I moved! There was no corroded drum in there when my dad left work Saturday night. Christ Almighty, there weren't *any* drums. All the drums were in the storage shed across the back lot."

ALEXANDER'S SONG

Charlie, who was younger than Alex and Frank by two years, gave in first. "Who would've done it?" he said in a voice that was filled with traces of wonder, fear, and something that might have been simple excitement.

Alex didn't know, but he intended to find out.

Frank laughed loud and long, apparently forgetting what he had just learned, that his best friend's father had been a victim of foul play. There was no sympathy in that laugh, no sorrow. It was a laugh of ripe amusement.

"It's a grand day, ladies and gentlemen!" he cried, leaping to his feet and announcing this news to the uneasy waters of Preston Lake. "Mr. Holmes is back in residence at 221B! Look out, all you purloiners of jewels, you robbers of banks, you spillers of kerosene and strikers of matches! Look out, because Mr. Holmes will—"

He must have remembered the situation then, because he broke off suddenly, his face flushed. His gaze darted away from Alex and he became extremely interested in the tag alders growing in a scrubby tangle to his left.

"I'm sorry," he muttered. "I lost my head. I'm a shit, Alex. I wasn't thinking."

"It's all right," Alex said, determined not to let on how hurt he was. "I'm being an ass. I'm sure you're right. But how would you feel if it was your dad, Frank? Charlie, what about you? If your father had been killed, could you just let it go? Wouldn't you want to dig into things and try to understand? Could you even look at yourself in the mirror if you knew you'd just walked away and done nothing?"

It seemed to Alex that that last word echoed back to him from across the lake, an undying chant—*nothing...nothing...nothing....*It went immediately like an arrow to his heart, summing up what he had done about his suspicions—nothing!—what he really knew about what he was saying—nothing!—and what he could honestly hope to do about it now—nothing and nothing and nothing!

He was a little surprised that he didn't feel better after the telling. The knowledge had, after all, been a weight on his soul from the very first day, and it had only grown worse as the weeks went by. When he had

345

tried to tell Elwood McFarren what he knew about the drums of kerosene, he hadn't been able to do it. Facing the stern and always gruff constable had reminded him too much of his run-ins with the man, when he and Frank had been caught smoking cigarettes behind the market, or when McFarren had discovered him with Jeanette Comstock, the two of them in each other's arms under the shingled roof of the gazebo in Memorial Park. Those memories had tied his tongue in front of the man. They had made what he knew about his father's death seem wrongheaded, a fantasy that the little boy he no longer was might have made up, constructed out of a runaway imagination and a refusal to accept a God who allowed accidents to happen.

And so he had said nothing.

And so he had felt even worse.

But releasing the pent-up news at last to Frank and Charlie hadn't helped. Maybe it was the way Charlie was looking at him with those eyes that were full of awe and also traces of fear, and it probably had something to do with Frank's expression as well, that disbelieving, slightly mocking look that was still there even after his apology.

Andy felt all this in his dream. As this creature who was two-men-in-one, this Alex-Andy, he was intensely in tune with these feelings of impotence and the fear and helpless rage that resulted from them. He understood that he, as just Andy alone, had been dealing with the same emotions much of the time lately, and that understanding made his empathy all the more acute.

What have you done?

Nothing._

What can you do?

Nothing.

"I think you're right, Franko," Charlie was saying. He went on after that and said several more things, but Alex, or rather Alex-Andy, was still listening to the imaginary sound of his mournful echo coming back to him across the lake. He was sorry now that he'd opened his mouth, sorry now about almost everything, and from the depths of his self-pity he heard only the last few words.

"What's that?" he said, sitting up a little straighter, his fishing pole and the McCready's bottle of wine forgotten at his side. "What did you say?"

Charlie looked embarrassed. "I was just joshing around with Frank. It was nothing important. I...I'm sorry about your pop, Alex. I never thought—"

"No, no!" Alex snapped. "You said something just now. What was it?"

"Aw, don't make me say it again. I wasn't serious."

Alex stood up and walked over to the boulder where the boy was sitting. He glared down at him. *"What was it?"*

Charlie squirmed uncomfortably. He muttered, "Shit," but Alex continued to glower, and finally Charlie was forced to surrender, unwillingly repeating what he had said to Frank.

"It was a joke, Alex. I was just fooling, but...but I said...I said this business with your pop sounded like a job for the Dupin Society."

"The Dupin Society?"

"I told you I wasn't serious! I'm sorry about your old man, honest I am. I sure didn't—"

"The Dupin Society?"

"Stop looking at me like that!" Charlie cried, close to tears.

"The Dupin Society?"

"Leave the kid alone," Frank said, stepping between them. "We both said things we didn't mean. We both apologized. Let it go."

"The Dupin Society?"

Alex was vaguely aware that they sounded like actors in a bad vaudeville routine. He didn't know about Frank and Charlie, but for his part, he was unable to help himself. That name seemed suddenly so important that he couldn't stop saying it. The Dupin Society...the very thought of it, as silly as it admittedly was on the surface, was like a key finally opening a long-locked door, a lamp being lit in a darkened room.

The society itself had been a game, something the three of them had done as boys. First it had been the Long John Silver Society and pirate adventures in the woods around town, and when they'd tired of that the Dupin Society was born. For some amount of time that Alex was no longer certain of—a few weeks, probably; no more than a month—he and Frank and Charlie had played at being great detectives, solving strange disappearances and hideous murders, tracking ruthless master criminals down woodland trails that had been transformed in their imaginations to the rooftops of London or the sewers beneath the streets of Paris.

After the Dupin Society it had been...he was no longer certain. It all seemed so long ago. Ivanhoe, perhaps, or Camelot. At any rate, it was something to do with knights and grails. And after that? After that, they had grown too old for such games.

Obviously it wasn't the idea of the Dupin Society itself that excited Alex now. That would have been ludicrous. It was the idea *behind* the idea, the thought that perhaps the three of them actually could do something, ask some questions, look around, maybe go so far as to comb what was left of the fire site at the mill for clues. Before, he wished that he had done something, he longed for something to do. Now here it was, presented by Charlie and laid into his lap in the form of a memory seven or eight years old.

Forget that bastard McFarren and his ignorant deputies.

The Dupin Society.

Yes.

It was so simple. It was so clear.

You didn't need the officials when you could do it yourself.

The Dupin Society.

Get off your ass, he told himself. Get off your ass and open your eyes and act!

"Are you all right?"

Alex blinked and turned around. It was Charlie standing beside him, gently touching his shoulder, worried about the way he had drifted away for a second or two.

"Alex? I didn't mean to upset you, honest to God. I swear I was just making a joke. I mean, hell, your old man is dead, and here I go saying something—"

"It's all right, Charlie. It's fine. I'm not angry."

"You sure?"

Alex nodded. "Not angry at all. Far from it. You had a grand idea. We're going to become detectives."

Frank and Charlie each took a step back and stared at him, as though afraid he might have slipped a cog. Their expressions were so frankly ridiculous that Alex couldn't help himself.

He threw back his head and laughed.

8

EXCEPT THE SOUND that came out in Andy's dream wasn't laughter at all. It was high and sharp and jarring, as grating as nails on slate and as brittle as breaking ice.

It was almost like a scream.

9

HE AWOKE DRENCHED in sweat but shivering, cloaked in darkness and lost in that place between sleep and unconsciousness, partly himself and partly an Alexander Bassett sixty-three years gone. He looked left and right, frantically trying to find the faces of Frank and Charlie that were now lost in blackness.

He heard another scream, muffled and faraway. The sound made his heart take three or four stuttering steps, and at the same time made him realize where he was. Not at Preston Lake in the early summer of 1927 but in his room, Andy Gillespie's room on the third floor of the Sleep-Tite Hotel.

A sound that might have been scuffling footsteps in the corridor outside (or perhaps it was just the uneven rasp of his own breath) seemed to fill the room. He sat up and fumbled for the bedside lamp, almost knocked it over, righted it, and tried desperately to find the switch.

When his fingers closed on it at last, they were too slick with sweat to turn it. He cursed.

Screams...footsteps ....

At last he got it. The light was like a knife driven into the space between his eyes, blinding and painful. Through a dancing field of black and red dots he saw his watch lying on the nightstand. Six-thirty...midnight...quarter of nine...no...no. He drew a breath and calmed himself. It was three-fifteen, and he remembered now: leaving Wolf Island at eleven-thirty; the long journey across the lake in a boat that was now his, or almost his, leased from Seward's Outfitters on a weekly basis; the drive into town; collapsing into his bed sometime after one with the story of The Dupin Society and what had happened to them still fresh in his mind.

And then he remembered the screams.

He listened, but the night was silent now. No voices, no cries, no footsteps. Even the pipes in the bathroom, which always seemed to make a constant racket of hissing and clanking, were quiet. He couldn't even hear the wind outside his window.

Andy tried to piece things together in his mind, to determine if what had awakened him and what he thought he'd heard immediately thereafter had been real. He finally decided it had not been. It had been a fragment of dream, sleep residue, something like that. And on the off chance he had really heard it...if that were the case, then it hadn't been in the hallway but outside—dogs fighting, drunks roaming around in the alley alongside the hotel, something common and harmless like that, an every-night sort of sound.

"Keep a good thought," he muttered thickly, and so saying, fell back asleep almost instantly.

10

HE DID NOT recapture the dream, or at least he didn't pick up the threads in the same place he'd dropped them. He did skip briefly past the images of Frank Hale and Charlie McCready, but this time it was horrible.

Beyond horrible.

Unspeakable.

He saw blood flying, swirling through the air like mist around a storm cloud. He heard dreadful cries and the sound of an ax chopping wetly through tissue, grinding through bone. He saw Hale in a puddle of gore, McCready trying to run, being pursued by Jens Carlson, or someone he thought was Carlson—a gigantic shadow, a faceless mountain of destruction. And all because they had reformed the Dupin Society, all because they had uncovered the murderer of William Bassett and had confronted him, had told him what they'd learned and promised to go to the constable.

Andy heard all this and watched all this from the trees on the edge of a forest clearing. He covered his eyes with his hands and cried silently, wept soundlessly, screamed inside himself. He felt small, infinitesimally tiny.

He felt helpless.

He *was* helpless.

And then the dream moved on, and if he dreamed any more he forgot by the time the insistent ringing of the telephone dragged him out of bed at seven that morning.

He was dazed and almost unbelievably groggy as he stumbled toward the phone, and he half imagined that the coppery smell of blood clung to the insides of his nostrils, although he couldn't for the life of him imagine why.

11

"HELLO?"

His voice was thick and dull, a voice from out of an ancient tomb, and it occurred to him in shorthand fashion that this experience was killing him. He was living on coffee and cigarettes, not getting nearly enough sleep, his only energy coming from the dangerous adrenaline cocktail of mystery and stress.

He said it again, speaking into a line that was clotted with static and a sound like rumbling engines: "Hello?"

At last, out of the chaos, a reply: "Gillespie!"

He pulled the receiver back from his ear, startled, suddenly wide awake and at the same time remembering that last bit of dream: Hale and McCready and a shadow-man's ax doing its deadly work.

"Who...who is this?"

"Is that you, Gillespie?"

"Who are you?"

"It's Robert Jackowicz."

"Bob?"

He couldn't have been more surprised if it was a phone call from the pope. He had spoken to Joanne's current lover only once in the last year, and even that had been an accident. He had called Jo about some mail that had been mistakenly delivered to him, Jackowicz had answered the phone, and they had spent an unpleasant minute or two engaging in something that could only charitably be called small talk.

"Bob? What's up? Is Joanne okay?"

Jackowicz made a noise somewhere between a grunt and a growl. "You tell me."

"What're you talking about?" Andy rubbed his eyes with the back of his hand. "Is she there? Let me talk to her."

A sizzle of static on the line swallowed the answer the way the explosion on Wolf Island had swallowed Bassett's stairs.

"Bob?"

Noise and nothingness.

"Bob, Jesus, let me talk to Jo."

There was an angry sound that Andy at first took to be more interference. Then, a split second later, he realized it was Jackowicz growling again, fiercely swearing.

"Bob, for Chrissakes, *what's wrong?*"

The line went dead.

TWELVE

THE WIDENING GYRE

1

It took over fifteen minutes to get Jackowicz back on the phone. In that time Andy had to endure several dialing attempts that went nowhere but into Michigan Bell's mystical ether, the siren sound of a line out of service, and several busy signals that he hoped were Jackowicz simultaneously trying to reach him. When the phone in Orlando finally rang, he was leaning against the dresser, a cigarette twitching between his lips, his small address book with the imitation leather cover gripped in the trembling fingers of his right hand.

She's dead, he was thinking. It was a car crash, a fire, some kind of disaster. Jackowicz was calling to break the news. Why else would he call, at seven in the morning or any other time? He was calling to tell him Jo was dead.

"I hope that's you, Gillespie."

The connection this time was dramatically better, and Andy felt both relief and terror in equal measures.

"It's me. What's going on there? What happened to Jo?"

There was the sound of Jackowicz sighing. "Don't play games with me, you lousy prick. She's there, isn't she? Right there in your room, probably sitting next to you, laughing her ass off. I won't stand for it. If I'm the cuckold, then dammit, have the balls to come right out and tell me."

Andy couldn't make sense of any of that. The wild image that came to mind, of a horned Bob Jackowicz running down the streets of Orlando, didn't fit with anything he had been thinking just a few seconds earlier. Cuckold? Jo in his room? Laughing? Then, in a moment of clarity, he thought he understood what the man was trying to tell him.

"Jo's not there?" he said softly.

"You're a funny man," Jackowicz shot back. "You're a goddamned laugh riot. Now let me talk to her."

"You're saying Jo's here, in Rock Creek. Is that right?"

"You know fucking well she's there in Rock Creek, and I'm giving you approximately three more seconds to quit yanking my chain and put her on the line."

"Bob, slow down." Andy heard something in his voice, something very thin and frail, laced with fright. Doubtless it was only the outward expression of what was going on inside, but at the moment he didn't feel *anything* inside. He had gone cold all over. He was numb. "Jo's not here. I haven't seen her in over a year. I haven't talked to her in…God, I don't know…four days, maybe? Are you telling the truth? She was coming to Rock Creek?"

There was a moment of silence that felt to Andy like an hour. Finally: "Aw, what a fucked up mess this is. I don't know what's happening. Maybe you're being straight with me. Maybe you don't know, either. But she left here yesterday morning. She said she was going to find you. She was supposed to call me when she got up there, but—"

"Hold on. She was coming here. To find me. For godssakes, why?"

"Do you think I know? She said she was worried about you. She said you sounded terrible on the phone the last time she called. She said you sounded sick and…and frightened. She said you sounded frightened of something. She tried calling you again on Friday, but the people at that inn or boarding house, whatever it was, wherever you were staying, told her you'd checked out. They said you were going back home to Chicago."

ALEXANDER'S SONG

Andy swallowed and felt a lump in his throat. "Go on."

"She spent all day Saturday trying to reach you at home. When she didn't get you by Saturday night she called the boarding house again. They were very abrupt with her, rude. They said you were gone and that was that. They had some kind of emergency going on there and couldn't be bothered. So she waited until Sunday morning, yesterday, and when she still didn't reach you, she called our travel agent and took off for Michigan."

"But that's ridiculous! I told her I was fine! I told her not to worry!"

"Yeah. Right," Jackowicz said.

Andy fumbled a fresh cigarette out of the pack and lit it. It tasted dry and stale, like hot sawdust on his tongue.

He was still having trouble making sense out of the news. It was disorienting at best, a rug being placed under his feet and then quickly yanked away. The thought that Jo, with whom he had parted on less than amicable terms, would be concerned enough about his well-being to travel all the way from Florida to Michigan looking for him...the concept seemed incredible to him. Helping with his research, finding the Bassett and Kretchmer journals, was one thing—odd enough, perhaps, but still understandable. This information, however, was something he couldn't seem to grab hold of. He couldn't even begin to find a grip.

"I'm worried about her," Jackowicz said. "Unless of course you're lying to me and she's right there with you, just like I thought."

"She's not here," Andy heard himself say. "But don't worry. Rock Creek's kind of off the beaten path. Getting here's not like one of your business trips, flying to New York or L.A. I'm sure she'll be getting in soon, sometime this morning or—"

"She should be there now. I've got her itinerary right in front of me. She left Orlando at eleven-fifteen yesterday morning. She was supposed to layover a few hours in Chicago and take some commuter airline to a place called Houghton. According to this, she got into Houghton at ten-thirty last night."

"Maybe there was a delay," Andy said, knowing right away how foolish that was. A nine-hour delay? And in that unlikely event, wouldn't she have called home?

"No delay," Jackowicz said. "I checked with the airline. Of course the assholes wouldn't confirm whether or not she was on that flight, but the plane landed in Houghton seven minutes early last night."

"Then maybe she stayed over there."

"That's what I thought. But then I called the airport and talked to someone at the Hertz desk. She rented a car from them last night. How long does it take to get from there to Rock Creek?"

"I don't know. Forty-five minutes, maybe an hour."

"Then she should've been there by midnight at the latest."

"She still could've stayed in Houghton," Andy said. "Maybe she rented the car and drove to a hotel. She might have been too tired to drive these back roads late at night."

"Maybe." Jackowicz said, but he sounded thoroughly unconvinced. "You didn't see the hurry she was in when she ran out of here yesterday. I tried to talk sense into her, but she's headstrong—shit, you know that, right? I wanted her to wait a few more days. Maybe you were taking your time driving back home to Chicago, I said. Maybe you were on the road somewhere in between, spending a few days in Milwaukee or something. She wouldn't hear of it. She said I hadn't talked to you on the phone last Thursday, I didn't know what you sounded like. She was worried. I don't think she would've wasted the night in some hotel, when it was only a matter of an hour's drive to get to Rock Creek."

Andy bit his lower lip. "How did you find me? If she couldn't, how did *you* track me down?"

"Accident, I guess. Either that, or we get back to the fact that you're slinging bullshit at me again."

"What do you mean?"

"She jotted down everything on this itinerary—everything *but* the name of the hotel where she'd be staying in Rock Creek. So I called the agent. She said it was the Sleep-Tite. But when I called there and asked for Jo Gillespie, the old bat on the phone connected me to you."

"Oh. I get it now. Now it makes sense. You thought you'd gotten Jo's room. You were expecting to hear her voice, and I answered the phone instead. The lady at the desk—her name's Marilyn, by the way—heard you ask for Gillespie and thought you wanted me. You had no clue I was staying here. I was the last voice you expected to hear and...Jesus."

"Yeah. Jesus." There was a long moment of silence. "You have to tell me, Gillespie. You've got to be straight with me. She's not there with you, is she? You're telling the truth about that? This wasn't some kind of crazy scheme of hers, to go running back to her ex? And you didn't take her in with open arms?"

Andy sighed. The cigarette had burned out in the ashtray on the dresser, almost untouched, and he stared at the long column of gray ash with ridiculous interest.

"Gillespie? Talk to me, goddammit."

"I'm telling the truth," Andy said. "She's not here. I didn't know she was coming. But I also have to tell you that I think it's too early to worry. Jo's smart. She wouldn't get into trouble between Houghton and Rock Creek. I'm sure she spent the night at some hotel up there. She'll probably be pulling in here any minute, all rested and ready to chew me out for having her worried."

"Do you really think so?"

"I do." Andy paused. Something else had just occurred to him. "You know, Bob, she might even be right here at the Sleep-Tite. Maybe Marilyn just got confused when you asked for Jo Gillespie and connected you to my room. But that doesn't mean there isn't *another* Gillespie in *another* room."

"Christ!" Jackowicz said, with clear relief. "I never thought of that! I got so pissed when I heard your voice on the other end of the line that... well, maybe I got carried away."

"I guess I can understand that," Andy said softly. "Look, I'll tell you what. There's not much more you can do from that end now, so let me

PAUL F. OLSON

check on it. If she's here in the hotel, or if she gets here later this morning, I'll have her call you right away. Fair enough?"

"Yeah. Yeah, fair enough. I appreciate that."

There was, thank God, no pointless small talk after that. Andy hung up, picked up the receiver again right away, and dialed down to the front desk. But Marilyn said that no one had checked in at all last night or so far this morning. Not Joanne Gillespie, not anyone else.

"You ready to fill me in on all your deep, dark secrets?" Marilyn asked. "You going to tell me why you've been running around like an alley cat at all hours of the night? Or are you just going to piss off this partnership we've got before it even gets going?"

Andy brushed away the question. "If someone by that name—Joanne Gillespie—checks in here, send her up to my room right away. She's my ex-wife. It's very important."

"Your ex? What in Sam Hell does she have to do—"

But Andy cut her off by putting the phone down into its cradle.

2

FROM THE RESEARCH *notebooks of Andy Gillespie:*

Well okay. Now I understand how A.B. became a socialist, or at least I think I understand it.

McCready, Hale, and A.B. found out that Jens Carlson had set the fire in the mill. That, by the way, was easier than they'd thought going in. There were questions that the cop, McFarren, should have asked. But he didn't. Too quick to write the thing off as an accidental explosion. But the Dupins asked, and they found out from residents around the mill that Carlson had been seen skulking around there late on Saturday night, 3/5/27. Someone had even seen the guy rolling something through the weeds between the storage shed and the mill office. They couldn't see what it was, but to A.B. it was obvious. It

ALEXANDER'S SONG

was a kerosene drum, of course. Why didn't McFarren discover that? Why didn't the locals come forward? Their explanation: they thought Carlson was working there, at the mill. He was an odd-jobs kind of guy, worked a week here, a month there, an afternoon doing something else. They just assumed he'd gotten his most recent job at the Manitou Mill. Okay. That's understandable. But it still doesn't excuse McFarren for his sloppy investigation.

Anyway, the Dupins confronted Carlson, and before Carlson got around to making his death threats against the three (and making good on two of them) he laid out for them the whole sordid tale. He told them about W. Bassett's murder of Haag, about the way W. had tried to buy off Carlson's father, and when that didn't work, how he killed the man and made it look like a confessional suicide. He said his murder of W. was strictly revenge, or as A.B. quoted him: "The sumbitch did away with m'daddy because m'daddy was too goddamned honest to play his game! I kept that inside a'me too long, boyos. I hadda do somethin' about it or I woulda busted up from holdin' it in."

Well Christ.

Here's A.B., a thoughtful, poetic kind of kid. He'd always worshipped his father—the good provider, the family man, the successful entrepreneur, a man for all seasons and times. But he was wrong about that, and suddenly he realizes it. He realizes that his father was just another rich sleazy bastard who would kill a man over (as best anyone knew) an attempt to organize a union. Then he had tried to buy his way out of trouble. And then he had killed again.

A.B. was enraged. Who wouldn't be? All this death over money, what amounted to a handful of pocket change for William Bassett. And it only got worse. When Jens Carlson killed McCready and Hale, and almost killed Alex himself, the death toll had risen. Four people were dead, essentially because of W. And later, when Alex went after Carlson, and they fought, and Carlson fell off the pier into Green Lake and presumably drowned, well, that made five. Five dead.

It would've made me question the values I was raised with, I'll tell you that. It would've made me wonder about the corrupting power of money. It would've made me hate my father, if I were in A.B.'s shoes.

Would it have turned me into a socialist?

I don't know. The idea seems almost silly, quaint in today's brave new world.

But times were different in 1927.

They were different just a few years ago.

Christ, A.B., I heard the story from your own lips. I heard you tell it, old man. I saw you weep when you talked about what your father had done, what it meant to you when you found out.

I think I understand you a lot better than I did yesterday.

3

ANDY PUT DOWN his pen and walked from the tiny desk to the window overlooking Michigan Street. He scanned the street in both directions, as he had been doing every few minutes all morning, looking for some sign of Jo. It was almost eleven. He had told Bassett he'd be back at Wolf Island by noon. He didn't think he was going to make it.

She's going to arrive safely, he told himself, not for the first time. God knew why she was coming—he had told her not to worry—but she *was* coming, and there was nothing he could do about it now. She was coming. She would get here. She was fine.

But while that had been easy to believe at seven, it seemed less and less likely as the hours ticked by.

Bob Jackowicz had already called back twice, and each time Andy had repeated his earlier advice. "Relax," he had said. "Jo's smart. She wouldn't get into trouble between Houghton and Rock Creek." And yet the fact remained that Jackowicz had put her on a plane in Orlando twenty-four hours ago, and presumably that plane had arrived in Chicago on time.

ALEXANDER'S SONG

Presumably Jo had sat out her layover and boarded a commuter flight for Houghton, and that flight had landed seven minutes early. She had rented a car. She had left the airport and gone—

Stop it! he thought. You're just torturing yourself.

Any minute Jo would come breezing into his room, full of her usual sarcasm and hard-edged cheer. She would have a story to relate, something about a flat tire on a lonely stretch of Rock Creek Road, an overheated engine, a series of wrong turns. She would forcefully ignore the fact that he'd had nothing directly to do with her trip to Michigan and instead chastise him for making her worry. They would argue. Then they would probably laugh. But even if they didn't find the humor in the situation, everything would be fine. One way or the other it would be okay.

He checked the street one more time, then turned toward the door. He stared at it with an expression that was a cross between trepidation and determination, the look of a mountain climber gathering the courage to tackle a difficult peak.

Ten minutes ago, as he'd been putting the finishing touches on his most recent notebook entry, he had paused in the act of writing and suddenly looked up, staring across the room at nothing in particular. For the first time that morning he had remembered the screams and the sound of footsteps he had imagined hearing somewhere in the hotel late last night. What time had that been? Three-fifteen? He had thought about those sounds, and he couldn't help wondering if he'd actually heard them. He remembered thinking at the time that they were all in his head, but maybe....

Where had they come from? Not directly outside his room; he was sure of that. But where? Somewhere downstairs, on another floor or in the lobby? On the fire stairs? Outside in the rear parking lot?

He was going to have to get this over with. Whether he wanted to or not, he was going to have to cross the room, pull open that door, and look for a message in an envelope.

He realized that he was walking close to the edge. He had been over that edge once, panicking in the street. Now he was tempting the heights again. Thinking that the Gardener might have Jo was crazy. It was a bad, sick joke. But those sounds, which had been so easy to dismiss at first, were echoing now through his mind. He heard them over and over again, a muffled scream, the sound of scuffling steps, another scream. Each time the loop played in his memory, it seemed less imaginary, more concrete, more authentic.

"Do it," he said, and started toward the door.

He was almost there when someone knocked, hard and fast. He actually jumped, and bit down on his tongue sharply enough to draw blood.

"J-Jo?"

"It's housekeeping. You want me to come back?"

For a moment he couldn't find the sense in what he'd just heard, as if the woman on the other side had been speaking in a foreign tongue. Then he understood and felt a wave of despair wash over him. He'd been so sure it would be Joanne, certain that she'd arrived at last, safe and sound.

"Sir? You want me to come back later?"

He swallowed and tasted blood. "Yes. Please. In fact, you don't have to come back at all today. The room's fine."

"Okay, then. I'll leave some fresh towels here for you and check again tomorrow." There was a pause. He almost thought she'd gone away when she said, "Sir?"

"Yes, what is it?"

"Do you know you got a note on your door?"

4

HE DIDN'T MOVE for at least ten seconds, a span of time during which his mind, at least on the conscious level, was blank, a span of time during which he stared at the doorway and soaked in the sight of it—the grain of the wood, its tiny cracks and blemishes, the tone of the stain, the posted rules and regulations sign, the floor plan marked with the locations of fire exits and ice machines, the tarnish on the knob and lock—without really registering any of it.

"Sir? Did you hear what I said? You've got a note out here."

Feeling like an apparition in someone else's dream, Andy went forward the last two or three steps. He reached out slowly and was vaguely aware of his fingers wrapping themselves around the knob. He turned and pulled, stepping back as the heavy door swung inward, and only then, when it was already too late to stop or protect himself in any way, did it occur to him that he was doing a stupid thing. It might be a trap, not a maid at all but a companion of the Gardener, maybe the Gardener himself using some kind of voice trick to fool him and—

The door was open.

The girl standing in the hallway was short and plain, forcing an on-the-job kind of smile. She was only about nineteen, dressed in a gray sweatshirt with the legend L'ANSE PURPLE HORNETS, faded jeans, and sneakers. Around her waist was a short half-apron, the kind used by waitresses for storing order pads and change. Nosing out of the pockets of the apron were a can of Pledge, a feather duster, and a bottle of generic blue window-cleaning fluid. In one arm she held a folded white bath towel and set of washcloths. In the other —

"Here you go," she said, thrusting into his hands a plain white envelope that still had a strip of tape attached to one corner. "You sure about the room?"

Andy looked up from the envelope, which had his last name printed across the front. "I'm sorry, what?"

The maid sighed. It was clearly an effort not to roll her eyes in exasperation. "The *room*, sir. Are you sure you don't want me to make it up today?"

"Not today...no...no, thank you."

"Well, if you change your mind before three, just call down to the desk and ask them to send me up. After three you're on your own. That's when I get off."

Andy waved her away. "Thanks. Bye-bye now."

He swung the door shut, checked to make sure it was locked, and tore open the envelope. His hands were trembling again—they trembled almost all the time lately—but after several failed attempts he was able to pull out the piece of paper inside and unfold it.

He read the message in those now-familiar block letters and was temporarily confused, frustrated and irritated by that confusion. It was like getting a phone call in the middle of the night that turned out to be a wrong number, a piece of personal mail addressed to your neighbor. He knew full well how weird and nonsensical the Gardener's messages could be, but this time he had been hoping (perhaps against all reasonable hope) for something plainer, easier to understand, something to address his fears directly.

But this…this message was brief and cold. This message meant nothing.

THEN THERE WERE TWO

"Two," he muttered under his breath. "Two *what*, for Chrissakes?"

And then, as soon as he asked the question, the answer hurtled out of nowhere and struck him full force. If it had been a punch, he would have dropped like a stone. If it had been a wave, he would have drowned.

He tried to stay calm, forced himself to take slow, deep breaths, and attempted to ponder his next step. But it was useless. For the next minute or so he moved about the room like a dithering old man, picking up the phone and getting halfway through Bob Jackowicz's number before hanging up again, starting toward the door with the intention of going down to see Marilyn before hesitating and changing his mind.

He wondered if this, now, changed everything. Did he finally have a reason to go to the police? Did he now have a clue that he and Bassett could use?

"Goddammit, Jo, I never asked for your help! I never suggested that you come here!"

But on the heels of that he felt something different, something he hadn't felt before in quite this way. It took him a second to sort it out from among all the other thoughts and feelings roiling through his brain, to recognize what it was, but he finally identified it as a sense of pure, almost righteous anger—scary in its unfamiliarity, energizing in its raw intensity.

He hadn't asked Jo to come —that was true enough—but what did that mean? Was that supposed to be some kind of excuse? Was that supposed to forgive the Gardener for whatever he had done? Jo hadn't asked for that. None of them had asked for what had befallen them. Certainly Ginnie hadn't, or Grace Mahler, or Constance Warren. Calvert Drummond hadn't asked for it. Jack Kretchmer hadn't asked. Even Bassett hadn't asked, as far as Andy could tell.

I didn't ask, either, he thought. I came here to write a couple of lousy articles.

Maybe Bassett was right. Maybe the Gardener was nothing but accident and chaos, a flaw in the fabric of the world, a cosmic wrinkle without a cause, beyond explanation or justification.

Maybe.

But so what? Andy wondered. Was he simply supposed to accept that?

Where were you when I made the universe? God had roared to Job.

Where were you when I decided to set my hooks into Bassett? the Gardener's phantom voice might also ask Andy.

"Fuck that," he said now, addressing the phantom voice in return. "Fuck *you*. That's not good enough."

He looked down and saw that he had ground the latest message—THEN THERE WERE TWO—into an unrecognizable ball. It was clenched in the bloodless knuckles of his right hand, a hand that was suddenly no longer trembling.

"Fuck you," he said again.

He understood then that he had reached a decision of sorts. None of them had asked for the Gardener, but the Gardener had not asked for him, either. The police, even if they could do something, even if they believed him, even if they didn't throw him into a cell for concealing evidence or obstructing justice, weren't good enough for the Gardener. Norman Paquin wasn't good enough. Jeff Lamoreaux wasn't good enough. Betty Rhodes wasn't good enough. Coffin of the FBI wasn't good enough.

It's me, you son of a bitch. You brought the game to me. Now I'm going to bring it back to you.

He didn't stop to question the wisdom of that decision or the essential foolhardiness behind his new determination. He didn't dare. Instead, he blotted out everything in his mind but a double image, two faces, Ginnie's and Jo's.

A moment later he was on the phone to Florida.

"Christ, I've been waiting for you to call back," Jackowicz said. "I was about to track down the cops up there and report this to them."

"Don't bother," Andy said. "She got here a little while ago. She's fine."

"Well, let me talk to her. Did she—"

"She can't talk right now. She'll call you soon."

"But what about—"

"She's here. She's all right. That's all you have to know."

"But what happened? Dammit, Gillespie, why was she so late? Did she say—"

"Goodbye, Bob."

"*Gillespie!*"

The receiver made a satisfying thunk as he put it down.

On his way to Harker's Landing, he detoured to Victory Street and stopped for a short time in front of the bed and breakfast. For the first time in a week there were no police cars out front. He supposed the search had been called off, or had taken on some new reduced form. Why not? As Carrie Ives had said, "Kids run off." As Jack Seely had said, "Once they hit sixteen-seventeen, you can't keep 'em around." You couldn't waste taxpayers' money forever looking for one disaffected runaway kid, could you?

The rage inside him went up a notch, boiling. It was like a thin red veil that colored his vision, the inside of the truck, the landscape around him.

ALEXANDER'S SONG

"Fuck you," he said again.

Apparently that was his new battle cry, and he couldn't seem to stop saying it.

5

HE WAITED A long time at the door of the cabin, knocking, listening, knocking again, but Bassett didn't answer. He refused to allow himself the dubious luxury of fear, and instead kept rapping on the door at regular intervals.

After a while, he became aware of a sound from inside the cabin, a common and familiar noise that he nevertheless couldn't place. It was a distant sort of tapping, a harsh rattle that came in slow, methodical bursts broken by brief bouts of silence.

Suddenly, the grim expression that Andy had been wearing for the last two hours melted away. It was replaced almost instantly by a slowly rising smile, a grin that spread until it stretched across his entire face. He stopped knocking and opened the door, went in, crossed the cluttered living room to a door on the far side of the cabin, and pushed that open as well.

He could have said something. He *should* have said something. But at the moment he could think of nothing to say. Words—and there were a lot of them buzzing around inside his head—seemed woefully inadequate in light of what he was seeing. He felt history hanging in the air of that little corner room, an almost somber aura of great importance that touched everything around him. If his anger had tinted things red before, this feeling turned everything a faint and shimmery gold. It was lovely. It was fabulous. He doubted that many people, even in days gone by, had seen what he was seeing now.

A few minutes passed that way, and then something happened. As though the excitement Andy was feeling had somehow become tangible and crossed the room to announce his presence, Alexander Bassett looked up from his old manual typewriter. He cocked his head to one side and turned slowly to look at Andy with an inscrutable expression.

"You're...you're working," Andy said.

"Very observant."

"No, I mean...Jesus, you're *writing*."

"Yes, Andy. That's what I do."

He stood up, and Andy got his first good look at Bassett's workspace. Pushed up to a window that overlooked the woods north of the cabin was an old kitchen-style table draped in oilcloth, the top of the table mostly hidden by an Olympia office model typewriter. By the standards of the computer age, the ancient machine looked large and boxy and downright clunky enough to be a cartoon. Scattered around it were six or seven manila folders crammed to overflowing with scraps of paper—notes, he guessed. And finally there was the manuscript. It sat next to the Olympia, a tower of white. Andy, who as a teacher had a habit of postponing the grading of tests and lessons as long as possible, was no stranger to mountains of paper. Still, nothing in his experience had prepared him for something so *huge*. It had to be at least a thousand pages, and even that was probably a conservative estimate.

"That's it?" he asked, pointing at the manuscript. "That's the magnum opus?"

Bassett flashed a gloomy smile. "That's it. The results of almost thirty years work. Impressive, no?" He laughed shortly. "Empires have been born and fallen in less time than it took to write that."

Andy shook his head. "It...it's so big."

"Well, actually, that's two-and-a-half drafts. The first draft came in slightly under four-hundred pages. The second was close to four-fifty. The draft I'm working on now...ah, who knows? I'll die before I finish it."

"May I?"

Bassett stared at him blankly for a moment before giving in with a casual shrug. "Be my guest. Read a page or two. Laugh in my face. I laugh at myself every time I type a sentence; it's nothing new."

Andy crossed to the table like a convert approaching the baptismal font. He reached out as if to touch the manuscript, but jerked his hand away at the last second, as though the paper were giving off fierce heat. He read the title page from afar.

THE CHILDREN'S SONG

a novel by

Alexander Bassett

"*The Children's Song*," Andy murmured. "It's not—"

"I'm afraid so. A sequel to my first book, *A Daughter's Song*."

"But the main character...Dorothy dies at the end of that book."

"So she does. Thank you for pointing that out."

"But if she's dead—"

"Oh, my. I had no idea this meeting today was going to degenerate into an interview." He crossed back to his writing chair and sat down, looking up at Andy. "You know the first book fairly well, I suppose. Dorothy Billings, the young idealist, murders her father, the evil military man—the symbol of everything my work always stood against. She ends up being employed as an aide to a compassionate senator, but gradually he falls prey to the power of government corruption, and so too does Dorothy—or at least she *almost* surrenders. When she remembers her ideals and stands up for her beliefs at the crucial moment, her dark deed from the past is exposed by political enemies. To make a long story short, she flees prosecution for her father's murder and lives in hiding—much as I ended up doing myself some years later, though I had no idea at the time that I was writing a form of prophecy. She falls in love, marries, dies in childbirth. Does that describe the book, Andy? Is it a fairly accurate summary?"

Andy nodded. "You left a lot out, but—"

"Well, we don't have all day now, do we? The sequel you're looking at is about her child, the one born as she died. It's about that child, a son, and his children, and their children. It's about the ideals they discover when they go searching for information about Dorothy. It's also about the way her buried, violent past follows them through the generations. It's about trying to reconcile faith and hope and optimism with the darker things that live within our soul.

"When I started it, I saw the book as a way to close the doors I had been opening all the way through my career, a bookend, the finish of a long cycle. I'm sure you can also see some parallels to my own life—all that hogwash about the past influencing the present and trying to find hope in the midst of despair."

"Except it's not hogwash, is it?" Andy said. "I mean, hell, look at your life. Everything you've done, everything you *are*...it's all been influenced by the past."

"So it has." Bassett closed his eyes, opened them again a moment later, and sighed. "It's the rest of it that's hogwash. Hope out of despair—an impossibility."

"Do you really believe that?"

"Let me make a confession to you, Andy. Hear me out, and then decide for yourself. You were late today. You were supposed to be here by noon. That's what you told me last night. When twelve-thirty came, and then quarter to one, and finally one o' clock, I had occasion to wonder if perhaps the Gardener had gotten to you last night. I decided that the odds were very good that he had. I thought about that. I tried to care. I tried to muster some feeling, anything, some sorrow, some bitterness, some high-minded anger—literally anything at all.

"Do you know what I said to myself? Can you guess? I ended up saying to myself, 'Well, what of it? He was a friend of sorts, so you can add him to the list. But if the Gardener got him, well then, the Gardener got him. You haven't written anything in a week or two, Alex. Why don't you take this opportunity to get some work done?' That's what I told myself, Andy. That's the hope and compassion and righteousness I could dredge from the depths of my despair—'I think I'll go do some work.'"

Andy didn't know what to say. He picked up the title page and set it aside, turning to the first page of text. He read the opening sentence: *At*

ALEXANDER'S SONG

a time in his life when he was extremely impressionable, when anything at all could have bent him like a willow, Gilbert Tucker discovered the scrapbook that had belonged to his dead mother.

His eyes began to burn, but he wasn't aware for another few seconds that they had actually filled with tears. He wiped them away savagely and turned to look at the old man.

"I guess I can't expect you to care, not after what you just told me, but the Gardener has my ex-wife. He took her sometime last night and left a note for me. He...he took...he...oh, shit."

That was it. The rage he'd felt earlier, the worshipful awe with which he'd watched Bassett pound the keys of the typewriter, the confusion and frustration and fear, the worry, the wonder, the wondering...it all came together in a swirling storm and grew until it reached critical mass.

Andy wept.

The tears burst from him with the power of an explosion, and he sagged down against the table, his hands over his eyes, his body shaking violently, wracked with a series of tremendous shudders that passed through the table itself to the floor of the cabin, making the mineral samples on the top shelf of a nearby bookcase rattle on their faded cardboard squares.

"Andy—" Bassett began, his voice both gentle and slightly alarmed.

"No...no...never mind, damn it, never mind." He spoke into the palms of his hands; his words were muffled, garbled. "You said you didn't care... that's what you told me...and you know...you know, I think I can understand that. I...I'm not asking...I'm not asking you to care...that's not what this is about."

"Andy, listen to me."

"Did you hear what I said? I said the Gardener has my ex-wife!"

He took his hands away from his eyes and fumbled in the front pocket of his jeans. He pulled out the crumpled ball that was the Gardener's latest message and threw it in the old man's direction.

"Then there were two. That's what it says. Then there were two. I heard him taking her, I heard it last night, I was dreaming and I woke up and I heard it, the scream, the struggle, I actually heard that and I went back to sleep, so I guess that means I'm no better than you, no different." He paused, still crying, his breath coming in a ragged pant. "You close your eyes and go to work, and I...I just close my eyes and go back to sleep."

"Andy, it's not your fault."

"Of course it's not," Andy said bitterly.

"It's not!" Bassett stood up and approached him. "It's not your fault, any of it."

"Yeah, I know that. We didn't ask for it, right? I've been telling myself that all day. We didn't ask for it. But that's really not the question, is it? I thought it was, but Christ, it's not even close. It's here, whether we asked for it or not. The Gardener's out there with Ginnie Turner and my ex-wife, and I'll probably be next, and the question isn't whether we asked for it. The question is, what the fuck do we do about it? Can you tell me that? Do we just do what you said before? Run away? Hide? Do we re-form the god-damned Dupin Society? And what possible difference would that make, anyway? He's out there. His circle of death is getting bigger and bigger. He's coming for us, and we can't hear him. We don't see him until it's too late. You know that better than anyone. You've had years of experience, haven't you? You go about your business, or maybe, if you're feeling really tough, you actually pretend to be the hunter. But it's really him that's hunting you. It's useless, just useless. But of course you don't care. The past keeps haunting you, and there's no hope, no light. It's all darkness. It's all despair."

He stopped, suddenly unable to catch his breath. He wiped the tears again and saw a blurry image of Bassett looking back at him. The old man was slack-jawed, his milky eyes open wide.

"I thought I was beginning to understand you," Andy said, his voice a little softer than before. "I felt sorry for you. I had empathy. I hurt at the way you'd been victimized. I got angry on your behalf. And now I find out what a waste that was. You're tired, you're sad, you're worn out, so you give up. If you'd really tell the truth, you were secretly hoping the Gardener *had* gotten me last night. Isn't that right? Then you could go back to living the way you have for the last fifty years, without the meddling outsider to ruin your days. I guess you put so much compassion into your books, you don't have any left for the people around you."

"Stop it, Andy."

"Why? Does the truth hurt the truth-seeker? Does it hurt to have your real nature exposed? You thought you had me fooled the other night, didn't you? When I talked you into helping me find Ginnie, you thought you'd snowed me. And now you let the real story sneak out. You didn't give a fuck about Ginnie. You don't give a fuck about anyone. You're just words on paper, that's all you are. You're a goddamned paper man."

They stared at each other across a distance of no more than a foot or two, a distance that might as well have been light-years. The moment stretched out in silence, charged with quiet electricity. Andy was still weeping, and the old man's eyes sparkled. They were breathing hard, both of them.

"I'm not a paper man," Bassett said, his voice a whisper, the words a prayer.

"I was counting on you," Andy said.

The old man nodded.

"I can't do this without you. I thought you understood that. I really thought you understood."

The old man nodded again.

"I need you."

The old man said something. It was too low for Andy to make out. He thought it might have been *I need you, too*, but perhaps that was just his own fervent hope. He was too afraid to ask Bassett to repeat it.

The moment spun on and on.

At last, Bassett opened his frail and skinny arms, held them wide. Andy hesitated, but not for long. He stepped into the ancient, fragile embrace, and he wept again, this time against the old man's bony shoulder.

THIRTEEN

THE DUPIN SOCIETY, THEN AND NOW

1

Andy spent the next twenty-four hours on the island, engaged with Bassett in an orgy of history. Their research was intensive, putting all their previous efforts to shame. They poured over notebooks. They reviewed old newspaper articles. They studied things like the Kretchmer journal and the small packet of letters (written mostly in a primitive code) that Bassett had exchanged with Earl Rappala.

But mostly they talked.

Bassett, eyes closed much of the time, puffing on one of Andy's cigarettes, reached back into his past and opened up in a way he hadn't before. He spoke at greater length about his friends, Hale and McCready, and about Jens Carlson, and about what his own father had done in the six months preceding Alex's birth. He talked for the first time about Jerome Wandry, the actor, who had so resembled Jens Carlson that Alex had succumbed to his fear and paranoia, physically attacking Wandry just days before the opening of *To Raise Brave Men*, catching him outside the prop room and throttling him, smashing his head back against the wall repeatedly while shrieking like a demented Poe narrator, *"You're supposed to be dead! You drowned in the lake! You're not alive! You're dead! You're dead!"*

For the most part, though, he spoke of his other friends, those who had perished at the Gardener's hands—Mahler and Warren, the only two women he had ever truly loved; Cal Drummond; Henry Oglebay; Dwight and Lonnie Gulliver ("The truly absurd injustice of it is that they didn't even know who I was," he said. "They thought I was Hoffer. We were fishing friends. They'd come out here and have a beer or two and we'd take their beautiful boat out for walleye. They were on their way here to share an Independence Day dinner I was preparing. A barbecue. Ribs. Corn on the cob. Afterward, we were going to shoot a few fireworks off the cliff. Real old-fashioned, harmless fun between friends. But they never got here that day. They were found murdered near the public boat landing across the lake, perhaps the ultimate innocent victims.").

The stories were a search for clues. As Bassett painfully revealed what he knew of each murder—the manner of death, the location, the time of day, what, if anything, the police had discovered about each case, what the Gardener's notes had said afterwards —Andy took assiduous notes, looking again for that common thread, that elusive connection. He knew that somewhere in there, lost among all the history, buried under a mountain of years, was an answer, *the* answer. Yet as the hours went by and the stories unfolded, one after another, forming a continuous chain of bygone misery and ancient sorrow, no answer was revealed.

Andy grew discouraged, although with a little effort he found that he was able to keep much of his frustration in check by focusing on one simple fact: for the first time they were working as a team. They were no longer two separate people with their own agendas, two almost-enemies suffering each other's presence and trying to ignore the wall of tension that existed between them. They were a unit, an honest-to-God machine that was finally functioning efficiently, hitting most of the time on all cylinders. The cross-purposes were gone. The almost-enemies had become nearly-friends. And of course they were in complete agreement about the nature of the *real* enemy.

2

SOMETIME IN THE middle of that long night together, Bassett finally broke down. His spirit was still willing, his newfound enthusiasm still there, but his body had reached its limit. His voice, always weak at best, had grown scratchy and thin. His back had bowed farther than ever. His movements had slowed to the point where he gestured like a Disney robot with a short circuit somewhere in its crucial wiring. His face was pale, his eyes sunken deep above dark bruised circles. And though he said nothing about it, Andy had noticed the old man absently massaging his chest from time to time, as though his heart pained him.

Andy bundled him off for a few hours of sleep, fully intending to take his own nap on the couch. Yet once he was lying down in the darkened main room, he discovered that he couldn't relax. His mind kept zipping off on unplanned little journeys, going back over the terrain they had already covered, looking ahead and trying to guess what terrain still awaited them.

After a half hour or so of uncomfortable tossing, he got up and went to the bookshelves on the other side of the cabin. He picked up a Faulkner novel here, a volume of Wallace Stevens' poetry there, but he felt restless and distracted, incapable of concentrating long enough or well enough to settle into any writer's rhythms. He was about to pick up a copy of Bassett's own *The Biggest Angel* when he was struck by a better inspiration.

In the corner room that overlooked the woods, he sat down in front of that gargantuan typewriter. He turned on the tabletop lamp, took a deep breath, and began reading *The Children's Song*.

It was like magic.

By the time he reached the second page he was gone, completely consumed by Bassett's fictional world, at one with the characters, alive in the setting, pulled through the story by the ceaseless tug of the perfectly-balanced, wonderfully-metered language. None of it was a new experience for him—it happened every time he picked up a Bassett novel, even one he'd read a half-dozen times before—but there was still something extraordinary about it this time around, a special sensation he hadn't felt before and couldn't quite identify.

By the time he came up for air at last, he had been living next to, living *inside of*, fifteen-year-old Gilbert Tucker, whose mother was the late Dorothy Billings Tucker, for close to four hours. The sky was growing light, the trees outside the window gradually materializing out of a pre-dawn mist. They looked like prehistoric aliens slowly appearing at the edge of a wilderness encampment, and Andy stared at them for a long time, as though in a trance, suddenly understanding what he was feeling.

There was enchantment in any work by Alexander Bassett. In the best of it—*The Pharisee, To Raise Brave Men*, some of the poetry in his first collection, *Fields of Fire*—it was the enchantment of finding yourself in the firm, confident hands of a master writer. In some of his lesser work—*Doctor Howell, Peter Wept*—the enchantment came from watching a steady and reliable craftsman making the best of difficult material.

This time, in *The Children's Song*, Andy was seeing a novel that left even the man's previous masterpiece, *The Pharisee*, in the dust. Never before, at least in any of his published works, had Bassett conjured such a perfect blend of ideas and action. Never before had he propelled a story forward with such relentless energy. Never before had he molded language into such beautiful yet completely functional forms. It was prose-as-poetry, as sound as bedrock, as fine as a great painting.

And the special thrill that Andy finally understood: it was, for now at least, all his. His alone. For the first time ever he was reading a novel by Alexander Bassett and not having to share the pleasure with anyone. No editor had blue-penciled this book. No readers had snatched published copies off bookstore shelves. No reviewers had gone over it with a fine-toothed comb, picking it apart. No academics had analyzed it. No students had butchered its meaning in rambling, incoherent essays.

ALEXANDER'S SONG

The Children's Song was ore taken straight from the ground, raw material that came directly from the miner's shovel into Andy's hands, no smelting, no middlemen, nothing dulled in transit or spilled in the process of marketing.

Mine, he thought. It's his, but it's mine too, like a secret that nobody else knows.

Had Bassett really said he laughed at himself every time he wrote a sentence? Could that be right? Was his self-confidence and his sense of the work so blunted by time, so savagely torn apart by the darkness of his past, that he honestly didn't realize what he had here? Didn't he know, couldn't he see, that *The Children's Song* was a genuine contender for the title "Best Fiction of the Twentieth Century?"

"This is it," he whispered to Bassett's typewriter. "This is finally it—the goddamned Great American Novel."

He read another hour and finally, with tremendous reluctance, put the manuscript aside and went to check on the old man. He was still asleep, in the precise position he'd been in when Andy helped him into bed, his eyelids gently fluttering with dreams, his dentureless mouth slightly open, snoring.

"Keep resting," he said softly, and went back into the main room to return to work.

3

FROM THE RESEARCH *notebooks of Andy Gillespie:*

> Essentially I've heard the story of Jens Carlson and The Dupin Society twice now, and I'm convinced the answer lies somewhere in that story. Never mind that A.B. disagrees. I think he's so determined to forget those days ever happened that he just won't acknowledge it. But the answer is there. It has to be.
>
> The best thing to do, I think, is list the vital points and go over them again. I'll try not to think about how important this is. I'll try to do it

automatically, as unconsciously as possible. Maybe the act of transferring what I've heard to the page will make some difference. Please. A deep breath, pinch the nose, and dive in. Here goes:

1) Dupins learn about Carlson.

2) They go to Carlson's cabin in the woods. Now, let's face it, that was probably crazy, but they did it anyway. Angry, A.B. says. They were angry, and young and brash and cocky. They actually thought they could convince Carlson to surrender to the authorities—<u>Give yourself up, evildoer! We've got the goods on you!</u>

3) Carlson confesses right away, but pretty much laughs in their faces at the thought of turning himself in to McFarren. In the ensuing argument, Carlson punches Hale, threatens them with a shotgun, and all three Dupins end up fleeing the cabin, screaming as they go, "If you won't do it, then we will! We'll go to the constable and tell him all about you!" Carlson shouts back, "You do an' you're dead! I'll kill all'a ya!"

4) They don't go to McFarren, at least not right away, and that's their fatal mistake. Instead they spend too much time talking it over, pondering Carlson's death threat. The net effect is to raise doubts in their own minds—doubts that weren't there before. Their basic fear is that if McFarren dismisses them as nosy kids (which I guess his track record indicated he might do), or if Carlson is brought in but the evidence against him doesn't hold up, then they're all in mortal danger.

5) They vote. It comes out 2-1 in favor of keeping quiet for the time being, perhaps trying to find something more concrete to prove Carlson's guilt. A.B. says that was probably the real beginning of his long streak of cowardice. Charlie McCready was the only one who wanted to go to the cops right away. Hale and A.B. voted against.

6) Time goes by, the argument goes on, but they are unable to find any indictable evidence. When they sort of offhandedly ask some of the people who live around the mill if they might be willing to testify against Carlson, the responses are less than positive. Several of the witnesses, when they get the scent of a possible courtroom appearance on the wind, say in effect, "What night was that? What drum of kerosene? Jens <u>who?</u>"

7) Twice over the summer, the Dupins run into Carlson downtown. The first time, McCready sees him coming out of the market and quickly turns away—but not before Carlson sneers at him and says, "Where ya goin in such a hurry, boyo? You ain't afraid a'me, are you?" The second time, a few weeks later, all three of them bump into Carlson outside the bank. Nobody says anything. Carlson just grins a huge, toothy, wolfish kind of grin.

8) August 1927. If their plan to go to McFarren isn't dead, it might as well be. Over a month has gone by and they're more mixed-up than ever before. A.B. has become quiet, sullen, withdrawn, tortured by everything—what he learned about his father from Carlson, what he knows about Carlson himself. But still he's no different than the others. He too is afraid of the death threat and is paralyzed by that fear. Even McCready is now less than certain. They don't vote again, but if they did it would probably turn out 3-0 in favor of shutting up. When A.B., after drinking a little too much beer one night, says, "Hell, fellows, maybe my old man <u>deserved</u> to die. He was a greedy, manipulative, exploitative son of a bitch!" it could well have been the final nail driven into the coffin of their McFarren plans.

9) It didn't matter. They didn't know it, of course, but even without a visit to the authorities, the clock was ticking. When they'd visited Carlson at his cabin back in late June, they had effectively signed their own death warrants.

10) August 10. A hot day, temperature around ninety, humidity close to a hundred percent, thunderheads building in the west. The Dupins, who really aren't the Dupins any more than they are those other childhood characters, the Long John Silvers or the Ivanhoes, are at their favorite spot—a little clearing in the woods, a half-mile off Green Meadow Trail near Preston Lake. They're drinking beer and taking target practice. They have a shotgun (did A.B. tell me it was a thirty-aught-six? Is there such a thing? Christ, I never did know anything about guns) that once belonged to William Bassett and now belongs to

A.B. They're taking turns with it, trying to blow old elixir bottles off a fallen tree on the other side of the clearing. It's A.B.'s turn. He's a poor shot—only four out of ten bottles so far.

Suddenly, a voice behind them says, "Betcha ya boyos wouldn't mind usin' that thing on yers truly."

They turn around and see Jens Carlson standing there. He's shouldering an open leather packsack full of freshly cut stove lengths that must have weighed sixty pounds all together. He's sucking on a pint bottle of whiskey. There's an ax slung over his shoulder.

"Get out of here," Frank Hale says. "Leave us alone!"

Carlson laughs. It's clear even from a distance of thirty feet or more than he's been drinking. "Leave ya alone? Shit-n-piss, boyo, weren't me that come bargin' into *yer* lives, were it? Yer the big-asses that come pokin' around, showin' up at my house with yer smart talk 'bout clues and ev-ee-dence and that ijit cop, McFarren."

"That's over now," A.B. says to him. "You can forget it. There are no clues, there's no McFarren. You can forget you ever saw us that day."

"Ferget," Carlson says thoughtfully. "Ferget I ever saw ya." He laughs again. "Boyo, I don't think I can do that thing."

He takes a few steps closer, shrugging out of the packsack as he comes. It hits the ground and spills stove lengths everywhere. He throws his bottle down on top of the logs. It shatters. He brings the ax around and holds it up in front of him.

"Leave us alone," Hale says again. "We didn't do anything to you."

Carlson grins. "That's what *you* say. An' who the hell knows? Mebbe yer right. Mebbe you didn't do nothin' to me. But I got this aunt—sweet thing, she is—who's alwus sewin'. She makes pretty things for the friends an' fambly, know what I mean? She takes in mendin' from the neighbors. I heard her one day, she said sumpin' real smart. She said, 'Ya gotta watch out for them loose threads. One loose thread'll get ya every time.' Bright lady. Jest 'bout as bright as they come, I'd hafta say."

"You're crazy," Charlie McCready shoots back. "You're as crazy as a crow."

ALEXANDER'S SONG

Carlson laughs. "Could be, boyo. It goddamned well could be."

And he charges at Charlie with the ax.

It all happens very quickly. Charlie goes down with a scream, a gaping slash across his chest and belly. Frank rushes in to help him and receives Carlson's second murderous blow—across his back. Blood is flying. It's begun to rain lightly, and A.B. has a momentary impression that the rain is red.

Carlson raises the ax again and brings it down on Frank's body. Again he raises it and—

A.B. is frozen there. He knows he could do something. He has the damn shotgun in his hands! It's loaded. He calls out to Carlson to stop, orders him to put the ax down, but Carlson is chopping and slashing and A.B. has no choice. He lifts the gun and aims it. His hands are trembling, his finger unable to find the trigger.

Then he has it.

He calls to Carlson again. He warns him.

He sees Charlie trying to crawl away from the slaughter, one hand literally clutched to his belly, trying to hold in his intestines. He cries, "Don't worry, Charlie! Don't worry!" And he prepares to shoot at Carlson.

He would have.

He swears to this day he would have.

But Carlson turns at that very moment and faces him head on. The blood of his friends is smeared across Carlson's face like war paint. A bit of clotted tissue clings like an appendage to the tip of Carlson's nose. And yet he's grinning, laughing—a maniacal shrieking sound that fills the clearing.

"Rich boy!" he cries, and rushes at A.B.—

—who panics and drops the shotgun and flees.

He's blundering through the woods, sobbing, shouting out Frank and Charlie's names over and over again, tripping, falling, getting back up and charging on, and two sounds seem to follow him: that insane laughter and the dying cries of his friend Charlie McCready—"Help! Oh, for godsakes, Alex, help me!"

He didn't see anything that happened after he ran, but even I can imagine it. Based on what I know, it isn't very difficult to picture.

There's Frank dying, or probably already dead, lying in his own blood. There's Charlie, badly wounded, maybe even <u>mortally</u> wounded, trying to slither away from the madman's ax. And with A.B. gone, that madman goes after him again, raising his blade and dropping it on Charlie, raising and dropping it again, over and over, an endless, murderous machine that, now that it's started, can't be shut off again.

Carlson is a monster. He's a pure killing animal, a raw force wielding that ax like some kind of lumberjack. But not a real lumberjack. A supernatural lumberjack. An inhuman lumberjack. He's like a—

Oh.

Oh, man.

Oh, shit.

4

IT WAS MID-MORNING and they were sitting at the kitchen table, drinking coffee, smoking Andy's cigarettes again. Bassett had just finished reading what Andy had written in his notebook. He looked up expectantly.

"Yes? So?"

Andy sighed. He produced the sheet of paper he'd pulled from the stack of the Gardener's messages and laid it on top of the notebook:

**THE GARDENER WAS ALONE
AMONG THE TREES
CROUCHING WHILE THE
LUMBERJACK WORKED**

THE TREES SOBBED AS THEY FELL

ALEXANDER'S SONG

THE STANDING TREE WAS SPARED

THE NIGHT SEEMED NEAR AS THE SKY WEPT

A TREE WALKED AWAY LIKE A TRAITOR
LOVE BROKEN AND SLASHED

THE GARDENER WATCHED

"Oh," Bassett said softly. "Oh, my. Jesus."

"That's one way of putting it," Andy said.

Bassett looked stunned. "My problem was, I never saw it that way. Me, the big-time poet, Mister Imagery, and I never pictured Carlson as a lumberjack. Even when I got this note all those years ago, I never made the connection between felling trees and…and my friends."

"Somebody did. Somebody was there that day. Somebody besides you and Frank and Charlie, besides Carlson."

"The Gardener," Bassett said. "The Gardener was there."

"Either that, or he heard about it afterwards. But Christ, it's all there, isn't it? The ax. Hale and McCready. The rain that was falling."

"And me," Bassett said. "I guess I'm the final tree. The one that was spared."

They fell silent, looking down at the note, up at each other, down at the note again, as though not quite able to come to grips with their new knowledge.

"One of Carlson's brothers," Andy said at last. "One of Halvard Borg's other illegitimate kids. Do you think that's possible? Are any of them still alive?"

Bassett shrugged weakly. "The thought had occurred to me once, a long time ago. I had Earl Rappala check into for me. He was, after all, living right here in Rock Creek."

"And?"

"It was impossible to trace. That was all a long time ago, the turn of the century. He had quite a few children, apparently, and as you just said, they were illegitimate. None carried the Borg surname; they had their mothers' names, or the last names of men who'd adopted them. And when you looked for birth certificates...hell, if they existed at all and hadn't burned up in some old town hall fire or washed away in a flood, they were usually unreliable.

"Earl did find two descendants, I remember that much. There was a woman by the name of Julia Crowley, an old lady schoolteacher down in Arkansas. And a man by the name of Rahilly, Jim or John Rahilly. He was serving a life sentence at the state prison in Waupun, Wisconsin, for a series of armed robberies and murders—one of your typical highway kill sprees. He'd been put away in 1953, before the attack on Jack, or Connie's murder, or any of the rest. There was no chance it was him."

"But we know there were others."

"Were," Bassett said, nodding. "Even if that *were* is really an *are*, the trail is cold."

Andy frowned. He studied the note again. Was the writer, the Gardener, angry at the standing tree that was spared, or at the lumberjack? And the traitor, the tree that walked away...that had to be Bassett, didn't it? But why was he a traitor? Because of the things his father had done? If so, then one of Halvard Borg's other offspring might indeed fit the picture. If not...no. It didn't add up any other way.

"It has to be," he murmured. "One of Borg's bastards. He was furious at you because of what your father did to Halvard. And later that day, when your shame at running off drove you to track Carlson down to Green Lake, and you found him drunk out of his mind and fought with him and he fell in the lake and never came up, and you ran—"

ALEXANDER'S SONG

"Yes, yes," Bassett said impatiently. "Then two Bassetts had killed two Borgs. I told you I'd considered all of that. Once I got over the insanity of thinking that Jens Carlson was still alive and stalking me around New York, not to mention the even bigger insanity of believing that his vengeful ghost was following me, I turned to that idea immediately. For all we know, it may even be right. That may be the *why* of the whole matter. But it doesn't help us one whit on the *who*. There might be a thousand of Hal Borg's children still running around out there, with ten thousand children and grandchildren of their own. But we don't know who they are."

Andy smiled. "We don't," he said, his heart starting to pound, his body beginning to tingle with excitement. "But somebody does."

5

COMING BACK INTO town late that Tuesday afternoon gave Andy an uncomfortable feeling, a sense of dislocation, of being ripped out of the second world and deposited back into the real one. If that feeling was mitigated at all, it was by the fact that he was still aware of the second world and knew that it was close, very close. He couldn't quite see the overlapping edges, but he could sense that they were there. It was like picking up a fading radio signal from faraway or catching a distant smell riding on a gentle breeze.

But for all his discomfort, he was eager too, feeling revitalized. Once he had convinced Bassett of their only course of action, they had committed to it completely. The back of Andy's truck was loaded with their notes and files, manuscripts, notebooks, journals. Even the box that contained the annals of the Dupin Society was back there, despite the fact that Bassett had told him it was filled only with worthless childhood memorabilia and contained nothing from that crucial summer of 1927, the year of Jens Carlson.

In short, they had brought everything with them. They were moving their base of operations.

They found Marilyn in the lobby of the Sleep-Tite, having what appeared to be a mild argument over rent money with the brother and sister owners of the Angler's Rest. She looked at Andy with disdain as he approached, then noticed Bassett standing several steps behind him.

"Hoffer, isn't it? I see this boy's got you suckered too. You want to watch out for his bullshit. He tells you you're partners, but he leaves you standing in the cold, freezing your goddamned ass off."

Andy cleared his throat. "We need to talk to you, Marilyn."

"Oh, do we now?" She laughed. "Suddenly I'm on the inside again." She gave a sweeping look that took in the entire lobby, Bassett, and the confused siblings. "And why should I sit and listen to whatever you've got to say?"

"Because it's important?"

"Crap."

"He's right," Bassett said. "It is important. You might say it's critical."

"Mr. Hoffer, with all due respect, I don't know you from an effing hole in the ground. We've talked…what was it? Once? Years ago? Why in the name of Christ should I listen to anything you—"

"Hey, there you are!"

They all spun around, but the exclamation from across the lobby was directed at Andy alone. At first he didn't recognize the girl who was hailing him, but then he got it. It was the maid he had seen the other day, the one who had wanted to make up his room and had found the message taped to his door.

"Jeez, you're a popular guy," she said as she approached.

Andy frowned. "Pardon me?"

"You're popular," she repeated, stowing her feather duster in an apron pocket and folding her arms across her chest. "I put them all on your dresser."

"What?"

"I put them on your dresser. When I cleaned your room this morning."

"Put what?" Andy said. "What're you talking about?"

"The letters, silly." She said this bluntly, as though stating the obvious. "Someone sure writes to you a lot. You had three different envelopes on your door when I got there."

Behind his back, Andy heard Marilyn gasp.

6

TWO HOURS LATER they were sitting in Andy's room and Marilyn was looking at Bassett, shaking her head. "I'm too effing old to be surprised by anything," she said. "But this comes close. Damn close." She turned to Andy and thumped him on the back with one of her tiny troll hands. "How about that, hon? I was right. You *are* serious-minded. You found your man, and you didn't even have to rob any damn graves to do it!"

Andy gave a distracted nod, looking for perhaps the hundredth time at the three messages from the Gardener. They were arrayed side by side on the desk, each more disturbing than the one before.

**THE GARDENER HAS WORKED
LONG AND HARD
AND SOMETIMES HE MUST PLAY**

**INSTEAD OF PRUNING
HE HAS CHOSEN TO PERFORM TRANSPLANTS**

THIS IS MORE FUN

I HAVE THEM

and:

PAUL F. OLSON

**THE POET SAITH THE DAYS ARE LONG
BUT THE GARDENER SAITH THAT
EVEN THE LONGEST DAYS
MUST EVENTUALLY END**

**THE TRANSPLANTS ARE NOT TAKING
THE FLOWERS ARE WILTING**

**NEXT TIME IT MIGHT BE EASIER TO PRUNE
AGAIN**

**WHAT IS A TRANSPLANT BUT A WAY TO STALL
DEATH
IT MIGHT BE FUN
BUT PRUNING IS MORE EFFICIENT**

and finally, worst of all:

**THE GARDENER HAS EXAMINED
THE TREE CLOSELY
AND HE SEES THAT IT IS DYING**

**HE MUST ASK HIMSELF IF IT IS DYING
QUICKLY ENOUGH**

ALEXANDER'S SONG

MANY FLOWERS ARE GROWING NEAR ITS BASE THESE DAYS

TRANSPLANTING OR PRUNING BECOMES DIFFICULT WHEN THE BLOOMS OUTNUMBER THE TIRELESS GARDENER

IT WOULD BE EASIER TO KILL THE TREE

CHOP CHOP CHOP CHOP

CHOP CHOP CHOP

CHOP CHOP

CHOP

"You've heard everything now," Andy said to Marilyn, dragging his gaze away from the messages. "Will you help us?"

"Help you?" She leaned toward him, her nose almost touching his. "Isn't that jumping the gun a little bit, hon?"

"But you said—"

"I said you found your man. All that means is I believe this old fart—" she waved a hand in Bassett's direction "— is your commie writer. Well, I do. It's strange as hell, but I buy it. I'm not half as sure about all this other bullshit, these nasty rumors about my poor dead nephew, Jens."

"That poor dead nephew of yours was an ax murderer," Bassett said coolly. "I'm afraid I can't show you any pictures; you'll just have to take my word for it."

"And if that's the case," Marilyn shot back, "then you're a murderer, too. Isn't that right?"

"Right enough," Bassett said. "But my crime was unintentional, brought about as much by the liquor your nephew had consumed that day as by anything I did to him with my fists."

Marilyn grunted. "And I suppose if he hadn't drowned in the lake, you would've dragged his ass down to the police and turned him in."

"Of course I would have."

"At least then there would've been a trial and we'd have heard the truth of it, one way or another."

"You're right about that," Bassett said with a sigh. "Unfortunately, I can't do anything about the past. What we're trying to do here is change the future."

"And that's why you want my help. You think I can help you change the future by telling you about my tosspot nieces and nephews."

"In a manner of speaking, yes."

"In a manner of speaking," Marilyn said, "this whole business sucks." She turned away from Bassett and faced Andy with a quick, apologetic smile. "I feel for you, hon, I really do. This Gardener is obviously real, and he's a son of a bitch. I'd like nothing better than to help you find the Turner girl and your ex, but I'm not sure I can work with the man who killed Jens."

"Marilyn—"

"I don't care if Jens did crisp the commie's daddy, and I don't care if he made mincemeat pie out of those two kids. He was my goddamn nephew, my brother's boy. He took care of me when my mama died, made sure I had food on the table and the roof over my head stayed patched. Yeah, he was a drunk and a no-good, but bloody hell, we were all drunks and no-goods back then. Rock Creek was full of drunks and no-goods. That doesn't change the family relationship. He was my drunk and no-good nephew, and this goddamned communist here killed him."

Andy threw up his hands. "I don't believe this! Marilyn...God, don't you see that none of that matters anymore? Everybody was guilty! William

ALEXANDER'S SONG

Bassett murdered Royal Haag and your brother. Your nephew killed William Bassett and two innocent teenagers. And this man right here accidently killed your nephew. If you're going to start assigning blame, you'll be here all day. And meanwhile, Joanne and Ginnie are in danger." He picked up the Gardener's second message and waved it in her face. "He says the flowers are wilting! Don't you know what that means?"

"Yeah, I suppose I do," Marilyn said. "And like I told you once, I feel for you. But I won't—"

"All right, okay! Jesus!" He slammed his fist down on the desk, scattering the other messages. "Just answer one question. We'll never bother you again if you just answer this: From what you've heard here, do you agree that the Gardener might be one of your brother's children? Is that possible?"

She shook her head slowly, and Andy thought he heard a trace of admiration in her voice as she said, "You don't know how to quit, do you? Your mama never told you the one about not being able to get blood out of a stone. But I'll answer you, because it sure as hell can't hurt anything. The answer is no."

"You mean—"

"I mean what I said, hon. No."

"Why?"

"That's another question. I only agreed to answer one."

"Marilyn!"

She laughed. It sounded chilly, but not altogether unfriendly. "The answer is no, Andy, because none of Jens' brothers or sisters is still alive. I knew them all, more or less. That doesn't mean I would've thrown a life jacket to some of them if they were drowning, or even given them the time of day. But I guess I knew who they all were and where they all lived.

"The one you mentioned before, the highway bandit. His name was Johnny Rahilly. He popped off one night in his cell more than ten years ago. Old Julia Crowley died before that. The others are gone too, some before, some after. The last one, old Wally Pickleman, went by cancer at the hospital over in Marquette two years ago next month."

PAUL F. OLSON

Andy closed his eyes. He felt a little bit like a rubber ball with a small, slow leak, gradually deflating, losing substance, vanishing. He had been so sure that one of Borg's illegitimate children was responsible. It had seemed so easy—get the names of the surviving offspring from Marilyn, contact them, eliminate, discover. Now, with that chance taken away, it was back to square one.

A small moan escaped from the back of his throat, and he saw the Gardener's warning flashing like a neon sign against the black screen of his closed eyelids:

THE TRANSPLANTS ARE NOT TAKING...THE FLOWERS ARE WILTING.

A hand gently touched his shoulder, but he didn't know if it was Marilyn's or Bassett's until he opened his eyes and looked up. The old man was standing next to him, gazing down with an expression of genuine pity, his ancient eyes communicating many things at once: sorrow and companionship, sympathy, support.

"Oh, this is great," Andy said softly. "This is just fucking great. I'm down so low that *you* have to buck me up. You, who lost more friends to the Gardener than I've ever had. You, who didn't...I mean you never...." He trailed away, shaking his head in frustration.

Bassett squeezed his shoulder, then turned to Marilyn, speaking in a low, quiet voice. "It appears you're free to go now, Miss Borg. You answered our question; we're grateful." When she didn't get up immediately, he went on: "I would ask that you keep what you heard this afternoon a secret, but whether or not you do is between you and your conscience. I only told you what I did because Andy said you could be trusted. I hope that trust was well placed."

"You talk real nice for a son of a bitch who's a murderer."

Bassett opened his mouth but closed it again quickly. He pursed his lips, thinking, looking for something better to say than whatever had first popped into his mind.

ALEXANDER'S SONG

"Miss Borg," he finally said, "what happened between Jens Carlson and me at Green Lake was not murder. It took me many years to realize that. I regret what happened, but I won't apologize for it. As Andy told you a few minutes ago, we were all guilty, but my crime was cowardice, not murder. I wanted to beat up your nephew, not drown him. It never should have come to that. I should have shot him in the clearing, before he slaughtered my friends. And that wouldn't have been murder, either. It would have been self-defense."

Andy glanced up, watching the two of them staring at each other like old stone idols. If either was giving so much as an inch, he couldn't see it. All he could see was pride and determination, an unbreakable resolution in both of them.

"I'll keep your effing secret," Marilyn said then, getting up and going to the door. "Who would I tell, anyway? You think anybody actually cares if some old-timey commie's still alive or not?"

"There's at least one person out there who cares," Andy said.

"And I wish you good luck with him. Sounds like you're going to need that and more."

She went out the door and shut it firmly behind her.

7

DINNER ARRIVED AT six o' clock—cheeseburgers and fries and onion rings, along with two bottles of beer, all of it delivered by the young, bearded bartender from the Angler's Rest.

"We didn't order this," Andy said.

"That's right," the bartender said with a grin. "It's already bought and paid for. Tell you what, though. I wouldn't mind a tip."

Andy gave the man two dollars and watched him stroll happily back to the elevator. Then he shut the door and turned to Bassett.

"Marilyn," he said. "She's more on our side than she wants to let on. Unfortunately, I think we've gotten from her everything there is to get."

"Just as well," the old man replied. "If she was any more involved, she'd become another potential victim—more innocence for the Gardener to take advantage of and destroy."

"Innocence," Andy repeated, and fetched a dismal sigh. "Yesterday, out at your cabin, you said the Gullivers were the ultimate innocent victims. But they were all innocent— Oglebay, Mahler, Drummond. I'm innocent, although I have to admit I don't feel it at the moment. God knows Ginnie and Jo are innocent. And you. You're innocent, too."

"A nice sentiment," Bassett said, "but false."

Andy shook his head. "I don't mean that stuff about cowardice. You were eighteen years old—a kid, for godsakes. And before that, you didn't make your father murder Royal Haag. You didn't make him bribe and murder Halvard Borg. You weren't even born for another three months! You didn't make Jens Carlson spill that kerosene and strike that match, and you didn't make him go crazy in the clearing. You're innocent, all right. The only guilty one is whoever was watching Jens that day."

"Perhaps," Bassett said simply.

Andy rubbed the bridge of his nose. He was silent for a time, and then said, "He's coming for you, you know."

"Yes, I know. I'm the tree that's not dying quickly enough. I'm the tree he'd rather kill."

"I don't think he likes the way things are going," Andy said. "I think he wanted to play a game with me—and you too, by association. He wanted to tease us, torture us. But he didn't expect you and I to become allies. He doesn't like that. He didn't think it would go that far. So because I didn't quit, because I latched onto you and stayed with you and talked you into fighting…because I did all that, he's going to go after you."

"I hate to tell you this, Andy, but you're not off the hook either."

"No. Nobody is. Not yet." Andy laughed, low and throaty, a sound filled with ice and gravel. "I feel like we're the new Dupin Society. Except that every time the Dupin Society gets together, horrible things happen."

ALEXANDER'S SONG

Bassett nodded and picked up the grease-stained white bag on the desktop. "At least we new Dupins will eat well tonight." He opened the bag and took out the cheeseburgers. "Oh, my. Beware, heart and arteries. It was a generous thought Marilyn had, but it might kill me before the Gardener ever—"

He stopped abruptly, causing Andy to spin around. "What's wrong?"

Bassett didn't answer. He was holding a cheeseburger in one hand, a wax-paper bag of French fries in the other. The bag was upside down, raining golden fries around his feet, but he didn't appear to notice.

"Mr. Bassett?"

Nothing. The old man's face was pale again, the sickly grayish white of dying flesh.

"Mr. Bassett…Alex…what is it?"

Bassett inclined his head, gesturing at the bag. Andy frowned and went to the desk. He looked into the bag, saw nothing for a moment but some onion rings and a handful of folded paper napkins, and then finally realized what the old man was looking at.

He didn't need to take it out to see it clearly, but of course he did. Even had he wanted to leave it in the bag, he didn't think he could have. His movements were other-directed, beyond his control.

He reached down inside, nudged the napkins out of the way, and picked up the picture that was lying there. It was color for a change, not black and white, and showed a young woman huddled in a dark corner of a dark room. Her legs were bound together at the ankles by what appeared to be a length of chain, and her hands were tied behind her back, cinched tightly. Not much of her face was visible, covered as it was by long strands of dark hair that fell across her forehead and spilled down her cheeks in knotty tangles. But there was one white irregular crescent of her left cheek still open to the camera, gleaming out of the blackness like a moon.

Andy didn't need to see any more than that.

"Jo," he said. "Oh, Christ, it's Jo."

On the back of the picture, in large block printing, were three words:

397

YOUR FINAL MEAL

The picture slipped from Andy's hands and fluttered slowly to the floor, disappearing beneath the desk.

He shut his eyes tightly, squeezed them closed until they ached. But it didn't help. It didn't help at all.

The image of the photograph, every line and shadow, every curve and angle, every detail of Jo's suffering, had been burned indelibly into his brain.

FOURTEEN

DANNY

1

When the breakthrough came, it came not with a bang or with a whimper but with something in between—a soft poof, Andy thought later, like a slightly damp firecracker wrapped in heavy cotton.

It was eight o' clock. The door to the room was locked. The drapes were pulled snugly shut. Most of the lights were off except for the small lamp atop the desk, where Bassett sat hunched over, reading Andy's most recent notes, the ones about that August day in 1927 and what had happened in the clearing off Green Meadow Trail. The dim reading lamp next to the bed was on, too. Andy was sprawled across the covers, halfheartedly reading the old newspaper clippings about the murders, searching fruitlessly for anything that would offer even the slightest hint that someone the police had spoken to in the aftermath might have witnessed what Carlson had done.

They had thrown the meal, which Bassett (without a trace of a smile) had referred to as "the Gardener's love offering," into the wastebasket right away. Now the stench of grease filled the room like the odor of nervous sweat, settling over everything, pervading, permeating, penetrating. Every few minutes one of them would glance up from his reading with a vague look of distaste, although neither was consciously aware of doing so.

"Hopeless," Andy muttered. "How many times do we have to read these things before we admit it? 'Mr. McFarren urges anyone with information to step forward immediately.' That's all we're going to find. They interviewed you, because they were your friends; they talked to both families; they grilled the fisherman who found the bodies; and they begged for information from the public. That's all. There wasn't anyone else."

"Nothing in your notes either, I'm afraid," Bassett said. "You have a frighteningly accurate recreation of the events, but no clues." He stood, and even from the other side of the room, Andy could hear the sad pop and creak of the old man's joints. "I think that's about it."

"What do you mean?"

"I mean we've arrived at the end of the line. Research has taken us as far as we're going to go. You made a real breakthrough today with your lumberjack connection. I had honestly come to believe that our wicked friend couldn't possibly have anything to do with Frank and Charlie, but you proved me wrong. I'll admit that. It's a step forward. But we'll never identify the other person in the clearing at the rate we're progressing now."

"So what? Give up?" Andy sighed. "I really don't want to have this same argument again, Alex. I'm not strong enough for it right now. I've fought with you too much, and trying to persuade Marilyn today took the rest of the fight out of me. I know it seems like we're at a dead-end, but I can't quit. Not now. Of all times, not now. Not after I saw that picture of Jo."

"Andy, slow down, my friend, slow down and listen. I'm not suggesting we quit, as attractive as that might seem to me. I'm merely saying we should try something new. It might be time to think about throwing our notebooks aside and...well, taking to the streets, so to speak."

Andy raised his eyebrows.

"We should think about setting a trap for the Gardener."

ALEXANDER'S SONG

"A trap," Andy repeated dully. "You mean we should dig a tiger pit or something? Cover it with vines and wait for him to fall in?"

Bassett's smile was thin. "It would be nice if it was that easy, wouldn't it? What I'm talking about is something I'd planned to do after I staged my death and moved back here. I never worked out the mechanics of it because I never had the chance. My rough ideas were based on the Gardener making contact with me, which, as I told you before, was a very basic mistake. He thought I was dead, and obviously he wasn't going to make contact with a dead man. For almost twenty years I was a corpse to him and he was completely out of my sight, no notes or pictures or anything. By the time he realized I was alive and living as Hoffer, it was too late. He killed the Gullivers, and his appearance like that out of the blue so shocked me and depressed me that I couldn't do anything but surrender to him all over again."

"But you had a plan?" Andy said.

"No. I had a concept, which is a very different thing. Roughly, it involved catching the bastard in the act of committing one of his deeds or leaving one of his messages. Instead of hiding from him…well, I'd still be hiding, but instead of hoping he'd just give up and go away, I'd be hoping for the opposite. I'd be waiting for him to arrive."

"Sounds too easy," Andy said, frowning.

"Perhaps it is. But I think we've exhausted all our other avenues—unless you've changed your mind and want to pay a visit to Chief Paquin."

"I don't think so."

"No, nor I. That would just be transferring the impossible from our shoulders to his, and frankly, I think we're better equipped to deal with it right now."

"But—"

"We have to try, Andy. It might be too easy, too simple to work, but I don't know that for sure. The Gardener's twenty years of inactivity took the chance to find out away from me. But now…it's safe to say he's seldom been *more* active than he's been these last few weeks."

Andy knew Bassett was right. They could keep going the way they were, reading the same notebooks and articles for the twentieth time, looking for things that weren't there, or they could take some kind of action. The first choice might seem infinitely preferable, but while they were reading and jotting and pondering, time was clearly running out. It was probably even worse than Andy dared think. The transplants, after all, weren't taking. The flowers were wilting. And he and Bassett had been served their final meal.

He lit a cigarette but couldn't stand the taste and immediately crushed it out. He sat up and let his feet dangle off the edge of the bed. He was momentarily dizzy, but refused to consider the truth, that his lack of sleep was catching up with him again and would soon prove dangerous. It was easier to pretend that his head wasn't aching, that his throat wasn't sore, that his eyes weren't dry and burning, that his bones weren't aching and his muscles weren't throbbing, that his stomach wasn't burning with fiery acid.

"Okay," he said, with a brightness and determination he didn't feel. "You're right. Let's hear it. Tell me exactly what you have in mind."

2

BASSETT DIDN'T ANSWER.

The old man had gotten up from the desk and was standing with his back to Andy, apparently studying something in the messy jumble of books and papers heaped on top of the dresser.

"Alex?"

For a terrifying instant, Andy was certain that Bassett had found something else from the Gardener, another communication they had somehow missed earlier.

Oh Jesus, he thought, panicky and crazy. He was here, right here in this room, sometime today, before we got back from the island. He came to leave another calling card and he was standing right where Alex is now. That means that locking the door isn't good enough. It means—

ALEXANDER'S SONG

Bassett turned around with a strange half-smile playing on his lips. "This is incredible," he said, holding up Andy's copy of A *Daughter's Song*. "Do you realize what you have here?"

Still thinking of the Gardener, Andy nodded impatiently. "Yeah, sure. Your first book. A signed first edition. A real collector's item."

"Where did you get it?"

"Does that really matter right now? Is it important?"

"Important, no. Fascinating, yes."

Andy shrugged, and told Bassett about finding the volume at the used bookstore in Chicago, dickering with the store's owner, paying eighty dollars and coming away with the centerpiece of his collection.

"Fascinating," Bassett said again. "I remember signing this one."

"Is that so?" Andy said. His immediate impression was that was nothing out of the ordinary. Then he realized how many inscriptions a famous writer—even a relative hermit like Bassett—must sign in the course of a career, and he said with more genuine interest, "You honestly remember it?"

"Oh, yes." He opened the book to the title page and read aloud: "To Danny, Thank you for dinner and the most stimulating conversation. You are a fine young friend, and I suspect our bond will endure—forged in sadness, never to be broken. You have all my best wishes as you sail forth. Yours for peace, etcetera, December 21, 1941."

He held the open book up to his chest, like a young lover clutching a picture of his betrothed. Andy was amused until he noticed the tears trickling slowly down the old man's cheeks.

"Danny," Bassett croaked. "Daniel Martin McCready."

Andy's jaw went slack. If he could have thought of something to say, he would have said it, but his mind was suddenly floating away from him.

Daniel McCready? Charlie McCready's brother? Did he even *have* a brother?

But he remembered now, recalled that day at the cemetery on Oak Hill Road, standing in front of McCready's tombstone.

PAUL F. OLSON

CHARLES GRANT McCREADY
Loving Son of Matthew and Nora
Devoted brother to David, Elizabeth and Daniel

He put his hand on the old man's arm. "Are you telling me that I have a copy of a book that belonged to Charlie McCready's brother? That somehow I lucked onto this, years before I even knew there *was* a Charlie McCready outside the pages of *Brave Men?*"

Bassett wiped away his tears and nodded. "Verges on the unbelievable, doesn't it? Danny was Charlie's youngest brother, years younger than us. I saw him all the time when he was a boy and had a number of contacts with him as he grew older, in those eight or nine years between the time I graduated from college and the time I ran away from Grace's death.

"I remember the night I signed this book. It was right after Pearl Harbor. Danny must have been twenty, twenty-one years old. He'd done what almost all young men did in those wild, frightening days. He'd enlisted in the service—the Navy, in his case. He came to New York for a quick visit on the eve of shipping out. We had dinner. We talked about Rock Creek, about mutual acquaintances, about Charlie…of course about Charlie. And just before we said goodbye, he presented this book. It had just been published a few months earlier. He told me he'd read it and loved it, and he asked me to sign it for him."

"A bond forged in sadness," Andy said. "Incredible."

"He was a remarkable young man—quiet, polite, thoughtful. I'm sure the war was difficult for him, but of course it was for all of us, even those of us who stayed behind and advocated peace."

"I still can't believe this," Andy said. "I prided myself on having a signed first edition Bassett in mint condition. And all the while, I never dreamed—"

"I think I have a picture of him here someplace. Would you like to see it? In fact, I'll give it to you; you can add it to the book. I'm afraid it won't

ALEXANDER'S SONG

increase the resale value at all, but it'll make a nice conversation piece some day."

Andy nodded, and the old man went over to the wooden trunk, the one with the decoupage portrait of Poe on top and ANNALS OF THE DUPIN SOCIETY carved into the front. He lifted the lid and rummaged slowly through the contents—a tattered leather-bound copy of Poe's complete stories and poems; a smaller volume, a chapbook, containing illustrated versions of three Dupin stories, "The Murders in the Rue Morgue," "The Mystery of Marie Roget" and "The Purloined Letter"; a long document in someone's childish handwriting describing at length the "Rules of Deportment for Dupin Society Members"; a hand-drawn map of the Quad Lakes area; a piece of tarnished jewelry that looked amazingly like an old cereal-premium decoder ring; a quickly-scrawled "Oath of Membership"; and dozens of other leftovers from those days just before the dawn of the roaring twenties, when Alexander Bassett's biggest concern had been where to throw a ground ball with one out and men on first and second.

"Aha!" the old man said. "Just when I thought I'd been mistaken...." He straightened, and Andy saw the photograph in his hand. "There's your man."

Andy took the picture, which was faded and yellowed and brittle at the edges. He stared at it, perplexed.

Two things bothered him. One, and most obvious, was that it wasn't a picture of Daniel McCready at all. It was a snapshot of the Dupin Society itself, although perhaps taken somewhere in between the two incarnations of that organization. It showed Frank, Charlie, and Alex standing in front of a house with their arms around each other. In almost all respects it was remarkably similar to the first picture he'd seen, the one Ginnie had stolen from Wolf Island.

The other thing that troubled him was...he wasn't sure. Oddly enough, this feeling was stronger than the first. He couldn't help thinking of the second world, its corners and edges almost lining up with this world but not quite achieving the seamless, geometric perfection necessary to remain unnoticed. He felt that same vague sense of distortion, of something a little bit unright, something out of place, something important that kept eluding him.

"Right there," Bassett said, reaching over Andy's shoulder and pointing with a gnarled finger. "There's Danny."

"Where? I...oh. Okay. Kind of an unusual place to sit, isn't it?"

Bassett was pointing at a whitish blob in the lower left corner of the picture, just to one side of the three friends. The blob appeared to float inside the neatly-trimmed hedges that surrounded the house, like a diffuse circle of lamplight in the depths of a forest. When he brought the picture a little closer and squinted, that blob at last materialized into the face of a little boy, a little boy who had apparently crawled into the shrubbery to hide but nevertheless couldn't resist the opportunity to poke his head out and watch a photograph being taken. Now Andy saw more detail: a bit of dark-colored overalls, a tiny shoe and some leg, a white hand rising to pull back the branches in front of him.

The boy was grinning, no doubt proud of his achievement: *I can see you but you can't see me.*

Bassett was chuckling over Andy's shoulder. "Unusual hiding places were Danny's specialty. Charlie would go to call him for dinner, or to tell him to get ready for church, or whatever, and it would take him an hour just to find his brother. Sometimes he'd hear Danny giggling, but the giggle would move—behind the couch, in the closet, out in the yard behind a tree. Sneaky kid. Charlie called him 'the little spook.'

"I remember when my mother took this picture for us. It would've been...oh, '25, I think. Frank and I were sixteen, so Charlie would've been fourteen, and Danny...Danny was five. We didn't know he'd been right behind us until the shot was developed, but it wasn't too surprising to see him there. He followed us everywhere. We'd go fishing miles from town, turn around, and there would be Danny. We'd ride our bikes out Rock Creek Road to the old bridge and find out later that Danny was right

ALEXANDER'S SONG

behind us. We'd go up Silver Mountain—Danny. We'd hike to the old cave, near the abandoned mine at Lake Manabozho—Danny.

"Frank and I took it all right. We thought it was rather flattering that he always wanted to be around us. But it drove Charlie crazy. 'I'm not a magnet, kid, and you're not a piece of iron,' he'd say. 'Get some friends your own age.'

"And of course it was a real inconvenience for Charlie, too. Every time we'd get somewhere and find out Danny had trailed us there, Charlie had to turn around and take him all the way back home. And then Charlie's mother would yell at him for being so coldhearted. She'd say, 'Let your brother play with you, Charles. He needs a good influence, and lord knows he worships you. It's good for him to be around his older brother.' But Charlie would say, 'Let the spook play with Liz. She's closer to his age.' And then he'd rush out of the house and hurry back to wherever we were waiting for him. It was a running joke with us. Charlie, the magnet, and his adoring brother, the spook."

Andy frowned. It was a cute story, one to which every kid with a younger brother could relate. Andy himself remembered friends he'd had growing up, baseball buddies who were always fighting a losing battle to keep their annoying younger siblings out of the game. But a nagging thought had entered his mind. It was flatly ridiculous, but once it was there, he couldn't get rid of it.

"You don't suppose..." he said slowly. "I mean, you don't...no. Never mind."

"What are you thinking?"

"Nothing. It's absurd. But what you said about the way he always followed you, up on the mountain, out to the mine, down to the lake. What about out to the clearing in the woods? What about out to Green Meadow Trail?"

The old man stared at him. Then he uttered a shrill laugh. "Danny? Danny *McCready*? The Gardener?"

Andy felt himself blushing. "It was just a thought."

"Well, that's one thought you can banish from your mind. It's impossible."

Andy nodded. But he was thinking about the inscription in the book. *Our bond will endure—forged in sadness, never to be broken.*

That was when he first became aware of that gentle poof, the sound and sensation of a damp firecracker, wrapped in cotton, going off inside his head.

3

"I KNOW YOU think I'm nuts," Andy said. "But humor me for a minute. Put my mind at rest. Where's Danny today?"

Bassett opened his mouth to give a quick reply, but hesitated and scowled. "I don't honestly know the answer to that. Since he'd be seventy years old right now, I'd say there's a fair chance he's dead."

"Could be," Andy said. "But since I'm sitting here talking to an eighty-one-year-old man, and since there's an eighty-three-year-old woman downstairs in the lobby of this hotel who seems to be in better shape than I am, I don't think I'd be too quick to give up on someone who's only seventy."

Bassett conceded the point with a small shrug. "I lost track of Danny years ago. The last time I saw him was that night in New York, 1941, just before he shipped out with the Navy. I heard about him a few times after that, however."

"And?"

"This would've been in the early fifties, I think. Yes, late '50 or early '51. *The Pharisee* had either just been published or was about to be. I got a letter from Danny's older sister, Liz. She was two years younger than Charlie, grew up, went off to teachers' college, and was working at a private school in Minneapolis. She wanted to know if I'd consider coming out there to speak to her students. I couldn't…or wouldn't…but I thanked her for the interest and we struck up a correspondence that lasted several years. Somewhere in the course of those letters, I found out what had happened to the rest of her family.

ALEXANDER'S SONG

"Her mother had never really recovered from Charlie's murder. She became chronically depressed, was ill much of the time, and passed away a few years later. I'd known that, of course. It happened while I was a senior in college. The things I didn't know were about her father, who died of a massive heart attack in late '39, a few months after I'd moved to New York, and about her older brother, David. David was maybe four years older than Charlie. The year that Charlie died, he'd already been in the service for several years. He was a career military man, Navy officer. Liz told me that he was dead, too. He was killed about a year after Pearl Harbor, when his aircraft carrier was hit by some Japanese Zeroes—dawn attack."

"One tragedy after another," Andy murmured. "Almost like the family had a curse on it."

"Perhaps."

"And what about Danny?"

"Well, that was interesting. Liz said Danny went AWOL about a week after learning of his brother's death. That was January of 1943— don't quote me, but I think that's right. Yes…yes, I'm sure she said it was right after the holidays. His ship had steamed into Hawaii for a week of repairs and resupply, and Danny vanished the very first night.

"David McCready's burial was a few days later at Arlington National Cemetery. Liz attended, of course. She said the service was chocked full of police and shore patrol and the like. Obviously, they were expecting Danny to show up there. But he didn't. He didn't show up anywhere.

"No one heard from him for several years. Liz had started to convince herself that he was dead, when suddenly he got in touch with her. He wrote her a letter from London, told her that she was the only one he could talk to. Not only was she his sole surviving family member, but she was the only person in the world he'd trust to keep his whereabouts secret. Of course she understood. The war was either still going on or had just ended around that time, and either way it was easy for her to imagine the big trouble he'd be in if the Navy caught up with him.

PAUL F. OLSON

"It continued that way for a while. She was never able to write back to him because he was on the road constantly, but he'd send her letters and postcards from everywhere. She got notes from London, Paris, Rome, Chicago, Detroit, San Francisco, New York, Washington—"

"Hold on," Andy said. "New York?"

Bassett sighed. "Yes, New York. Everyone in the world comes to New York at least once in his life. Is that so surprising?"

Andy shrugged, and nodded for him to continue.

"The communications lasted several years, then stopped. She had no idea what became of him. And a few years after she and I started corresponding, she got married, quit her teaching job, and I never heard from *her* again."

"Which means," Andy said slowly, "that no one knows what the hell happened to Danny. He disappeared in January '43, popped up again briefly, and then really dropped off the face of the earth."

"Yes, but surely you must know—"

"Alex, I don't know a damned thing. Maybe I *am* off base. I didn't know the guy. But how well did *you* know him? He was ten or eleven years younger than you."

"But I saw him several times in the years after college. I saw him the night I inscribed that copy of A *Daughter's Song*."

"Which doesn't mean anything," Andy said. "Think about it. Form a psychological profile. If it helps, don't think about Danny. Just think of some nameless person with a similar background. This person worships his older brother, and that brother is brutally murdered when the person is only six or seven years old. A few years after that his mother is dead, then his father, then his other older brother."

"Yes, all right," Bassett said. "You're describing a very difficult situation, a great deal of personal tragedy and heartbreak."

"Now carry it one step further," Andy said. "Just for the sake of argument, throw something else into the pot. Assume this person actually *saw* that older brother being murdered. Remember, he's only seven years old.

He followed his brother because…well, that was the game. It was something he did all the time. He's somewhere near the clearing where his brother and his friends are shooting at old medicine bottles. He sees the murderer arrive. He sees the argument. He sees his beloved brother being attacked with an ax. And he sees his older brother being betrayed by one of his friends."

"*Betrayed?*"

"Relax, no one's blaming you. I'm talking about a seven-year-old's perspective. He sees his brother being attacked, practically dismembered before his eyes. And he sees his brother's friend with a gun that could have saved the day. But the friend doesn't use the gun. He runs away instead. He could've been his brother's savior, but instead he only saved himself. To a seven-year-old, that would be betrayal."

"I suppose it would to most other people, too," Bassett said softly. "Lord knows it was to me. For many years, it was."

"Well, okay then. That's what the seven-year-old sees. It's what he thinks. Or maybe he doesn't think about it at all. Maybe some kind of protective mechanism kicks in and he doesn't remember anything. He represses the whole thing. He blanks it out. He knows the brother he worshipped is dead, but that's all, at least until some point in the future when the memory comes back, appearing in his head out of nowhere, brought out by stress or shock or just the passage of enough time."

"Oh, Jesus Christ."

"Maybe it didn't happen that way," Andy said. "It's all just speculation and guesswork. Maybe he blanked it out, maybe he didn't. Or maybe it isn't Danny at all. Maybe Danny wasn't even in the clearing that day. Maybe Danny was killed by roadside bandits in Spain in 1947. Maybe he developed lung cancer and died in a hospital in Arizona. Maybe he's still alive, living peacefully with a wife and kids and grandkids in Mississippi. Guesswork, Alex, nothing more. But do you concede it's possible? Will you admit that the psychological profile might fit?"

The old man didn't answer with words but with a ragged nod.

"It's the closest thing to an honest motivation we've found so far," Andy said. "And if nothing else, we at least know that Danny was troubled. Guys with nothing on their mind don't go AWOL in the middle of a war."

"Oh my god," Bassett whispered. "Danny...oh, you poor, sweet boy...."

He looked up at Andy, as though beseeching him to make it all go away, tell him it was all a mistake, a miscalculation, a little joke.

It made Andy's heart ache to see the old man that way, and he felt a weak, quivery feeling deep inside, as though he had brought not only Bassett up to the brink but himself as well.

Yet he felt angry, too. This was it. Their first tangible lead. Their first genuine advance. This was the breakthrough, and he didn't want to see it diminished or taken away by sentiment. If he was right, if all the speculation was even halfway close to the mark, then you could feel sorry for Danny all right. You could definitely hurt a bit for that little boy who had seen too much.

But what about the man Danny had become? What about the goddamned Gardener? Understanding was one thing, but forgiveness? The Gardener was a murderer. Andy couldn't forget that; how could Bassett? Sympathy was fine, but they were talking about mass killings. That was an awfully large hook, and Andy didn't want the Gardener sliding off that hook and getting away.

He went over to the pile of notes and rummaged through them until he found what he was looking for. It was the list he had made at Bassett's cabin, the one containing names of victims and dates of death.

"There's something pretty interesting here," he said, laying the sheet down in front of Bassett. "You said Danny disappeared from his ship at the beginning of January 1943. And look at this—Cal Drummond murdered in New York City two weeks later, on January 15."

"I don't want to hear this," Bassett said.

"Yeah, but you have to. You have to listen. He goes AWOL. He kills Drummond. Then maybe he lights out for a while, traveling around, writing to his sister from all over the world. But maybe he comes back to New York...here...in November '45...just in time to kill Henry Oglebay."

"No!"

But Andy persisted. "When did *Brave Men* get published? Wasn't it right around that time?"

Bassett blinked. "*Brave Men?* Yes. It came out in late October of that year."

"Well, there you go," Andy said. "Maybe he saw a copy of your new book and didn't like the way you used his brother as a character. Maybe he decided to come back from wherever he'd been hiding and punish you again."

"So that's what this is all about," Bassett said. He was massaging his chest absently, the way he had done at his cabin the night before. His breath was coming in shallow gulps. "In your theory, Danny's punishing me over and over again for allowing Jens Carlson to kill his brother."

Andy shrugged. "I'm not a psychologist, but it makes sense to me."

"Oh, hell," the old man said. "Me too. God help me, Andy, but it makes sense to me, too."

4

A FEW MINUTES later Bassett pointed to the list. "What about this?" he asked. "Grace was killed in 1939, four years before David McCready died in action and Danny went AWOL. And my mother died eight years earlier than that."

Andy nodded. "I've been thinking about that. First of all, we don't know for sure that the Gardener killed your mother. She might have been pushed down those cellar steps, but she might just as easily have stumbled and slipped."

"Granted. But what about Grace?"

"I don't know," Andy said. "You want a guess? Maybe he thought she was going to be a one-shot. Maybe he wanted to kill her as a way to get retribution, and he thought it would be enough. It's possible that he never intended it to go beyond that. But then his surviving brother dies in combat and Danny gets crazier and decides that one murder *wasn't* enough after all. So he does more, and he starts the note-writing campaign, really goes off the deep end, and commits the rest of his life to hurting you."

"It's possible, I suppose."

"There's only one other thing I can think of," Andy said, "and that's the possibility that he didn't push Grace in front of that train at all. He would've known about it, of course; he was still living at home in Rock Creek at the time it happened. So when he fell off his mental cliff a few years later, he decided to take credit for *her* death too. Maybe he even convinced himself that he did it, getting a vicarious thrill from the death of the woman you were engaged to."

"Yes," Bassett said, nodding thoughtfully. "Yes...perhaps. When you follow this scenario all the way back to the beginning, then turn around and come forward to today, it makes a dreadful kind of logic. Danny thought that I was responsible for the death of the thing he loved most, his brother. And so what does he do? He spends the rest of his life removing the things that *I* love, the things that *I* was close to. It fits so neatly."

"Sure," Andy said, "just look at all the notes. Anything that grows too close to the tree must be removed. Anything that helps the tree succeed must be pruned away. You're the tree, the one spared by the lumberjack, that *ran away* from the lumberjack. Whatever twisted mess is inside the head of that man, whatever synthesis there is of a seven-year-old's nightmare visions and a very sick grown-up's logic...that's what creates the Gardener and makes him do the things he does."

Bassett clumsily got out one of Andy's cigarettes and lit it. He inhaled deeply, coughed, and said, "Of course we might still be wrong. We talk about how neatly it fits, but when you're writing novels you quickly learn that there's such a thing as fitting *too* neatly. The critics will savage you if you use too much Dickensian coincidence."

ALEXANDER'S SONG

"This isn't coincidence, though," Andy said. "It's cause and effect, from your father and Royal Haag all the way through to Ginnie and Jo. There's nothing coincidental about any of it. It's a house of cards, one laid on top of the other. It's a chain of events, and every event is linked to the ones that went before."

Bassett coughed again, hard enough and long enough that his eyes watered. He put down the cigarette and folded his skinny arms across his chest.

"It's horrible, Andy. I close my eyes and I see that day in the clearing. I see Charlie trying to escape with his guts literally spilling out of his belly. I see Frank, dead probably right away, as soon as Carlson struck the first blow. I see the way Carlson looked to me as I sighted down the shotgun, and I can feel the trigger under my finger right now, just the way it felt back then. I can feel my finger twitching, wanting to pull, wanting it so badly."

"You can't change history."

"No. But it leaves me wondering if things could have been different. Would shooting Carlson have mattered? Would Charlie have lived then, or was he too badly wounded? If he died, would Danny have absolved me from blame, because at least I'd killed the lumberjack?"

"But you *did* kill the lumberjack," Andy said. "Or at least you and a lot of whiskey helped him kill himself."

Bassett nodded slowly. "Nobody knows that, however. Certainly the Gardener doesn't know it. You and me and now Marilyn Borg, we're the only ones who know about the fight at Green Lake."

He picked up the picture of the three friends with their arms around one another, gently touching the blurry face that grinned out of the bushes. "Ah, Danny, I'm sorry. You were such a good boy. It shouldn't have ended up this way."

Andy looked at the picture in Bassett's hands and felt that unidentifiable sensation again, that distortion, that feeling of not knowing something he should know, missing something that shouldn't be missed. He stepped back a pace but didn't take his eyes off the snapshot.

"Lamplight," he said, the word coming out of nowhere and making him jump.

Bassett looked up sharply. "What?"

"Nothing...it's nothing."

But the image was in his mind now, an old-fashioned gas lantern casting a welcoming glow. With it came a strange feeling of descending, as though he were no longer standing still in his hotel room but going downward. He swallowed hard, took a deep breath, and caught the imaginary scent of dirt and well-seasoned leather.

Bassett said something and Andy turned around, coming back almost unwillingly from wherever he had been.

"What did you say?"

"I said we should probably look in the phone book," Bassett told him. "We should see if there's a listing for a Daniel McCready."

Andy couldn't help laughing. "Do you really believe he'd be living under his own name? After everything he's done—always assuming, of course, that he's the Gardener?"

Despite the skepticism, he opened the desk drawer and removed the skinny Rock Creek phone book with its white and yellow sections totaling no more than fifteen pages.

"McAllistair, Horace...McWilliams, Tom and Sandy. No Dan McCready. And look—no listing under 'the Gardener,' either."

He put down the book and picked up the picture again. For a moment's time he felt nothing, but then everything returned, a gentle wash of fragmentary images, bits of sound and smell.

"Alex? Where was this picture taken? Whose house is this?"

The old man seemed startled by the question. "Why, that's my house. Well, not precisely mine—my parents'. That's the house where I grew up."

"Oh." Andy felt defeat now, side by side with his confusion. "Torn down long ago, I suppose?"

Again Bassett seemed surprised. "Not torn down. Abandoned long ago, yes. But it's still standing. Or it was the last time I looked. It's about two miles outside of town on the Manitou Road, not too far past the meadow and the old mill."

And then Andy remembered where he had seen it before. He had stopped by there just last week, when he'd been coming back from Green Lake. His intention had been to go to the meadow and check on the progress of the search. But first he had seen the house, and something about it had made him slam on the brakes, something had brought those same images to him—lamplight and stairs, old books standing on deep shelves.

Why?

Had he somehow known the house was Bassett's? Had someone told him about it on one of his first days in town? Had he forgotten it, but tucked the knowledge away in some corner of his mind, so that when he passed the house again he thought of the writer, which made him think of books, which made him think—

"No!" he cried suddenly. "It was a dream! Alex...my god, I dreamed about your house a long time ago, before I'd ever met you. I dreamed about that house before I knew it was yours—Christ, before I'd ever even *seen* it!

"Is that so?"

The old man looked hopelessly baffled, and why not? *Andy* was baffled. What he was talking about was crazy. It didn't make the least bit of sense. And yet....

"No," he said at last. "I guess I'm wrong. It couldn't have been that house. That would be...well, it would be impossible, wouldn't it?"

"That's the word that comes to mind."

"It must have been some other house," Andy said softly, as though trying to convince himself. "Another house that just looks like yours."

"Andy, I'm afraid I don't understand a word you're saying."

"Neither do I," he said with a sheepish smile. "Let's just forget it. I'm tired. I'm hallucinating. We have to get back to business. We have to figure out a way to find Danny."

5

HALF AN HOUR later they were sitting in the truck in front of the house on Manitou Road. Looking at it, Andy thought of a carving done on a piece of flat black rock, the dark lines of the house standing out in stark relief against the even darker trees behind, the cheerless filigree of coal-colored weeds that consumed the front yard.

It needs a moon, he thought. Some kind of light. Anything, just so it wouldn't look so black. But then he decided that was no good either; it would only make the place look haunted.

"I'm sorry about this," he said. "I don't know what we're doing here. I know it's a waste of time, but I...I just couldn't get the place out of my head."

Bassett grunted. When Andy turned he saw the old man only in silhouette, leaning back against the bench seat, his walking stick looking like a thin third leg.

"I want to go in," Andy said.

Bassett grunted again. "You've lost your mind."

"Yeah. Maybe."

Without waiting for anything else, Andy popped open the door and climbed out. He went around the other side and helped the old man lower himself to the ground.

"I can do this alone, you know," he said, but Bassett only waved the comment away sourly.

They went slowly up what was left of the driveway, the old man shuffling along, leaning on Andy's arm for support, probing the weeds and rocks in front of them with his stick. They went up the creaky front steps, moved cautiously around a gaping, splintered crater in the front porch, and pulled on the door that Andy was sure would be locked but wasn't. For just a moment he looked back over his shoulder, and something he had sensed without seeing finally broke through to his conscious mind.

"Someone's been here," he said. Bassett gave a startled jerk. "Look." He pointed back into the yard, at several series of parallel ruts that had been chewed into the mud. "Tire tracks."

The old man shook his head. "Somebody turned around, that's all. They realized they were on the wrong road and wanted to swing back toward town."

Andy nodded, unconvinced. The tracks didn't appear to mark a U-turn, a K-turn, or any other kind of turn. They appeared to enter the yard and come right up to the house, where they stopped abruptly. It was as if someone had driven in, done whatever business he or she was there for, and backed out again along the same lines.

They went inside.

Bassett said, "You didn't think to bring a flashlight, I suppose."

"No."

"Have one in your truck?"

"Sorry."

"Of course you are." The old man moved away from him, suddenly leading the way, and Andy had to jog a few steps to catch up.

He had been slowly piecing together the memory of his dream—Bassett, a man he had assumed dead, summoning him from his room at Turner's; a night drive; the house; the stairway; the cellar library and talk of the second world—and he stared around him now, catching what he could of the shadowy rooms, the ghosts of old furniture, trying to make everything fit.

It didn't.

With dawning relief that was tempered somewhat by an inexplicable disappointment, he understood that this was not the house of his dream after all. Nothing was the same, except for the stench of rot and mold that was the property of all abandoned places. The rooms weren't right, not the correct shape or size, nor in the proper order. The furniture wasn't the same. When they came to the kitchen, he looked immediately for what he remembered—the collapsed portion of outer wall that had allowed in years of weather—but discovered the room to be intact. The old iron cookstove wasn't there. The rubble and plaster dust weren't, either, although there was plenty of regular dirt and grime, and cobwebs that dangled from the ceiling like spectral curtains.

"The cellar door," he said, pointing to the corner where he had dreamed it. There was nothing there now but two broken old chairs pushed up against the wall.

"The cellar door is outside," Bassett said, giving him a strange, frightening look in the darkness. "You have to go down that hallway and out the back door."

Andy sighed, realizing how truly wrongheaded and insignificant his dream must have been. Once again, that knowledge was both good news and bad.

In a hurry now to finish, to put paid to what suddenly seemed like a ridiculous delay in their real business, Andy persuaded Bassett to go with him at least as far as the cellar. They went down the corridor, past more rooms that hadn't been in his dream, and out the back door, which was hanging aslant from broken hinges. They crossed a porch that was a smaller version of the one up front and went down into the back yard. The cellar door was standing open just to their right.

"I know what we're going to find," Andy said. "It's a party spot for kids, I'll bet. We'll see beer cans and empty Doritos bags and used condoms. We might even find a fire ring, if they use the place in the winter."

"Yes," Bassett said. "So for the life of me, I can't understand why you want to go down there."

Andy walked away from him, struck his lighter, held it up like a lamp, and started down.

There were only about ten steps, another fact that proved his dream false. That was one of the things he remembered most clearly, that endless stairway, the descent so ungodly long that going down had begun to feel like going up, like floating. At the bottom he turned around, holding the lighter up for Bassett, who limped his way down to join him.

ALEXANDER'S SONG

"Looks like I was right," Andy said. The cellar was just a cellar, not a library, and certainly not a repository of hidden secrets. "Beer cans…paper…garbage…nothing."

When Bassett didn't respond, Andy turned to look at him, expecting to see another expression of disdain or confusion, perhaps both. But the old man was staring past him, taking in the short length of cellar that was visible in the flickering yellow glow of the lighter.

"I guess we can go," Andy said.

The lighter had grown too hot to hold. He had to drop it suddenly and let it cool for half a minute before picking it up and striking it again. When he did, Bassett was still staring at the cracked stone walls, the hard-packed dirt floor, the half timbers overhead.

"Alex? You ready?"

"I was just thinking. It *is* odd that you dreamed of this place."

"Except that it *wasn't* this place, just an old dream house. I was wrong."

"We used to gather down here, Frank, Charlie, and I. In winter, or if it was raining and we couldn't go to the woods, this is where we'd be. We had Dupin Society meetings here. Before that it was the Long John Silvers; later, the Ivanhoes. When we got older, that last summer, it was the Dupins again. And in between, when there was no group at all, this is where we talked about girls and smoked our stolen cigarettes. Sometimes Danny would sit back there on those steps, about halfway down, and watch us. We couldn't shoo him away no matter what."

"It wasn't this cellar though, Alex. The dream didn't mean anything. I wasted our time by dragging—"

Andy stopped. He shut off the lighter again, just in time to save his thumb and forefinger from burns, and in the darkness was struck by a fleeting image he didn't understand. He saw the cliff on Wolf Island. But it wasn't an ordinary picture. It was canted to one side, tipped at an almost forty-five degree angle.

"Danny would watch you," he murmured as the image vanished. Once again he struck the lighter. "Danny knew about the Dupins and all the rest."

"Oh, I suppose Danny knew everything about us. He was iron, after all, and we were magnets."

Andy nodded distractedly. He thought in an abbreviated fashion that something was trying to come through to him again. It was a faint idea, something that was almost but not quite there. A phantom thought. A ghost concept.

He forced it away. He had more than enough on his plate without worrying about vague images that refused to come clear.

"Ready?" he said again, turning to go.

His foot kicked an empty Budweiser can. It hopped into the air and came down, clanking against others of its kind. When he looked down he saw a piece of paper lying there, half crumpled, its white surface covered with writing.

"Alex...."

The writing stood out starkly in the weird yellow glow of the lighter's flame. Words. Bits and pieces of sentences, some complete, some half-finished and crossed out with savage strokes.

"Alex."

He knew that handwriting. It was all straight printing, block letters, capitals.

"Alex!"

He bent down and picked up the Gardener's paper.

6

THERE WERE OTHERS, perhaps fifteen or twenty in all, each a rough draft.

This was the place where the Gardener composed his communications, the place he came when he worked out what he wanted to say. The notes were covered with familiar words and phrases—LUMBERJACK CUT, PRUNING, TRANSPLANTS ARE FAILING, WORK IS NEVER DONE, TREE IS DYING—each one put down in that same block printing, crossed out, put down again, moved by means of carets and arrows that slanted across the pages.

ALEXANDER'S SONG

"He edits himself," Andy said with childlike amazement. "He thinks of what he wants to tell us and then hammers it out like a…like a goddamned writer, a poet or something."

He was staring at a sheet that trembled in his hands, obviously an early version of one of the hotel room notes. In three separate places the Gardener had tried saying that transplanting and pruning were getting to be too much for him, that killing the tree outright would be easier. Finally, he had reached the bottom of the page, crossed everything out with lines heavy enough to rip through the paper in several spots, and moved on.

"It gives you a rather different feel for him, wouldn't you say?" Bassett asked softly.

Andy knew what he meant. Looking at the papers scattered around him, he felt a fresh rage stirring deep in his belly and boiling upward, wanting to escape. This was more than childhood trauma carried deep, more than tragedy-twisted brain cells and runaway emotions. This was deliberate. This was cold, calculatingly planned, straightforward, direct.

He cooled the lighter again, allowing the darkness to soothe some of his anger, and when he struck the flame for what was perhaps the thirtieth time since they'd arrived, he almost felt better. Then he picked up another page and stared at it.

"Here he's talking about transplants again. Look, he tries dying and drying and withering. He tries all of that before he settles on 'the flowers are wilting.'"

"Oh, Danny, Danny," Bassett said, sighing the words like a grandfather crooning to an infant. "I felt sorry for you, Danny. I felt sorry for you, my boy. But this is a different kind of sickness. This is…." He couldn't seem to find the right words and trailed away into silence.

Andy dropped the page he was holding. It fluttered to the dirt floor, landing upside down between his feet. There was writing on the back—writing that he almost ignored until he realized what it was. He had thought it was more of the Gardener's rough drafts, but it wasn't. This writing was typeset across the top of the page, printed in green. Andy knew that if he reached down and touched it, he'd be able to feel the letters. They would be embossed, slightly raised. They would feel professional and expensive.

"I should've known," he murmured. "I should've gotten it earlier. Of course. Christ! I was so stupid! I was *blind!*"

"What are you saying, Andy?"

"The things he told me, the things he *knew!* Nobody else could've possibly known those things!"

Bassett touched his shoulder and leaned in close, concerned.

"I know who Danny is," Andy said flatly. "Take a look at that."

The lighter was hot again, but he ignored it, beyond caring. He bent down, retrieved the paper, and held it up for the old man to see.

"I don't understand."

Andy waved the letterhead the Gardener had used to compose his threats.

"Read that!"

"I did, but—"

"Read it again! *Look!*"

He held the paper still so the old man could see what was printed there.

THE TRADING POST
111 Michigan Street Rock Creek, MI
Martin Visnaw, prop.

Before either of them could say a word, the cellar door above them slammed shut with a hollow bang.

FIFTEEN

IN THE PREDATOR'S DEN

1

"Who in the name of God is Martin Visnaw?" Bassett said, but Andy had already pushed past him and was charging up the steps. The lighter went out as he ran. He dropped it, climbed to the closed door in total blackness, and slammed against it before he realized it was there.

He grabbed the knob and pushed. The door rattled. He pushed again. It creaked and groaned.

"Andy?" Bassett's voice came floating up out of the darkness like a corpse rising to the surface of a black lake.

Andy didn't reply. He was listening to the sound of the wind beyond the door. It had apparently picked up a great deal while they were in the cellar; he could hear it shrieking out of the woods, roaring around the corners of the house. But a moment later he realized he was wrong. It wasn't the wind but the thunder of his own panic rolling through his brain.

"Andy! Something's happening upstairs. I hear—"

Andy threw himself against the door. It groaned again, and there was the crackling pop of old wood splintering, but the latch held firm. Again, hard enough this time to drive a hot spike of pain into his arm. Again, and colorful stars exploded in his head, raining downward.

"*Visnaw!*" he cried. "*I know you're out there!*"

This time when he dove forward, the latch gave way. The door cracked almost in half, flying open and spilling Andy to the ground. He lay there for a handful of seconds, dazed, then scrambled to his feet with the Gardener's name once again exploding from his lips—"*Visnaaaaaaaw!*"

He sized up what was happening. The Gardener was driving away. He heard the sound of tires tearing through mud and whirled around just in time to see a red flash of taillights vanishing up the Manitou Road. When he turned back he got the rest of the story.

The sound he'd heard inside had not been the roar of the wind, but neither had it been the mental shriek of his own terror—not completely. It was the sound of fire, the noise of destruction, the monstrous bellow of flames chewing their way with eager hunger through what had once been the home of Alexander Bassett.

The first floor was already gone, or going fast. Walls and doors and the few things Andy could make out beyond them had been swallowed by great sheets of flame. Over the sound of the fire itself he could hear the shattering of heated glass, the rumble of collapsing beams. And when he lifted his gaze, he saw the first bright orange tongues already licking away inside the windows of the second floor.

"Andy, I can't—"

Bassett's cry from the cellar disappeared beneath a tremendous crash. Andy had a brief image of the old man going down as the ceiling above him gave way, drowning in a sea of smoke, dragged down forever by a tide of flaming lumber.

He went back to the cellar steps and scrambled down, slipping halfway, flailing at the old stone walls and catching his fingers in a wide crack just in time to stop the fall. When he reached the bottom, he saw that he was at least partially right. A portion of ceiling toward the back had indeed given way, allowing the hellish light from above to come through. The entire area was filling rapidly with churning clouds of smoke.

"Alex!"

"Andy...over here...."

He found the old man on his knees, the only thing supporting him his walking stick, which he had planted firmly against the hard dirt floor. He was leaning forward against the stick, hacking, sputtering, his eyes wide and filled with tears.

"C'mon, I'll get you out of here."

"Can't...no...breath...."

He didn't waste time helping Bassett stand. He didn't worry about hurting him, either. The smoke was getting too thick, the heat from above increasing too fast. He just grasped the old man under the armpits and literally dragged him across the floor. Bassett shrieked with pain, but Andy ignored it, pulling him like a sack of stones to the base of the steps and upward, upward, and out across the yard until they were both standing, coughing fiercely, a hundred yards from the burning house. Even there the heat was alive and strong.

"He...he followed...us." Bassett gasped.

"Or he was here when we showed up. Maybe we surprised him in the act of writing more notes."

Everything in the house seemed to surrender all at once. With an explosion of sound that dwarfed even the detonation of the stairway on Wolf Island, the roof caved in onto the second floor, which collapsed upon the first, which then tumbled into the cellar. A cloud of smoke, as huge and seemingly solid as a mountain, roiled into the sky, surrounded by an expanding halo of flying sparks.

"So fast," Bassett murmured. "It all went up so fast."

"Old wood," Andy said. "And I guess Visnaw knows his tricks. Like that bomb or whatever is was back on the island. What did Danny do in the Navy, anyway? Demolition? Ordnance?"

Bassett shook his head. "Don't know." He coughed again. "This...this Visnaw...who is he?"

But before Andy could answer, another sound reached their ears. It was distant now but getting closer. It rose and fell like the cry of a lost soul—the wail of sirens approaching from town.

"Hurry," Andy said, half command, half plea.

They stumbled around the side of the house, through weeds and grass that looked strangely alive in the dancing orange light. Bassett was struggling, breathing harshly, still coughing every few seconds. Andy held tight to his hand and helped him along as best he could. At the truck, he lifted the old man in through the passenger door and hurried around the other side, pulling himself up behind the wheel. The sirens were much closer now. He thought he could hear two of them, even three, one of them perhaps a police car or an ambulance accompanying the fire trucks. He slammed his door and fumbled for his keys.

In the instant that he twisted the key in the ignition, black fear blossomed in his mind. *There's a bomb under the hood*, he thought. *We're going to blow sky-high*. But the engine caught, roared to life, and the only explosion was another crash as the back wall of the house crumbled inward.

He shifted and tromped on the gas. The truck stuttered a moment before lurching forward. He spun the wheel and they plowed across the remains of the driveway, cutting through the weeds, bouncing up onto the gravel shoulder and the asphalt of Manitou Road.

Andy looked only once into the rearview mirror. It seemed to him that there was no house left at all anymore. If there were any sections of wall remaining, any floors, windows, doors or ceilings, he certainly couldn't see them. The scene was one long wall of fire, flames reaching impossible heights on their quest to find the sky.

A half-mile down the road toward town the volunteers sped past them—a tanker, a pumper, and an ambulance. They roared by in a heartbeat, huge and dark, like beasts racing to the scene of a slaughter. The truck was buffeted in their wake, and Andy had to fight the wheel with a surprising amount of force to keep them from hopping across the centerline or going off the shoulder.

2

HE TOLD BASSETT everything he could in such a short amount of time. Speaking in rapid, broken sentences, he talked about Visnaw's interest in the writer, about their two meetings, the strange airplane ride over Wolf Island, the storekeeper's irritating habit of turning everything into a riddle or a joke, his knowledge of Frank and Charlie, Grace Mahler, the Dupin Society, his talk of death, and that strange statement about friends killing friends—directly or through cowardice and omission. Bassett listened with a look that was blank, impossible to read.

"Daniel Martin McCready," he said when Andy was finished. "Martin. Martin Visnaw. You might be right."

"I have to be. Who else could've known about the Dupins? It was a private club, wasn't it? Who else would've said those things about friends? It has to be him."

Andy pulled into the Shell Station at the edge of town. It was closed for the night, the pump islands dark, the inside of the building lit faintly by a dim overhead bulb and a row of three vending machines.

"Wait here," he said, climbing out and hurrying to the pay phone on the side of the building. There was a cord dangling there, but no phone book attached to the end of it. "Of course not," he muttered, and sprinted back to the truck.

He found a book at the same phone he had used the other day, the one outside Good Folks Rexall. He flipped to the last white page, jumped a little when he actually saw Visnaw's name listed there, and cursed when he read the useless address: Route 1.

Just on the outside chance, having absolutely no idea what he would say if Visnaw answered, he dialed the number. The phone rang ten or eleven times before he hung up.

"No address," he said when he got back to the truck. "Are you sure you don't know him?"

The old man thought for a moment before shaking his head and sighing. "I may have met him. I can't say. As much of a hermit as I've been these past twenty years, it's still an awfully small town. I suppose I've bumped into almost everyone here at least once."

"Oh, I'm sure you bumped into him all right. Probably in the summer of 1987."

Bassett frowned. "How could you possibly know that? Oh. Of course. Dwight and Lonnie."

"Sure. He thought you were dead since '69. But one day he bumps into you—the grocery store, the bank, who knows where. And some time after that he kills the Gullivers."

"But I didn't recognize him."

"How could you have? You hadn't seen Danny since you had dinner with him in New York. That was, god, forty-six years earlier. But he'd seen you a lot more recently than that. Forty-six years is a long time, but a person doesn't become unrecognizable in eighteen. Especially if the person in question's been the focal point of your entire life."

"That must be it," Bassett said. He coughed and rubbed his mouth with the back of one gnarled hand. "What do you propose we do?"

"I don't know. I'm thinking." He closed his eyes and put his head down, his chin on his chest. "We've got to find Visnaw, that's obvious. But *how* we find him is another question. That's his store right over there." He pointed diagonally across the street to the Trading Post. "Closed. Dark. We *have* to find his house. After that...I don't know, Alex. I really don't."

They sat like that, cloaked in silence, for a few minutes more. Andy remembered writing down the directions to Visnaw's house on the night he had almost gone over there. With a shudder, he realized what might have happened if he *had* gone. He could well be dead, or held captive along with Jo and Ginnie. Thank God, then, that he had refused. Thank God

ALEXANDER'S SONG

he had scheduled that aborted breakfast instead—even if it meant the directions he so desperately needed now had been thrown away.

He sighed.

And then he hit on his answer, or what would have to pass for an answer until something better came along. He started the engine again and drove to the end of Michigan Street, pulling up in front of the hotel. He parked, got out, and went around to help Bassett down.

It was eleven-fifteen.

3

"SO YOU'RE BACK here on your effing hands and knees," Marilyn said, as though the idea didn't exactly displease her. "And you're going to beg me for help no matter what I said to you before."

"I don't know what else to do," Andy said. "I'm a stranger in town, and Alex might as well be a stranger. It's late. None of the stores are open, the post office is closed. You're the only one I could think of who might know Visnaw's address."

Marilyn stared at him, that slight hint of a smile still dancing on her lips. When they'd rung the bell, she'd appeared from her apartment behind the desk wearing pink slippers and a faded gingham bathrobe. She pulled the belt of the robe tighter now, cinching it, and took the cigarette out of her mouth, blunting it out in the big ashtray next to the registration book.

"What makes you so sure he's the fellow you're after? When I talked to you last, you had no idea. You were busy trying and convicting all my dead relatives. What happened?"

Andy groaned. "We don't have time for this, Marilyn. The address. Either you know it or you don't. Either you'll give it to us or you won't. Just tell us yes or no, one way or the other."

"Please," Bassett said over Andy's shoulder. "What happened between your nephew and me was—"

"Yeah, yeah, yeah. We played this game once already today. I don't have the strength to rake through all that shit again."

She turned back to Andy. For all the wry amusement etched on her face, he thought he saw something deeper at work. He saw the gears in her brain whirling, her heart searching as she wrestled with whatever private demons were troubling her. Then, abruptly, all of that cleared. She appeared to reach a decision, or perhaps a point of comfort, although she was silent for another moment or two.

"I don't know the address," she said at last, "but the house is out on Waterman Road. You know where that is?"

"No."

"Take Oak Hill Road. Not as far as the cemetery. More like halfway, I'd say. Waterman branches off to the left. You'll pass a few houses —trailers and shacks, mostly—and just before you get to the summer cabins on the bluff you'll see it. It's either the big red one or the smaller one right next to it; I forget which."

"Marilyn, thank you. I don't know what to say. I really don't."

"Go, hon. Don't waste my time with your bullshit. Go. Take the commie with you. Get out of my sight. Go catch yourself a Gardener."

They were almost at the door when she called out: "Bassett?"

The old man turned, startled. "Yes?"

She stared at him for a long time, silent, studying. Then she shook her head and smiled.

"Nothing," she said. "Go on with you. Get the hell out of my hotel."

4

IT WAS THE smaller one, around the bend from the big red one, nestled at the base of a hill atop which sat a handful of summer places looking across two miles of forest at Carver Lake, the tiniest of the Quads. The name was on the side of the mailbox in reflective letters, two of which had fallen off: V SN W.

ALEXANDER'S SONG

"Now what?" Andy said as he eased the truck onto the shoulder, shut off the lights, and killed the engine. He wasn't asking Bassett, or at least he didn't think he was. The question was directed at himself. It was probably unanswerable.

"We have to talk to him," Bassett responded anyway. "If he's there, that is. That business stationery and the things he told you—they're damning, but we can't sentence him without a trial."

"Right," Andy agreed, although he found it hard to imagine how they could hold a sensible conversation with a man who might have killed as many as ten people, who might very well meet them at the door with a flashing knife or blazing gun.

But it didn't appear that Visnaw was home. The house was dark. The drapes on the front picture window were open, and the shadows within, almost as dark as the shadows of the surrounding wilderness, gave the place a definite look of abandonment. There was no light on over the stoop, no car parked in the drive.

To Andy, Visnaw's apparent absence was evidence enough. They weren't in Chicago, after all. Where would he be in Rock Creek at this time of night, if not out setting houses ablaze and tending his transplanted flowers? But he knew Bassett was right. There was far too much at stake to risk being wrong. They needed irrefutable proof, absolute certainty.

They left the truck and walked up the driveway to the front door. There was a bell and a knocker (the latter a carved woodpecker that tapped against an artificial log when you pulled the rope; Andy had seen those for sale in the Trading Post), but neither summoned anyone to the door.

Andy peered through the window and found himself looking into a kitchen. He went to the picture window and looked in there as well, but nothing he could make out in the big living room was evidence of either innocence or guilt. When he got back to the door, Bassett was rattling the knob.

"No luck," the old man said. "It seems we've struck out."

Andy nodded, but then, on the strength of a dark whim that surprised him, he tried the kitchen window and found that it slid up smoothly.

"Breaking and entering?" Bassett asked.

"Why not?"

"Because..." Bassett hesitated, floundering. "...because, like it or not, the old saying is true. Two wrongs don't make a right."

"They do this time," Andy said. "We're talking about mass murder on one side, unlawful entry on the other. You tell me which one tips the scales."

Before the old man could respond, Andy added, "You wait here," and snaked through the open window into the house.

He went through the kitchen and into a small entryway, every nerve jangling. It was mostly fear, he knew —fear of what they might find, fear that Visnaw might appear from the back of the house at any moment, fear that he might pull into the driveway, even fear that the place might be booby-trapped, like a bandits' hideout in an old movie, crisscrossed with tripwires that would fire guns or drop bundles of bricks from overhead.

But there were other feelings working on him, too: anticipation, eagerness, righteousness. They were justified in doing this. He had to believe that. He couldn't allow any doubt to creep in and stop him now.

He opened the front door, and Bassett shuffled in without a murmur of protest. They went immediately to the living room. Andy found a small table lamp with a three-way bulb and turned it on to the dimmest setting.

"Oh!" Bassett cried, startled and dismayed.

The room could have passed for an Alexander Bassett shrine. There were many books by many different authors on the shelves along the far wall, but another set of shelves next to the fireplace held nothing but Bassett titles, reminding Andy again of the dream he had just recently remembered. There were multiple copies of every novel, every poetry collection, the play, the essays. There were hardcovers and paperbacks, foreign editions, student abridgements. In a cardboard box on the bottom shelf were reams of newspaper clippings—articles and interviews from the forties, when Bassett had his biggest successes. There was a *Playbill* and a program from the Broadway

ALEXANDER'S SONG

version of *Brave Men*. There was a *Publishers Weekly* from 1947, containing an interview. Next to that was a *New York Times Book Review* with *The Pharisee* prominently featured on the front page.

That wasn't all.

On the mantle was a framed picture of Bassett, the same one that had graced the jackets of several of his novels. Hanging on the wall was a framed cover from *To Raise Brave Men*. A little farther down, also in a shiny gold frame, was the lengthy obituary from the *New York Times*, headlined *Highway Accident Claims Former Literary Master—Alexander Bassett dead at 60*.

"He's a fanatic all right," Andy said softly. "But this doesn't prove anything yet. Ginnie told me about all this stuff when she put me onto Visnaw in the first place. Hell, I've got most of it myself. I just don't display it so nicely."

Bassett was trembling, shaking his head.

"What's wrong?"

"I don't know. It's just that this is all a little surprising…disconcerting. You expect fans, you *want* fans, but to this extent? I'm a writer, just a man with a typewriter and a few ideas. I'm not any kind of damn movie star."

Andy sensed that some of the old man's distress was feigned, that he was almost as pleased as he was upset.

"When this is all over, you can visit me in Chicago and look at all my things. You'll go through the roof."

"Yes…well…." Bassett looked shyly at the floor. "What next?"

Andy knew what was next but was hesitant to say it. They had reached the moment when undiluted fear overwhelmed all his other emotions. It was the moment they had come for. Never mind that business about talking to Visnaw, giving him a chance to tell his side of the story. Without admitting it aloud, Andy knew that they had really trekked all the way out here to the woods for just one reason: to find Ginnie and Jo.

If Visnaw was Danny, if Visnaw was the Gardener, then where else would he be holding his prisoners? In the back of the Trading Post, where

435

any straying customer or visiting sales rep might discover them? No. He would be holding them here. The question was where, which part of the house? And the bigger question was, would they still be alive, or had the wilting of the petals progressed all the way to death?

He didn't have to say any of this—he knew that Bassett understood it as well as he—a fact for which he was grateful. Instead, he led the way out of the living room and down a long, narrow corridor that went toward the back of the house. They investigated as they went, opening doors and looking into two empty bedrooms, an empty bathroom, several storage cupboards full of linens and towels and toiletries. When they reached the end of the hall they stopped, looking into each other's eyes, stalling, still not ready to express their fears in words.

"Well, it's only a one-story house," Andy said at last. "But there *is* a basement."

"Yes," Bassett said. "There is, isn't there?"

They turned to look at the final door. It was standing ajar, offering a peak at a staircase going down. A light, cool draft seemed to rise up those steps and swirl gently past them, moving down the hallway. Despite that, the back of Andy's neck prickled with heat and his palms were slick with sweat.

"It'll be faster if I go alone. You'd better stay here."

"No!"

"Yes. You can go back to the living room, watch for a car pulling in. If you see one, shout."

He hurried down before the old man could argue again, but even at that he heard some soft grumbling as Bassett headed back toward the front of the house, unintelligible words punctuated by the *thump-thump* of his walking stick.

Once Andy reached bottom and located the light switch, he was struck again with that same odd sense of relief and disappointment he'd felt at Bassett's house on Manitou Road. This was not the place, and the thought that they had been completely wrong about Visnaw leapt to the front of his mind.

ALEXANDER'S SONG

It was immediately obvious that Ginnie and Jo weren't there. The basement was nothing but a basement, and there was nothing there that didn't belong. A work bench with scattered tools and jars full of different-sized nails. A faded floral-print couch with the stuffing poking through in spots. A pool table with worn green felt. An apartment-sized refrigerator. A few random-looking stacks of boxes. A desk in the far corner with an old transistor radio on a shelf above it.

Not him, he thought. But who?

That question was blown out of his mind when he walked over to the desk. One look was all he needed. One look was confirmation. One look proved that Visnaw was more than just an eccentric old Bassett fan who had somehow allowed a few business letterheads to fall into the wrong hands. Everything arrayed across the desktop seemed alive when he looked at it, clamoring for his attention, screaming out the word *Gardener* at a hundred decibels.

Mostly, the things on that desk were the same bits and pieces of Alexander Bassett's career that were upstairs in the living room. There were duplicate copies of the books standing in precarious stacks, duplicate articles paperclipped together, photographs and copies of photographs arranged in rough chronological order, youngest (1941 or so) to oldest (early fifties).

There was a difference, though, Andy noticed with an uncomfortable shiver, and that difference was all the answer they would need.

Every item had been defaced in some way. The novels and poetry collections had been scribbled in, almost every page mercilessly marked in pen or pencil or crayon. On some, the dust jackets had been torn. On others, the author's name had been neatly clipped out and thrown away, leaving a gaping hole below the title. On several of the jacket photos, a heavy black slash mark had been drawn diagonally across Bassett's face, like a brutish political statement left on someone's campaign poster.

When he turned to the stacks of articles and interviews, he saw that most of Bassett's words, his comments or responses to questions, had been blotted out, as though by a vicious censor. In a copy of the *Times* obituary, the section that read "Publicity shy his entire life, Bassett became a recluse in his later years, his whereabouts known only to a few of his closest acquaintances" had been circled twice in red. The statement "Whether writing about kings or commoners, the corridors of power or the alleys of a slum, whether hinting for change or stridently demanding it, Bassett's love and concern for mankind always shone through in his work" had been crossed out with a series of perfect, frighteningly neat black Xs. The single word *Charlie* had been written three times next to it in the margin.

With hands that were cold and slow, Andy slid open the center drawer of the desk. He thought he was prepared for whatever he might find there—surely it couldn't be any worse than what he'd seen already—but he still let out a startled squawk when he saw the photograph.

It was an oversized enlargement of that same dust jacket photograph that was framed on the mantle upstairs. In it, a Bassett of perhaps forty-five was standing in front of a shelf of leather-bound books, his dark, thick hair swept back from his forehead, his moustache neatly-trimmed, jaunty and daring, his lips just barely hinting at a smile, his eyes sad and yet challenging you with their directness. A cigarette burned between the fingers of his left hand. His right hand was thrust casually into the pocket of his dark suit jacket.

Visnaw...or Danny...or the Gardener...whoever or whatever he was... that person had used a blue ballpoint pen to draw thirty or forty little arrows bristling out of various parts of Bassett's body. The immediate effect was almost comical, like finding a student's surreptitious amendment to a yearbook portrait of a hated teacher. But the longer you looked at them, the stronger the icy statement made by those crude little arrows became. It wasn't, after all, like stumbling across something in an angry child's room. It was more like walking into the apartment of a bombing suspect and finding a floor plan of the victim's house hidden beneath the glue and the gunpowder and the little snippets of colored wire.

ALEXANDER'S SONG

Andy touched the photograph and felt a strong jolt, as though the picture itself carried an impossible electrical charge. He lifted it out of the drawer quickly, dropped it on top of the desk, and looked at what was underneath.

More photos. Copies. The same photos that Andy had already seen, that had been left in envelopes on the door of his room. The same photos that Bassett had been sent over the years. Graveyards. Tombstones. Calvert Drummond. Henry Oglebay. Constance Warren. Dwight and Lenore Gulliver. Others.

Then came a picture of Charlie McCready's grave marker in the Oak Hill Cemetery. Andy sighed when he saw it, and sighed again a minute later when he identified the three or four tiny blotches that marred its surface—the permanent marks left by the salt of Danny's tears.

He backed away from the desk, groping through his mind for the right words, some way to describe what he felt. The place was like a predator's den, a psychopath's sanctuary, a museum of death and twisted impulses. But Andy felt he had seen more than that. He felt that he had somehow glimpsed several different levels of Danny in just a short time. There was the living room upstairs, where, as in his shop downtown, he put on a human face for the public. There was the cellar of the old Bassett house on Manitou Road, where he went to tap into his past and plan for the future. And finally there was this desk, this corner of the basement, where all the masks were removed and everything else fell away and there was nothing left but the insanity itself, black and living, pulsing, pure, huge.

Andy was frightened, yes, disturbed in precisely the way anyone would be under the same circumstances. But those feelings came wrapped in sorrow. He found that he ached in a spot he couldn't quite pinpoint, in a way he couldn't describe. The sorrow made him angry. The anger made him angrier still. And finally, he was brought around again to the sadness, as though nothing else mattered, as though there really wasn't anything else.

There was one final picture in the drawer, not a photograph this time but a sketch, a line drawing done in pencil, faded and smudged by years of handling. Andy recognized the face, the mature yet curiously childlike eyes, the slightly puglike nose, the lips pulled back in a world-beating grin. He didn't need the one-word caption to identify the subject, but that word was written there nevertheless, printed in those familiar and bold block letters: CHARLIE.

He might have stood there like that for hours, no longer a rational being but a tangle of living emotions, the tear-stained photo of Oak Hill in one hand, the pencil sketch of Charlie in the other, had not Bassett cried out to him. The crowlike squawk came down the basement steps and made him jump.

"Andy! Andy, come here! Quickly!"

He could think of only one thing such a cry might mean. Danny was back. The Gardener was home, and they had been caught.

With his heart pounding out a violent distress rhythm, Andy dropped everything back into the drawer and slammed it shut.

"Andy! For godssakes!"

He hurried back across the basement, lurching, bouncing off the pool table like a drunk in a bar, and raced up the steps to the main floor. If Bassett had been quick enough and seen the car pulling into the driveway, then perhaps there was still time for them to sneak out the back. Of course their truck was parked out on the side of the road, a dead giveaway, but if Danny stopped to puzzle over it, that might actually be to their advantage, giving them time to make it into the woods and hide.

The old man was in the living room, and it took Andy a few breathless seconds to grasp the situation. It wasn't the arrival of the Gardener that had caused the outcry, but something Bassett had found tucked between the end of the couch and the bookshelves.

"They weren't down there, were they?" Bassett said. He looked as though he had aged another ten years. His breathing was still ragged, his skin still the unhealthy shade of gray it had been all night, but now the wrinkles looked deeper too, the hair finer. It was standing up on his pale scalp like the hair of a mad prophet. "Turner and your ex-wife—they weren't there?"

ALEXANDER'S SONG

"No, but how—"

"I know where they are, Andy. I'm quite sure of it, almost positive."

"But...."

The question died when he saw what the old man was pointing at, what he'd discovered hidden next to the couch.

There were two wooden crates nestled there, side by side. They were filled with junk heaped in random disarray. Except that it wasn't just junk. Andy saw that immediately. Oh, some of it might have been. There were crumpled papers and an empty white bag with the logo of The Place printed on the side and several empty Coke cans. But those weren't what he was really looking at. What he was looking at were the two lengths of chain tossed into the first crate and the length of heavy rope coiled in the second—items that instantly brought back the image in the photograph, the picture of Jo bound in the darkened corner of a darkened room.

Partially hidden beneath the rope was a piece of clothing. He knelt down and grasped it, pulled it free and inspected it, although he really didn't need to. He recognized that piece of clothing—Ginnie's faded sweatshirt with the Utah Jazz emblem emblazoned on the front. She had been wearing it when she left for school on that Monday morning more than a week ago. Now it was damp and dirty, grime streaked on the sleeves, something that looked like an oil stain ground deep into one shoulder. And the worst: a large brown splash of dried blood down the front, almost forming a question mark, covering up the T and A in the word Utah.

"It's hers," he whispered, for his benefit or Bassett's or both. "It's Ginnie's."

"I thought it must be."

Andy grasped the shirt a little tighter for a moment, then let it drop. It fell open across the first crate, covering it like a sheet.

"I don't get it," he said. "How does any of this stuff tell us where they are?"

"Just look," Bassett said, pointing at the crates.

"I did! It doesn't tell us anything we don't already know! He's got them! But that's old news! We need to find out—"

"Andy, calm yourself. The sides. Look at the sides of the crates."

Andy frowned, but did as he was told. He lifted the sweatshirt out of the way and looked at what was stenciled on the slats. The letters were old, perhaps as old as a hundred years, dating from a time when the crates had held nothing more damning or harmful than...what? Coal, maybe? Machine parts? Tools? Scraps of wood? The age of the letters had not made them any harder to read. The answer to their question was there, as neat and bold as the Gardener's printing, as stark as the inscription on Charlie McCready's tombstone:

MANITOU MILL   ROCK CREEK

5

"PROMISE ME SOMETHING."

They were halfway back into town, bouncing along Oak Hill Road just before it met the outlying portion of Ontonagon Street. The world seemed to grow darker as midnight came and went, and Andy was too busy keeping the truck on the road to hear Bassett's statement.

"Andy, please listen. I'm exacting a promise from you."

"Hmm? Oh. Yeah. Whatever."

Bassett grunted unhappily. "Not whatever, Andy. This is important. Stop the truck."

"Whatever."

"Andy! Stop!"

Finally, the words broke through his fog of concentration. He didn't stop, but he did glance over long enough to see the expression of utter seriousness on Bassett's face.

"What're you talking about?"

"I'm telling you to stop the truck. I want you to promise something."

Andy almost laughed. "I'll promise anything you want, but I'm not going to stop. Don't you understand? We've got him now. We know who he is. We know where Jo and Ginnie are. Talk while I drive, that's fine, but I'm not going to waste time pulling over."

He thought he heard Bassett sigh, but he wasn't sure. He was still having trouble putting his attention anywhere but on the road, and when he did succeed in turning it elsewhere, it jumped inevitably to their next step. The mill. Of course. But then what? There were too many possibilities to even consider them all.

To begin with, there was always a chance they might be wrong. They might arrive at the abandoned mill and find it just that, abandoned, no one there at all. Or perhaps the Gardener would be there but Ginnie and Jo would not. It was counterproductive to think along those lines, but he couldn't help himself. And even assuming that all three of them were there…what then?

They would have to attempt some kind of rescue. That was a given. It was their whole reason for going in the first place. But they would have to deal with the Gardener first, and how did they plan to do that? Charm? Reason? He doubted that would work. He would have doubted it before, and after seeing the contents of that corner desk in the basement, it was the next thing to certainty. Violence, then? An attack? That was a pathetic joke. The two of them, a schoolteacher and an old man, attacking the Gardener who had killed so many and so often. With no fighting skills. With no weapons.

The Gardener's old too, a voice in the back of his head whispered. *He's seventy. He's got to be beatable.*

That might be so, Andy realized, but he had seen Visnaw walking through the woods at a pace that would leave most younger men winded. He had talked to the man and felt his energy. He had looked into his eyes and *seen* it. And there was the little matter of practice. The Gardener had a skill for mayhem that had been honed to a deadly edge over the years.

"Andy, please, pull over. It won't take long. We won't lose any more time than we've lost already. But I want you to listen to me—really listen—and hear what I'm saying."

Andy glanced over again. Bassett's gaze was more than serious now. There was an urgency shining from his eyes, something bordering on panic in the way his nostrils flared, the way he wet his lips with a nervous dart of his tongue, the way his hands curled around the walking stick.

"Oh, hell," Andy growled, but even as he said it he was pulling over, easing up to the intersection of Oak Hill and Ontonagon. "This better be good."

Bassett nodded once, shortly. "I've been thinking," he said.

"Yeah, so have I."

"But not about this, I'm sure. I've been thinking about what we're doing here, or what we're trying to do, what we *hope* to do. I've been thinking that we're trying to accomplish the nearly impossible, without a plan or even so much as a clue where to begin."

"Me too," Andy said, still impatient. "Get to the point."

"I...this is very difficult. I don't think...at least I don't *expect* that I'll come out of this alive. No, no, let me finish, don't argue with me yet. *Maybe* I'll survive. Is that better? I don't want you thinking I'm just a whining, self-pitying old man. I don't expect to escape alive, but I might. There. Optimism tempered with realism, or the other way around.

"The point is, no matter what happens, I'm prepared. After all, I've been dying for a long time. I said it before and I'll say it again: I've lived longer with a weak heart than any man would have a right to hope. There were times I was so sick, physically and emotionally, that I prayed to die. There were times I felt better and wanted to live. But whether wishing for extinction or immortality, I've always been prepared for the worst. A life with someone like the Gardener in your shadow will do that to you."

"Go on," Andy said, interested despite himself.

"Go on. Yes. I said I'd keep this short, didn't I? It would be foolish of me to go into this any other way. To just assume that someone like me, at my age and in my condition, could jaunt off to the old mill, conquer a murderer, and rescue two women—even with the help of a younger, stronger man—would be naive. That's why I said what I did. That's why I told you I expect to die tonight.

"That's where you come in. That's where we come to the promise I want you to make. Listen to what I'm going to tell you, and then we can discuss it—if we must. I'd prefer that you didn't feel the need to talk about it or to object, but that's up to you, of course."

Andy nodded. "I'm listening."

"If my fears prove true and I don't survive the next few hours, I want you to become my executor."

"*What?* Alex, I couldn't—"

"Remember what I said, Andy. Listen to me first."

"But you don't seriously mean—"

"I want you to become my executor," Bassett repeated. "My literary executor, that is. You wouldn't have to worry about the island or the cabin. Nor would you need to be concerned with any of my collectibles—the rocks and minerals, the antiques and such—all of those things which were handed down from my grandparents to my parents and eventually to me. All of that was taken care of by Earl Rappala's astute planning twenty years ago. He acquired the island, stocked the cabin with my family's things, tutored me on the lies he wanted me to tell, and told me never to worry about it again. It's all accounted for in Edward Hoffer's will, which is in the hands of a Houghton law firm.

"For the really important things, however, I reserved the right to name an executor at a later date. I'm talking about my paper goods. Things like the book collection. Things like the early notebooks and journals I have left, the ones that weren't donated or sold. Things like the copies of my original manuscripts. And, of course, my work-in-progress."

"*The Children's Song?*" Andy said.

"Exactly. I initially assumed that Earl himself would become the literary executor, but I ended up outliving him by a good many years. Then I thought for a time it would be my book dealer friend, Hedda Fogerty. When she died and the Gullivers came along, I toyed with the idea of revealing my true identity to one of them. Most likely I would have picked Lonnie, a very smart woman, an extraordinary reader. Now, today, I'd like it to be you. And lest you think you're an executor-of-convenience, chosen because time is short and there's no one else handy, you're wrong. I'm happy with my choice. I think you're the best of the bunch for what I now have in mind."

Andy swallowed hard. He didn't really want a cigarette but found himself lighting one anyway. "You'd better tell me what that is," he said.

"Well, it's quite simple. I want you to tell the world about this. I don't want you to abandon the articles you planned to write just because my life turned out to be much different than you thought going in. Maybe you haven't even thought of abandoning them, but maybe you have, and I don't want you to do that. In fact, I want you to expand on the idea. I'd like you to do a full-length book. Tell everyone the *real* Alexander Bassett story. Tell them about my father and Royal Haag, Hal Borg, Jens Carlson, Frank and Charlie. Tell them about the Gardener. Tell them about all my poor lost friends, about the way I ran and hid, about Earl Rappala and George O'Callaghan, and about the men-who-weren't-men—Hansson and Paasch and Hoffer. Lay it all out. Hold nothing back."

"But why?" Andy said. "Why do you want the story to come out now?"

Bassett gave a long, exhausted sigh and leaned back in his seat. "That's a difficult question to answer. Maybe I'm still trying to make things right for Frank and Charlie. God knows immortalizing their names in my work didn't help. It didn't make the guilt or my sense of responsibility go away. And now, as horrible as it might sound to you, I even find myself feeling I owe a little something to Danny, too, something I doubt I'll have the opportunity to give him if we meet face to face. Can you understand that?"

"Yes," Andy said, a little surprised at his own answer. He was thinking about that aching sense of sadness that had come over him as he'd looked at Danny's desk. "Yes, I think I can."

"Good, because that's some of it. The rest of it is just selfishness on my part. Self-importance. I suppose I'd like the literary world to know

ALEXANDER'S SONG

that they were wrong about me. It wasn't Joe McCarthy and a few bad reviews that stopped my career cold. Nor was it a nasty drinking habit. It was something worse. I've always had the impulse to make that known, to stand up for myself, to let everyone hear my eloquent defense, but I never had the chance. Now I have you, a real writer. My chance is here at last."

"Christ," Andy said softly. "I'm not a writer. I've never written *anything*, aside from a few tests and essay critiques."

Bassett gave him a thin smile. "A mere technicality, Andy. You have it in you, I know you do. You wouldn't have stayed in Rock Creek, asking questions against all odds of success, if you didn't have the makings of a writer. And you wouldn't have dragged every last shred of my story out of me, either. "

"No, Alex, you're wrong. I can't believe you want me to do a book. A *book*, for godssakes! I couldn't. I mean, oh my god, I couldn't possibly write—"

"Listen to the rest of it," Bassett said, cutting him short. "I want you to tell my real story. And then, when that's published, I want you to follow up with *The Children's Song*. You've read it, haven't you?"

Andy's first impulse was to deny it. Feeling something like panic, he responded exactly like a thief, an intruder caught in the act. He stumbled and stammered, trying to say something non-incriminatory, but stopped when he saw that Bassett was smiling, almost laughing at his distress.

"It's all right," the old man said gently. "If you'll remember, I *told* you to read it. And this afternoon—yesterday afternoon now—before we left the cabin, I went to lock up my office and noticed some of the manuscript pages were out of order. So tell me what you think. Is it good?"

"More than that," Andy said. "It's great. It's…it's a masterpiece."

"Yes, I think so too," Bassett said. "Well, maybe not the masterpiece part—it would take more gall than I've ever had to think that. But I'm confident that it's good. I wouldn't have struggled and strained through almost thirty years of illness and writer's block and fear and sadness if I didn't think so. If I didn't feel strongly about it, I would have burned the manuscript long ago. That's why I want you to have it. I don't care what you do with it, just so long as you see that it's published. Put it out the way it is now, unfinished, with perhaps two hundred pages left to go. Annotate it, if you'd like, add notes and references of your own. Or finish it. Use all the early drafts and outlines to wrap it all up in orderly fashion. Just do it. One way, the other, I don't care. I just want it between covers."

Andy tried to speak. He searched gamely for the proper words, but couldn't seem to find them. He felt dizzy, strangely giddy, as though he'd been hit over the head with a huge mallet made of foam rubber.

"It's selfishness again," Bassett was saying. "I can't deny that. But it's important to me that people know what happened, that they know I didn't lose everything in the fifties. That's where your book would come in. And after that it would be necessary to follow the claim up with the proof. That's *The Children's Song*. I want you to do that, Andy. I *need* you to do it. It's up to you to show the world that I still had it, right up to the end. You're the one, my conduit, my mouthpiece. You have to let the world see that I still had the talent. You have to prove that my ideas and beliefs, my politics, everything I always stood for, still mattered to me. And you have to show that they were still valid at the end."

Andy put his head down, forehead against the steering wheel. "Alex," he murmured, "you've got the wrong man."

"No, I don't."

"But I can't. Jesus, I couldn't."

"You have to, Andy. I'm counting on you."

Andy let out a small groan. He couldn't deny that the prospect was enthralling. The real Alexander Bassett story—that was it, the bestselling book he'd barely dared dream of before. And *The Children's Song*. That had been beyond imagining, and no matter what the old man said, it still was. Tantalizing. Oh, yes. But impossible.

"I think you're being premature," he said at last, slowly raising his head to look Bassett in the eyes. "You're writing yourself off too quickly."

Bassett shrugged. "I prefer to think of it as being realistic."

"Well then, you're putting too much faith in me. If we meet the Gardener tonight, what makes you think *either* of us will survive? How do you know I won't die right alongside you?"

Bassett smiled. "Because you can't."

"That doesn't make any sense."

"Oh, but it does. You can't die tonight."

"Why not?"

"I already told you, Andy. You're my executor. I'm counting on you."

"Alex, no."

"Yes. Now, go on. It's too late for argument. It's already in writing, or—" he withdrew a small spiral notebook and a pen from his shirt pocket "—it will be by the time we get to the mill."

Helplessly, Andy watched the old man flip open the notebook and begin to write in the glow of the dashboard instruments.

"You're making a huge mistake," Andy said weakly.

"Drive, please," Bassett said.

After a moment, Andy did.

SIXTEEN

THE SOUNDS OF HISTORY, THE FIRES OF THE HEART (ALEXANDER'S SONG)

1

It was not quite a setting from a gothic novel, Andy thought, but it was awfully damn close.

The mill, that huge and ancient building, ran for almost a quarter-mile along Manitou Road, a man-made divider between the vast meadow and the woods that ran for another mile or so before reaching the edge of the old Bassett property. In the darkness it looked like a long, low, flat-topped plateau, a hulking shape you had to stare at for a while before the outlines of corners and doorways and boarded-up windows revealed themselves to you.

They pulled into the grass and gravel parking area, stopping next to a leaning sign left from the building's last incarnation:

ROCK CREEK YOUTH ACTIVITY CENTER
OPEN TUESDAY - SUNDAY
3:00 P.M. - 11:00 P.M.

"No car here," Andy observed.

Bassett mumbled something and fell silent.

They got out.

The temperature had dropped a few degrees, settling nervously in the mid-thirties. Snow flurries as fine as metal dust whirled around them. The wind, not strong but not gentle either, hummed a low, moaning tune as it moved over and around the mill in its endless flow. To their left, above the black of the forest, the sky still held a faint orange glow, an afterimage of the fire they had escaped.

"You know your way around in there?" Andy asked, nodding toward the mill.

"I did," Bassett said. "That was over sixty years ago."

"Will it come back to you, do you think?"

"It might."

There didn't seem to be anything left to say, yet neither of them moved. They were like figures in a sketch, poised between meadow, woodland, and building, trapped there for eternity or until time turned the picture to dust.

Andy wasn't sure who moved first. He thought he took the first step, but it might have been triggered by Bassett, a casual shifting of position, a twitch of the walking stick. Whatever the case, one moment they were standing there and the next they were walking toward the building. It seemed to rise up to meet them as they approached, growing taller, looming. Andy had a brief impression that it would have been just as intimidating in the bright sunlight, as its shadow fell over them a little bit at a time. But then the feeling passed. What did it matter? he wondered. It was intimidating enough right now.

"Alex...about this executor thing...."

"The case is closed."

"No, it's not. I respect your wishes, I really do. I understand what you said about wanting *The Children's Song* to be published. It makes sense. I read the thing. It'll prove that you weren't washed up in the fifties better than anything else ever could. But why me? What about your family?"

ALEXANDER'S SONG

"Family?"

"Your sister, Ruth?"

"Dead. Stroke. 1970."

"Her children?"

"The boy died of polio in the forties. The girl, as far as I know, lives with her husband in England. I never met her, never spoke to her. For all I know, she's dead, too."

"But there must be someone."

"No."

"Ruth's grandchildren? Her daughter's children?"

"No."

"But—"

"Andy, I can't answer your question in any way that's ever going to satisfy you. You ask why I chose you, and all I can say is that I have faith in you. I've seen you work. I read the notes you made, and the story you pieced together out of all those bits of random nonsense, long before you knew I wasn't just a man named Ed Hoffer. It wasn't all correct. Probably less than half of it was. Yet you still managed to build a credible case out of nothing, and you were right on the mark with my father and Haag, Frank and Charlie, all of that. I trust you."

"That's it?"

"Not all of it, no. In a way, I'm trying to thank you. You brought me back again, dragged me out of hiding. I hadn't thought of fighting the Gardener for twenty years, and not only did you make me see how necessary it was to do it, you made me *want* to do it. I was back under my rock, and you pulled me kicking and screaming out into the daylight. If I die tonight, I'll die fighting, not cowering. I'll die the way I was ready to die the day I chased the Gardener in Central Park, the way I was ready to die when we staged my death and I moved back to Rock Creek. I had thought that fire inside me was long gone, and you proved it wasn't. You kindled the flame again. That's worth something to me, and I'm paying you back.

453

PAUL F. OLSON

"The things I'm offering you—the biography, the rights to *The Children's Song*—can make you very rich. I'm well aware of that, and it makes me feel good. Now are you going to stand there and say that you don't *want* to be rich? Or that you want to deny me the one last thing that can make me happy?"

Andy was silent. They had reached the main entrance. Once it had been a high archway. Now it was a crumbling hole in a wall of rotted wood.

"I was never a wealthy man, Andy. I donated almost all of my inheritance. At the height of my success, I gave away most of what I earned. Even when I was in hiding, living my false identities, the majority of my income went to charity and causes. Now you're my cause. I'm giving you the last major income-producers that are mine to give. Don't turn them down."

Still Andy didn't say anything. Snow flurries swept across the meadow, scraping his face like sandpaper.

"The time has come, O Brave Knight," Bassett said softly.

And so they went in, leaving the night and the cold and the wind behind.

It was as though the mill had devoured them.

2

ANDY TURNED ON the flashlight he'd taken from Visnaw's kitchen. The beam showed a long corridor stretching away before them like a tunnel. At regular intervals along either side stood doorways with small frosted windows. A sign taped to the wall between the first and second door read B.BALL AND ROLLER SKATING, with an arrow pointing down the hallway. A little farther on was another sign: DANCE FOR AGES 14 & UP!! FRIDAY 12/16/77!!

"These were offices," Bassett said softly, almost whispering. "I remember that much. It was mostly the lower-echelon employees back in those days—clerks and bookkeepers, white collar sweat. My father and the other bigwigs had their offices in the cross-wing, directly overlooking the meadow."

ALEXANDER'S SONG

"That's where the fire was?"

"Yes. The whole wing was destroyed, but they'd rebuilt it by the time I went off to college a few months later. The storage shed where Carlson got the kerosene was on the edge of the meadow itself. And back then, there were houses just across on the other side. That's where we found our witnesses, the ones who saw Carlson that night."

Andy shivered. He gestured forward with the light, indicating that they should go on. Bassett nodded and they started off, moving slowly, navigating around the piles of debris—chunks of fallen plaster, scraps of fallen wood—that were scattered everywhere. The farther they went from the entrance, the thicker grew the smell of the old building. Not a smell at all, really. A stench. Rot and mold, dead animals, animal droppings, animal urine.

Just before they reached the north-south cross-wing, they passed an open door. Andy stopped, laid a hand gently on Bassett's arm, and went back. He shined his light through the opening and felt his breath catch in his throat.

The old office had been remade into a crude bedroom. There was a cot covered with a jumbled heap of blankets, one of the Manitou Mill wooden crates containing a quilted jacket and a pair of jeans, and another turned up on end next to the cot, serving as a night table. On top of the table was an old-fashioned gas lantern with a circular lens, an empty Styrofoam cup, and a hardcover book.

"*To Raise Brave Men*," Andy said, playing the flashlight beam across the dust jacket. "I guess we know who sleeps here."

"Yes. We also know he's not sleeping now."

Andy felt another involuntary shiver, and he turned to regard Bassett's expression. Surprised? Interested? Fearful? But the old man's face was hidden in heavy shadow, and Andy didn't have the heart or the courage to turn the light on him and have his question answered.

They left the bedroom, turned into the cross-wing, and almost instantly became lost. Either his memory of the place was faulty, Bassett remarked, or the wing had been added on to over the years. There was no other explanation for the difference between the way he recalled it—as a straight row of office space—and the way they found it now—as a maze of intersecting hallways, a rash of doorways on every side.

They took a left turn, followed by another left, and came up against a wall that blocked further progress. Backtracking, they went right, right, right again, then left, but it seemed as though the funhouse went on indefinitely, as though that warren of corridors and rooms could trap them there for hours or even days.

After several minutes Andy began opening the doors they passed, probing each room with the light, but most of them were empty of everything but cobwebs, a few others occupied only by broken-down desks, chairs missing legs, empty crates and dusty shelves. The tenth door he opened fell off its hinges, the frosted window shattering with a nerve-snapping crash. They retreated as quickly as they could back to the relative safety of the main corridor.

"What's down there?" Andy asked, motioning to the end of the building opposite the entrance; it was still so far away that the flashlight beam couldn't cover the entire distance.

Bassett sighed. "As best I recall, more offices, storage rooms, old supply closets. Somewhere at the far end was the mechanical part of things. There was the boiler room, a machine shop, a tool shop. At the very end was a right turn. That took you into the mill itself. It was all in one gigantic room, all the saws and chippers and conveyor belts and pieces of equipment I never knew the names of, much less understood. Beyond that was the warehouse."

"Jesus," Andy said. "This could take us till morning."

"Yes," Bassett said with an air of defeat. "And of course my memories are of an old sawmill, not the pulp mill it became later, or a youth center. Who knows how much more was changed around after my time?"

Andy nodded. His hands had curled themselves into fists. His nails were digging painfully into the palms of his hands. The muscles of his forearms were aching.

ALEXANDER'S SONG

He wasn't surprised by his frustration, either its presence or its ferocity. Between the hours of eight and midnight, everything had happened so quickly. There had been the discovery of Danny, the trip to the old house, the identification of Visnaw, the fire. Since then, although their sense of urgency had increased, their speed had dropped almost to a standstill. Not only did they have no idea what they were going to do if they finally located the Gardener, they were incapable of finding him in the first place.

Unaware of what he was going to do until he did it, Andy suddenly threw back his head and roared at the top of his voice: *"VISNAW!"*

Bassett recoiled. The sound his old throat emitted was somewhere between a choking cough and a bleat of dismay, but he recovered himself quickly enough, stepped forward, and put a hand on Andy's shoulder, cutting off any further shouts.

"Wait," he whispered.

Andy shrugged away from Bassett's grasp, but held his peace and listened. For the first time since they had entered the building, all was silent. With no footsteps or harsh breathing, no tap-tap of Bassett's stick, no murmuring between them, the mill seemed impossibly quiet, still.

And yet it wasn't still at all. It was filled with a hundred, a thousand different sounds: the creak of old timbers; the hushing of wind caressing distant windows; the crypt-whistle of that same wind forcing its way through cracks in the siding and holes in sagging shutters; the scrape of a tree limb on some outside wall; the skitter and patter of dozens of unseen rats.

Bassett touched his shoulder again, then spoke down the corridor, his voice soft and gentle but surprisingly firm: "Danny?"

From somewhere near the end of the hall, in the area that had once held the mill and warehouse, Andy heard a whispered reply. A moment later he knew that he had only imagined it. It had to have been the wind-sound, twisting itself into a phantom *Yessssss?*

"Danny? Are you here?"

Andy held his breath and waited.

"It's Alex Bassett. Let's get this over with, Dan."

This time there was no doubt about it. This time Andy was positive that it wasn't the wind, or the creak of old wood, or the rustle of rodents. This time it was a real reply, a voice as soft as Bassett's own and filled with layers of meaning, implication, insinuation.

"Chop," that voice said. "Chop. Chop. Chop."

3

AN ACOUSTICAL TRICK: the voice came from no one particular place. It was simultaneously behind them (back near the main entrance) and in front of them (down near the end of the corridor) and off to one side (from within that dark warren of hallways in the cross-wing).

Andy stiffened when he heard it, as though every nerve ending had been coated with liquid nitrogen, his spine encased in frozen steel. His heart momentarily seemed to constrict, but then it swelled full again, pushing out blood with urgent force.

"Danny," Bassett said, "let's talk, shall we?" His voice was still calm and strong, the tone that of a man completely in charge and untroubled by the responsibility.

It had to be an act, Andy thought. He was pretending, posing, somehow keeping his wits about him enough to portray a decisiveness he didn't feel, a composure he couldn't possibly possess.

That voice from everywhere and nowhere responded at last: "The Gardener doesn't talk. The Gardener prunes."

Bassett's eyebrows went up slightly, but it seemed to Andy that he gripped his stick a little tighter, as though renewing his determination.

"You really ought to drop that charade," he said. "You're not the Gardener. The Gardener doesn't exist. You're a man named Martin Visnaw, aren't you? A man named Martin Visnaw, who used to be a man named Dan McCready, who used to be a little boy named Danny. That's who you really are. Why don't you tell the truth?"

"Chop, chop."

ALEXANDER'S SONG

Andy put his hand against the wall for support. The plaster was cold, damp, and as soft as a sponge beneath his fingers. Nevertheless, he needed it. Each "chop" that came floating to them out of the black made his heart stagger again. He felt dazed and stupid, his head filled with dark clouds. The muscles of one thigh were doing a crazy twitch, making that leg jitter and jump.

The voice of the second world, he thought in a muddled, distant way. The second world is talking, and of all the things it could be telling us, it's saying *Chop, chop.*

"Listen to me, Danny," Bassett said. "Just put your little ax of memory away and listen for a bit. I want to deal with you. You have prisoners here. There's no point saying otherwise; we know it. I want you to let them go. You do that, and you can have *me*. That's a promise. It'll be just us, just Alex and Danny, and you can do whatever you want to me. Whatever it is you've been trying to do through this slow process all these years, you can finish in a few seconds. No more playing, no more fooling. Just us and whatever you've got—your knife or your gun or your rope—you and me."

For a bewildering instant, Andy felt everything that anchored him to reality drop away, no more floor under his feet or mildewed wall beneath his fingers. Freefalling, he felt as if the air around him was suddenly filled with hallucinatory ghosts, each one an embodiment of a different emotion, scrabbling to catch hold of him, jabbering at him in voices that formed a dizzying, cyclonic rush of sound. There was simple amazement at Bassett's strength and courage, and an intense pride in the old man that he had no right to feel but couldn't help. There was the icy realization of exactly what Bassett was proposing to the Gardener, and there was the anger, fierce and well-grounded and yet somehow irrational, that came flying in on the heels of that. How dare he? How dare he make himself a sacrifice? Ginnie and Jo were *his* responsibility, and so, in a way, was Bassett himself. Andy had found him. Andy had uncovered his hidey hole. Andy had dragged him into the fight. Andy had to make sure he survived. How could Bassett just throw himself away without consultation or consent?

Like a child awakening from a nightmare, seeking to confirm reality, he bit down hard on the inside of his cheek. His mouth filled with metallic pain, his eyes began to water, but the ghosts were banished in the blur of a second and he was back again, no longer tumbling through space but standing in the corridor with the remnants of a once-grand tile floor beneath the soles of his shoes.

"Alex—"

"Shh." Bassett spoke without looking at him, still gazing steadily, almost serenely down the corridor from where the voice of the Gardener may or may not have come. "Danny? Did you hear me? I made you an offer. What's your answer?"

There was no response but the sounds of night and mill.

"Danny!" His voice was louder but still under rein. "Answer me, boy."

Andy tried again: "Alex, maybe—"

"He's here. You heard him. Be quiet and let me talk to him."

"But what you're suggesting—it's crazy!" He lowered his voice to a whisper, though it sounded more like a savage hiss. "He'll kill you!"

Bassett seemed not to hear him. "An even swap," he said down the corridor. "The two women for the tree that was spared. What do you say, Danny? Isn't that what you really want? They didn't do anything. It's me you should be after. So here I am." He hesitated. For just a moment his resolve appeared to weaken. A tremor passed through his body and into his stick. His breath came out as a long, windy sigh. "Here I am," he said again, and added, "after all these years."

The snap of a settling board.

The drip-drip-drip of a distant leak.

Bassett turned to him. "Obviously, we're back where we started. He's not going to come out, so we'll have to find him."

Andy nodded. He was better than he'd been just a minute earlier, but he still felt slightly off-balance. He wasn't sure he understood anymore what they were doing there—staging a rescue, fighting the Gardener, or condemning Bassett to death? Was that it? Was that what this was all about?

ALEXANDER'S SONG

If so, he couldn't seem to grasp his own role in the affair. The thought of locating Danny just to turn over the old man made him ill, but he wasn't sure he was within his rights to resist.

He could tell himself all night long that *he* was in charge, that Ginnie and Jo were *his* people, that whatever battle might be waiting belonged to *him*. But there was a half-century of history telling him otherwise, a death roster of Alexander Bassett's friends that said, *You're wrong, Andy. Just stay out of it.*

"Okay," he said, pulling himself straight and managing, he thought, to sound determined. "What do you think? Down there, toward the end of the hall? That's what it sounded like."

"Down the hall," Bassett agreed.

They hesitated only one moment longer before starting off. Andy aimed the flashlight in front of them as before, but following an urge for secrecy brought about by the sound of the Gardener's voice, he hooded the beam with his hand, narrowing it, cutting their field of vision down to ten feet or less. Their pace was slow, and only charitably could it be called steady. They went a few steps, paused, listening and looking, and crept forward again. They jumped each time the buckled floor beneath them creaked.

After fifteen minutes and perhaps a hundred yards, the offices along each side disappeared and were replaced by the larger rooms Bassett had spoken of. The signs on those rooms—SKATE RENTAL, PINBALL—spoke of a modern day rec center, but Andy knew they had crossed the line of demarcation from those old lumbering days. William Bassett and his ruling class had dwelt in the rooms up front, the ones with the solid oak doors and fancy glass windows. The working class, on the other hand, had been relegated to this end of the mill, toiling in tool and machine shops, pushing carts and dollies from one supply room to another, from the warehouse to the loading docks.

A faint, unamused smile flickered on his lips. Being here was having an effect on him, besides the obvious nervousness and fright. He was starting to think like an activist himself, seeing the mill the way he guessed Bassett had seen it after learning what his father had done. Ruling class, working class, almost as though the building had been a sweatshop or a prison instead of an honest workplace. In a way it had been, he supposed, but it was still peculiar to find himself thinking in such outdated terms.

Suddenly, Bassett stopped. They were almost to the end of the corridor now, about to turn right and enter the heart of the mill. Andy pulled up short beside him, waiting to see what was going to happen next. The dripping noise they'd heard before was louder now, closer, the sound of a slow leak finding its way through rotted roofing and striking something metallic far below. The odor of the place was stronger here too, a stench of great age, lost vitality, unstoppable decay.

Before Andy could ask about their next step, Bassett called out for Danny again in that same soft, firm voice he'd used earlier. Where before the sound of his words had seemed to be swallowed by the building itself, going out into a cottony nothingness and disappearing, now they bounced back, echoing—a plea for understanding and a faint, mocking reply.

The Gardener didn't answer. If he was listening—and surely he must be, Andy thought—he was choosing to play with them again. His silence left them baffled. It was as maddening and unhelpful as the years full of cryptic messages. It extended the dance of cat and mouse.

But which is which? Andy wondered.

"We may as well go the rest of the way," Bassett said softly. He jabbed a crooked finger toward the bend in the hallway. "If he's not in there, we'll have to backtrack, but—"

Whatever he was going to say next was severed by a loud crack and thump, a crash of splintering wood. Andy was briefly aware of several pinpricks of bright pain on his cheeks and neck, and then he was grabbed from behind and spun swiftly around. The flashlight tumbled out of his hand and skidded across the corridor, where it struck the far wall, beam tilted uselessly toward the cobwebs that swooped down from the ceiling.

"Andy, what—" he thought he heard the old man cry in the darkness, though in the confusion of the moment he supposed it could have also been a question in his own brain.

A hand was holding him from the front, bunching up his jacket and gripping it tightly, the way a schoolyard bully would pin a smaller child, the way a violent guard might handle a prisoner.

He felt hot breath on his face and tried to pull away, but the grasp was firm, cruel, unrelenting. Somewhere behind him, Bassett was talking fast, spitting out questions or expressions of concern that Andy was unable to focus on or properly hear. He picked up shards and fragments only—*who... why is...are you*—and then those too seemed to disappear.

He reached out and swung weakly at his captor's arm, missed, tried again, and struck a pitiful, glancing blow off what might have been an elbow or a wrist.

Then he was turned sideways and slammed up against the wall. Colorful skyrockets went off in his head. A bullet of pain ripped through his shoulder. He smelled wet plaster. He heard voices again, and the gravel rasp of labored breathing.

Just above him now he noticed a misty, floating shape. He stared up at it in drunken wonder, blinking, and groggily realized what had caused that splintering crack, what weapon the Gardener had swung at them from behind. He saw the dark handle of an ax growing out of the wall, its black shadowy blade buried deep in plaster and lath.

"Chop, chop," he slurred, as another trailer of fire and sparks drifted downward through his brain. "Coulda been...my...skull...."

Then something struck him like a hammer between the eyes, and after that even the sparks were gone.

4

WAKING UP WAS like breaking the surface of a bottomless lake only to find himself mired in mud. Every single movement—the twitch of a finger, the shifting of a leg—was a slow struggle. Every breath was hopelessly difficult, dangerously short, frighteningly inadequate. His head throbbed in the low bass range of a gigantic engine, and when he tried raising it, or even tilting it to one side, sharp bands of pain bit in and seemed to scrape deep furrows in his skull with their razored edges.

He laid very still after a time and tried to find some basic understanding of where he was, but his memory of things was as muddy as everything else. He remembered talking to Marilyn Borg about...something. He remembered a note from the Gardener about wilting flowers and another that had been crossed out and nearly obliterated by revisions. He had vague images of a pool table, a faded sweatshirt, a dark hallway, a frosted window, a length of chain. After a moment, he had a stronger picture of flames leaping upward into a late-night sky.

You're my executor...promise me, said a weak voice from the back of his mind.

Achingly, he put a hand up to his face and touched a knot above the bridge of his nose. It was just slightly smaller than a golf ball, and probing it with his fingers sent bright tendrils of pain spiraling through his face. Moving downward, he found a jagged splinter protruding from his cheek. A little lower was another. A third angled out of his chin like a ghastly whisker. His hand grew sticky with blood.

In the dim light that surrounded him, he could make out a ceiling high overhead, huge and timbered and vaulted like the ceiling of an ancient church. A hole that might have been the size of someone's living room couch looked out onto a black sky, and snow flurries spun through it, coming crazily downward in a tight little whirlwind.

He realized for the first time how cold he was. Whatever room this was, whatever *place*, was unheated and damp. He didn't know if he had been here long or not, but the chill had burrowed under his skin and wrapped itself around his bones in an unfriendly embrace.

Another image stirred in his mind, this one of a low building seen from a short distance. It sat on the side of a country road, surrounded by fields and trees, and was so long that it appeared to stretch, moving away from him like something alive, vanishing into darkness. He thought he had seen this building before, in fact he knew he must have seen it to be thinking of it now, but like everything else, the identification would have to wait until he could think a little more clearly.

At last, inevitably, he tried to sit up—a very bad move. The throbbing in his head opened up into a full-throttle blast of agony, searing fire that consumed him, originating in that knot above his nose and spreading everywhere instantly, burning away all thought or further hope of movement.

He groaned and sagged back to the floor, gritting his teeth, willing the pain to leave him. If it wouldn't do that, he prayed that at least it would lessen, let up, let go just a little. As soon as it did, he was aware of a sudden silence, and only then did he understand that it *hadn't* been silent before. There had been voices talking softly somewhere nearby, a conversation going on. Apparently, whoever it was had stopped when they heard him stir and cry out.

That was when it came to him.

He remembered coming to the Manitou Mill, prowling the dark corridor, the ax biting into the wall just above his head, being caught, twirled around, thrown against the wall and struck between the eyes. In the same instant those memories returned, he knew where he was. He realized that this must be the large main room of the mill, the place where once great felled trees had arrived and perfect lengths of lumber had departed.

Slowly this time, he turned to one side. Blinking rapidly, trying to clear his blurry vision, he gradually discovered a floor made out of narrow strips of varnished wood. It had buckled upward in several places and the boards had completely warped and separated in others, but it still had a familiar look to it, a look that made him think of high schools and shrilly cheering kids and the not altogether unpleasant smells of sweat and hot dogs and soda pop.

Ten feet away, he saw a wide black line painted on the floor, a black circle surrounding it, overhead a metal framework onto which was attached a cheap wooden backboard with a netless orange rim that sagged on weary bolts. The central room of the Manitou Mill. The real home of that old downtrodden working class. Turned more than a decade ago into a community youth center. Turned not long after that into an abandoned, rotting hulk.

The voices resumed again, and now he had no trouble identifying them. Alexander Bassett and the Gardener were talking. It seemed unlikely, unnatural, even impossible, but there was no mistaking the strained, frail tones of the writer and that slightly sharp, slightly ironic voice that Andy had first heard as the voice of a shopkeeper named Martin Visnaw.

"...moved to the city," Bassett was saying. "But little did I know that the death would follow me there, as well."

"It had to," Visnaw responded. "The death would have followed you anywhere, eventually. You bought it that day in 1927. It was yours. You had to keep it."

"You knew that from the start?"

"Of course not! I was a stupid little boy! I was shocked beyond reality! Do you really think I could have come out of the woods that day understanding what I saw? I don't think I even realized my brother was dead until after the bodies were found and McFarren showed up at the door.

"That was days after the disappearance. My parents were worried about me. They would have been even more worried if they hadn't had Charlie's absence to keep them busy. I hadn't been eating or talking to anyone. My sister told me a few years later that I'd been hiding under the bed most of the time. But did I *know* anything? I don't think so. Oh, I knew that I was frightened. And I knew that I hated you. Even so early in the game I knew that. You, who was always like another older brother, another Charlie to me, Big Brother Alex—suddenly, without understanding why, I hated your stinking guts. But the real truth was hidden somewhere in my mind. I wasn't conscious of the facts, you might say.

"Even when I'd reassembled everything years later, even when I'd decided something had to be done, I didn't know the extent of the death you'd purchased for yourself. I tried once to remove my nightmares. I thought that would be enough—more than enough."

"You're talking about my mother?" Andy heard Bassett ask.

The Gardener laughed. "I didn't kill that whore, though I wish I had. I was only eleven when she died, still busy working things out in my head."

"Then you're talking about—"

"Gracie. Your lover girl, Alex."

"She was the first, then."

"She was the first—the only, I thought. You were responsible for the death of my loved one, so I would remove a loved one of yours. It seemed a simple enough equation, but it didn't help for more than a few months. The blood-dreams kept boiling inside of me. Dreams, day and night, awake and asleep, that's what I'm talking about. A kid's nightmare of his brother as a tree being felled by a lumberjack was eventually translated into more adult images, more concrete images, more realistic images—but *worse* images, for all of that.

"So I visited you in New York. I don't know quite what I expected from you, but I think I was hoping to be wrong. I didn't want to kill again, do you see? I wanted it all to be over, but for that to be, I had to hear the truth from you. I needed to hear your story, proving that you really *had* done something, tried to help Charlie in some way that my little six-year-old eyes had missed or my older mind had forgotten. I wanted to love you again, as I once had. I wanted my mind put at rest. I wanted to leave that night as your friend and go off to the Navy and put Charlie and everything else behind me for good.

"But that didn't happen. You pretended to talk very openly about Charlie, saying how terrible and tragic his death was, how you still felt it all those years later. You thought you could fool me with that bullshit. You dared to act miserable in front of me. Me! Who felt it more than anyone else could have! You lied to me. You told me how awful you felt when you came back from your out-of-town trip and discovered what had happened in your absence. You didn't even confess to being there, let alone to running like a coward when the ax started to fly.

"I left my dinner with the big hotshot, the newly-crowned master writer that everyone was buzzing about, the success story, the budding legend, and I went back to my flophouse hotel. And that night the blood-dreams were worse. I sailed off to war like a good boy, but I never could put it behind me. That's when I knew you'd bought the death forever. That's when I knew it was yours for life."

Andy hugged himself against the cold and closed his eyes. The voices seemed to rise and fall as they came to him, grow and fade, strengthen and diminish. It was because of the blow to his head, he knew, but he thought there might have been more to it than that.

He had always considered the act of looking back at history to be a bit like experiencing the Doppler Effect. No one was really aware of it as they lived through it, of course, but to an observer from the future it was all too evident. That observer could see someone at a single moment in time. He could study that moment—a war, a birth, a death, a marriage, a life—and hear the psychic sound the person made, the high-pitched building whine as he moved out of his past toward that cataclysmic event, the fading drone as he moved off again into the future.

As he listened now to Bassett trying to explain what had really happened in the clearing that day, he heard him as he was, an old man trying to deal with the wreckage of his life. But for those few seconds it was also Bassett as a teenager, barely more than a frightened boy, fighting to comprehend an incomprehensible horror even as he lived through it.

It was the same with Visnaw. As he'd spoken of that dinner in New York, Andy had been able to hear a second voice beneath the first, the voice of Danny, the voice of the striving young man he had been at the time, someone wanting desperately to put tragedy behind him and move on to a better, brighter life.

The Doppler Effect. The mill was filled with it.

If they heard the sound of their own lives at all, it was as a steady, even hum, moving along in a darkly linear fashion toward one conclusion or another. Only Andy was aware of the rest. They were experiencing the present, while he stood firmly in the present, looking back. He alone could hear the struggling boys they had been in the men they had become, hear the men they would be in the boys they once were.

Like the spot beside the freeway where you stood and listened to the whine and drone of passing trucks, this mill was the looking-back point, the promontory, the place to hear the frantic sound of eager hopes and the dying whisper of lost or faded expectations.

Gritting his teeth again to hold back any involuntary cries of pain, he tried once more to sit up. This time he made it. Turning his head slowly, he saw them at last. They were on the opposite side of the big room, forming a weird tableau. Bassett was standing in the corner, his back against the wall, his skinny legs spread wide and his walking stick planted firmly. Twenty feet in front of him, the Gardener sat casually cross-legged on the floor. His hands were folded, his ax resting lazily across his lap. They were looking at each other intently, Bassett's head inclined toward the Gardener, the Gardener's tipped up at a curious, inquiring angle. An antique gas lantern, the twin of the one they had found in the converted bedroom, sat on the floor, lighting that scene and the rest of the room with its weak and eerie glow.

"...not right away," he heard Visnaw saying. "I kept my real name for many years. Not that it mattered. Dan McCready, Jim Smith, Jack-Fucking-Frost. I could have been anyone, for all the difference it made to the rest of the world. What I really was...I was a nobody, an invisible man, a wanderer, working odd jobs for a month or two at a time, but mostly just rooting through garbage cans to stay alive."

"But Martin Visnaw?" Bassett said. "Where did that come from?"

"I stole it—part of it, anyway—from the first man to give me a job when I arrived in New York after jumping ship. His name was Artie Visnaw. He'd been a fighter pilot in the war, but was shot down in the first few weeks. He was wounded and lame, very bitter, and when I knew him he ran a flower shop in Manhattan. He treated me well. He taught me to fly. He didn't ask questions. Martin from my given middle name, Visnaw from him. Simple."

"A flower shop," Bassett said, and even from across the room Andy could hear the wonderment in his voice.

"That's right, a flower shop. The Gardener." He gave an abrupt, grating laugh. "Of course, I only needed to steal the Visnaw name many years later, when I moved back here."

"But wait—I don't understand. If you were so poor, how in the world did you survive in Rock Creek? You have a business here. How could you possibly afford that?"

"Quite easily. For openers, the Trading Post wasn't my first business. In the sixties I borrowed a good deal of money from my sister, who had inherited it from my parents."

"You mean Liz knew about—"

"She knew some of it. I'd been out of contact with her for a few years, but sometime around 1963 I reached her again and told her as much as I dared. She knew I still wanted to remain hidden, but not why. She assumed it had something to do with my escape from the Navy twenty years earlier. I told her not to ask, and she was a good girl, she didn't. I used her money to open a small import gift shop in New York. It was tough sledding, I'll tell you. I was almost broke again when I decided to come back here. I had nothing to lose by doing that. You had no close friends for me to tend to, and I could write letters to you from Michigan as well as I could from New York. No one here would recognize me, or remember a boy they'd last seen in 1941. All I needed was a new name and enough capital to get set up in the tourist trade here—and I had at least that much. So I came."

"And I followed you a few years later," Bassett said.

"Yes." Another brittle laugh. "But your death trick was a damn good one. You had me completely fooled until the spring of '87, when I saw you shopping in the drug store. To say the least, I was thunderstruck. I thought, my god, it's him, the cowardly son of a bitch actually tricked me properly for once. But still I followed you to be sure. I trailed you on all your errands, to the post office, the grocery store, the bank. I drove behind you back to Harker's Landing. I watched you putter off in your

ALEXANDER'S SONG

boat to the island. By then I was positive it was you. I knew who Edward Hoffer really was."

Andy felt some of his pain begin to fade beneath a numbing analgesic of rage. Listening to their conversation, at once bizarre and perfectly logical, completely transformed the flimsy image of the Gardener that he had constructed in his mind. That was no gibbering lunatic over there. It wasn't a tortured, damaged Danny McCready, all grown up and incapable of distinguishing moral values, of knowing right from wrong. He might have been that way once, but now...now...now he was the murderer who carefully edited his notes before sending them, a cold and calculating man, someone capable of rational thought, of premeditated action, someone who did the things he did not because he couldn't help himself but because he wanted to.

He shifted a little, and with a jolting start saw the Gardener's prisoners for the first time. They were huddled close to each other, perhaps fifty feet down the wall from where history was replaying itself in the form of that long, strange conversation.

Ginnie was bound with chain, face down on the floor, the short-sleeved cotton tee that had been underneath her sweatshirt matted to her back with dried blood. Next to her was Jo, also bound, also bloody, curled into the fetal position, her face turned toward the wall.

Neither of them moved.

Neither of them appeared to breathe.

He watched for a very long time but didn't see so much as a single muscular twitch.

He told himself they weren't dead. They couldn't be. They had to be breathing shallowly. It was only because he was so far away from them. It was only because the light from the gas lantern was so weak. That's why he failed to see any signs of life.

He turned back to Bassett and the Gardener. That whine and drone of history was still going on. The Gardener's back was to him. He thought it might be possible—always assuming that Bassett didn't see him or give him away in some manner—to crawl across the floor, sneak up behind the Gardener and...

And what?

Reach over his shoulder and grab his ax?

Yes, that might work. And even if it didn't, he could die with the satisfaction of knowing he had tried. He wouldn't surrender the way Bassett had. He certainly would not go down holding a pleasant conversation with the bastard. No rehashing of old events for him. No happy talk, like two old friends meeting again after a long time.

He rose to his knees. The pain swept through him with miserable, burning force. A cloud of dizziness fogged his brain, and he had to clench his fists and grit his teeth for a third time to keep from passing out.

"...because all acts of cowardice have their price," the Gardener was saying. "Didn't I explain that before? Don't you *know* that? There's cowardice all through your past—it's a goddamned Coward's Hall of Fame. Take your father, for instance. He was a coward. There's no way to know for sure, obviously, but I'll bet he lied when William Bassett approached him. William was a reasonable man. At least he was a good *business* man. If your father had shown enough guts to level with him, I'm sure they could have worked something out: money in exchange for secrecy, a quick midnight trip out of town, anything like that. But I'll wager a bundle on the fact that your father lied. He wouldn't come clean to William about what he'd done and—"

"What are you talking about?" Bassett said. His voice was shaky, puzzled, suddenly fearful. "My father? William *was* my father."

"Oh, come now!" the Gardener cried, sounding thoroughly disgusted. "After everything I just said about lies? After you heard what your deception in New York cost you? Of all the people in the world, I'm the one you should be truthful with. We're old buddies, right? And I know everything about you."

"Then w-w-what are you trying to say?"

"Oh, spare me the dramatics. If you don't know...Jesus, you *have* to know! If not, you'd better start using that educated brain of yours to do some simple math."

ALEXANDER'S SONG

"I...I still don't—"

"Add and subtract, Alex. It's simple. Just add and subtract."

Andy's head was thundering with the implications, although for the first time he wasn't thinking about himself. He wasn't wondering what kind of impact this latest news would have on his research or what it might mean to his work.

He was thinking about Alex.

What was going through the old man's head right now? To suddenly discover, as apparently he just had, that his entire life, all the darkness of the last eighty-two years...to learn that all of that had different origins than he'd always believed? To find that all the death and horror did not, after all, trace back to an act of unbelievable greed but to something else entirely? Simply toying with the possibility made Andy feel uprooted, misused and abused. What in God's name must *Alex* be thinking?

"It's not true," Bassett said weakly. "It can't be. Not my mother. No. She wouldn't have. She couldn't. And I would have known about it. I would have found out."

The Gardener chuckled. "Suit yourself, Alex. You stick to your story, if it makes you feel better. You say whatever you have to say. What *I'm* saying is that your father might have been able to save himself, but he was a coward. And William was a coward, too. He did what he thought he had to, but then didn't want to face the music. He went looking for someone to take his blame, and because of that he burned for his sins."

Andy thought sickly of disembowelment and castration, of the search for a scapegoat and a suicide to assure continued secrecy. It fit. Oh, yes. But was it right? Was it the truth, or only more of the Gardener's demented non-logic?

"Danny...please...."

"Danny, please," the Gardener spat back in a mimicking voice. "Please what? Please say it ain't so? Please save you from the truth? I can't, Alex. Face it. It's what I said, and it's all about cowardice. Your father and your mother and William Bassett led to Jens Carlson and you. You committed your own act of cowardice—the *supreme* act of cowardice. You had the means of rescue in your hands but you turned away, you whimpered and ran. Now you pay the price. I suffer, you suffer. What could be more fair?"

"Do you think I haven't suffered?" Bassett said. "Do you think I'm not suffering right now? Do you really believe that?"

"What I believe is that your miserable little handful of friends wasn't enough. A *hundred* friends wouldn't be enough, or a thousand."

Andy was sure he heard Bassett sigh. "I'm not talking about that," he said. "I'm talking about Charlie. Don't you think I've suffered for that?"

"Oh, I doubt it. You ran away that day, and you ran even farther a few weeks later. You abandoned him and you abandoned your town. You went off and made a huge success of yourself. That's suffering?"

"Yes."

"Well then," the Gardener said, sneering, "you have a damned funny notion of what suffering is all about."

Andy's thought his pain and weakness might be starting to fade. He convinced himself that it was gradually but steadily getting better, that everything was diminishing to a single point, a steady throbbing flutter in the very center of his body. To get over the shock, the pure emotional jolt of what he'd just heard, would take longer, but he couldn't afford to wait for that.

He gauged the distance across the floor at seventy, perhaps eighty feet. There was no way to do it obliquely, approaching undetected from the flank. It would have to be straight across, no fooling around. If Bassett noticed him—and how could he not?—Andy could only hope he wouldn't say anything or betray him with a stray expression of surprise.

Hope.

Under the circumstances, it seemed ridiculous to even mention the word, but it was all he had left.

Going down on all fours, like a prowling animal, he started across the floor.

ALEXANDER'S SONG

"To suffer you have to pay a price every day, the way I have," the Gardener told Bassett. "You have to try to make amends, set things right the way I do, the way I've always done, by dealing with whoever gets close to you."

"You're not setting anything right," Bassett said, anger creeping into his voice for the first time. "You're just playing games. That's all they are—your sick little notes, your mystical poetry, kidnapping people who don't even know me, the violence and murder—pointless, vicious, stupid games."

"And yet I try," the Gardener responded. "Every day I try to repair what happened to my brother. Am I supposed to care that my methods aren't the ones you'd choose? At least I've chosen. I haven't hidden in the shadows and refused to even make the attempt."

"Oh, Christ," Bassett said. "You're so wrong about me, Danny. You think you understand me, but you don't. You're not even in the neighborhood. You're not even close."

Andy was underway. He crawled forward a few steps, rested, crawled forward, and rested again. Something in Bassett's tone made him pause a little longer this time, although he wasn't immediately sure what it was.

"You say you've read all my books. You sit there and tell me you've studied the poetry, picked apart the essays, devoured the interviews, and I have to wonder how that could be. You've followed me all my life, and yet you still don't have the faintest idea what I've been doing."

Now he had it. The old man's face was masked by shadow, but Andy didn't need to see his eyes to know that Bassett was crying.

"Every day since your brother died, I've been striving to make up for it. All my work, every last word of it, was about courage, about doing the right thing, about helping those in trouble and those less fortunate than you. I dealt with ideals, losing them, finding them again, and holding on to them in the face of incredible odds. You can call it socialism if you want—lord knows everyone else did. But I never thought of it as socialism. To be brutally honest with you, I'm not entirely sure what it was, but I think it may have been idealism more than anything else."

475

The Gardener hissed, "And what does idealism have to do with Charlie? Tell me that."

"Oh, I'll tell you, Danny, I'll be more than happy to tell you. I lost my own idealism that day on Green Meadow Trail. It had already been slipping for a few weeks, ever since I'd learned what my...my...my f-f-father....Well. Well. Indeed. It appears I might have lost something else here tonight. But my point, Danny...my point is that I'd suffered a loss of hope and faith that summer. I'd lost much of my belief in things. The few shreds that were left, they vanished when I saw what mankind was truly capable of. Watching Jens Carlson swing that ax at your brother and Frank ripped off the last of my blinders. I saw tremendous cruelty, hatred, violent oppression of others—all of the things that you saw in the form of your lumberjack. I finally understood that evil wasn't just some theoretical biblical concept, and it wasn't just an isolated case like my f-father. *Everyone* was capable of viciousness toward their fellow man. Everyone was a potential oppressor, a potential killer, a potential monster.

"So what did I do? Did I stand up to the cruelty? Did I fight it? No. You know what I did. I had my chance and dodged it. I gave in. I broke and ran, and accidently knocking Carlson into the lake later that day didn't patch up the hole in my life that act of cowardice had made. I'd gone there only intending to blacken an eye or bloody a nose, maybe drag him back to McFarren's justice in town. But none of that would have fixed what I'd broken by fleeing that monster earlier. And drowning him by mistake didn't fix it, either.

"I had seen my ideals shattered. Worse, I'd shattered most of them myself.

"That day burned inside me after that. Not for a few weeks or months. Always. It was a flame in my brain, a fire in my heart, a message branded on my soul. Mankind has the power to destroy, Alex. That was the message. Mankind has the power to destroy, and the only way to make sure it doesn't happen is to cling to your ideals no matter what, to stand up to that power, lash back at it, fight it whenever it rears its head, in whatever dreadful form. Build, don't tear down. Repair, don't break. Hold, don't throw away. Love, don't hate.

"It's all there inside of us. That's what I said in *The Pharisee*. You read it—do you remember? When the blind man tells Norman about the valleys and the mountains? They're all there, the depths and the heights. No one's better than anyone else; our job is to *try* to be better—better than ourselves. We've got to climb all the time. We're got to climb away from the low ground. We've got to climb toward the high. And it's not easy. Gravity works against us and the terrain is always slippery.

"I've fallen a lot over the years. I gave up more than once. Just recently… it was just a few days ago that someone had to pick me up, put me back on the stairway, and give me a push. But if we fall, or how far we fall, or how often we fall—that's not important. What counts is that somehow, eventually, we start climbing again.

"We have to conquer all the different destroyers that live inside us, Danny—the villainy, the greed, that goddamned urge to be superior and hold everyone else down in the gutter so that we have someone who's inferior to us. You pick your demon, your weakness, your vice, your flaw, your human fault, your human frailty, your human evil. Whatever you pick, rest assured that it's real and it's out there. It's always out there. It's always waiting. Always. Our job, then, is to beat it.

"That's what my work was about, and whether you believe it or not, it was all because of what happened to Charlie and Frank. It was because I regretted what I'd done, what I didn't do, what I should have done. Because I ached and mourned over it. Because I wanted to get right what I tragically bungled that day in the clearing.

"Charlie and Frank were the wellspring of my *new* idealism, do you understand? *Can* you understand? They were the spark that fired everything else. I took them into my heart and I allowed them to burn in there, writhing around in that flame I told you about, melting down, slowly being refined into something new. And *then* I turned them loose. I sent that flame back out, stronger and brighter and better. They became a message about what I had learned, a message that went straight from my heart to the world."

Bassett finished, gasping for breath.

Halfway toward his target on the other side of the room, Andy stopped too. He realized that his eyes were stinging with tears, and it seemed that for the first time since their arrival the mill was genuinely silent. He didn't hear his own strained breathing, and after a moment the sound of Bassett's faded as well. The drip of leaking water had apparently stopped. The rats and mice were still. Nothing settled or creaked, shifted or groaned, and for an unknowable span of time nothing moved.

"Very pretty," the Gardener said then, shattering the spell. "Quite lovely, actually. But it doesn't do anything to bring Charlie back."

Andy started crawling again. He was now just thirty feet away.

Bassett gave a wistful sigh. "Is that what you've been trying to do, Danny? You told me you were just trying to set things right. That I could understand. I clearly disagreed with your methods, yet the motive was pure. But to actually *change* things? To bring him back? How could you possibly do that?"

Twenty feet.

"It doesn't matter," the Gardener answered. "Maybe I misjudged you, after all. I always thought you wrote with some kind of twisted, perverted glee. I thought you were writing for me, *to* me, poking at me, laughing at me, trying to rub my nose in what happened. But I might have been wrong. It wasn't glee. It was...a coping mechanism, wasn't it?"

"Yes," Bassett whispered. "It was."

"We all do things in our own way, I suppose. You write. I kill. None of it helps in the long run, but it feels good when we do it."

Fifteen feet.

"You don't mean that, Danny. The killing makes you feel *good?* You find joy in knifing and torturing, in what you've done to those poor women over there?"

Ten feet.

"I find what I need to keep me going. That's enough."

Five.

"So what's next?"

Three.

"You should know, Alex. The tree was spared. But even the oldest, strongest redwoods eventually end up as pulp."

Andy paused just behind the Gardener. He held his breath and looked up. For a single moment his eyes met Bassett's, and he waited, prepared for the cry of dismay that would betray him, the stray look that would give him away. But the old man's gaze was cold, passionless, rock steady.

"Pulp," Bassett said, raising a hand from his stick and absently massaging his shoulder. Now his expression did change, but it wasn't the tip-off Andy had feared. It was a sour, wincing grimace, as though something inside him ached quite badly. "So your chain of death is going to lead to me at last. Wouldn't it have been better to just come to me in the beginning and spare all the others?"

"Ah, but you said it yourself, on the night of our dinner. Do you remember? You signed my copy of *A Daughter's Song*. Unfortunately, I lost it. It had to stay behind when I left ship in Hawaii. But I've never forgotten what you wrote. 'Our bond will endure, forged in sadness, never to be broken.' You were right. And who was I to break that bond before it was time?"

Andy moved.

He crawled forward the final few inches to the Gardener's back—and his right knee came down squarely on a buckled floorboard, snapping it in two.

He froze, but it was too late.

The Gardener was on his feet, pivoting with uncanny speed and grace. As he turned, Andy saw the ax in one hand and the thing he *hadn't* been able to see as he made his way across the room. It was a gun, and it was coming up, leveling, aiming right at his face.

5

ANDY SCRAMBLED TO his feet.

He saw the silvery, dancing gleam in the Gardener's eyes and knew that he'd been right all along. The man was insane. He had been lost on a hot and rainy afternoon sixty-three years before, and he had never been found again. His was a special kind of craziness, perhaps, one that could masquerade as normality, could put on a face that showed only an odd, ironic sense of humor, could speak in rational sentences, in tones of human sadness or gaiety, whatever was required. But for all of that, down at the bottom, deep inside, it was craziness all the same.

"Well, hello there," the Gardener said, as conversationally as if he really were a man named Martin Visnaw and the two of them were exchanging pleasantries over the sales counter at the Trading Post. With a cheerful grin he tossed the ax to one side and put both hands on the revolver. "I guess I didn't hit you hard enough, did I? A small slip in the excitement of the moment, nothing more."

"Danny, no!" Bassett cried.

In his periphery Andy saw the old man lunge out of the corner, take a staggering step forward, fight to maintain his balance, and then come charging. His walking stick went up, up, going high over his head like an executioner's sword—or a woodsman's ax.

The Gardener turned in response to the yell. The gun went off at the same time, splitting the air with a furious *crack*.

Andy watched, horrified, as Bassett stopped in his tracks, eyes bulging out of their sunken sockets, mouth sagging open in a drawn O of surprise.

He tried to understand what he was seeing. On one hand it seemed dreadfully obvious. Bassett had been shot. What else could it be? But if that was the case, why was the Gardener staring at him with as much shock and dismay as Andy himself? And why were there no powder burns on the front of the old man's jacket? Why was there no blood pouring from a wound?

ALEXANDER'S SONG

As if someone had punched him in the stomach, Bassett's breath suddenly gusted out of him in a long, wheezing moan. He tried to pull in fresh air, but apparently couldn't do it. His mouth opened still wider and great cords of muscle appeared from beneath the folds of loose flesh on his neck. His Adam's apple bobbed up and down. More air out, no air in. His lips began to color, taking on a tone that must have been dark blue but looked black in the lantern light.

Andy realized what was happening. Bassett hadn't been shot. The gun had gone off, yes, but that had just been the Gardener's startled reaction to the old man's cry. The bullet had whizzed off harmlessly in some other direction, and Bassett was having a heart attack.

The signs were there all night, he thought. Why didn't I see them? The trouble he was having catching a breath, the paper-gray skin tone, the way he rubbed his chest every few minutes—even a clueless layman should have picked up on those things.

The old man's luck had finally run out. He remembered Bassett saying he was living on borrowed time. That was true for all of them, of course, but perhaps a little more true for Bassett. He had been existing beyond the odds for years, and the price for that had just come due.

"What the hell are you doing now?" the Gardener barked at Bassett. In any other situation it might have been comical. As it was, Andy felt both saddened and chilled. "No tricks, Alex. I didn't follow you all these years, watching you, eluding you, just to be taken in by some cheap ploy now. If that's what you've got in mind—"

"He's dying, you bastard!" Andy cried. "Don't you see what's happening to him? He's having a heart attack!"

Bassett tried again without success to pull in a breath. The result was a high-pitched whine, followed by a gasping rattle of phlegm, both of which seemed very loud indeed, deadly and final.

"He's pretending," the Gardener said, though his voice suddenly lacked conviction. He turned to Andy, back to Bassett, back to Andy again. His lunatic's eyes were darting wildly left and right. The gun wavered in his hands.

"Get out of my way," Andy said.

He pushed past the Gardener and started toward the old man.

Bassett had lowered his walking stick, putting it down at an awkward angle and leaning on it, about to topple forward. His arms trembled with the effort of holding himself upright. The muscles in his throat were pumping furiously now. His eyelids began to flutter.

"*Stop!*"

Andy looked just long enough to see the Gardener's revolver trained on him again. He hesitated, halfway between one old enemy and the other.

"I've got to help him," he said.

"No. Stay where you are. No tricks."

"It's not a trick! Jesus Christ, he's *dying!*"

"If he is, so be it. A heart attack would be quite wonderful. Step back a bit. I want to watch."

A hundred responses flooded into Andy's mind, yet he couldn't get even one of them out. He looked into the Gardener's eyes again, mesmerized by that mad, glittering gaze, overcome with revulsion at a mind that could actually want to see such a thing, actually want to watch another man die helplessly right in front of him.

"Is it true, Alex?" the Gardener asked. "Is that pathetic heart of yours finally giving out?"

Bassett's knees began to buckle. Andy saw him fight to stay erect, struggle to remain on his feet. He felt as though he were being physically ripped in half, wanting to rush to his friend's side and do whatever he could, yet frozen by the thought of the weapon in the Gardener's hands.

"Tell me, Alex. Is this it? The tree is dying, not from an ax wound but from old age? Surely I deserve to know the truth. Is this the way it all ends?"

Andy took advantage of the moment to inch closer to Bassett, but the Gardener noticed immediately and commanded him to stop. In his mind's eye he imagined himself ignoring the order, hurrying to the old man's aid. He could feel the bullet punching through him and the gray, dull ebbing sensation of his life draining away.

ALEXANDER'S SONG

Was it worth it?

The easy answer was, obviously not. No matter what he might have thought before, whatever lies he had told himself about protecting Bassett, the current situation was not his fault. He wasn't the one who had offered himself to the Gardener, and he shouldn't have to take a bullet in the back just because Bassett had seen fit to do so.

You're the one who decided to talk to him, Alex, not me. It was you. You got yourself into this. I'd like to help, I want to help, but—

"Step back," the Gardener told him again. "You're blocking my view."

Andy turned to stare at him, but his gaze went somewhere else instead. It went past the man's shoulder and fell upon the two huddled forms farther down the room. He swallowed hard and felt another burst of that unfamiliar protective instinct, a burning rush that filled his chest with something he didn't quite recognize, something big and brilliant, enveloping, nearly overpowering.

It was almost absurd. He barely knew Ginnie, and Jo was little more than an enemy combatant these days, connected to him mainly by memories of dysfunction and despair and endless pints of spilled emotional blood. Why should he feel that strange, unnamable sensation in his chest or the sudden need to risk his life for theirs?

"An…dy…."

Bassett's voice was weak, barely there. The old man was holding his stick with one hand, the other reaching out, floating toward him like the hand of a drowning man, trying to touch Andy, catch hold of him.

"I told you to step back!" the Gardener shouted, and then he also reached out, apparently to shove Andy out of the way.

The moment had come.

Bassett was crumpling, falling forward in unnatural slow motion.

The Gardener was coming toward him, off balance, groping for his arm.

Andy moved.

He lunged for Bassett, waiting to feel the flash of pain as the bullet took him, but it didn't come, not right away. He caught Bassett in the crook of one arm, at the same time taking the walking stick from him and swinging blindly around, connecting with the Gardener's skull.

A fierce vibration traveled up the stick, into his hand and arm. There was a soft crack, which was almost completely covered by the roar of the gun going off. He felt a tug at the sleeve of his jacket, a nip of fire that wasn't too bad at all. And then he saw the Gardener lying on the floor, his head tipped to the side at a grisly angle, a ribbon of blood trickling down past his ear.

Bassett was gasping, trying to talk. He murmured something that might have been *best* or *rest*, but his breath failed him and his eyelids dropped shut.

Andy lowered him gently to the floor and went to the Gardener. Only after he was standing over the man did he notice that he still had the walking stick in his hand. It felt incredibly heavy. He saw absently that there was a clump of hair and skin clotted on the end.

The Gardener moaned.

"It's over," Andy said. "You wanted to know how it ends? Well, this is it."

The Gardener's eyes were barely open, heavy-lidded as if with sleep, but his arms were starting to move, reaching backwards. Andy was suddenly aware of just how close the ax was, what a short distance it had traveled when the Gardener tossed it aside.

"Flowers...prune," the Gardener said, his voice seeming to come from light-years away, his fingers approaching the smooth wooden ax handle, brushing against it, closing around it. "Chop."

Andy nodded, and answered softly: "Chop."

He sighed wearily and raised Alexander Bassett's walking stick high above his head.

6

IT TOOK HIM several minutes to find any signs of life in the Gardener's prisoners.

He went to Ginnie first and cradled her head, shocked at how wasted she looked, how pale, how light her body seemed. A dark but fading bruise covered most of the left side of her face, clearly showing where she'd been struck the day she disappeared. Her jaw was broken and her right arm was twisted at a terrible angle.

He couldn't find a pulse at either wrist or throat.

"C'mon," he muttered, and put his cheek to her lips. After a very long time he felt a gentle wisp of breath. He waited. He shook her, heedless of her injuries. He waited longer. He was about to give up, dismissing the first breath as hallucination, when he felt another, and a painful length of time later, a third.

Jo was better. When he rolled her over he knew immediately that she was alive. Her face was also bruised, and crisscrossed with lines of dried blood. There were faint red marks around her neck, ghosts of the Gardener's chokehold. But her breathing was strong, fairly regular, and her eyes fluttered open right away.

"Jo?"

She took him in with foggy, dazed confusion. Her gaze hovered on his face for a moment, then drifted listlessly to the vaulted ceiling overhead.

"It's going to be all right," he said. "You're going to be fine."

He hurried back to Bassett's side and found the old man conscious again, though barely.

"Alex? Can you hear me?"

The head moved just slightly.

"You're going to be okay, Alex, I'll make sure of it. Ginnie and Jo are alive. I'll get all three of you to the hospital. Just hang on."

Bassett said something Andy could not decipher. He leaned closer.

"Heart?" the old man whispered.

"Yeah, I think so. Just sit tight a minute. I've got to find a way to get everyone out of here."

"You...did...." A strangled gasp. "You did...well."

Andy nodded perfunctorily.

"I'm dead," Bassett rasped, making Andy's blood run cold. "Dead... serious...."

"It would've been hard to do any less after that speech you gave the Gardener."

"S-speech?"

"Never mind. Be still. Rest. I'm going to get the truck."

He started to stand but hesitated, struck with the overwhelming certainty that time was short, the overwhelming need to do this right.

"Alex? Do you need anything? Anything at all I should do? Anything I can get you?"

"Yes...."

Andy waited for the rest of it. It came a second later.

"A ...cigarette."

Andy laughed, and Bassett's lips pulled back into a wintry smile.

"Cig...a...rette," he said again, and Andy simply couldn't help himself. He laughed even harder.

7

IT WAS ALL over by the time he got back.

Ignoring the pain, he had run full speed to get his truck. He pulled it around to the side entrance, slammed on the brakes, then crept forward again a few feet at a time, steadily maneuvering until the right edge of the bumper shattered through the old wooden door, opening a gaping hole into the mill.

When he came back into the gym Jo was sitting up and staring at him, dumbfounded.

"Andy?" Her voice was soft, as though the simple act of talking was pure agony. "Andy, Jesus, is that really you? Where are we? What the hell happened?"

He was going to answer when he saw that Bassett had also moved. Somehow, he had pulled himself across the floor, over to where the body of the Gardener lay in a bloody heap. He had collapsed across the Gardener's chest, and Andy knew as soon as he raised the old man's head that he was gone.

ALEXANDER'S SONG

"Who is it?" Jo said, the chains that still bound her wrists and ankles clanking as she moved. "Who *are* all these people? Where *are* we?"

Andy shook his head, unable to speak. His tongue felt swollen, his throat blocked.

"He was talking," Jo said a moment later. "The old man there…he was talking to the other one. He said something like, 'Danny, you wouldn't believe it, but we were much more alike than either of us knew.' I think that was it. Does that make sense?"

Andy nodded.

"He said something else, too, right at the end. He said something about a fire and something else about a bond. Do you know what that means?"

He nodded again.

"Well, I wish to hell you'd tell *me* what was going on."

He felt the first tears burning tracks down his cheeks.

"And to think," she said dryly, "all of this…this whatever it is…whatever the hell all of this is…to think I used to find you dull and boring."

Andy turned, mustering the best smile he could. Then he sat down on the floor beside Bassett and found the cigarettes in his jacket pocket. He shook one out and lit it.

"Andy, are you crazy? What in the name of Christ are you doing?"

The smile became a grin.

The tears came a little faster.

He pulled in a large puff of smoke, held it, let it out.

"*Andy!*"

He hugged the old man's head to his chest and wept.

LATER...

THE DEATH OF A WOULD-BE WRITER

There were always choices, he realized in the end; options were unlimited. There were thousands of potential avenues to follow, whole worlds of possibility and consequence. But he came to understand that the answer lay in forgetting about those other worlds. The answer was to choose the one option that lived within your heart, to dwell in the *real* world, and to simply get on with it.

Alexander Bassett
from *The Pharisee* (Novel, 1951)

THE DEATH OF A WOULD-BE WRITER

1

Andy put down the phone and turned on the light over his desk, startled and more than a little pleased that he'd been talking to Ginnie long enough for it to grow dark outside. Every other conversation with her had lasted five minutes at most. Today, for the first time, she seemed happy to hear from him. They had chatted idly for ten minutes or so, then talked about more serious matters, until finally she had begun to fade. He could hear the change in her voice, then the disorientation he was so familiar with, the slightly odd questions and vague non-answers that told him she was beginning to wear out, that she was not quite there anymore.

Nine weeks in the hospital and probably another four still stretching ahead of her.

"They said I'll never recover all the way," she told him a week ago.

Andy had been horrified, struck by images of Ginnie forever curled into a fetal ball, unable to walk, scarcely able to think.

But they were only talking about her memory, she explained.

"The doctor said I'll never get it all back," she told him. "He said I'll hear all about that time, and say, 'yeah, yeah, right, of course,' but it won't really *mean* anything to me. It'll be like hearing a history teacher talking about something that happened before I was born."

She had explained all that in a cool, matter-of-fact voice, but Andy heard something else. He thought she sounded almost sanguine at the possibility of forgetfulness, of disconnection, as though the prospect secretly pleased her.

It was another blistering Chicago summer, and the house had grown noticeably warmer with the approach of night. He turned on the fan that sat next his desk and picked up the stack of messages that had been accumulating all day.

He read the first one: *J. Summerfield from Bellingham Publishers. Wants to talk about his offer again.*

The next: *Peter Horace called. Still willing to fly you to New York for a weekend talk.*

The third: *Jim Hayes, freelance scriptwriter. Call him. Says it's extremely urgent!!! (He ordered me to use three exclamation marks)*

Andy sighed. He felt the beginnings of the headache again, the dully throbbing pain at the top of his skull that waxed and waned but never entirely left him these days.

There were at least ten more messages to go, but he didn't have to read any of them to know what they were about. The best of them were from lawyers—proof of how bad things had gotten. The rest were from publishers, editors, agents, writers, movie people, television people, developers and packagers, producers and managers, men and women who wanted to discuss foreign rights, paperbacks, tabloid serialization, book club editions, talk show interviews.

It had gotten so far out of hand that he'd finally broken down and hired an assistant, a girl by the name of Shelley Hayward, a college freshman home for the summer and staying with her parents down the street. For the past three weeks, Shelley had been coming in every day to field calls and jot messages. She normally worked until four-thirty or five, but today she had gone home at three. The calls had continued to come in since then. The red light on the answering machine was blinking too rapidly to count.

ALEXANDER'S SONG

He turned back to the message slips, which were easier to deal with than the machine.

Someone called from the legal department of Renfield House (didn't catch the name—sorry!) He said they have first rights to any Bassett works, can prove it, and you better not think about selling anywhere else.

"Right," Andy murmured.

Another agent—Susan T. Fischer. Sounded like a car salesman, if you ask me. Said you HAD to give her a chance, see what she can do for you before you go anywhere else.

Andy dropped the rest of the slips. They scattered across his desk. The headache was worse, and he knew exactly what that meant. Following the normal progression, the pain would be raging out of control by midnight.

Reluctantly, he punched the button on the answering machine. The tape rewound an impossibly long time. When it reached the beginning and started to play back, he had a pleasant surprise. The first message was from Jo:

"Hey, you. It's me. You didn't return my call the other day, or, for that matter, the two before that. I know, I know, you're busy. Your secretary told me. *Secretary!* Who would ever believe that Andy Gillespie would have a secretary? Anyway, I was wondering…before we left Pebble Stream, when I was still in the hospital, we talked a little bit. Do you remember? You mentioned in passing that you might come down to Florida and pay a little visit. Anyway, I thought you should know that I'm game if you are. I'd like to give you a proper thank-you. And in case you're wondering, I'm not staying at Bob's place anymore; I'm on my own. So think about it, okay? Give me a call when your terribly busy celebrity lifestyle permits. Bye."

Andy's smile was short-lived. The next message was from a television producer he'd already heard from three times in the past week. The one after that was from an expert in publishing law. The next was the Renfield House legal department again, and after that it was Simon and Schuster, Harper and Row, Random, Putnam, Bantam, Paramount.

At some point in the droning cavalcade of voices, he simply stopped paying attention.

2

HE'D FOUND HIMSELF thinking a great deal lately about duty, about sacrifice. At odd moments—coming out of the shower, taking a break from his writing, eating a sandwich at the local Denny's—the things Bassett had said to the Gardener came back to him. They had come back again tonight, talking to Ginnie on the phone.

"I can't get over it," she said early in the conversation, when she was still sounding bright and alert. "He was alive all that time, living in Rock Creek, right under my nose. And I never got a chance to meet him."

"But you did," Andy said. "You stood right there in his house and talked to him about poetry."

"No, that was Ed Hoffer. It's not the same, you know? It's like sitting next to a stranger at lunch and later realizing it was a famous movie star. You think about all the things you could have asked him, everything he could have told you."

"Yes," Andy said, "I see what you mean."

"What about you? Did *you* talk to him? Did you talk about the important stuff? Did you get a chance to talk about books and ideas? Did you ask him about his politics? Everything you and I wondered about—did you talk to him about *that?*"

He wanted to explain it to her. He wanted to make her understand that there simply hadn't been time, not nearly enough time. He wanted to say that by the time he discovered Ed Hoffer's real identity there were more pressing concerns to deal with. But he didn't know how to say those things. There was still so much about those days that she didn't know, couldn't comprehend.

He closed his eyes, trying to decide what to say and how to say it, and it was then that Bassett's talk with the Gardener came back to him.

ALEXANDER'S SONG

"C'mon, Andy," she pressed. "You talked to him about all that stuff, right? You learned things from him?"

"Yes," he said, and had to draw a deep breath before he could continue. "Yes, Ginnie, I learned a lot from him."

3

HE'D LOST CONTROL of his office more than a week ago.

Shelley Hayward tried to keep up with the mess as best she could, but eventually even she surrendered, saying their only recourse was to stop fighting and apply for federal disaster relief.

Now he surveyed everything in the waning light, looking from one end of his desk to the other, and felt his headache grow by steady leaps.

In addition to the most recent messages, there were stacks of those small white slips piled in every available spot, arranged by day of call and caller's name. Down at the other end, next to his new personal computer, sat a mountain of notebooks and journals, and next to that his growing manuscript—seventy-nine pages as of dinner time. The working title had been suggested by something Bassett and the Gardener had talked about: *Making Amends: The Dark Life of a Literary Master*.

Many of the calls over the past month had dealt with the rights to that story—rights half the world was interested in and the other half insisted they didn't need.

"If you won't deal with us, Mr. Gillespie, we'll simply do our own version of the story," a publishing executive said to him one day. "There's nothing at all to stop us from doing an unauthorized biography. Is that how you want to be remembered? Is that how you want Alexander Bassett remembered?"

Those who weren't interested in the biography (or at least pretended not to be) were after the other item on Andy's desk: the one thousand pages of manuscript that comprised *The Children's Song*.

The majority of the callers were interested in both books, of course, and those people tossed around obscene figures as casually as most folks chat about the weather.

One afternoon a week ago, as he sat daydreaming, gazing absently out the window at the new four-door Blazer he'd purchased in expectation of his coming windfall, Shelley bustled into the room carrying a stack of newspaper articles—part of her latest attempt to create order out of chaos.

"What does that mean?" she asked. Andy looked up, surprised to realize that he'd been scribbling on a notepad, absently writing the same word over and over again.

Shelley pointed at the pad. "Is that important, or should it go in the circular file?"

Andy looked down and saw the word *climb* printed seven or eight times down the center of the page.

"I guess it's important," he said. "I'll hang onto it for a while."

She gave him an odd look but said nothing.

The paper had disappeared since then, but not the feeling that he'd gotten from looking at that word, and not the growing sense that it was more important than he had known at the time.

Would Bassett have made him his literary executor if he had known what was going to happen? More to the point, would he have wanted an executor at all?

You have to prove that my ideas and beliefs, my politics, everything I always stood for, still mattered to me. You have to show that they were still valid at the end.

There was a problem, though. As each day went by, Andy was more and more convinced that the publication of *Making Amends*, followed by publication of *The Children's Song*, wasn't going to prove anything at all—except perhaps the maxim that where you have clowns and noise and color, you have a circus.

He would be lying if he said he was completely revolted by everything the circus offered. Certain aspects of it, particularly those embodied by

ALEXANDER'S SONG

that shiny Blazer and the new computer and the CD player in the living room, were actually quite wonderful. But every time he thought about that, his mind would immediately start turning in a different direction. Eventually, it would find its way back to that word—*climb*—or one of its brothers—*sacrifice* and *duty*.

He knew now what Alexander Bassett's life had been about. In some ways, of course, he had always known it, but the talk he'd overheard in the old mill on that chilly spring night had brought the disparate threads together into a fabric that was whole and complete.

Would Bassett approve of what was happening now?

The man had inherited more than three million dollars from his family and had earned almost a million more by writing. Yet he had always lived like a pauper. He had ended his life with an identity far different than the one he'd been born with, but he was still the same for all of that.

Still the same.

What would he think of the messages on Andy's desk? What would he think, that man who had given most of what he made to charity, that man who wrote stories and offered them as gifts to editors in need, who dedicated his novels to causes and donated all of his royalties to the poor, the hungry, the homeless and helpless and hopeless?

Sacrifice.

Duty.

Doing what was right.

Standing up to those who used the weapons of oppression—power, wealth, the ax—to bend others to their will.

Climbing.

It was never about money, and it certainly was not about the relative merits of one economic system over another. To Bassett it was simpler than that, purer. It was about fighting against the night, standing up against those who thrilled at the suffering of others, the way the Gardener had longed to watch Bassett die, to relish the very moment that his heart stopped pumping.

It was about leaving darkness, reaching for light.

Andy thought about that, and he thought about Rock Creek. He thought about Jo, traveling fifteen-hundred miles because she sensed he was in trouble. He thought about Marilyn, swallowing her hatred of the man who had killed her nephew to stand up against someone worse. And he thought about Bassett himself, coming out of hiding to do what *he* knew was right, offering himself to Danny, and at the end, lunging forward in an attempt to save Andy, even as his heart was beating for the very last time.

And what about me? he wondered. I stayed in town when I was in danger, just to help Ginnie. I risked the Gardener's bullet to go to Alex's side. That was a sacrifice too, wasn't it? Why would I do that? Because of what the old man said?

He didn't think that was it, at least not all of it. In the end, he had gone to Bassett without really thinking about what he'd heard, without thinking about *anything*. In a moment of crisis, a lifetime of selfishness had been thrown aside on instinct alone, because the moment called for proper action and the proper action was clear.

That was the *real* message of Bassett's work, the real ideal for which he'd stood. You had inside you the power to do what was right, to reject the darkness, to choose light, to climb beyond all your baser impulses, and to use that power at the moment it was needed, without review, without debate, without analyzing or agonizing over it. You did it because it was necessary.

That's what Bassett had learned in a clearing off Green Meadow Trail.

That's what Andy had learned in an abandoned gymnasium on Manitou Road.

The phone rang. Irrationally hoping it was either Ginnie or Jo, he snatched it off the hook. "Hello?"

"Mr. Gillespie? *Andrew* Gillespie?"

His heart sank. "Yes."

"I'm glad I caught you, sir. My name's Hogan, and I've got a helluva proposal for—"

ALEXANDER'S SONG

He put the receiver down quickly.

"What am I supposed to do about this, Alex?" he asked his study.

His headache was getting worse.

He turned off the light and sat there, alone in the darkness.

4

THE NEXT MORNING, an hour past dawn, he stood fully dressed in his living room, feeling surprisingly rested after a night of stormy dreams, tossing, turning, waking and slipping fitfully back to sleep in endless cycles. In front of him was the big stone fireplace that dominated the room—the reason he and Jo had bought the house five years before. Piled between the andirons was a fantastic drift of paperwork: white message slips by the score, folders full of scribbled notes, and manuscript pages, lots of them—more manuscript pages than anything else. The titles of two books were clearly visible from where he stood.

The telephone rang.

His headache gave a little kick. He winced. But he let the phone keep jingling, unanswered, and that alone did wonders for the pain.

You have to prove that my ideas still mattered...that they were valid at the end.

He struck a match and dropped it. It landed on the first page of his own work-in-progress. At first nothing happened, but eventually the paper began to smolder and smoke. A moment later the first finger of flame appeared, weak, tentative.

Andy had a moment of panic. He almost leapt forward to rescue everything before it was too late, but then he realized that his headache was gone, completely gone for the first time in days, and he held his ground.

The telephone was still ringing, promising riches beyond counting—money to pay for the computer, the Blazer, trips to see Jo in Florida, trips back to Rock Creek to visit Marilyn and spend time with Ginnie as she recovered and reclaimed her life.

Well, there was always teaching. The classroom would be there in September. The kids to whom he owed something would be there, too. They always were. They always would be.

Sometime after that, he could deal with the copy he had made of Bassett's novel, now securely tucked away in his office safe. A year from now, three years, five, when the clamor had faded and the spotlight was turned off...after that, there would be a publisher. There would be a small press somewhere, a non-profit group, someone who could do it the right away. There would be no riches. It might even mean money out of Andy's own pocket. But that wasn't the issue. The issue was that a request had been made, a request that Andy wanted and needed to honor.

That first page was gone now and the pages underneath had caught. He could feel the warmth beginning to radiate from the fireplace.

Is this right? he wondered. Can this possibly be the right thing to do?

But he pushed the question away, not wanting to think about it.

Instinct. Action.

He shook his head and watched the fire, marveling at the way it made him feel like a dead man, a new man, a frightened man, a better man.

The telephone rang on and on, the unending music of the valley he was leaving behind.

You have to prove that my ideas still mattered...

"I will, Alex," he said.

He turned and left the room, while the phone continued to ring and the flames danced in the fireplace like a message from the heart.

> To sing of death is easy. But to sing of life? To sing of hope?
> Ah, there, my friends, is the challenge of the ages.
>
> Alexander Bassett
> from *The Children's Song* (Novel, unpublished)

ABOUT THE AUTHOR

PAUL F. OLSON debuted as a fiction writer in 1983, with his short story, "The Visitor." His first novel, *The Night Prophets*, followed six years later. In the late 1980s, he published and edited *Horrorstruck: The World of Dark Fantasy*, a trade magazine for horror fans and professionals. With the late David B. Silva, he co-edited the anthologies *Post Mortem: New Tales of Ghostly Horror* and *Dead End: City Limits*, and created the award-winning newsletter *Hellnotes*, which he and Silva produced weekly for five years. Following Silva's death, he teamed with Richard Chizmar and Brian James Freeman to put together the tribute anthology *Better Weird*. Some of his short fiction is available in the collection *Whispered Echoes*, which includes the World Fantasy Award-nominated novella "Bloodybones." He lives in Brimley, Michigan, not far from the shores of Lake Superior.

CEMETERY DANCE PUBLICATIONS
PAPERBACKS AND EBOOKS!

SAVAGES
by Greg F. Gifune

An island of horror...unstoppable evil... there is no escape!

"This was a great stranded-on-a-deserted-island story. Fun characters. Interesting villains. Gifune does a great job making the struggle for survival feel real. One of my favorite novels of the year."
—Tim Meyer, author of *Malignant Summer*

JEDI SUMMER
by John Boden

A boy and his little brother wander through the loosely stitched summer of 1983. It was a magical one. Full of sun and surrealism, of lessons and loss, and of growing up.

"Delivers honest self-reflection without ever venturing into saccharine sentimentality or maudlin self-pity, and his picture of the uncanny summer of 1983 is as clear as a never-played VHS tape right out of the box."
—Bracken MacLeod, author of *Closing Costs*

THE MAN IN THE FIELD
by James Cooper

A remote village, ruled by the Word of God. An enigmatic man who comes every year. A rigid system of ritual and tradition, and the one woman who dared defy the order.

"Like other folk horror that centers on appeasing old gods, *The Man in the Field* is a tribute to the works of Shirley Jackson. Fans of the literary spectrum of horror will enjoy this tale of small-town terror, reminiscent of the early works of Laird Barron and John Langan."
—*Booklist*

Purchase these and other fine works of horror from Cemetery Dance Publications today!
https://www.cemeterydance.com/

Made in the USA
Middletown, DE
07 October 2022